THE WILD WOLF'S REJECTED MATE

The Five Packs
Book Five

CATE C. WELLS

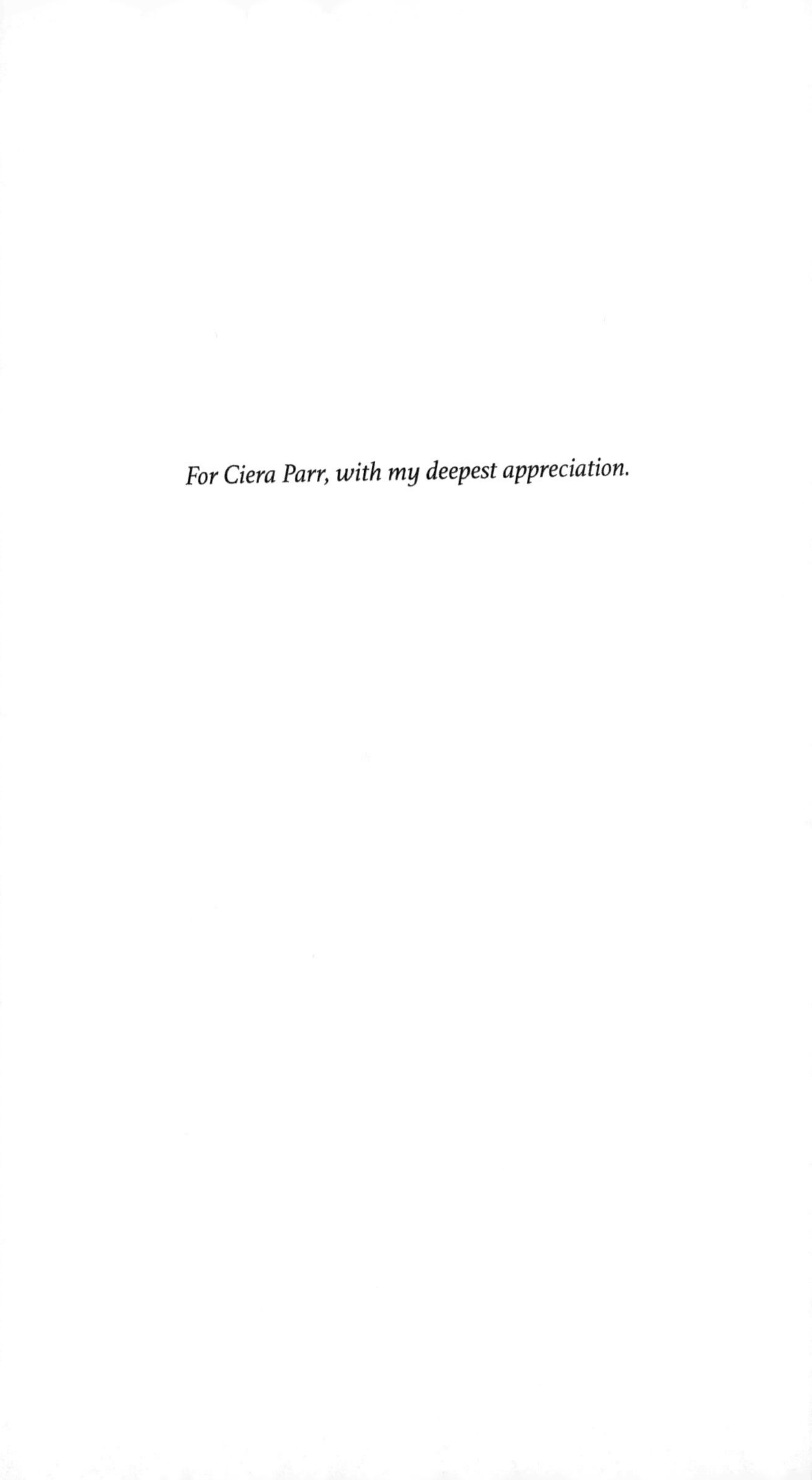

For Ciera Parr, with my deepest appreciation.

AUTHOR'S NOTE

This novel contains explicit scenes of violence as well as a biologically compelled mating. For more detailed notes, please visit the author's website.

1

ANNIE, AGE EIGHTEEN

There's something wrong with me.

Beyond the usual.

It's November, and I'm sweating through my long jean skirt.

The yellow school bus bumps along, winding back to Quarry Pack territory from Moon Lake Academy, and I slide back and forth on the plastic bench, leaving streaks of sweat on the dark green seats. I scrub the dampness away with the cuff of my flannel shirt, but then the bus takes another hairpin turn, and I've got another streak to swipe.

What if it's wasting sickness?

A memory flashes into my head—the stink of camphor, Ma's rattling lungs, the white sheet almost flat on the mattress except for the knobs of her knees and ridges of her hips.

But it can't be wasting sickness. The big brains at Moon Lake cured that years ago. Besides, sweating isn't a symptom.

The sharp, pecking voice that lives in the back of my head pipes up. It can never be silent for long.

You know what causes sweating.

The bus barrels around a curve. I brace my knees against the seat in front of me and press my spine into the back so I don't slide.

It's heat.

If I ignore the voice, it'll get louder and more insistent until I melt down. If I listen to it, I'll work myself into a panic attack. I don't know which is worse. I've tried to experiment, but I don't make a good scientist when I'm balled up in a corner, rocking and digging my nails into my forearms.

Sometimes I hate myself. I want to unzip myself like a pair of footie pajamas, step out of my skin, and walk away.

I want to cut the nagging, beaky voice out of my brain with a pair of scissors. I know the voice is me, but I hate it because it's always full of doom and gloom, and it's always right.

Heat causes sweating. And it makes unmated males stink. What's that smell, Annie? You smell it. I know you do.

It's three dozen kids at the end of a long day, crammed into a metal can with windows that only open halfway.

No, it isn't. It's different. Mustier. Nastier.

My stomach gurgles queasily. I switch to breathing through my mouth.

I'd give anything for a knob that would turn the voice off. Or down. I'd take down.

You're in heat. You know it. Your mate is here. Time's up.

If the voice had a body, I'd take a tire iron to the back of its head. In this pack, I'm the shyest and quietest female my age, the scaredy cat who wouldn't say shit if she had a mouth full of it—but if the voice were a person, I'd crack its skull open.

Your mate could be any one of these males. You don't get to pick. Fate decides, and you have to take it. And then he can do whatever he wants to you.

The pecking voice throws up images of the worst males I know—Lochlan Byrne, smirking as he slinks out of a broom closet, tucking himself back into his gym shorts while a female with raccoon eyes follows in his wake, head high and defiant, her face sickly white and her hands shaking.

Alfie Doyle, shoving little Frankie Duffy down the steep bus steps, laughing when the poor guy sprawls in the asphalt.

Brody Hughes, leaning on the fence beside the track while we run past during human sport class, jeering at us to pick up our feet while he ogles our chests.

Somehow, my innards twist tighter. I wouldn't have figured that was possible. My stomach already hurts worse than it usually does at the end of the day. I'm too scared to use the bathroom at the Academy—not around females from other packs—so I'm always bloated and crampy after lunch. If I poke my lower belly, it'll be rock hard.

I need privacy and a shower. Then I'll feel better. Maybe I'm making myself hot. I do sweat when I freak out.

Not this hot. Not this much sweat. And what about that smell?

My wolf whines and trots her worn path inside me, back and forth, deepening the rut with her pacing. The beaky, pecking voice drowns her out, but I know what my wolf grumbles low in her throat—run and hide, run and hide, run and hide. That's all my wolf ever says. But run from what, though? And where? And hide from whom? How?

You can't stop heat. It's a greased metal chute into the unknown. Like life.

I stretch my neck and peek over the seat in front of me at the back of my classmates' heads, many of them male. None of them seem special or different. I glance up at the rear-facing mirror over the driver, and I can see a few more males behind me, laughing and messing around, chewing food with their mouths open, propping themselves up with a knee on their seats, as close as they can get to standing without getting hollered at to sit down.

I sink as low in my seat as I can without looking weird. None of the males make me feel anything except scared and uncomfortable, and I always feel that way.

It's going to be worse when one of them owns you. It's going to be hell. You need a plan. Now.

My wolf adds her standard two cents—run and hide, run and hide, run and hide.

I blot my slick forehead with a damp sleeve as we careen around the last bend before rumbling through the Quarry Pack gates. As we pull into the commons, I gather my bag so I can bolt as soon as the bus rolls to a halt.

Mari and I have this part of the ride choreographed. She sits in the seat in front of me. As soon as the bus's brakes screech and the door opens with a whoosh, she pops into the aisle, and I slip in behind her. She leads us down the steep steps and away from the crowd that spills out behind us.

We used to be permanent seatmates, but during one of our honest, late-night conversations between fellow insomniacs, Mari admitted that my fear stench was a little overpowering by the end of the day. Now we sit together on the ride to the Academy, but we split for the ride home.

It's fine. I get it. I can't stand my own smell, either.

Mari glances back at me. "Ready?" she mouths.

I nod.

The brakes screech, and the door whooshes. Mari hops

up. I fall in behind her, stumbling forward when a male's swinging gym bag whacks me in the back.

Run. Run. Run!

The pecking voice joins my wolf and becomes a blaring alarm in my brain. I ball my fists. My muscles tense, preparing to bolt. I slam my foot on my own internal brakes.

No.

I am not under attack.

It was an accident.

I force my balled hands to relax. I'm okay. Nothing is wrong except this bus is a freaking oven, and it smells like everyone has a piece of rotten fruit in their lunch box that's been in there since the first day of school.

I take another second, and as soon as I'm confident that I'm not going to freak out and try to fight my way off the bus because I got bumped by a duffel bag, I hustle down the aisle.

As soon as my boot hits the ground, I scurry clear of the crowd spilling from the bus and drag in a lungful of fresh air, lifting my flushed face toward the late afternoon breeze rolling down from the hills.

It's fresh. Heavenly. There's an odd note in it, and it's not bad at all. An earthiness. My cheeks cool, and my stomach muscles relax.

Mari grabs my hand and takes off toward home. I let her drag me along.

What *is* that scent? It's not a usual November smell, not dry leaves or waterlogged wood. It's closer to freshly tilled garden, but it's also rich and spicy like the inside of the crone Abertha's trunk or the cabinet where she keeps her oils and unguents.

"Do you smell something?" I ask Mari.

"Yeah," she says, grimacing. "Don't worry. You can have first shower."

My cheeks heat again, and I pick up the pace.

Our cabin isn't far, but it's past the commons and up a fairly steep hill. Killian, our alpha, doesn't want us lone females living close enough to the unmated males to tempt them into doing something they shouldn't. That's why we have to dress modestly and serve at meals instead of sitting at tables with the rest of the pack.

In my opinion, the rules are mostly in place to give Killian a false sense of security. Clothes aren't armor, and if a male wants to hurt you, he's not going to decide against it because he's got to hike an extra quarter mile uphill. I don't chafe against the rules as much as my roommates Mari, Kennedy, and Una do, though.

A quarter mile is a head start.

A long skirt with thick tights can get in a male's way long enough to give you a chance to escape.

Run and hide. Run and hide. Run and hide. My wolf chants her mantra as she dashes along the border between us. She's really amped up, even for her. She's noticed the scent, too, and she's on alert, but she's not terrified and pissing herself in some corner of my subconscious, which is usually her M.O.

I don't hate my wolf—not like I hate the voice—but she's kind of a bummer. On the one hand, I want to meet her, but on the other, I'm so scared that she's going to be scrawny and weak. One of my worst nightmares is being stuck inside a runt of a wolf who is incapable of protecting herself.

Just the thought of it makes my panic rise.

I take a deep breath, and that earthy scent hits me again. I scan the wildflowers and trees on either side of the path, but I don't see anyone or anything out of place.

Because it's behind you. Somewhere you can't see. Better run while you still can.

I check over my shoulder, but there's nothing but the empty, winding path. Down the hill, everything appears peaceful—the cabins clustered around the commons and pups playing in the grassy park in the center of it all. The young males wrestle and chase each other around the females sitting in a circle, their heads bent together, intent on some game.

What if it goes after them? The voice rises to a scream. *Go! Now! Warn them! They need to run!*

I force myself to calmly turn away. The pups are safe. Their dams are on their porches, watching them. There are males close by. There are always at least a few training in the gym for the shifter fights, and besides, the patrols would have raised an alarm if something had encroached on our territory.

The danger isn't real. It's in my head.

Always in my head.

I trudge the final few feet to the steps to our cabin and peel my damp shirt from my back to let air reach my skin. Maybe the weird smell *is* me. I give my pits a quick sniff. Mari wasn't lying. I am rank.

Per usual, Mari leads the way inside, hollering, "Kennedy!"

"In the kitchen," Kennedy calls back.

She's a year older than Mari and me, so she doesn't have to go to the Academy anymore. She works in the kitchens with us at breakfast and dinner. During the day, she goes up to Abertha's with Una to work on our super-secret mushrooms, jams, herbs, and honey business that we run under the alpha's nose.

Instead of weird smells, I should be worried about how

we're inevitably going to get busted selling our wares at the human farmers' market in Chapel Bell. But that's a real fear. I don't worry about those.

Mari and I drop our bookbags on the floor and traipse down the hall. Kennedy is bellied up to the kitchen counter, eating cheese. She's using its plastic wrapper as a plate and a butter knife to cut slices and ferry them to her mouth. With her free hand, she's scrolling on her phone.

Mari goes directly to the refrigerator and throws the door open. I grab the tea kettle from the stove and fill it at the sink. My crampy stomach eases a little more. It's tea time. The best time.

"Is that all the cheese we've got?" Mari asks Kennedy.

Kennedy hums a cheerful affirmative around a mouthful of cheddar.

"Can I have some?" Mari sounds tetchy, but we all know that she rips through the cheese the quickest. Kennedy's lucky there was any left.

Kennedy slides the cheese closer to her own chest, and her wolf rumbles a warning. My wolf yelps and drops to her belly inside me, baring her neck and burying her head in her forelegs.

"My bad," Kennedy says, wincing.

I smile ruefully. Everyone in the house is used to my skittish wolf. We've lived together for a long time now. I know that Kennedy's wolf would never hurt mine, but there is nothing in the world that will convince my wolf of that fact. Kennedy's wolf is male. Males are killers. End of story.

Frowning, Mari sticks her nose deeper into the fridge. "Who ate the summer sausage?"

Kennedy and I grimace at each other behind her back. I left half. Kennedy must've finished it.

"There are Slim Jims left," I suggest.

Mari turns up her nose, but she still snakes past me to fetch them from the cabinet over my head. Her big blue eyes shine with anticipation as she upends the box, expecting a windfall.

A single Jim drops onto the counter.

"Really?" She scowls at me. "You left one Jim?"

I shrug. "There was at least half a box left last night."

Mari glares at Kennedy. Kennedy stares back with wide-eyed innocence as she pops another piece of cheddar into her mouth.

Mari huffs, drops into a chair at the kitchen table, and snaps into her meat stick. "Is Una still up at the cottage?" she asks Kennedy.

Kennedy takes her snack to sit in the chair across from her. "Yeah."

"What did y'all do today?" Mari asks.

"Brought in the last of the squash, and then we canned apples. Una thinks they'll move at the market."

"Everyone sells canned apples." Mari scarfs down the last of her snack, licks her fingers, and looks longingly at Kennedy's cheese.

"Yeah, but ours were grown, picked, and canned by real, live shifters." Kennedy waggles her eyebrows. "That puts a premium on them."

I will never understand humans. They're afraid of us, but they're also fascinated. The humans with booths at the Chapel Bell farmers' market resent us for stealing "their" business. They tell stories behind our backs about how we go on killing rampages during the full moon, but darn if they don't make sure to come by our stall before we sell out and get themselves a few of whatever we've got on offer. They probably resell our stuff online with a three-digit markup.

I hate going into town. Sometimes my nerves and my wolf won't let me, but if I can take my turn, I do. The money we make buys my tea and yarn and Wi-Fi and our streaming services. Without my little coping mechanisms, I'd be even worse off than I am. I'd have nothing to drown out the voice.

I dab my sweaty forehead with a dish towel and flip open my wooden tea chest. I need something to cool me off. Mint? Lemon? I draw in a breath to let my nose choose, but there's that strange scent again, wafting in from the cracked window above the sink. Maybe because I have tea on the brain, I feel like I can make out notes of oolong or yerba mate.

My stomach unfurls, somehow making more room for my lungs so I can take another, deeper breath.

The kettle screams.

My heart explodes.

I fling my arms into the air. My legs skitter on the floor tiles, and then I drop, crouch, and tuck to protect my soft parts, huddling against the oven door.

The knife! In the block! Grab it!

Run and hide, run and hide, run and hide.

The voice and the wolf shout louder and louder, trying to top each other.

Oh, hell. I forgot to flip the whistle up on the teapot.

I curl my fingers around the handle on the oven, squeezing until my knuckles blanch so I don't snatch a knife and bolt out the back door.

I don't need to run.

There's no one to fight.

It was only the teapot.

I try to talk myself down, and it's like talking in the middle of a hurricane. Nothing in my body—not my nerves, my muscles, my adrenaline, my cortisol—*nothing* is listening. I'm not fleeing the cabin like my heels are on fire, though, so it's a win.

I used to run all the time when I was a pup. Once, the door was locked when I had a freak out. I hit it at full speed, and it didn't give, so I bounced backward, landed flat on my butt, and bruised my tailbone. My brain broke, and I crawled under the kitchen table and wouldn't come out for hours.

Eventually, Una crawled under the table after me, despite her bad leg. She dragged me out and held me on her lap, rocking me until I fell asleep. She couldn't walk the next day, her leg was so stiff. That was the last time I made a run for it because of a sudden loud noise. Sometimes, shame is more powerful than fear.

Sometimes.

In the here and now, Mari and Kennedy politely ignore me while I force my fingers to release the oven door and take a few deep breaths. The weird smell is stronger. When I finally rise on my shaking legs, I peer out the window. There's nothing but the deck, the flower bed, our tiny yard, and then beyond it, the steep bank to the ridge that runs behind our cabin. I don't see anything.

Whatever it is, it doesn't smell like danger. That's a change of pace. Usually, everything unfamiliar smells like a threat.

I unwrap a bag of orange pekoe, pour the water, and carry my tea to the table. My hand is still unsteady, so the cup rattles in the saucer. Kennedy pushes my chair out for me with her foot, and I sink into it with as much grace as I can muster.

For a second, we're silent, and then all three of us exhale a long sigh in unison. Mari drops her head back and closes her eyes. Kennedy slumps forward and slices herself another hunk of cheese.

I know exactly what they're thinking. It's been a long day already, and we're not even halfway done. In a few minutes, we have to head down to the lodge to prep for dinner. Then we have to serve and clean up and prep for breakfast, all while ducking and weaving around the meathead males of the pack.

I'm so hot and sweaty. I feel like a wrung-out washcloth.

I slump forward, push my teacup forward with the tips of my fingers, and lay my cheek on the cool linoleum table.

"What's wrong with you?" Kennedy asks.

"I think I have a fever."

"Shifters don't get fevers." Mari reaches over to feel my forehead. Pups get fevers, but we grow out of it by the time we're old enough for the Academy. I haven't had one since before Killian became alpha and moved me in with Una and the others. "You're really hot."

Kennedy reaches over and feels my face for herself. "Gross. You're all wet."

I blow out my cheeks. "I know."

I can't see Mari and Kennedy exchange looks, but I hear them shift meaningfully in their chairs. Neither dares to say it for a minute, but finally, Kennedy takes the leap.

"Do you think you're in heat?" she asks.

I squeeze my eyes shut. "I don't know. How can you tell?"

There is a long pause before Mari ventures an answer. "Well, I guess you get really hot and turned on, and you recognize your mate. Do you know who he is?"

I moan. "If I knew who he was, I'd know that I was in heat."

There should be a class on this at the Academy. I can solve for X, and I know that iambic pentameter has ten syllables made up of alternating stressed and unstressed syllables, and that each of these pairs is called a foot, and each foot is called an iamb, and the opposite of an iamb is a trochee, but my body is burning up, and I have no idea if it's *heat*, and I don't even write poems.

"Well, are you horny?" Mari asks.

I turn my head so my nose and lips are mashed against the cool tabletop. Your mother is supposed to tell you this stuff, and if she's not around, then your grandmother or your aunts. My aunt lives in Salt Mountain, and even if we did talk, I'd never ask her about this in a million years.

I don't think Una knows any more about heat than we do, and I'd feel weird asking her about it. She's kind of like the nun from the movie with the singing children. And besides, if we talked about it, I'd let on that I'm terrified of the whole thing. My brokenness makes her sad, so I try to play it off like I can't wait for a mate like Mari.

"Well, do other males smell bad to you? I've heard that when you find your mate, other males stink until you do the deed." I can picture Mari's turned-up nose from the tone of her voice.

"Do any males smell *good*?" Quarry Pack males smell like unwashed gym socks. High-ranking Moon Lake males smell like too much human cologne, and the low-ranking ones smell like pipe tobacco and swamp water. Salt Mountain males smell like chewing tobacco and gasoline.

You know they do. Don't pretend. Face facts. It's heat. You need to run.

Kennedy snorts.

"Well, when we get to dinner, you can take a good whiff, and that'll be your answer," Mari says, her chair screeching as she shoves herself back from the table.

Suddenly, the idea of doing the usual—showering,

changing, hurrying to the kitchens, rinsing, chopping, mixing, serving, sweeping, wiping down, mopping, all while trying to stay invisible as I trail fear stink all around the lodge—feels unbearable. Insurmountable. I sigh, and my breath fogs the tabletop.

"I can't do it tonight," I say quietly. I'm never one to complain or shirk. The voice would never let me. If I'm not useful, I'm expendable. Maybe even a liability.

"Then don't," Kennedy answers like it's nothing. "We'll cover for you."

Don't you dare. You don't want them to think you're slacking. What if they decide you don't need to eat since you're not working? What then?

The voice flashes an image of the lodge basement in my mind, frozen in time ten years ago when the old alpha was alive.

It's enough. I hoist myself up.

I feel like wilted lettuce. Right now, I can't summon up any worry about getting my food cut off. The thought of eating anything makes my stomach churn, and besides, my rational mind knows that sort of thing doesn't happen anymore now that Killian is alpha. Most of the time, my rational mind wins out, but that doesn't mean the voice shuts up.

And that doesn't mean she doesn't know exactly what button to push in my brain to keep me vigilant.

What if they decide you're only worth one thing? Better go anyway. You don't want to draw attention to yourself.

The only people who'd notice if I was missing are Mari, Kennedy, Una, and Old Noreen. I'm furniture in this pack, and that's how I want it. It's safer.

You're never safe.

And you're boring, I want to say, but the voice doesn't care about what I think any more than my belly button or my left foot does. Argument is futile. Ignoring is the only thing I can do.

"Are you sure you're cool to cover for me?" I ask my roomies.

Mari and Kennedy both nod. "Take a long bath and veg out," Kennedy says. "You'll feel better."

"Everything'll be fine," Mari adds, and they both head to their respective rooms to get ready to leave.

Neither of them actually believes what they said. If this is heat, I won't feel better until I let a strange male mount me, and then I'll be stuck with him for the rest of my life.

Killian Kelley. Lochlan Byrne. Alfie Doyle. Brody Hughes. Vaughn Lewis. Art Floyd. Dangerous, cold, mean, cruel, violent, heartless—it won't matter who or what he is. Fate decides, and that's that. Females get on their hands and knees and beg for it. If you somehow manage to resist the urge, the male descends into rut and makes you.

My stomach roils. The tea sloshes.

I push up from the table and trudge down the hall like a zombie. I need a shower. Ice cold. Maybe I'm lucky, and I just caught some human flu. I've never heard of it happening, but that doesn't mean it's impossible.

Some of the tension seeps out of my shoulders after I pop the lock in the bathroom. It's not strong enough to keep anyone out, but if someone forced the door while the shower is running, it'd be loud enough to give me warning. I slide the wicker hamper in front of the door for good measure, wedging it as best I can under the knob. Then I get the wooden broom out of the linen closet and lean it on the wall next to the tub so it's within reach.

I know a male shifter can burst through a standard door like it's nothing, and this broom would probably break if I hit him with it, but I need the ritual so I'm strong enough to ignore the voice and take my clothes off.

What are you doing? You can't get naked. What if you have to run? You've got no shoes. Nothing between you and them. Nothing to stop them.

I undress quickly, hanging my skirt, shirt, bra, and panties over the towel rod so that I can slip them back on as soon as I dry myself. I am a very efficient bather. Even with turning the water off a couple times to listen for phantom noises, I can wash, shave, shampoo, and condition in five minutes flat. The key is using shaving cream as soap and buying a two-in-one for your hair.

I actually stay a little longer than usual under the spray and run the water ice cold. For several precious minutes, the relief is more powerful than the voice. After I turn the faucet off, I press my palm to my chest. My skin is still rosy and hot to the touch, and my breath is shallow.

It's heat. Run before you're trapped. Get the hell out of here.
And go where?

The voice is silent. It always is when I call it out. It doesn't have answers, just fear and hysteria and prophecies of doom and disaster.

I wish I could carve it out of my brain. Skewer it with a hot poker. Kill it with fire. Give it what it wants.

What does it want?

I pat myself dry and pull my skirt and shirt back on. I can't bear the thought of squeezing my tender breasts into an underwire bra, and my underwear is ruined. I shove them deep in the hamper, covering them with one of Kennedy's oversized sweatshirts and Mari's flouncy party dresses.

I splash my face with cold water and brush my teeth. Like always, I dribble on my shirt, but there's no help for it.

I'm not about to stand in the middle of a room in nothing but a towel.

I moisturize and comb out my wet hair. It's brown, like my eyes. I'm a very ordinary-looking female. I have a long torso, and my arms and legs are kind of gangly, but other than that, I'm pretty unremarkable.

My left breast is a B cup, almost a C. My right breast is a C, almost a B. My butt is square. My hips exist. Barely. I have a few moles, but none that show when I'm dressed.

I tie my hair back into a tight ponytail and check the effect in the mirror. Bland. Commonplace. Garden variety.

Will my mate be disappointed? Will he want me to wear crop tops and short skirts like Haisley and Rowan and the other young, mated females?

Acid rises in my throat as my adrenaline spikes.

He can make you do whatever he wants.

Run and hide. Run and hide. Run and hide.

I force myself to move the hamper back where it belongs, unlock the door, and walk at a steady pace to the back of the cabin. I'm not going to run. I'm just going to look out the storm door and remind myself that I can leave at any time. I'm not trapped.

Your mate can smell you. Once he mounts you, he can track you by the bond. Pull you by the leash. You'll never get away.

My trembling hand grabs the knob, and I can't stop myself from pushing the door open. I'm not going to run away. I don't do that anymore. The last time, Una had to trek all the way up to the blackberry bramble in the west woods before she found me, and her bad leg was so sore the next day, she couldn't make it up to Abertha's cottage. I've outgrown running away. Years ago. I can control myself.

I venture to the edge of the deck and lower myself to sit at the top of the steps that lead to the small yard. The earthy smell is stronger now. I breathe it in, and for some reason, it slows my thudding heart. My wolf drops to her haunches and peeks out at the physical world, eyes narrowing, ears perking.

Someone is out there.

I steel myself for another round of run and hide, but she's quiet. She cocks her head.

I scan the yard, the beds of purple phlox and salvia—not long for the world now that the first frost is coming any day —the sunflowers and pink panicle hydrangeas, the yellow strawflowers on the slope leading up to the ridge above our cabin.

The sun is sinking in the west, but it's not reached that angle yet where the rays are blinding. There aren't stark shadows cast on the grass. It's like someone's turned down the dimmer on the world, so the outside seems mellow and lovely and close and safe.

I take another deep breath. It feels amazing. Like my lungs can suddenly hold more.

It's a trick. There's something out there. Lurking. You just can't see it.

It's stupid to feel safe. It's a delusion. I know that. No female is ever really safe. The reminder should spur my wolf back to her pacing, but she stays still, listening. Her nose quivers.

I take another look around, slower this time. Blades of grass flutter in the faint breeze, and so do the flower petals.

And so does the fur on the strange wolf hiding in the strawflowers.

Watching.

With gold eyes.

Every muscle in my body freezes.

Inside my head, I scream, but my throat has choked off my air. My lungs have seized mid-inhalation.

Don't make a sound. Don't move an inch. Don't breathe.

No, no, no—this is the moment to run. I need to *run.*

I can't. I don't have the strength to stand. My legs are weak from terror. A droplet of warm pee dribbles down the crease of my thigh.

The wolf in the strawflowers rises to his four feet, up and up and up. He's huge. A full-grown male. I can't see his teeth, but they'll be razor sharp. His ears are up and canted forward, like he's listening for something.

My lungs seize.

My heart pounds louder, too loud. It thunders in my ears, ready to burst into mangled, meaty chunks.

The wolf lifts himself even higher, his head swiveling on his neck, scanning the horizon. He's scouting for danger. Are there others?

I track his gaze, but I don't see anything except flowers and shrubs and the shed where we keep the mower.

He lifts his snout in the air, his nostrils flaring. His furry brow knits. He's confused.

He strides forward. I shrink in my skin. I want to squeeze my eyes closed, drop to the ground, and curl into a ball, but I can't move, and besides, I need to see it coming for me.

It's worse if you don't see it coming.

I brace myself, pulse pounding, as he bulldozes his way through the bed of phlox and salvia, his huge paws trampling tender stems into the dirt. I cower in place, frozen and quaking at the same time. At any second, he'll be on me. His teeth. His claws.

He pads across the lawn. A yard away. Ten feet. Five. A soundless scream escapes my throat, nothing but air.

At the last moment, he veers right and dashes to the

perimeter of the yard, following it until he disappears around the cabin. Before my lungs can finish a gasp, he reappears around the other side and skids to a halt in front of me.

He stares at me, his bushy brow furrowed, leans forward in my direction and sniffs. His lip curls, showing black gums and shiny white fangs. I whimper.

His head snaps left, then right, like he's trying to catch someone sneaking up on him. Finally, he bounds away up the slope to the ridge and stands there, outlined by the setting sun, surveying the landscape in three hundred and sixty degrees.

What is he looking for? What's out there?

I need to run while he's distracted, while he can be a decoy for whatever bigger danger he's looking for.

I dig deep inside myself for the strength to move, but all that's down there is blind terror, so I stare at the strange wolf, helpless and small and frozen.

Again.

He's huge. Well, not as big as Killian, but still—massive. And he's mangy. His mottled fur sticks up randomly in tufts, and it's matted along his left haunch. Is that a twig stuck in it?

He's not a natural wolf—he doesn't have that way about him—but he's not a pack shifter, either. Is he feral?

The sunset bathes him in light, and I can make out smaller details. The edges of his ears are ragged, and he has a bald patch on his side that runs on either side of a puckered scar. He's young, not much older than me, but his body is battle worn, like the older generation in Quarry Pack who came up under the old alpha. They had to fight for food. Not in a ring, but for real.

How did this wolf get onto pack land without the patrols catching him?

The bottom drops out of my stomach. If he's here, so far into our territory, I've been right all along. Safety is an illusion. Patrols can be dodged, locks won't hold, doors won't stand in anyone's way, the alpha's assurances are lies.

The voice is right. It *knows*.

I need to call for help, but the fear strangles my throat too tightly.

High on the ridge, the strange wolf takes a long final look around and trots back down the hill. When he comes to the yard, he keeps coming, but he slows down. Like he's trying to be stealthy.

Like he's stalking prey.

No. That's not exactly right. He lifts his paw so carefully that the move is almost comical, and then places it daintily down before he lifts another. A wild thought pops into my mind. He looks like a pup playing red light, green light.

What is he doing?

He reaches the circle of dead grass where the bird bath used to be before Kennedy's wolf accidentally bowled it over during one of her angry shifts. He's close enough now that he could be on me in a single bound. My shoulders rise to my ears while my hands curl into fists.

He stops, his eyes trained on my face. The gold is so smooth and bright that they hardly seem real. They certainly don't match the raggedy rest of him.

Slowly—very, very slowly—he lowers his hulking body to his belly.

I let out a shallow breath that I can't hold anymore.

With exaggerated slowness, he rolls onto his back and cocks his rear leg.

I can see his butthole. And all the rest of his business, too. My face catches fire.

He cranes his neck and studies me, his ears perked.

His belly fur is filthy. The small patches on his back and haunches that aren't matted and caked are a nice pale tan, but there aren't many of them. It looks like he deliberately rolled around in a mud puddle.

Is he a lone wolf, on his way to going feral? Or is he Last Pack?

I desperately try to remember everything I've heard about them. They sleep in dens and feed on rodents and grubs and the occasional deer or hog. They live like animals, spend most of their time as wolves, and they kidnap females, who are never seen again.

What happened to their own females?

You know what happened. They killed them. You know what males do.

Another wave of panic crashes through me, spiking my blood with a fresh hit of adrenaline.

The wolf sniffs, his face screwing up like he's caught a whiff of something foul. A tendril of embarrassment worms its way through my panic. My fear is really pungent.

He stares at me. I stare at the ground, neck tilted and bared, but I track him from the corner of my eye. He sprawls on his back and wriggles in the grass, his enormous balls drooping, not an ounce of shame or modesty. He's not afraid.

Why would he be? I'm not a threat.

After a few more rolls, he gets bored and flips onto his flank to check my reaction. I'm not stupid. I know this is a display of submission, but I also know it's a lie. He's easily twice my size, and under the filthy, matted coat, his muscles are honed. If he attacks, I won't have a chance against him.

He scrambles onto four feet.

I try to make myself even smaller, tucking my forearms to my chest and dipping my chin to emphasize my own submission.

I'm on my own here. No one will be home for hours. Which is good. I don't want anyone else to be in danger. I need to pull it together enough to run.

I'll head away from the commons. Lead him toward Abertha's cottage. She's old, but she can handle anything. She has nerves of steel, and I've smelled metal and gunpowder in the back of her pantry.

My brain sifts manically through escape routes while my body cowers and the strange wolf trots over to the flower bed with an exaggerated nonchalance.

What is he doing now?

He sniffs a sunflower and then glances over his shoulder to see if I'm watching. I am. I can't tear my eyes away. He's the clear and present danger. For once, it's not in my head.

He casually wanders to a hydrangea bush and sticks his muzzle deep into the pink blossoms. The flowers are on their last leg, so when he delves his snout into a bunch, a handful of petals flutter to the ground. He sneezes. Another bunch of petals burst into confetti and drift down, sticking to his fur.

He glares at the bush, startled and a little put out. Then he casts me another look. This time, it's expectant.

What does he want me to do?

He waits.

My stomach knots tighter and tighter the longer he stares. If my intestines were rope, they'd be frayed close to snapping.

Sometimes I marvel at all the ways I can mess up my body with the power of my mind—all the parts of my body that I can make ache. My belly, my head, my neck, my shoulders, my jaw. I wonder which part I'll break first. Probably my teeth from grinding them while I sleep. And anytime I'm around the males of the pack.

I am so tired of myself, and I'm tired of cowering here, soaked in sweat and terrified, while a feral wolf makes a mess of our flower bed.

"Just do whatever it is you're going to do," I call to him. In my mind, my words are loud and clear. In reality, they splutter out of my mouth, mumbly and faint.

The wolf cocks his head. He's meandered behind the sunflowers so he's standing with all four paws in the mulch, facing me. His brow scrunches, as if he's lost for what to do next. Then his ear twitches, knocking against a sunflower stalk. It sways, bopping his muzzle, and he startles, his clumpy fur bristling like a porcupine's quills.

I can't help it. A tiny smile flashes across my face, half hysteria, half reflex. I mean, he freaked himself out by accidentally whacking himself in the snoot with a flower. Totally something I would do.

His golden eyes light up, and he bumps the flower with his muzzle again, closely observing my reaction.

I gawk back at him. Is he *playing*?

He sits back on his haunches, reaches up with a paw, and bats the sunflower, watching me, waiting.

What am I supposed to do?

He picks up a paw and gently presses down on the stalk until the sunflower is touching the ground, and then he lets it go. It flies up and boops his snoot. His wooly brows rise in expectation. My eyes round. He cocks his head and blinks.

He's being silly on purpose.

Quarry Pack wolves don't play, at least not like this. When the males are in their fur, they act like animals. They might wrestle or chase each other, but they'd never fool around in a flower bed. They'd never be *silly*.

He's looking around now, and I can see his gears turning. Suddenly, inspiration strikes, and he trots to stand between two flowers with small blooms growing close together. He shoves his shoulders between them, stretches his neck, and simultaneously shoves the bottom of the stalks together with his front paws.

He's given himself sunflower antennae. He tilts his head left and right, showing off for me.

My lips curve again, of their own volition, and so do his, revealing wickedly sharp incisors. Fear snatches at my heart. I moan, my smile disappearing.

His wolf snorts a sigh and flops back down on his belly. Now he has really long sunflower antennae. He raises an eyebrow. It's a question, but I don't know what he's asking.

He waits, watching and listening, but I can't give him any reaction. Even if I knew what to do, my body wouldn't let me. At the Academy, we learn about fight, flight, freeze, and fawn, but I've only got three in my repertoire, and if I can't run, I'll be playing possum.

Once, a possum got into Abertha's cottage when someone—ahem, Kennedy—left the door open. The little guy freaked out and played dead in the middle of the kitchen. Abertha just picked him up and carried him outside like a baby. He didn't move a muscle the whole time, his paws sticking straight up in the air and his glazed eyes wide open. I've never seen anyone more committed to a bit.

Sometimes, I imagine someone picking me up like that, carrying my stiff body outside and dropping me by the compost heap. It would be a relief.

The strange wolf is losing his patience. First, his tail begins to flick, and then he wriggles restlessly in place.

When he gets bored enough, he begins to army crawl forward, keeping his body low to the ground. The closer he gets, the tighter every part of me clenches.

I don't think he wants to hurt me. Obviously. The sunflower antennae were a giveaway. My body doesn't believe that though. Neither does the voice that has reverted to tossing images in my mind like a game of fifty-two pick up.

Fangs tearing muscle. Fists pummeling flesh. Heart wrenching cries. Male laughter. Sightless eyes, staring at nothing. A mouth twisted in a frozen scream.

My hands shake in my lap. I curl them until the nails bite into the meat of my palm, and the pain doesn't make it better at all, but it's something else to think about besides the sharp-beaked birds of memory swooping and pecking at my brain.

I would give anything to not be this way.

"Please go away," I mumble, but I can't even hear my own voice.

The wolf keeps coming, and when he's a few feet to my left, he casually turns so that we're both facing the ridge with Salt Mountain rising beyond it in the distance. He sits beside me, watching the sun sink behind the peak for a long moment. My shallow breath is jagged and loud in the quiet.

He scooches his butt a little closer. I can really smell him now. The earthy scent is definitely him. It wafts from him like a just-opened air freshener. My wolf likes it. She sits very still at the edge of the boundary between us and peeks at him from the corner of her eye.

This wolf is my mate.

The heat, his smell, the fact that he's here at all in our pack's territory—my head might be jam-packed with all kinds of wild and unfounded fears, but at the same time, I don't tend to delude myself. He's here for me.

I swallow. I can hardly get the spit down my throat.

"Y-you should leave," I say. "B-before they find you here."

He glances at me out of the corner of a golden eye and snorts.

"They won't care that you're my mate. You're on Quarry Pack territory without permission. My alpha will kill you."

He blinks, unfazed, and keeps watching the sunset, but I know he's as aware of me as I am of him. The silence stretches. My nerves would, too, if they weren't already strung as tight as they can go.

"This isn't going to work anyway." I stare at the scuffed toes of my boots, peeking out from the hem of my long denim skirt. "I'm...I'm not right. I can't do this. I can't have a mate."

His tail twitches, brushing the grass. My heart lurches at the sudden movement, and I gasp. He jumps to his feet, searching the distance, looking for the threat.

Kennedy's wolf does the same thing when I freak out. He smells my fresh burst of fear, and in the second before he remembers that I'm just messed up, he starts howling, ready to shift and fight for our lives, and then he gets pissy when there's no one to beat down. It's a whole thing.

"There's nothing out there," I tell the strange wolf. "Ignore the smell."

He either doesn't believe me, or he doesn't understand. Growling at me to stay put, he races up the ridge, and when he doesn't see anything, he trots the perimeter of the yard and circles the house again before coming to sit beside me. Closer.

He glances over, considering me, a question in his eyes. I shrug a shoulder. He bends his head to sniff himself and then frowns back at me, clearly having trouble believing that whatever's bothering me could possibly be him. It shouldn't be a hard leap for him to make. He's huge, and he looks feral—there's a burr stuck in his belly hair and dirt inside his ears. I can't believe females are easy in his company.

"You need to go," I say with the softest, sweetest voice I can muster. "I can't be your mate. I'm sorry."

It's not that I don't want a mate. A home of my own. Warm and snuggly pups. A bright fire, thick walls, strong doors with solid bars, and a male made for me who'll watch for danger while I sleep. It's the kind of dream that's so achingly sweet you don't dare want it lest Fate snatches away what little you do have as punishment for your audacity.

Maybe that's why Fate sent this wolf. I can't mate him; there's no way. He's either a lone wolf, or he's from the Last Pack. Either way, he lives in the wild. No walls, no doors, no locks. I couldn't. Not in a million years.

And he'd want to—mount me.

There are knives in the kitchen. There is a baseball bat in Kennedy's closet. You can run. You've got a clear path.

But I can't move. I'm stuck here because my survival instincts are cross-wired. I'm a possum in a wolf's world.

"Please go," I murmur, knowing he'll do what he wants. He's male, and he's big.

He slowly rises to his feet again, turning to gaze at me, narrow-eyed as if he's trying to figure me out. I stare at my feet.

I know I don't really have a choice. Sooner or later, I'll go into full-blown heat, and then it won't matter that I'm scared. I'll get on all fours and stick my butt in the air until he takes me. Or, if I manage to fend off the heat long enough, he'll break first and go into rut. He'll pin me down, and it won't matter how hard I fight. I won't have a chance against him.

A fresh wave of terror barrels through me like a freight train.

The strange wolf growls as he takes a few steps away, but this time, he doesn't scan the horizon. He keeps his gaze riveted on me. He's figured out that he's the danger.

He stands at a distance a little longer, his head cocked, waiting. Confused. Or disappointed.

Sweat trickles down my face, but I can't even raise my hand to wipe it away with my sleeve.

"Please go," I mutter into my lap.

After a few more seconds, I hear him pad away. His scent fades, and my lungs can finally expand to take in a full breath. My muscles go slack, and I slump forward, resting my forehead on my knees.

What do I do?

I listen for the familiar, almost reassuring chant of *run and hide* from my wolf, but she's silent and shaking. She knows it's hopeless. We're trapped. There's no way out but through.

This is happening.

There's no way to stop it.

We're going to have to live through hell.

Again.

2

JUSTUS, AGE EIGHTEEN

My mate's name is Annie. She's beautiful, but she smells bad, and there's something wrong with her.

She sent my wolf away. That's not surprising. Colm's female screamed at him every time he got close to her for moons and moons when he first brought her back from North Border, but she still *ate*.

Annie wouldn't eat the squirrel I brought her. She took it out to the backyard and buried it. I thought she was hiding it from the other females so she didn't have to share, but she just left it there. She did the same with the black snake and the hare.

Maybe she's picky. I hope so. If she's sick—

No. I can't think that.

I drop the dead goose dangling from my maw onto her front porch, spitting out as many bloody feathers as I can. When I'm done, I've only got a few still stuck in my teeth.

She should definitely like this. Goose is delicious, and this particular one is plump and juicy. My wolf and I definitely earned our fair share after the hassle of hunting it down, but we decided to settle for a little taste, saving most of it for her. She's not got enough fat on her for winter, let alone for bearing pups.

My blood heats at the thought. I can't wait to see my seed dripping from her pussy crack. When I knot her, she's going to look over her shoulder at me with those big brown eyes, and there won't be any fear anymore. She'll know that I can take care of her, and she'll stop stinking as if I'm about to attack her.

I pad away from the goose and sit further off, angled so that she'll see the bloody goose bite on my haunch when she comes out. The wily fucker managed to nip a chunk out of my butt cheek before I ripped its throat out. I guess that means I've eaten my own ass.

At least no one from the pack saw. I'd never live it down. Annie doesn't know it was a goose that got the drop on me, though. For all she knows, maybe I fought off a natural wolf for the goose. Or a feral.

I fix my face, trying to look like even though I'm in pain, I'm suffering stoically. Females love fussing over every little injury. At least that's what I remember from when my dam was alive. It was a long time ago, but I do remember that.

Maybe if Annie sees me injured, she won't be as afraid. It's a small scratch, so she won't think I'm weak, but she'll see that I'm a wolf like any other.

Or maybe she'll think that I'm the kind of sad, sorry wolf who gets himself hurt taking down a bird?

Shit. I quickly rotate so my uninjured side is facing the door.

I wish I could just fight someone and take her. I feel like an idiot, skulking around this cabin, bringing her meat she won't eat, hoping she gets used to me enough to stop smelling like I'm a monster come to murder her.

Mating a female is the least dignified shit I've ever done. I should have brought her straight to the dens, but no, I listened to Max. He said if I stole her, she'd cry and make me wait, and it'd be better in the long run to hang around her territory, where she feels safe, until she presents. He said she won't fight so hard afterward once the bond is in place.

I don't know about that. It doesn't smell like she feels safe here, and she's crying and making me wait now. I'm sleeping outside under the bushes and hiding from the Quarry Pack patrols like I'm scared of them. It's embarrassing.

She keeps saying that her pack is going to kill me, but they'd have to catch me first, and they're not going to do that patrolling the same routes every day at the same time. That's what happens to you when you spend so much time as a man. You start thinking like a human and ignoring your instincts. Wolves don't follow the same trails day after day. Because it's *dumb*.

As soon as I get her back to the dens, that's the first thing I'm going to teach her. She takes the same paths every day at the same time. She needs to vary her routes. And another thing—someone's going to steal her if she doesn't pay more attention to her nose. Every time I approach her, she startles. I haven't bathed since I got here. My wolf should not be able to sneak up on her.

At least I think she's close to presenting. She didn't go to the lodge this morning or up to the witch's afterward, thank Fate. I hate it when she goes to the witch's place. I track her there, but I don't get anywhere near the boundaries of that female's territory. I like my balls attached, and the witch has been clear. If you trespass without permission, she says she'll go "collecting nuts."

What is my mate doing in her cabin now? I know she's in

there. The spicy scent of her heat wafts from the open windows, a dinner bell to a starving male. It makes me hungry to take my skin, and I'm never excited to become the man, not like I crave the wolf when it's been too long.

My wolf rises to his feet, restless, and trots over to peer inside a window. The large front room is dark. It's filled with all kinds of human equipment like the stuff we find abandoned in the woods. I press my nose to the glass, teasing out the scents. Plastic. Metal. Chemicals. Teabags left seeping and biscuit crumbs. Traces of the three females she lives with—the hobbled one, the blessed one, and Mari.

Despite whatever's wrong with Annie, I'm happy that Fate gave her to me. She is the prettiest of the females I've seen, either here or back home, and she has the best tits. One is a little bigger than the other so it spills over her bra cup, and it shows through her shirt. I want to bite that little pooch. But gently.

She's also clever with her fingers. I snuck up to the porch when the others were at dinner last night and watched her in her rocking chair, knitting. She knew I was there— of course, she did—and she tensed, terrified, but her fingers kept looping and hooking the yarn, despite the shaking. She dropped stitches, but she caught and mended them all. She will make good blankets to keep our pups warm and to trade for the things we can't get ourselves.

I don't know how to make her understand that I won't hurt her. I keep low around her, but I'm a big wolf. I can only make myself but so small. I show her my neck, too. Doesn't seem to make a difference.

She'll be calmer after I mount her. Then she'll know she has nothing to fear and that I know what I'm doing.

I will be very careful to please her. Lelia and Diantha both let me mount them when they're needy, and they're the pickiest females in the pack. I must be decent with my cock. It's thick, but Alroy's is much thicker, and they won't let him near them.

Once Alroy asked me why they liked me and not him, and I didn't want to tell him it was because I do exactly what they say to do when I mount them, so I told him it was because I had a deeper rumble. He spent a month rumbling as deep as he could whenever the females were around, annoying the hell out of everyone.

I pad quietly along the porch and peek in the next window. The room is dark. It belongs to the hobbled one. She's not old, but she acts like a dam to my mate and the others. They follow her like ducklings up to the witch's cottage and down to the lodge, slowing their pace to match hers.

My dam died during the wasting sickness that fell during the year of the late frost, not long after my sire passed from injuries he got fighting a feral. My mate's parents are gone, too. I'm happy that Annie has had a female to care for her.

I don't remember my dam very well anymore. I can't recall her face, but I can picture perfectly how one side of her mouth curled higher than the other when she smiled. I remember random things—her ginger cookie smell, her wolf's rough tongue lapping crumbs from my snout, her gentle yips calling me back when I ventured too far afield.

I was an adventurous pup. For a long time, I thought that's why Fate took her. Because I didn't keep a close enough eye on her like my sire asked me to do before he passed.

I'm grown now. I've lived eighteen years, and I've long since figured out that Fate doesn't have reasons for what she does.

An owl hoots, and my fur bristles.

Why does Annie not come out? She's not even creeping to the door to see what I've brought her.

I growl softly to let her know that I'm coming closer and then leap over the porch rail, continuing alongside the cabin to her room. Her heat is heavy in the air. I don't know how she's held out this long. If I were in human form, I'm sure I would have gone into rut days ago.

I reach her window, peer through the glass, and come eye-to-eye with her peeking through her curtains. She startles, screams, and bolts. Her footsteps pound toward the back of the house. The kitchen door slams.

My wolf sighs. We made noise. We brought a goose. How did she not smell the goose? Its blood is all over my face.

My wolf trots after her. We give her lots of space. Maybe if she runs long enough, she'll be too exhausted to be so afraid.

She races up the hill, down the far side of the ridge, and into the woods. I let her get far enough ahead that I can't see her through the trees. It's no trouble tracking her with the scent of terror and the noise she's making. She must be whacking into every low branch she passes. Thank goodness the patrols are east and west at this time of day. There's no one between us and the border of Quarry Pack territory.

Of course, she's going to reach the river first. Will she try to cross it? It's wide, deep, and fast where she's heading, and I doubt she swims much. I've never seen her without a shirt buttoned up to her chin and a skirt down to her ankles.

If she tries to swim for it, I'll have to shift. My wolf is an otter in the water, but he can't very well fish her out of the rapids with his paws. I can only imagine what she'd do if he tried to bite her by the scruff to haul her out.

My pulse races as I think of her neck in my mouth. I can't wait to mark her. My bite will look perfect on her delicate, willowy neck. I'll teach her to hold her head high so everyone can see. She doesn't need to bow down all the time anymore. Now she has me, and I don't show neck to anyone.

Thankfully, when we reach the river bank, she doesn't even consider jumping. She whirls to face me, her tits heaving, her eyes wild. Her pupils are pinpricks. Her heat is riding her hard.

Is she gone yet?

She has to be very, very close. She's finally stopped shivering and shaking and squeezing her hands into little fists. Her gaze is darting around as if she doesn't know how she got here.

Hell, I feel the same. I never dreamed I'd be lucky enough to find my mate, let alone that she'd be from one of the lost packs. No wonder she's behaving so strangely. She thinks it's normal for the air she breathes and the food she eats to come out of machines.

Do her people mate differently, too? Do they have a machine for this, too?

Her wild brown eyes meet mine. She's needy. I recognize the look. There's still fear, though.

I hunker down so she doesn't feel like her back is against a wall. I don't think she's going to tell me what she wants like Lelia and Diantha, but I'll follow her lead.

Her gaze drops, and she sinks to her knees and begins scooping the dry leaves from the maples and oaks overhead into a pile. Shit. She's making her nest. Right out here in the open. This is not ideal.

I sniff the air. Quarry Pack does keep their territory clear. I don't even get a stale whiff of four-legged predator. There's no trace of their males, either. We're pretty far from their nearest patrol path. They let the river act as a boundary here, which is stupid. Ferals can swim if they're hungry enough, and so can humans, and they're worse—they won't be looking for food.

Annie pauses with an armful of leaves, her eyes clearing for a moment as if she's woken from a dream. A wave of fear rolls off her. I remind my wolf not to growl. Growling makes it worse.

"I don't know what's happening," she mutters, her lower lip trembling. "I can't stop it."

I wish I could take the fear from her, but she has a right to it. This is going to hurt her. The females always make a fuss after their first time and make their males fetch sweets or rub their backs. I'm pretty sure they're playing it up, but I've scented blood in the air after a new mating, so there must be some pain.

I don't want to hurt Annie. She's lovely. Like a sparrow. Or a swan with her long, graceful neck. And I sure as hell don't want her any more scared. Her fear already has my nerves on a hair trigger. My wolf's, too.

I creep forward. She doesn't pay me any mind. She's gone back to piling leaves and plucking twigs from the heap and tossing them over her shoulder. She mutters as she works, but I can't make out the words.

When I get to the edge of her nest, I stop. I'd never come closer without invitation. Nests are sacred, even a makeshift one made out of leaves.

My paw brushes a leaf, and she casts my wolf a baleful glare. What has displeased her? It could be so many things.

I haven't brought her home, so she doesn't know that I have a good, warm den for her. Besides the goose, the squirrel, the snake, and the hare, she has no proof that I can care for her, and females need more than just meat. They like sweets and pretty, soft, clean things, and they need to know that you're vicious enough to kill any threat so that they can sleep undisturbed. But they also need to know that you're not so feral or foul-tempered that you'd hurt the pups.

We don't have many females, so we all watch them closely, and as strange as they act sometimes, they're not complicated. They just want things to be safe and nice and tidy.

None of this is right. We should be in my den.

I've been trespassing on Quarry Pack land for almost two weeks at this point, and it's making my fur itch. Max said to stay here to see her through her heat, though, and he stole his mate Elspeth from North Border, and she seems happy enough. She lets him sleep in their den, and she never tried to run back home, not that I heard about anyway.

But mating out in the open? When I'm on the verge of rut?

I feel the vicious hunger pulsing inside me. When I shift to human, I'm going to need to focus harder than I ever have before so that I don't tear into her. I need to do the thing as gently as I can, then shift back, and get her home. Once she's in my den, she'll see that I can give her everything she needs, and she'll calm down.

She's slowing down with the nesting. She's flushed bright pink, and her hair has come undone. She looks tired. There are dark circles under her eyes.

"I can't make it any better," she says, soft and sad, and lies down on her side, resting her head on her upper arm. Her hand is over the edge of the nest. So close to where I wait.

I roll to my side and wriggle closer, mirroring her position. Her hand is near enough to stroke my belly now if she'd just lift it. I whine to encourage her. She looks at me with bleary eyes.

"You're not going to go away, are you?" she asks.

Never. At least, not without her. We're mates. She's safe now. Whatever is frightening her, I'll kill. If I can't, I know places where we'll never be found. We're going to be a family.

I don't know much about how it works—I was so young when I lost my sire and dam—but I remember a crackling fire and thick venison steaks sizzling on the grilling grate, my sire in his fur, pretending to snatch one away, and my dam giggling. I can figure out how to make that for Annie. I can't wait.

I scooch forward until my stomach brushes the tips of her fingers. She sighs, but thank Fate, she takes the hint and pets my belly. Her touch is hesitant. I can barely feel it through my fur, but still, it's the best thing I've ever felt. My blood surges through my veins, dosing me with adrenaline. If I were in my human skin, I'd have her on her knees and be sinking into her now.

"Can you be quick?" she asks.

I don't think I'll have any choice in the matter. Lelia taught me tricks to last long enough to please her, but I don't see them working with Annie. I'm too excited. Annie is mine to keep. I won't be alone anymore. I've wanted this my entire life. I'll be lucky if I last three strokes.

I bend my neck so I can nuzzle her fingers with my nose.

"When it's done, you'll go. It'll be over." She sounds so hopeless.

Why does she worry that I'll leave her here? Can't she feel that this is real? We'll both go *together*. This is just the beginning.

I roll all the way onto my back so she understands that

between us, she ranks. She doesn't need to worry. Whatever is wrong, I can fix. I can do anything for her.

Her fingers graze my sternum, hesitating at a clump of fur caked with dried goose blood. She must realize what she's touched because she grimaces and snatches her hand away. My wolf whines.

"Will you bathe first? Please?"

Yes. Of course. Females like their males clean. I know this. I clamber to my feet. She startles. Her fear scent thickens. Even though I hate leaving her even for a few minutes, it's good that the air will have time to clear by the time I get back. I really can't wait until we're bonded, so she stops going skunk on me.

My wolf races to the bank and flings himself into the rushing stream. The frigid water sharpens my mind. When I shift to human, I'm going to have to be quick. Rut is riding me, but I'm strong enough to hold it back and fuck her with care. I have to be. She's already so skittish.

I paddle in a few circles, letting the current rinse my pelt. I'm about as dirty as I've ever been. I mudded myself up real good before I crossed into Quarry Pack territory to hide my scent, and I haven't bathed since. I'll be keeping my fur squeaky clean from here on out, though. I want her to stroke me with those clever fingers all the time. All over.

My wolf's dick swells, which is impressive, considering that there's already a film of ice at the river's edge.

I need to do this before I lose the ability to control myself.

I paddle for shore, scramble out, and give myself a good, hardy shake. I'm only a few yards downstream, and I can see Annie's nest, but with the incline, I can't see her. She's buried in the middle of a huge leaf pile. I trot back, careful to keep my pace nice and slow. I make lots of noise so she can't possibly be startled again.

And then her scent hits me. It straight up punches me in the face. Full-blown heat. Spicy and yeasty and musky like a pussy that hasn't been washed in a while. Delicious. My wolf's throat rumbles. He yearns to taste her. Desperately.

I don't want to let him get near her like this, but I need to see the lay of the land before I shift, and very possibly, tumble into rut. I let him creep closer and lift himself onto his hindquarters to peer over the wall of leaves.

Fuck.

She's naked.

Mostly.

Her skirt and panties are gone. She's got her shirt on, but it's unbuttoned and hanging open. She's sitting up with her butt propped on her heels. Her belly and thighs are flushed. She has a dark, wiry bush, and along her slit, the curls are wet and matted from her slick.

My wolf growls. I muscle him down, reminding him of his limits. I am not like some in the pack. *I* rule *him*. He snuffs down the deepest breath he can manage. She still smells like fear, but the scent is overpowered by the rich tang of her wet pussy. She's getting herself ready to take my knot.

This is the best thing that's ever happened in my entire life.

My mate is the most beautiful female in the world.

I am the luckiest male.

A little pink tongue peeks out from the top of her slit like the meat of a clam. I can't tear my eyes away. My mouth waters.

She's making a strange sound, a low, hungry moan. I have to do this now.

Please, Fate, don't let me fuck this up.

I screw my eyes shut and become a man. Instantly, I recognize that my body is different. I'm bigger, swollen with muscle all over. Even my cock is thicker.

I feel like I've stepped out of a lake. That kind of unfamiliar heaviness. I shake out my arms and draw down a deep breath.

There's no need to freak out. I'm fine. It's normal. Mated males fill out. Max said he gained twenty pounds of muscle and an inch in girth overnight when he caught Elspeth.

I step forward and trip on a clump of leaves. Annie cries out.

Shit. My feet are bigger, too.

I steady myself on her shoulder. She cowers, ducking away, her neck bent so far that her chin is tucked to her chest. My wolf rumbles in my chest to reassure her, but instead of consoling her, it freaks her out even more. She wraps her arms tightly around herself and whimpers.

"It won't hurt much," I tell her, my wolf raspy in my throat. I pray that's true. If she cries in pain, I'll puke. I can hardly bear the scent of her fear with my human nose. My wolf doesn't like it, but he also kind of takes her fear as his due. He's huge, and he's got really sharp fangs. Fear is a natural response from a smaller wolf.

But my mate shouldn't be afraid around *me*. I'm not weak. I can protect her. And she must know I don't want to hurt her. "Don't cry, okay?" I say.

She moans louder.

"I'll be quick." It's the best I can promise, but again, it doesn't soothe her. She rocks, curling her shoulders forward as if to protect herself.

I don't know what to do. I crouch, my cock pointing due north like a flagpole. I still tower over her, but I can't make myself smaller, not in any way that'd make a difference.

I show her my throat, angling my gaze toward her knees. They're pretty. I don't know why. They're smooth and round, but really no different than most female's knees. But still. I like the look of them.

We sit in silence for a long time while the sun fades and the breeze grows brisker, picking off leaves from the top of the pile and flicking them along the ground. Every so often, I sneak a glance at her face. She's lovely, but she's also bright red. Like a beefsteak tomato. Her eyes are vague and wild, like she's eaten full moon mushrooms.

Finally, her breathing speeds and shallows, and the pitch of her whine changes, dropping deeper with more of her wolf coming through. Her rocking becomes less frantic, more intentional. She grinds her pussy against her heel.

"Let me make you feel better," I say, careful to keep my voice calm and even. My wolf is smart enough to keep his trap shut. The last thing either of us wants is to frighten her now.

She groans, and finally—finally—she reaches for me. She falls forward, her small hands landing on my chest. She doesn't weigh much, average for a female, I guess, but nothing a male my size can't handle. I press her hand to my heart. It's warm. And perfect.

She whimpers and blood rushes to my cock.

"Please," she whines.

I help her turn and settle herself on her forearms, and without me saying anything, she lifts her ass into the air and sidles her knees apart.

Fuck.

I can see everything now.

Her pussy is watermelon pink, and the inner flaps are

kind of frilled like a tulip bud. Her slick is the dew. Her little clit is popped from its hood, swollen and shiny. It even *looks* needy.

She works her knees further apart and arches her back, moaning low in her throat, urging me on. I shuffle forward on my knees.

Her hole is really small, and when I spread her lips with my fingers, I see it's not fully open. It's kind of divided by a thin strip of skin. That's got to be her maidenhead. Why the hell do they call it a head? It's more like a seal.

What am I going to do with it?

I stroke her ass and rumble while I consider my next move. I don't want her to feel neglected or worried that I don't know what to do. Neither Lelia nor Diantha were virgins when they invited me to bed down with them. What do I know about maidenheads? They've got a dumb name. That's it.

If it were me, I'd want it gone quickly. Rip the bandage right off. But I'm male, and I'm not skittish like Annie. Whatever I do, I better give her fair warning.

She raises her hips and rocks into my hand, growling her impatience. Yeah. Her heat is on her. She's ready.

I trail my fingers along her folds. I don't need to spread her slick around. She's already soaked. I slip my index finger into her hole and watch as the strip of flesh stretches to accommodate me. She snarls and bucks, trying to fuck herself with my finger. She likes it. Good, good.

My heart thuds in my chest. I'm fucking terrified. I can't afford to hurt her too much. Not when she doesn't know yet that I can care for her. She could decide she only wants me for heat, and that'd kill me.

I stroke her curving spine with my free hand. I can feel

each vertebra. She's so delicate. Definitely like a young doe, gentle and wary and sweet.

Regret claws at my heart. Her bare knees are in the dirt, and when she comes back to her senses, they'll probably be rubbed raw from digging into the hard ground with only a layer of dried leaves for a cushion. She'll be angry, and she'll have every right to be. I'm the one who chose to wait here for her to go into heat. I should have taken her home to the dens.

"I have quilts at home," I murmur as I work her with my finger. "A half dozen of them at least, and a snug den with a good pallet, and a nice oak barrel for bathing."

She groans, grinding against my hand. I slip another finger inside her. She's slippery and spongy, and I want to feel her gripping my cock so fucking bad, but the maidenhead has to be dealt with first, and I haven't figured it out yet.

"Do you like elk?" I ask her, finding her little swollen pearl and circling it with my thumb. "We've got a herd up by the camp. I'll bring you a nice fat cow."

She moans, and her thighs quiver. She's about to come. I hope she forgives me for what I've got to do next.

"You won't even have to skin it. I'll do everything," I promise her. "This next part might hurt, but don't be scared. It'll be quick." I give her time to complain, but she only grinds harder, so I slide another finger into her and scissor them, breaking that thin band of flesh.

She shrieks, bucking her hips, and then she groans again, loud and long, as her pussy squeezes my fingers. She's coming. Holy shit. My chest lightens. I'm doing okay.

"You're so pretty. Be easy." I hush her, running my palms down her back. Her skin is as soft as a baby rabbit's belly. I grab her waist and line my cock up with her plump, rosy slit.

"I'm going to fuck you now," I warn her, giving her another second in case she wants to tell me to wait.

Thank Fate, she drops her head to the ground, raises her hips, and says, "Do it."

My heart soars. I sink into her, and it's the most amazing thing I've ever felt. I wish I could stop time and live here, in this moment, with my mate's pussy gripping my cock as the power of her wolf's growls makes her ass vibrate against my thighs.

This isn't for me, though. This is so that she knows I can give her what she needs. I focus. I want to feel her come again.

Her channel doesn't give easy and strangles my cock. If she weren't so wet, I'd have to fight to get inside.

"So sweet," I mumble, doing everything I can to keep myself from shooting my seed inside her. I tense my abs and clench my ass and think about Max's gray pubes and his limp, saggy dick while he squats at the fire to stir the embers. Still, the base of my spine begins to tingle.

No. It's too soon.

That dead moose we found floating in the pond.

Spoiled milk.

Latrine duty.

"Shit. I'm going to come, Annie." No. Scratch that. I'm already coming. My cum explodes from my cock with so much force behind it that if my knot weren't already swelling, I would've unseated myself. As it is, my knot swells with blood so quickly that I get a head rush.

Annie grows very, very still. We're in a weird position. I'm bent over her, propping myself up on one hand so I don't put weight on her. I don't know what to do with my other hand.

I clear my throat. "Are you, uh, are you comfortable?"

She doesn't answer. She's trembling. Shit. She's probably freezing cold, naked and sweaty outside in the middle of November.

I can do better than this. "I'm going to sit us up, okay?"

Again, she doesn't answer, but she doesn't protest when I wrap an arm around her waist and lift her as I sit back on my heels. She's cradled on my lap now. Well, it's more like she's stuck to my lap, nailed in place by my dick, but at least she's upright, and I can wrap my arms around her.

She's stiff as a board, and she's shaking so hard her teeth clatter. I lean us both to the side so I can pluck her shirt from the scattered leaves. As soon as it's in reach, she snatches it from my hand.

I try to help her out by leaning back so she can get it on, but with the knot fusing us together, I can only give her so much room. She elbows me in the kidney as she shoves an arm into a sleeve.

I grunt, and she freezes. The insides of her thighs quiver helplessly against the outsides of mine like her muscles are about to give out. She's exhausted.

She needs water. Why didn't I bring any? I'm an idiot.

I rest my chin on her shoulder and rumble in her ear, breathing through my mouth so the fresh burst of her fear scent isn't quite as bad.

"Everything will be okay," I promise her. "The knot will go down soon, and I'll get you something to drink, and then we'll go to my den. You can sleep as long as you want, and I'll throw a few elk steaks on the fire, and you can take all the time you want to make your nest."

She doesn't react. She just shakes, fear rolling off her in waves.

How do I make it stop?

"I know where I can get chocolate." It'll cost me, but

Diantha has a stash, and she'll probably trade me for a nice shank steak. I hope I can get an elk so late in the season. The more I run my mouth, the more I've got riding on this bull I haven't even bagged yet.

Annie doesn't answer. She must be worn out. I stop running my mouth and focus on holding her and soaking in the amazing feeling of my knot pulsing against her warm, spongy walls.

As time ticks by, I become aware of the bond in my chest. It's a strange sensation that burns more than I thought it would, but I probably just need to get accustomed to it. Max never mentions his. He doesn't seem to notice it at all except when he wants to check and make sure that Elspeth is close to the dens. Then, he'll give it a yank and grunt when he's reassured that she's where she always is.

I can't wait to take Annie home and fuck her again when there aren't so many worries buzzing around in my brain. If her wolf has enough stamina, we can make it to the camp by tomorrow evening, and we can do this as many times as we want, in a warm, safe nest. *Inside.*

I'll feed her, and I'll show her off to the worthy males, and I'll find some excuse to fight a few of the unworthy ones, so she knows that I'm the strongest in the pack.

Maybe there is a pup taking root in her now. Warmth spreads through my chest. I don't care that I'm kneeling in the dirt far from home, freezing cold and baring my naked ass to anyone in Quarry Pack who happens along. This is everything I've ever dreamed of.

Too soon, my knot slips free. Cooling seed seeps out of Annie's pussy and drips onto my thighs. I sigh. I don't want to let her go, but we need to go.

I open my mouth to say so.

She heaves herself away from me, scrabbles onto her

back, and crab crawls out of the nest, scattering leaves in her wake.

"Get away from me!" she shouts, staggering to her feet.

I keep very still, painfully aware of my size and how wild my long hair and beard must look after so long in my fur. I must look frighteningly different from the Quarry Pack males with my tattoos and wolf-tipped ears and canines. I'd smooth them into human ears and teeth, but I've never bothered to before, and it's too late in this moment to figure it out now.

Her scent has taken on an acrid note, and her eyes are wild, the pupils hardly even pinpricks. I slowly raise my hands in the air.

"Stay away." She raises her palms to fend me off, even though I'm standing stock-still. She glances wildly over her shoulder at the river. "Don't come any closer."

Her gaze careens left and right. She's searching for the best way out. She's going to run. The intention blares through the bond.

"Don't run," I warn her. If she runs, my wolf will take our body and chase her. Normally, I could keep him reined in, no problem, but the mating exhausted me too, and honestly, it's a fifty-fifty chance whether I could stop him from taking our skin. I don't want to know what Annie will smell like if my wolf runs her to ground.

Shit. Is *that* the burning feeling in the bond? Her fear? I need to make it stop.

"My wolf won't hurt you," I tell her, just in case it comes down to it, and she does bolt, and my wolf goes after her. He'll tackle her, and he might bite her to hold her still, but he won't maul her or anything. "I won't either," I add.

She should know that, but clearly, she doesn't. She's acting like she's been attacked.

"Get away from me! Now!" Her voice is stronger than I've heard it yet.

I rise to my feet and take a small step backward. I'm not going anywhere, but I need her to breathe. My wolf is working himself up into a lather, priming himself to attack whatever's frightening our mate, and it doesn't even occur to him that it's me.

"Annie, please. Calm down."

She bolts, breaking right. My wolf surges forward to take our skin. I race to intercept her, and at the same time, I wrestle the wolf back, somehow navigating through inner and outer space in the same split second.

My head spins as my arms wrap around my mate. Her heel cracks against my shinbone. Her arms turn into windmills. She's silent as the grave while her fists and elbows drive into my shoulders and side and chest, anywhere she can land a blow. The back of her skull clunks against my jaw. I grunt. I can't stop her without hurting her. I have to let her go.

I drop her as gently as I can, but she's fighting so hard, she staggers and falls on her butt. I immediately sink to my knees and reach out my hands. Gasping in terror, she *crawls* from me. On all fours. In her human form. She's only got her shirt on. Her dirt-caked knees are cut. They're *bleeding*.

"Please stop," I beg. "What are you doing?"

In her panic, she's heading toward the river bank. Is she going to jump? Am I such a terrible mate that she would risk death to escape me?

"What's *wrong*?" If she'd only explain, I could fix it.

"*You're* wrong," she cries, scrambling to her feet. "*This* is wrong." She waves her hands wildly between us. "I don't want this. Why won't you go away? Just leave me alone. You got what you wanted."

No, I didn't. I don't want a mate who stinks like fear and crawls away from me like I'm a monster.

I want a mate. A family. What other males have. What everyone wants.

For the first time in these long, wretched weeks since I scented my mate on the wind, I let my temper flare. She's acting like I'm unworthy. Feral. Like I took her without care.

"You presented. You said 'do it.'" I heard her clear as day. She can't deny it.

She tugs her shirt tightly around herself. Her knees are knocking. "We had to get it over with, and we did. You can go now."

"We are *mates*."

She understands what that means. Even Quarry Pack males—with their pulley machines that they work at for *hours* and make *nothing*, their constant sparring, and their hoisting weights for no reason, over and over while they admire each other—even *they* haven't ventured so far from their roots that they don't bond with their fated female. Why does she say I can go? She knows I can't.

"You come with me." I reach out my hand again. "We'll go to our den now." I try to make my voice ring with authority like Max does when us younger males get out of line, but I only manage to snarl and scare her more.

I hate her fear stench. It accuses me, and I did nothing to her that I didn't have to do.

"N-no." She whips her head back and forth. Her breath comes harder. She's almost wheezing, her lungs working like she's run a mile. "D-don't c-come any closer. Don't t-touch me."

I take one step closer. That's all. I'm still six feet away, at least, but I might as well have lunged for her.

She shifts.

And it's *carnage*.

Her human body basically *pitches* her wolf out of her skin, and it's all wrong. Her wolf thrashes into being, bones cracking, tendons snapping, and muscles tearing. The shift goes on *forever*.

I reach for her, but there's nothing I can do to help, no part of her I can hold as her body rips itself to pieces, so my hands hover in the air, useless. My wolf gapes in horror as our mate seizes and writhes on the ground while her animal stitches herself together.

My gorge rises. It's a scene from a nightmare.

I know the lost packs have forgotten how to shift the right way, but I've never seen them do it up close. It's torture. Annie's screams morph into her wolf's agonized howls, and I'm powerless to help. I sink to my knees again, pounding my chest so that my wolf will rumble louder. It's all the comfort I can offer.

How can they do this to themselves? This must be why they spend so much time in their skin. To avoid this agony.

Finally, after what feels like an entire *minute*, her wolf staggers to her wobbling feet. Despite the horror, my heart warms. She's lovely, just as pretty as her human self, slender and shiny with a white topcoat, a light gray underbelly, and light gray socks. I can't make out her eye color. They're narrowed into slits.

"Welcome, beautiful," I say softly, offering her my fingers to sniff.

Her lips peel back.

She comes for me.

She launches herself at my neck, claws unsheathed, an unholy howl rising from her chest. She's coming for blood.

I snatch her from mid-air, pinning her forelegs to her sides, holding her away from my face to avoid her gnashing fangs. If I was a slower male, she'd have ripped my throat out. She still will if I let her go.

She hates me.

"What did I do?" I ask and shake her, just a little, just to calm her down.

Her wolf bucks and flails. The whites of her rolling eyes flash. Her teeth snap.

"Is there a male of your own pack that you want? Is that it?" I'll kill him. He doesn't deserve her. She lives in fear. No worthy male would allow it.

She struggles, all claws and teeth, fighting with every ounce of her strength while I try to keep her from hurting either of us.

It can't be another male. She was so afraid of me, if she had another male, she would have certainly gone to him.

She doesn't want someone else. She just doesn't want me.

Because she believes what her people say about us?

Of course. She must. And because I've always been honest with myself, at least, I have to admit that a lot of what her people think is true. We steal their females, and their pups, too, if the females can't bear to be parted from them. We live as Fate intended, and we don't do human shit like have an alpha who makes decisions for folks whose brains work perfectly fine.

The lost packs think we're a step away from feral, but ferals don't come from the camps. They were all born in packs who live in houses with walls and doors and locks.

Annie's wolf doesn't respond to my words. She's losing energy, but she doesn't give up and grazes my forearm with her small, sharp canines. I hiss. Fear floods her wolf's eyes.

My temper roars again. I've done nothing to deserve such a look. I'm not unworthy. I'm a good hunter, and I have never harmed a female or pup, nor would I. But she hated me from the first moment she saw me. She never gave me a chance. I didn't want a female from a lost pack for a mate, but I didn't try to fight Fate. I courted her, even when she scorned me.

She stunk and cowered, but I didn't treat her with contempt. Not like she treats me.

"Stop fighting, and I'll put you down," I grunt, grappling with her legs, so weak, but somehow as slippery as butter. She struggles harder, lunging at my face.

I can't bring her home with me. She won't come willingly.

There will be no family. No fire, no steak, no sweet giggles.

My heart is sick. I can't bear it. I toss her from me as far as I can. I try to be gentle. She lands in a heap, but she's on four feet in seconds. She bolts, but she's disoriented and picks the wrong direction. Almost immediately, she has to skid to a stop at the edge of the river bank.

She scrambles backward and wheels to face me, her crazed gaze darting left and right, searching for a way to escape as if she's trapped between me and the water. I guess she can't swim.

My cock shrivels. My mouth tastes like ashes. I disgust her. She thinks I'm nothing but an animal.

She let me mount her even though she didn't want me. I touched her, and the whole time, she hated it. Hated me.

I'm going to puke.

I take a step back. She whimpers.

Every move I make is a threat. I've done nothing to hurt her, nothing that I didn't have to do, and she looks at me with horror in her eyes.

Everything I never dared to dream of until a few weeks

ago—running with my own female under a full moon, cuddling our pups in our warm nest, a family, a real home—it will never happen. She doesn't want me. This scrawny, cowardly female thinks I'm not good enough.

"Tell me why," I growl, my voice deeper than it was even minutes ago. I sound like my sire. I haven't heard his voice in years, but here it is, coming from my mouth.

My mate's wolf cringes, her thin legs shaking. She tucks her chin. She's not going to shift and answer me. I'm not even worth her breath.

A spiteful rage rises in me like dust in a whipping wind, burning my eyes. What did I do to deserve this? To be left alone, over and over again?

"You've got nothing to say for yourself, do you? What a sad female you are. I don't want such a pathetic coward for a mate. What would my pack say if I brought *you* back?" My forced laugh scrapes my throat. "You smell more like food than female. You stink like prey."

I glare at the small, huddled ball, willing her to show a spark of life, to *care*, but all she does is quiver. She *is* food. She's a cowering mound of jelly.

I scoff at her, that gritty, dusty rage egging me on, drowning out my wolf. He's whining, urging me to calm her. He doesn't understand. She's turned the best moment of our life into something ugly and shameful. She rejected us. She's made us into the kind of foul, craven male who fucks unwilling females. She's trampled everything we've ever wanted under her foot. She's ruined our life.

I take a purposeful step toward her. She whines in fear, and I am glad.

"I will pray to Fate that I did not get a whelp on you." I sneer down at her. "A female like you would make weak, spindly young."

I stand over her. I want to pick her up and shake her. I want to give her something to be afraid of.

But I don't. My righteous rage deserts me in a sudden rush, and all I feel is cold and lost and far from home.

I square my shoulders, turn my back, and walk away.

With no pride.

No consolation.

And no mate.

3

ANNIE, AGE EIGHTEEN

As soon as our mate is far enough away that my wolf feels that she has a good head start to escape him if he changes his mind, she tears off in the opposite direction. She runs as far and as fast as she can, racing along the river until she can't stand the exposure anymore, and then she crosses into the woods, barreling through the undergrowth.

When her thin legs give out, she hides. Somehow, she finds her way to the blackberry bramble where we used to hide. She wriggles through the stickers, eyes squeezed shut, oblivious to the thorns scraping through her fur.

She knows he didn't follow us, but it doesn't matter. His words hurt, sharp as knives, and she might not quite understand them, but she knows she's been attacked, so she reacts accordingly.

When she's as deep in the thicket as she can get, she twists until she's facing the trail we blazed and primes herself to fight.

If he comes back, you won't have a chance against him.

The voice and I are stuck inside my wolf together now in

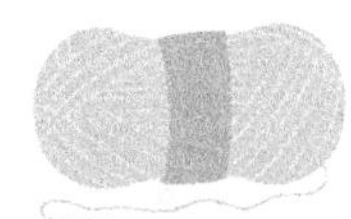

this strange nowhere place. The thicket is close and dark and barbed, sticky with the sweetness of overripe berries rotting in the black soil. Its words ricochet, amplified, booming like proclamations.

But he doesn't want you. He hates you. Did you see his face? You disgust him.

I saw his face—it's burned into my mind—and I can also *feel* his disgust, flowing through the bond. Horror. Loathing. Revulsion.

I can't breathe. My wolf is gasping, but there's no air in here.

He probably wants you dead. He's coming back to kill you. You need to run.

He's not coming back. I can feel him getting farther and farther away, and it's a relief—it *is*—or it would be, if I could breathe, but I can't.

Can you suffocate inside your wolf? What happens then? Does your wolf run around with the spirit of your decomposing body inside them? Would that smell better or worse than my constant, unrelenting stench of fear?

My wolf bares her teeth, raising up on her haunches so that she can better launch herself against whatever's threatening us, but like always, it's me, my thoughts, my utter inability to defend myself.

I let him touch me. I *told* him to do it.

I can't think about it. It didn't happen. It will be another bad dream.

I *can* breathe. I *am* breathing, even if it doesn't feel like it. I'm inflating my lungs, and if I'm really not, if I'm dying, then what will it matter if I'm lying to myself once I'm dead?

"You're not dying," a familiar, raspy voice calls into the bramble.

My wolf scuttles backward, snagging herself on a tangle of prickers. She whines.

"I mean, we're all dying, in a sense, but you're not dying right now. Probably. The odds are against it." Abertha clears her throat. "Well, it would be really ironic if you *were* dying." She's quiet for a moment. "Or would that be a coincidence? I can never remember the difference."

My wolf plasters herself to the ground, trembling. For once, the voice in my head has nothing to say. She recognizes the witch as a greater power.

"Is this going to be a long one?" Abertha waits for a response, but my throat is swollen shut, and so is my wolf's. "Okay, I'll assume that's a 'yes.' I'm just going to have a seat on this handy fold-em-up stool then." There's a scuffling sound and a long sigh. "Take your time, Annie-girl," she says and then mutters, "Goodness gracious, my dogs were *barking*."

The first jab of shame pierces my panic. *What a sad female you are. I don't want such a pathetic coward for a mate.*

I don't want to be cringing in a bramble yet again with no choice but to wait it out and feel lower than dirt afterward. I don't want to have to scrub one more humiliation out of my brain.

I am so tired of being sad and broken. I can't take myself another second.

Fueled by nothing but self-disgust, I force my wolf to crawl forward, inch by inch back out the tunnel she made on her way in, and she doesn't want to leave, but my will is stronger than hers. I drive her out of the dark thicket into the glaring late afternoon sun.

Abertha is perched on a plastic, three-legged stool, legs crossed, packing a pipe. She blinks, surprised, and smiles, flashing the gold tooth in the back of her mouth. "Atta girl,

Annie. I thought we'd be here at least 'til dusk," she says and slaps her thighs. "Let's go put the tea on."

She takes a second to tap the tobacco back into an old mint tin and return her pipe to its pouch, slipping it into a crossbody bag I made her. I embroidered her cat Apollonia on it wearing a snorkel since she likes to hang out in the bathtub. She's very strange for a feline—she likes wolves and water, and I swear, one time I saw her stick her paw out to prevent Mari from knocking a cup off the table by accident.

Once Abertha's got her bag adjusted, she tucks her stool under her arm and leads the way toward her cottage. My wolf trots at her side.

Occasionally, Abertha's long skirt brushes my wolf's flank, sending her skittering away a few steps, but then she comes back and keeps close. Abertha is safe, and she is fearsome.

She doesn't look it. She's older, her hair is silver-gray, but she doesn't have the brittle thinness that the eldest shifters get, like their bones have worn to pumice stone. She has her share of laugh lines and frown lines and red roses under her high cheekbones from decades of exposure to the sun. Sometimes, she looks fifty, and sometimes she looks seventy, and I'm never sure whether it's because of the light or her expression or how she's holding herself.

Unmated females, especially elders, are low rank as a rule, but I've seen males in their prime go out of their way to give her a wide berth. There's just something uncanny about her. She moves like a much younger shifter. She walks with a purpose. Like Kennedy.

And she's always coming and going, disappearing for days or weeks at a time. We don't stick our nose in her business, and besides taking a cut of our profits, she leaves us to our own devices with our farmers' market business.

Despite the mysteriousness, she's the only person that my wolf and I trust implicitly. She's the one who rescued us, after all.

When we get to her cozy thatch-roofed cottage, she holds the door open for my wolf. "After you," she says.

My wolf trots inside, instantly enraptured by the kaleidoscope of scents. It's like everything good about the outside has been brought into the safety of four thick walls—oils and herbs and spices and extracts and essences. Lemon, sandalwood, sage, calendula, fennel, bergamot, tea tree, and lavender. The scents all blend with years of woodsmoke, baking bread, and the oak from the exposed beams overhead and polished planks underfoot.

My wolf drags it into her lungs, and some of the oxygen finally reaches me, too. We both love it here.

"Let me see what I've got for you to wear," Abertha mumbles, throwing open the trunk at the foot of her narrow cot. She rummages until she finds a worn blue flannel and a denim skirt. The skirt is knee length and fringed at the hem, but beggars can't be choosers. I'm grateful for it.

She lays the clothes on her bed and says, "No rush. You stay in your fur as long as you need. I'll be over here, putting the kettle on."

For a second, my wolf considers the clothes. She's been through the wringer, and now that we're inside behind a barred door, she's more than ready to hand our body back. Her limbs are wobbly from running so far and so fast the very first time she's taken our skin. She braces her shaking legs, though. She's not going to abandon me if we're not safe.

I reassure her that we're okay now.

She's not convinced. I have claws, she points out, not in a cocky way. Like she's stating facts. She is better equipped to fight than I am, and even though she's bone weary, survival always comes first.

We're fine. You can rest. I draw her attention to the bar across the solid wood door and the rusty sword propped against Abertha's bedside table for some reason.

I have sharp teeth, my wolf adds.

Not sharp enough, the voice in my head chimes in. *You're no match for your mate. You're lucky that he left. If he'd wanted to hurt you, you'd be torn to pieces. You'd be—* The voice summons up the old memory and shoves it to the forefront of my brain.

Sightless eyes, staring at nothing. A twisted mouth frozen in a soundless scream.

With all the strength of mind I have left, I force the memory back, and breathing through the panic rising in my chest, I close my eyes.

Come on, wolf. Hand our body over.

She doesn't give in. She gives up, collapsing to the floor, and again, my bones crack and muscles tear. The pain is blinding, the reconstruction as violent as the demolition. I curl into a ball. Life has always been this way. It's never once been easy.

My mate went from wolf to a man in an instant. He flip-shifted, like Killian. No one else in the civilized packs can flip-shift, except Alban Hughes from Moon Lake, and he can only do it once or twice, like a party trick, not whenever he wants like Killian. Rumor has it that Alban Hughes was raised in the Last Pack, and they can all flip-shift there.

Is that where my mate is from? What's his name?

If he's gone forever, I'll never know.

Good, the voice says. *You're safe.*

Her reassurance doesn't let me relax like it usually does. My muscles are still frozen in knots as I drag on the shirt and skirt. My biceps ache. My thighs burn. Every part of me hurts, especially between my legs where I feel tender and torn.

My face burns, and I button the flannel all the way up to the neck. I'm not going to think about it.

I cross the room to Abertha's table, and when I sit, I don't let the pain show. I keep my back straight and my head up.

That hour by the river didn't happen. I wasn't there. It isn't real unless I want it to be, and I don't. I know how to make it so that ugly things didn't really happen. I know how to live *around* them.

Abertha plonks the teapot down on a trivet and returns to her kitchenette, coming back a minute later with a tray crowded with mismatched cups, saucers, a sugar bowl, a cream pitcher and a package of cookies from the store in Chapel Bell still in the wrapper.

I keep my hands on my lap. They're shaking like crazy.

After giving me a once-over, Abertha pours. She dumps a huge spoonful of sugar and a big splash of cream in both of our cups, gives me another look, takes a flask from her pocket, fills our cups to the brim with its contents, and then carefully pushes my saucer across the table.

I wrap both hands around the warm china, holding it close to my face so the steam bathes my cheeks and nose. I inhale. Valerian root and whiskey. Everything feels a tiny bit less dire. That's the power of tea.

For a few, long minutes, Abertha levels me with her cool gray gaze. Is she not sure what to say? That would be a first. She doesn't always make sense, but she's never shy about speaking her mind.

Finally, she blows across her cup and says, "So, I

suppose the most urgent issue before us is—do you want a pup or not?"

My jaw drops. My stomach follows. "Pup?"

My hands fly up to cover my mouth. Quicker than should be possible, Abertha lunges for a mop bucket and swings it onto the table beside my teacup. The pail hits the oak with a solid thunk, startling me enough that the urge to heave disappears. My wolf yelps and hides her head under her paws.

I lower my hands back to my lap and straighten my shoulders.

"We good?" Abertha arches a thin, gray eyebrow.

I nod.

"All right. So, circling back to the subject—pups?"

Dear Fate. Pups? I can't think about pups. I can't *fathom* pups. I can't wrap my brain around this moment, right here, right now. I'm not even wearing underwear.

What if I'm leaking? It feels like I'm leaking. The denim of the skirt should be thick enough to absorb it, but I'm not sure. At least the chair is wood. It'll wipe clean. I don't want to leak on Abertha's furniture. I want to go home.

I'm filled with a male's seed, and he's my mate, and I don't know his name, and he hates me, and I don't want a mate from a pack that lives like animals, but every angry word he said also sticks in my chest like a dozen knitting needles.

Sad female.

Coward.

Stink like prey.

A female like you would make weak, spindly young.

I can't think about it. It didn't happen.

Are Una and the others worried about me? How long

have I been gone? I have no idea. In order to figure it out, I'd have to flip back in time, and I won't. I'm erasing it.

I've known for a long time how to make things go away. It's simple. Every time your mind tries to go to the past, you yank it away and give it something else to think about. Anything else, but worries work really well.

If you do yank every single time, eventually, your mind doesn't go there anymore, and if it does, you quickly give it something else to worry about that *could* happen. You tell yourself that if you don't worry hard enough, it *will* happen. And that's how you deal with the past. It's simple.

Not easy.

But simple.

It's warm in the cottage, but I'm shaking like a leaf. Am I getting sick?

I lost my shoes back by the river. How am I going to walk home? What if I come across a rabid natural wolf? Or a feral? How will I run?

"Can I borrow a pair of boots?" I ask Abertha.

The corners of her eyes crease, the steely gray gentling, but her jaw sets. "Not yet, Annie-girl. No shoving this into a deep, deep worry hole quite yet. You've got to deal with the issue at hand."

"I don't want to," I say softly.

She exhales. "I know."

She is quiet for a time, sipping her tea, dangling the fingers of her left hand to lure Appollonia over from her basket by the fire to be petted.

Abertha does know. She was there that night, not in the middle of it, but when it was too late. When it was deathly quiet.

Aunt Nola forgot her bag.

I was eight. We'd just finished a full-moon feast, and Declan

Kelly had ordered the unmated females down to the lodge's basement. Aunt Nola left the bag I'd made her on the table. I'd made it from an old denim shirt and cross-stitched it with the treasures she always brought me back from her rambles—walnuts, blackberries, nettles, pretty stones.

She loved her bag—it was her favorite thing—so I decided to take it to her. To make her feel better.

When Declan bellowed for the lone females, her face went ghost white, and Ma smothered a cry with her fist in her mouth. Half of the great room went silent. The other half—the males—stomped their boots and howled.

While Ma was whisper-hissing with the other dams, I slipped away, down the stairs. I'd been in the basement many times before to help Aunt Nola clean. There were no windows, only fluorescent lights with the shadows of dead flies smudged against the plastic.

I tripped into the room. The lone females were clustered together, their fear blossoming in the air like skunk spray.

They saw me skid across the linoleum.

Heavy footsteps sounded at the top of the stairs.

They surged toward me as one, reaching for me with octopus arms, clutching me close and bearing me away. A palm mashed my lips into my teeth. Steel fingers curled around my wrist.

They lifted me, rushed me over to an old leather sofa against the wall, shoved me underneath, and kicked Aunt Nola's bag in after. The sofa was saggy, the cushions drooping over the warped wooden slats. I couldn't turn my head. There wasn't enough room. I had to stare out into the room, and all I could see were tiles, skirt hems, and dirty, scuffed boots.

Males laughed and shouted and brayed, their voices echoing off the low ceiling. The scent of liquor, sweat, aggression, and fear seeped under the edge of the sofa, burning my eyes.

The females' small feet were frozen in place while the males' boots stomped and dashed and rocked back on their heels.

Wedged so tightly between the underside of the sofa and the cold floor, I couldn't hear the males' words, but I understood them all the same. They were taunting the females. Lunging at them to make them shriek. As the fear stench grew thicker and thicker, their laughs boomed louder.

And then something changed. A female screamed in earnest. Then another. Feet dashed. Shouts rose, followed by guttural snarls. A rubber sole squeaked on the tile. The swampy air thickened with copper and salt and terror and pain and rage.

I didn't dare close my eyes.

A yard away, Iona Ryan fell to the floor by the leg of the pool table, cradling her left arm. It was hanging from the socket wrong. A male approached her, looming, squatting—

Aunt Nola crashed to her knees, right next to my head, holding her dress to her chest. It had been rent, collar to hem. She hovered there, bent over, shoulders hunched, her side pressed against the sofa, blocking me, shielding me while she shook, head tucked to her chin, arms tight to her ribs, protecting her organs.

The weeping and screaming and laughter whipped toward some kind of crescendo, and something inside me screamed run, but I couldn't move. I couldn't protect my soft parts; I couldn't even turn my head.

And then a distant door slammed into a wall as it was flung open. New shouts filled the air.

"Fire!"

"The commissary is on fire!"

Declan Kelly and his favored males rumbled in disbelief.

"It's burning down!"

They ran, stomping up the stairs, their frenzy put on hold like it was nothing at all.

The silence that they left in the basement resonated like an aftershock. It singed like ozone.

The males' heavy footsteps trekked across the ceiling, tracking away toward the front of the lodge. Aunt Nola rose to her knees, and I could see the others' bare feet as they picked through the clothes and shoes strewn about like they'd been caught in a tornado.

They moved slowly, silently, like haunts. Aunt Nola staggered to her feet and wandered a few steps away, so I could see.

A female on her back in the middle of the room, staring at me. Her eyes were dark and wide. They didn't blink.

It was Orla Sullivan.

I'd never really spoken to her. She was grown. I was only eight.

She was old enough to be mated, but she wasn't, and now she never would be.

I'd never spoken to her, but I'd heard her scream.

She rested in a pool of blood, her sightless blue eyes staring at me, her mouth twisted in a frozen scream. Red marks blossomed on her skin like roses.

We looked at each other, but she wasn't there, and neither was I. It wasn't real. It couldn't be.

Iona Ryan used her good hand to cover Orla's body with someone's torn dress. Blood soaked through the homespun linen. More roses.

"They didn't get her," the females whispered to each other as they circled Orla Sullivan's body, drifting into each other's arms, holding each other up.

"Where is she?"

"Under the couch."

"She alive?"

"Yes. She's safe. She's fine."

"Did she see?"

"No, no, Nola blocked her view."

"She's not hurt?"

"She's fine. They didn't see her."

The females murmured and wept—softly into their hands or with their faces pressed into each other's bare shoulders—until a sharp step sounded on the stair. They tensed and then exhaled as one when Old Noreen's raspy voice called down, "It's clear. I have the crone."

I couldn't see what happened then. Nola and a few others moved and blocked my view, but I heard Abertha's quiet orders, and I smelled the smoke that clung to her skirts.

"You, get her shoulders. You two, get her sides. You and you, get her knees. Wait. Hold a second. Let me cover her back up. Take her out through the kitchens. There's a wheelbarrow by the woodbin. Take her to my cottage. We'll clean her up there. Don't let her mother see. Keep your ears open and your eyes peeled. Go quickly."

There were murmurs and grunts and a thump, and then Aunt Nola and the others drifted apart, and Orla was gone. The green and white checkered vinyl tile where she had been lying was empty, except for the blood. The white tiles were smeared with bright red. The blood was so dark against the green that it looked black.

Aunt Nola bent over and offered me a trembling hand. "It's safe now, Annie. You can come out."

No, it's not, *a strange, new, blade-sharp voice had said in my head.* It's a lie. She knows she's lying. Look at her shake. It's a trap.

I tried to scrunch myself farther back, but I was lodged in tight, my cheek pressed to the slat holding up the sagging leather cushions.

"Come on, Annie," Aunt Nola begged. "We've got to get out of here." She darted a glance over her shoulder.

They're out there, the voice said. She knows they're out there, and she's afraid.

Aunt Nola knelt and reached for me. Somehow, I curled my fingers around a slat, puffing my body so she couldn't budge me.

"Annie, you've got to come now. What if they come back?"

See, she lied. It isn't safe. Don't let her take you.

Tears rolled down Aunt Nola's cheek. "Please, Annie. Please."

I couldn't tell her to leave me. I couldn't make a noise.

"Oh, for heaven's sake." *The crone's boots appeared next to Aunt Nola. The hem of her flowy skirt was stained with brown blood, already drying.*

Abertha lowered herself into a squat and peered under the sofa. Her face was gaunt and grim, but her gray eyes flashed like steel.

"Why is she down here?" Abertha asked.

"I left my bag on the table when they called me. She thought to bring it to me."

Abertha hissed softly through her teeth. "You were quiet as a mouse, weren't you?"

I was.

"Good girl. You did right. But you've got to come out now."

I couldn't.

"It's not safe here," Abertha said. "The males are still blood mad. They've left for now to deal with the fire, but they'll be back. It's not time for quiet mouths anymore. It's time for quick feet." *She snapped her fingers, and her bangles jingled.*

The voice in my head had nothing to say. Abertha was right, but I still couldn't move. Nothing worked, not my legs, not my arms. Even my fingers were frozen, curled around the wooden slat.

"Oh, hell," Abertha sighed. "Can you lift the couch, Nola? Maybe I can grab her..."

Foot falls sounded on the ceiling above us. Aunt Nola moaned in fear.

"Shit. Get out of here, Nola. Now. I've got the pup."

Aunt Nola swayed. The scent of her fresh terror lashed my face.

Abertha pushed her. "Go now. I can't see to both you and the pup. Go! I've got her." Her voice was as hard as stone.

Aunt Nola stumbled in the direction of the stairs, and then she ran. Her bare feet left trails in Orla's blood.

For a moment, the crone just stared at the couch, as if she was gauging its weight, but then she sighed and said, "I've got an idea."

She reached under her skirt and took a knife from her leather ankle holster.

She held it so I could see, and then she placed it solemnly on the tile in front of her, hilt toward me. "The tip is poisoned. You don't even have to stab someone. Just nick his skin, and he'll die in agony."

My gaze homed in on the blade. I wanted it so badly. It was so close. So sharp.

The crone nudged it forward. "You know who gave that to me? Darragh Ryan. The Mercenary. The Haunt of the Hills."

I'd heard of him—everyone had—even though he'd left the pack before I was born. The males got shifty when his name came up, but their dismissive laughs always rang false, like they were whistling past a graveyard.

"Go on, Annie-girl. Take it. We have to get out of here before they come back even angrier."

The voice inside me had nothing to say. Abertha was telling the truth.

All I had to do was reach out and take it. Let go of the slat and grab. It was so close.

I willed my fingers to let go of the slat. To reach and wrap around the knife's handle.

I sucked in my belly and scooted out from under the sofa.

Abertha held out her hand, her eyes pleading. "Good girl. Come on now."

Boots pounded down the steps, so quick, too quick for me to do anything but look at a huge male skid to a halt at the bottom of the stairs, his mouth curling into a sneer.

The knife slipped from my fingers, clattering to the floor.

"Shit," Abertha muttered under her breath.

"What have we here?" the male said. He bared his teeth and licked a canine. It wasn't human. It was wolf.

Run, my wolf urged me with all her might. Run, run, run.

"I can't," I whispered back. "My legs don't work."

Abertha moved to block me. The male laughed. "I have enough for you, too, witch," he said as his hand went to his belt buckle.

"Now or never, Annie-girl," Abertha hissed.

I looked down at the knife. So did the male.

Run, my wolf begged.

I bent. Curled my little fingers around the knife's hilt. The male came for me.

Abertha shielded my body with hers, covering every part of me except for my arm. That, she tugged forward, covering my small hand with hers, squeezing it like a vise, and with an impossible strength, she lunged and stabbed the male with the knife in my hand, tearing my shoulder from its socket as she plunged the blade into his stomach. Hot blood spurted over our hands.

The male blinked down at the red stain blossoming on his shirt.

Abertha bolted for the stairs, towing me by my blood-soaked hand, dragging my entire body when my legs buckled, faster than I'd ever have imagined she could.

I couldn't tear my eyes from the male. He was still standing. He glanced up from the knife, his gaze narrowing on us, his gray face twisting into a howling maw, his fangs descending.

"Abertha, he's not dying in agony."

He was wrapping his clawed hands around the hilt.

"Life lesson—magic doesn't always work, but your feet do," Abertha huffed. "Run, Annie-girl. Run!"

We scrambled up the last few stairs, tearing through the lodge and out through the kitchens, fleeing into the dark woods away from the eerie, red sky over the burning commissary.

I take a long sip of my cooling tea, bringing myself back to the present.

Until today, I don't think I've ever run so fast and far as I did when I escaped that basement. After that night, I became some kind of burrowing animal, living life hiding in plain sight with my eyes screwed shut. But I can't hide from this.

I mated a wolf from Last Pack. His seed is inside me right now. I can't pretend it didn't happen. Not yet.

"I can't have a pup," I say. A babe would be vulnerable. It would need me. I can hardly take care of myself, and I'm definitely not strong enough to protect it from this world.

Abertha doesn't even blink. "Are you sure?"

Am I sure? What choice do I have? You mate, and then, unless you get really, really lucky, you have a pup. And I'm not lucky.

I have heard whispers, though. Some females don't keep their babes. I don't even know where I heard that, or how I know, but I picked it up somewhere, the same way I learned how to pitch my voice when a male is angry and that when a male tells you to smile, that's a threat and he's dangerous.

There are ways.

The crone would know them.

"I can't—" The words stick in my throat. I can't be a mother. But I can't make the choice not to be, either. I don't have that power. I don't want it. I'm scared, too scared for any of it.

I want my mother. I want her back.

"Can't what?" Abertha asks, so very gently.

"I can't have a pup." And I can't make the decision not to. "But I—" I can't say it. Fate will surely strike me down if I do. What's done cannot be undone.

"There are ways," she says, pushing up from the table and padding to the kitchen. She takes a mason jar from an overhead cabinet and spoons loose leaves into a metal ball strainer. My nose twitches. The blend smells medicinal.

I watch her like a mouse watches an eagle. She shuffles back to the table, downs the dregs of her tea, and then drops the strainer in and pours a fresh cup of hot water.

Is that poison?

"I can't...can't do *that* to a pup."

Abertha's face hardens. She holds the strainer by its thin chain and dips it into the water. "We're not talking about a pup."

"We aren't?"

"Not at this point." She lets out a long, tired breath. "What do they even teach you at that academy?"

I shrug. "Literature. Geology. Calculus."

"What is that?"

"I don't know. It's math about figuring change. Continuous change."

"At least that sounds useful. Change *is* continuous." She gives her head a shake and returns to the subject. "You've learned no basic anatomy and biology, though, I'm guessing. How do I put this...we're not talking about a pup because there *is* no pup. No bun in the oven yet. Just ingredients. Or *possible* ingredients."

"What's a *possible* ingredient?"

"Well, to be specific, the egg. The egg is still in the fridge. It's not even in the mixing bowl yet. And an egg in the carton isn't an *ingredient*, right? Who knows what you're going to do with that egg. You might throw it at someone's truck. You might drop it."

I have no idea what she's talking about. I think the bowl is my vagina, but the rest—I'm lost. I did take biology and anatomy, but it was mostly about the mechanics of shifting and how we're different from humans, so we need to be careful not to hurt them by accident.

Abertha sighs again. "Okay, let me put it this way. Is an egg in the fridge a cake?"

"No."

"If you mix egg and flour and leave it on the counter, is it a cake?"

"No."

"To make a cake, you've got to mix the egg and flour and put it in the oven, and if you don't take the egg out of the fridge, or if you don't put the batter in the oven, all you've got are ingredients. No cake."

"Okay."

"The cake is a pup." Abertha is looking at me like I'm slow as molasses.

"I get that."

"The oven is your uterus. *Not* your vagina. And there's a difference."

My face heats. I didn't say that out loud. She can't know I was thinking it.

"We can shut the refrigerator door so no egg gets out. Get it? No cakes will be hurt. No cakes will ever exist."

"I get it." I kind of do. She can give me something that will make it like today never happened. Nothing and no one will be hurt. I can erase everything. That's what I want. My heart doesn't hurt at the thought. Those are just aches from a hard day. "Okay, yes, I want that. Is it sure to work?"

"It's very likely to work. Of course, if the cake's already in the oven, it won't."

"Will it hurt the cake if the cake is already in there baking?" I don't want to hurt anything. I just want it never to have happened.

"No, it won't. If you shut the refrigerator door after the egg gets out, it has no bearing whatsoever on the cake."

I stare at the dark green brew, and the thin tendrils of steam rising into the air. My mate is gone. I've already muffled the bond to a cold, fading shadow in my chest. Soon, I'll be able to consign it to the deep well where I consign all the bad things that have happened to me in my life. If I do this, that's it. It'll be me, alone, forever.

Safe, the voice whispers. *Safe forever*.

"All right. I'll drink it," I say.

Abertha blinks. "Oh, no, not the tea. That's for me. For my nerves."

She stands again to go rummage in her cupboard and comes back with a waxed paper box with green and blue swirls sealed in plastic. It's human. They love to seal paper boxes in plastic.

She passes it to me. "I'll let you open this. Humans do these things up like bear traps."

Out of habit, I reach for the knife in my ankle holster, but it's not there. I must have lost it during my shift.

A memory flashes in my mind. The knife clattering to the linoleum floor in the lodge basement. A wave of sick horror rises in me, clogging my throat, until I swallow it back down. That's the distant past. I'm not there, in that moment, anymore. I know how the story ends.

The male died. Somehow, in the confusion that followed, Abertha got the knife back and brought it to me. She said, "Life lesson—sometimes the magic needs time."

I take a deep breath and force my brain back into the moment. The text on the box comes into focus.

Plan B.

What was plan A supposed to be?

I try to pry the plastic apart, but my nails are torn from what happened by the river. Eventually, I use my teeth to rip the package open. In the end, after I unbox and unwrap everything, it's only a tiny white pill.

"This is it?" I ask. "It's so small."

Abertha hums in agreement and sips her tea. She's letting me make the decision, but really, it's no choice at all. If I can make it like this never happened, erase it without hurting anyone, of course I will. Keep the egg in the fridge

I pop the pill and chase it with a sip of lukewarm tea.

"It never happened," I say to myself.

"Didn't it?" Abertha raises an eyebrow.

"No." And in the rush of deciding for myself, a molten flood of frustration fills me. I don't *want* this.

I don't want to have a failed mating. I don't want to go back and tell Una and the others that I mated a strange wolf from the Last Pack, and I rejected him, and he walked away, disgusted. I don't want them to look at me with even more pity.

I can't bear for them to whisper about me behind my back and shake their heads yet again. It took years for the females to stop looking at me like I'm a ghost, a walking reminder of Orla's dead body and that basement and the horrors of Declan Kelly's time.

I don't think the pity would have ever stopped if Killian hadn't sent the worst-off females away to live in other packs. He sent my Aunt Nola to Salt Mountain. Before she left, she got so bad, she wouldn't leave the house. Once the ones who couldn't get over it were gone, the others let themselves forget, and they let me blend into the scenery like I wanted.

My failed mating is going to turn back the clock. They'll stare and whisper, and in their eyes, once again, I'll see nothing but regret that they couldn't save me from what that night did to my head—and that they couldn't save themselves at all.

It's too heavy to bear.

"Can you make it so no one knows?" It's a child's request, but I want it like a child wants magic to fix the unbearable, and I'm *sure* that she can.

"What do you mean?" Abertha narrows her eyes.

"Cast a spell. Make it so that no one notices that I'm different now."

She shifts back in her chair. "That's a big ask, little girl."

"I can pay." But actually, no, I can't. I have some money stashed from our farmers' market sales, but most of it slips through my fingers. There's a human at the market who weaves yarn from alpaca, and it's so soft, I can't resist, and I spend most of what I make before we leave town. "I can work off the cost."

A speculative gleam lights in her eyes. "You know, no one can dodge their fate forever."

That's what everyone says. You can't fight Fate. But Fate feels very far away, and honestly, part of me feels like I've been living on borrowed time ever since the basement. Who knows if I'll even be around when Fate decides to make me pay up. I need to get through tonight and tomorrow. I need to make this go away, and I can't if everyone is staring and wondering where my mate has gone.

"Please help me." I make myself hold her gaze, make her see—in me—the pup under the couch who she rescued, if rescued is the word.

I can tell the exact moment that she remembers she was too late that night, and like the rest of us, not nearly as powerful as we needed to be.

She sighs. "You'll owe me. One day, I'll come to collect."

"Whatever I have will be yours."

Her lip quirks. "Clearly, your instructors at that academy are not the only ones failing you educationally. Never promise a witch 'whatever you have' while drinking her brew in her cottage in the woods. Have you never read a fairy tale in your life?"

"Make it like it didn't happen, and I'll be in your debt forever." It's an easy vow. What do I have that's worth anything?

She sighs. "All right. It's not a simple spell, though. I'm going to need to fetch some ingredients. And you're going to have to watch Appollonia while I'm gone. Don't let her outside no matter how much she yowls. She's been digging up the yams again."

"You can really make it so no one asks any questions about why I can shift now?"

"Eh." Abertha piles the tray with our tea things and rises from the table. "I can make folks uninterested in the fact. I am becoming an uncommonly powerful witch, but still, it's hard to make people not see what they see, or not smell what they smell. It's very easy to make it so they don't *care*, though. That's just encouraging folks' natural selfish inclinations."

For the first time since I lost control of my will by the

river, I feel a glimmer of hope. I walk on wobbling legs to the kitchen and run the dish water, holding my fingers in the stream to feel for when the heat is right. Abertha sets the tray on the counter. For a long moment, we stand side by side, our shoulders brushing, and we stare together out the small window above the sink.

Dusk is almost done, but the garden and the woods beyond are still cast in a rich, royal blue. The color belongs to early summer—it's out of season—but the sky overhead is true to November, crisp and clear and smattered with stars. The moon is round and low. Inside my chest, my wolf stirs, shaken to her bones and exhausted, but still drawn to its glow. The moon seems wise, somehow, as if it knows things we can't.

Is the Last Pack male looking up at it, right now? Does he feel his loneliness, like I do? Is he still angry? I'm too scared to search inside me for that fragile bond. I don't want to feel his hate *inside* me.

He's probably back in his fur and miles away, happy to be done with me.

Which is good.

I'm grateful.

He doesn't want a female like me, and I don't want him.

Abertha will fix things. No one will wonder why I can shift if I have no mate. And in a few months, if I shove this away like I did the night in the basement, he'll never even come to mind.

And it's not the saddest thing; it doesn't break my heart at all.

I'm going to be safe.

I decided. I chose.

And if it doesn't feel like a choice, no matter.

I'm not trapped, I'm not hurt, and I'm not scared. And in my experience, that's pretty much the best you can hope for.

4

JUSTUS, FIVE YEARS LATER

"What the hell was that, Alroy?" I roar as I pin together Max's wolf's flailing forelegs so I can wrap the bloody gash that Killian Kelly ripped down his side. Max is not making it easy. The old dog has more fight left in him than I'd have thought.

None of our wolves escaped Killian Kelly unscathed. They stand around the clearing thunderstruck, listing side to side and dripping blood in the dirt.

Only Alroy and Khalil are on two feet, and only because I commanded them out of their fur and into their skin. Since we were pups, they've been the source of all trouble and a constant burr in my side. I'm not sure which is worse —Alroy's inability to think through an idea or Khalil's utter disregard for consequences.

Alroy paces, dragging his hands through his red hair. "It was supposed to be a straight trade. I made the deal with the younger Byrne. He said Kelly wouldn't be an issue."

Alroy's balls have long since dropped, but you wouldn't know from the high-pitched whine in his voice. He sounds like he shifted for the first time yesterday.

He almost got us all killed, and Khalil, with his death wish, was happy to egg him on.

"What did you trade?" I growl at Alroy. "Your ever-loving mind?"

Max nips my hand, taking advantage of my distraction to express his displeasure that I'm wrapping up his guts so they don't plop onto the forest floor. I hoist his carcass high in the air and give him a shake. "Enough, gray belly! You're bleeding all over the place. You'll leave a trail."

Finally, he sees sense and goes limp. His paws and tail dangle like a chastised pup's. I set him down on a log and finish binding the wound. He got the worst of it. It's a miracle no one died. Alroy and Khalil didn't recruit our best for this misadventure. Just our dumbest.

"Could you not smell a trap? Is your snout stuck as far up your ass as your head? Eh?" I tie off the bandage and pat Max's haunch. He grumbles and immediately starts gnawing at the shirt I used to staunch the bleeding. I whack his nose. He waits until I walk off a few paces before he starts back at it.

I get in Alroy's pasty face until it blanches so white, his freckles look like they're floating.

"I'm sorry, Alpha," he whimpers, baring his neck and backing away.

"For the hundredth time, I'm not the alpha."

All the males in the clearing, wolf and man, give me that look. I bare my fangs, and their gazes slide away and their heads tilt.

"I'm *not* the goddamn alpha." I repeat it loud enough to shake the remaining birds from their perches in the high branches. Signaling to Killian Kelly exactly where we are. Now I'm being a dumbass, too.

If I were the alpha, I wouldn't be here. Alroy would have

felt obliged to run his fool plan past me. I wouldn't have heard it from Max too late to stop this sad-sacked, Fate-forsaken pack of absolute shit-for-brains from crossing into Quarry Pack territory before I could reach them.

I wouldn't have seen *her*.

I wouldn't feel like this.

"By all rights, we should be dead right now," I snarl and swing my gaze around the clearing, and they stumble backward. "If Kelly wasn't more interested in the traitors in his own pack, we'd be worm meal."

Well, Alroy and his band of merry dipshits would. Kelly is a majestic fighter—unworldly—but he defaults to expecting his opponent to come at him head-on. That's how the lost packs fight—in roped-off stages with bells announcing the first blow. It's a good thing he wasn't raised in First Pack. He'd be invincible if he'd spent his pup-hood like us with his pack brothers leaping onto him from behind every boulder and every tree branch sturdy enough to hold them.

As it is, it'd be a toss-up whether I could win against him. He's clearly not the young, stupid male he was back when I found my mate.

Annie.

My guts knot, and my gorge rises. The old rage drags its claws down my skin from the inside. I ignore it, scanning my pack to see who else is hiding a potentially mortal injury. Elis is crouched low to the ground with his rear up in the air. I grunt and carefully keep my eyes focused on the others while I slowly sidle closer to him.

Killian has learned a few things in the years since I basically strolled onto his territory. His patrols still travel the same routes, but they're staggered, and they overlap, and he has sentries at the river now. And his reputation as a monster has even reached us. He must be fearsome indeed if even out in the camps, we hear tales.

He relies on his opponent being thrown when he shifts mid-air, though. He wasn't raised playing snatch 'em like we were in First Pack. I was king of that game. I could predict where a tail would appear, and I'd grab it and swing the wolf like a lasso and then let him go to see how far I could make him fly. Those were good times.

Maybe that's what's wrong with my packmates. I threw too many of them into tree trunks when we were pups.

"What the hell were you thinking?" I bark at Alroy, sneaking a glance at Elis's wolf. He's trying his best to hide a gash in his belly, but blood is seeping into the dirt around him.

"I was thinking three unmated females," Alroy answers, awfully defiant for how badly his hands are shaking.

I snort. Except for the blessed one, not a single one of those females was unmated, and I'd like to see any of my pack brothers claim the blessed one's wolf. He's a beast. You can smell his size. He must be as big as a moose.

"You're a fool."

"You don't understand," Alroy whines, his face flushing from white to red like beet juice poured into a glass of milk. "Fate gave you a mate. You had a choice."

A choice. Annie's stiff body and fear stench flash in my memory. I wouldn't call walking away a choice.

She's even thinner now. Her brown eyes are hollows, eating up even more of her face. Back at the Quarry Pack dens, while the Byrnes were strutting around and blustering like stuffed roosters, she didn't look at me once. Not even from the corner of her eye. Her fear stink was the same as I remember. My wolf almost took our skin. If I wasn't stronger willed than him, he would have.

I never told the pack that she didn't want me. I told them she was too afraid to live like a real wolf, that she was twisted in her head like the others in the lost packs, so I left her where she belongs. Where she wants to be.

I hate her, and I hate myself for it. It feels wrong to despise such a weak and cowardly female, so I am ashamed of myself, and I hate her for that, too.

"What were you planning to do when Quarry Pack came to fetch their females?" I ask Alroy to distract myself from that train of thought.

"It was a fair trade, not a theft."

"And what were you trading?" I ask. I bend over Elis and rest my hands on his sides. He tenses and whines. I wait for him to relax. The last thing I want to do is upset an injured Elis. When his wolf bites, he goes for your dick.

Alroy mumbles an answer that sounds like pelts and steaks.

He better not have fucking said pelts and steaks.

"What?" I ask sharply. Elis startles and presses himself more stubbornly into the dirt, whimpering when it hurts. Dumb wolf. I pat his haunch and rumble.

Alroy hangs his head. His expression is still ornery, but his face is turning green. His lips are mashed together. He's decided silence is his best move.

I look at Khalil and raise an eyebrow.

"Pelts and steaks," Khalil says.

My stomach sinks. "How many?"

"All of them," Khalil says, holding my gaze. He'd love for me to take it as a challenge. He's been angling for a real fight for years, but if he wants to go out in a blaze of glory, he can find someone else to do the dirty work. There is no room in the pack I carry for any more ghosts.

"Fate's own *idiots*," I groan, searching my memory. I don't remember seeing a stack of pelts and steaks at the Quarry Pack dens. "Tell me you hid the goods somewhere until *after* you had the females in hand."

Khalil's brown cheeks darken. "One of their males hauled it all into a den before you got there."

I lift my hands off Elis so I don't squeeze his guts out through his belly as my fingers ball into fists. "And you thought you'd make this trade right under Kelly's nose?"

Khalil shrugs. "Old Byrne said something's wrong with Killian's new mate. He said she's made him weak and distracted."

"And you didn't question how reliable the word of a male making deals behind his alpha's back might be?"

"We make deals behind your back." Khalil smirks.

"I am *not* the alpha."

Khalil shrugs again.

Every word from these idiots' mouths pumps more blood into my brain. It's going to explode. "The lost packs have alphas," I begin for the thousandth time. "*They* are the ones so lacking in pride that the stronger make themselves bigger by standing on the shoulders of the weaker, pretending that's *our* way. *Our* instinct. But that is *man's* way. Look at the natural wolves. You only find alphas in cages. In *zoos*. In the woods and hills, there are only *packs*."

My pack gapes at me, blinking.

They're tired of hearing it, and I'm tired of saying it, but damned if I can stop myself. "When the smoke shed is full, and the firewood is piled high, when everyone is cared for, from the weakest to the strongest, there is no need for alphas."

"Well, Alpha, I have some bad news for you. Don't know that the smoke shed is full anymore," Khalil says, raising a pointed black eyebrow.

My wolf snarls in my throat.

Khalil puffs his chest and opens his arms. "Well, come on," he says. "I've been waiting. *Alpha*."

My temper snaps.

We meet mid-air in a collision of fur and skin, limbs and fangs and feet and claws. He moves faster than the last time we brawled, but his weakness is still his weakness—what he really, truly wants is pain, not a win.

Except for Elis—who lies still and watches with his muzzle flat on the ground—the others edge away, licking their wounds while they enjoy the show. I don't fight much these days. No one will try me except Khalil.

He attacks with no strategy, snapping and swiping at whatever part of me he can reach, shifting to dodge and lunge without thinking about where I'm going to be or what I'm doing.

He leaps for my neck. I shift, squat, grab his hindlegs as he sails overhead, and swing him through the air at an oak, just like a game of snatch 'em. He hits the trunk with a meaty thud. I've still got it.

He shifts back to man as he slides to the forest floor.

"Stay down," I tell him, but his eyes are on fire. For all his nonchalance, he's angry that he had to walk away without a female.

I understand the feeling.

He leaps back to his feet and sprints at me. I wait until he's close, and I shift, clamping down on his calf with the full force of my jaw. I dash forward, dragging him so he lands flat on his back. He shifts to wolf, curling and writhing, trying to get a piece of me, but I hold him tight and shift again, knocking him across the dirt with the force of my bigger human body exploding into his wolf.

He comes at me over and over, in fur and skin, and I

carve him up like a bird at the full moon table. After his calf, I rip into his shoulder, and then a knee, and a hip. It takes him longer and longer to drag himself upright.

He's fighting to stop hurting. It doesn't work. I learned that the first few years after I walked away from Annie.

Finally, after a lucky hit directly to his human sternum that steals his breath, he falls onto his ass and stays there. When he's finally able to speak, he huffs, "We didn't know that the Byrnes planned to take Kelly out."

I grunt, spit blood from my mouth, and then crouch next to Elis to continue checking him out. "You should have bailed the minute you figured it out."

"It was too late. We already scented Kelly on the wind. Would you have had us run like cowards?"

I pluck a stick from the nearby undergrowth and hurl it at his head. He ducks, and it misses, nailing Tiny Jac's wolf in the side of his head. He yelps and skitters away.

"I wouldn't have had you do anything because *I am not your alpha!*" I shout, scooping up Elis since he's already startled and peeking at his belly. It's a mess. "But if I had been fool enough to join forces with a bunch of delusional lost packers trying to overthrow their battle-chosen alpha, then yes, I would have run when I realized I'd kidnapped his mate. Give me your pants!" I snap at Alroy. He's the only one of us who took the time to snag his clothes when we did, in fact, run.

Alroy immediately fumbles with his waistband. I quickly look down. Guts peek through the gash in Elis's underside. It still beats seeing Alroy's dick.

His pants land in a heap beside me. I amp up my rumble and murmur to the young wolf huddled and shaking in the dirt. "It'll be over quick, brother. A few moments to get your stuffing back in, and you'll be right as rain."

His sad whine tears at my heart.

"On three," I say. "One. Two." I roll him onto his back, pin him in place with one arm, and frantically pack his wound with moss before any more intestine pops out. He manages a few weak kicks and swipes before he passes out from the blood loss. I finish binding his stomach and then glare at the others. "Who else is hurt?"

They scuff their paws in the dirt, hang their muzzles, and keep their traps shut.

I raise my voice. "Who else? We're not leaving a trail for Kelly to follow. We're already going to have to move the pack. Did you even think of that? Kelly will come after us." I'm bellowing now. "Did you consider the elders and the pups? Do you think our females are going to be happy to leave their dens because you took it upon yourselves to kick a gods-damned hornet's nest? For nothing?"

I give my anger free rein. The rage is well-worn, as familiar now as breathing, but I still remember a time when I didn't feel it burning in my guts every waking minute. She gave it to me. My mate.

I had hope before. I knew the odds were against me finding a mate. The wasting sickness took so many of us, so many females. But if Max could find his mate picking flowers in a field beside the North Border wall, then maybe mine was out there, too.

And then I found her, and she cowered from me like I was a fate worse than death, and I would have done anything at all to ease her fear. To please her.

And then she invited me into her nest, and I thought everything was going to change, and I wouldn't be the male that everyone came to with trouble, who always slept alone. I was Annie's mate.

And she ruined it. Made it foul. I can't bear to remember,

but at night in the dark when I stroke my cock, I always think about that pile of leaves beside the river, and then when I'm at my weakest and about to come, the shame kicks me in the gut, again and again, and I spurt my seed onto my belly, disgusted with myself and hating her.

She has no shame. No regret. At the Quarry Pack dens, she clung to the other females, refusing to look at me, like I was the enemy, like I don't feel our bond in my chest every minute of every day, a constant aching empty reminder that there is no hope left for me. I am as alone as these sorry, mangy males slumped in a circle around me.

"Alpha?" Alroy's quavery voice brings me back to the moment.

My pack brothers are all hanging their heads, tails tucked. The stink of their shame drifts like the stench of scum on a warm pond.

I sigh, loud and long, and bend over to pick up Elis's limp carcass.

"Khalil, take Tiny Jac and Calvus up to the north camp and clear out those dens. Don't just check for bear. Look for snakes and lizards and such. The females don't care to share their nests with critters. Alroy, you take the others and tell everyone what you've done. Tell them to be packed by the time I return. Max, can you walk?"

He grumbles.

"Well, go on then. Go," I bark at my packmates. I cradle Elis to my chest like a baby to add pressure to the wound.

I'm last to leave the clearing, but I don't linger, and I don't look back toward Quarry Pack.

Annie didn't spare a look for me.

I have no choice. I walk away again.

5

———

ANNIE, ONE YEAR LATER

I hate beekeeping. I hate varroa mites more. I hate testing for varroa mites the most.

I shake a few hundred workers out onto a double thick sheet of newspaper and fold the paper like a funnel. Then, very carefully, I pour a cup of bees into the shake jar.

Is the queen in there? Better check.

No. I already checked a dozen times.

Better check again.

I know for a fact that the queen isn't in the batch of bees I took out for testing. I found her before I started, and I kept an eye on her as I drew other frames from their slots in the box. Then I went back and made sure she was safe and sound.

But are you really, really sure? Better check again.

I *know* that the queen is on a frame I left in the box.

But you should check one more time. Just to be sure.

I let the voice babble her litany of doom and gloom in the background and focus on the task at hand.

Even though it's early spring and in the low sixties outside, it's hot as hell inside my white suit, and loose

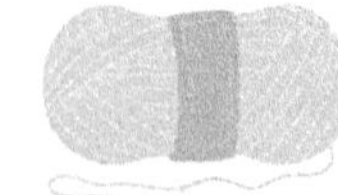

strands of hair are sticking to my sweaty face. There's nothing I can do with the mesh veil covering my head. I try to huff the hair away, but it's plastered to my cheek.

As quickly as I can wearing these thick gloves, I fill the jar halfway with alcohol. The bees panic while I screw on the lid, and my nose wrinkles at the chemical stink.

I hate murdering bees. Not because I'm fond of them or anything. They sting, and even when they're relatively calm, they buzz around you, skulking at the verge of your peripheral vision, and honestly, I don't know which is worse—a sting hurts, but it feels better once you slap some mud on it. The skulking gives me headaches and drives my wolf nuts.

Somehow, this job defaulted to me after Una mated Killian. Mari point blank refused to take over bee duty, and then she mated Darragh Ryan. Kennedy is really good at not being around when conversations about the divvying up of duties happen.

I'm an unenthusiastic beekeeper, but I'm a truly reluctant bee murderess. No matter how necessary I know it is, drowning them feels awful. I shake the jar as hard as I can, trying to give them as quick a death as possible. They're dying for the greater good, but they don't know that, and even if they did, I bet they wouldn't have volunteered.

I hate playing Fate.

After two minutes of shaking, I let the jar sit for the requisite two additional minutes. While the last of the bees give up the ghost, I survey our little kingdom.

Abertha is off on her travels, so her cottage windows are shut despite the warm weather. There's no one around except her cat Appollonia, although she's nowhere to be found at the moment.

These days, Una works down at the new greenhouse that Killian built for her near the commons. He wants her close to home, and now that she has a pup, she doesn't fight him on it. Mari still comes up here sometimes, but she lives with Darragh in a treehouse out in the woods, and since that's closer to our shop in Chapel Bell, she spends most of her time working there.

If Kennedy's not on patrol or training with the males, she's usually trudging around, doing something. She's handy, and she knows what needs doing, but she refuses to be pinned down to a schedule. It's always a surprise when I show up and the garden is tilled, or she's got buckets set up with spawn for a fresh crop of oyster mushrooms. I don't see or smell her now, though. I'm alone.

Always alone.

The hole in my chest aches, like cold water is pouring from it, but I can stand loneliness.

It's better this way. Safer.

It's beautiful up here at this time of year. Tender shoots and leaves and buds tremble in the breeze, and the ground is soft and dark and rich. There is a feeling that things are about to begin.

Not for me, of course, but for the world at large.

It's better that way.

Sometimes I find babies in the wildflower field or the woods. Bunnies. Squirrels. My wolf always hunts them, ferreting out their nests. Not to eat. She just likes to watch them nestle. The same with Una's baby. My wolf likes to watch him kick and coo. She stares, and then later, when we're alone at home, she paces, restless.

I pick up my jar of dead bees and tumble it, counting out another two minutes in my head.

I'm actually calmer than my wolf these days, now that Una is the alpha female. We don't have to hide our phones or the business or our trips to Chapel Bell anymore.

Of course, my brain has no trouble finding other things to worry about, but there's one hundred percent less sneaking around in my life now, and that's made a huge difference. My stomach ulcer is healing. I can eat Old Noreen's chili again.

I put the bee jar down and set up a filter in a funnel. Then, batting away the few bees that escaped the reaping, I screw a mesh lid on the jar and empty the dead bee water through the funnel. This is the part of varroa mite testing when the rubber hits the road. I take the filter, hold it up to the light, and examine it carefully. Nothing. Sweet.

I breathe a little easier. Varroa mites are the stuff of nightmares. They feed on the bee larvae and pupae, and then when the bees emerge as adults, they're missing chunks of their bodies and wings. You can treat for the mites, but that doesn't do the bees flying around with holes eaten out of them much good.

Justus's pointy wolf ears have jagged edges like they've been bitten. That's my mate's name—Justus. I finally learned it during last year's failed kidnapping attempt. He tried to trade for Kennedy, Mari, and me, but he acted like he didn't know me. Like I was no one to him.

He recognized me, though. I saw the hate before he shuttered his face and focused elsewhere.

Sad female.

Coward.

A female like you would make weak, spindly young.

The voice recites her favorite chorus. I let her. If I argue with her, she shouts over me.

After the showdown between Killian and the Byrnes at the old dens, when Justus shifted and ran, I saw his ears, and they looked chewed up. He looked rougher than he did when we mated. Bigger. More weathered. More scarred.

In my memory, he wasn't young when I met him, but seeing him now, I realize he hadn't even grown to his full height then. He was Fallon's age when we mated. Maybe eighteen or nineteen.

He's different now. Hard. Unforgiving.

I think a lot about his wolf, every time I have my tea on the back porch and look at the garden. I imagine him with his flower antennae, so worried about what was frightening me.

Does his wolf hate me, too?

My heart beats faster, and my hands shake as I unscrew the jar and walk over to the compost to toss the bee carcasses on the pile.

Regardless, the man doesn't want you. The voice reassures me. *Sad female. Coward. You would make weak, spindly young.*

He's the alpha of the Last Pack. I am his best—likely only—chance for pups, but when he saw me, he acted like he didn't know me.

I felt him in my chest, though. He is still so angry, angrier than he was when we mated. Despite the weakness of the bond, his rage *seared*.

I didn't know his name before that day. In my head, I called him the Last Pack wolf, and as soon as I thought about him, I thought about something else. And it worked. For a long time. Until Una mated Killian, and everything changed.

Kennedy is allowed to train and patrol now. The traitors who Killian let live are now on kitchen duty, so I'm expected to sit with the pack at meals. Una insists I sit with her, so I have a front row seat to the pups wandering up after dinner to show her the treasures they've found during the day or to give her baby crafts they've made for him—flower crowns and rattles made from pebbles in used plastic bottles.

And I'm happy for her—I *am*—but by the time I can excuse myself without causing concern, I'm sliced to ribbons. No one will ever love me like Killian loves Una, and I'll never have my own baby to love like Una loves Raff.

But you're safe. The voice is stubborn. Argumentative. Right.

I am safe, and it feels like cold, dirty dish water.

There's no sense in dwelling on what can't be changed. I shake it off and rinse out the jar now empty of dead bees. The sun is inching closer to the peaks of Salt Mountain. It's time to go home to change before I head for the lodge. I don't need to rush, but I should get going.

There's never a need to rush anymore. There's no one at the cabin hogging the bathroom. The days of us racing each other to the bathroom are over. Kennedy usually showers at the pack's gym.

Why am I so moody and mopey today? It's not that time of the month. I just finished my period.

I shake it off again, for real this time, and dry the testing jar before tucking it neatly in the metal toolbox where I keep the testing supplies. I peel off my beekeeping gear, hang it up on the hook on the back of the shed door, and tug my long skirt back on over the bike shorts I wear in the suit. The cool, early evening air is bliss on my sticky skin.

If I hurry, I have time for a cup of tea before I'm expected at the lodge.

Or.

The weather is beautiful. Patches of stark blue sky are framed by the low, stout clouds shaded gray from the fading daylight. The cottage's clearing and the fields and woods around it have settled into the kind of quiet that's punctuated with a rustling breeze and the dwindling calls of birds as they wind down and return to their nests.

Like I said, I don't have to rush.

I could walk home along the river.

My heartbeat quickens.

I always take the same path home—along the tree break beside the wildflower meadow and then down our well-worn track through the wood to the ridge behind the charred foundation of our old cabin. The traitors burned it down as a distraction on the day they tried to trade us to the Last Pack.

I know the way home like the palm of my hand—every exposed root, every place where the dirt washes out the trail when it rains. I know to the minute how long the walk takes. There's no section of the path that's exposed. If I had to run, I know exactly where I could hide.

The voice in my head is silent. She doesn't think I'll do it. Even the idea is twisting my stomach in knots.

The land beside the river is wide open. A few years ago, Killian cleared it all so the patrols have a clear view. Going along the river would actually take me away from the commons for about half a mile before it turns south. The river and its far bank are our territory, though. After the humans kidnapped Mari, Killian expanded our boundaries all the way to the rural route a mile to the north. Our territory is safe.

The voice snorts.

I have no reason to go home a different way today.

So you better not.

There she is. She can't let me make a decision without her.

Ferals can swim.

I can't even consider taking a slightly different path home without my brain conjuring the worst-case scenario.

Humans can swim. They have boats. Guns. Numbers.

What would happen if I didn't torment myself for once? An aquatic attack of swimming ferals and a fleet of gun-toting humans in boats? Beating myself up with my fears has no magic power. It can't stop Fate. Bad things still happen.

Remember last time by the river. You begged for a knot on your hands and knees in the dirt.

I gasp at the memory and stumble where I stand, alone in front of the shed. Shame burns my face. The voice is playing dirty.

I've walked by the river since then. Only a few months ago, during a full moon, Kennedy stayed on Quarry Pack territory for once and shifted. When the pack took their usual path eastward, he ran along the river.

Usually, on those nights, I'd shift and hide in my room, curled in a corner with the curtain cracked so a sliver of moonshine would fall in the window, but that night, something got into my wolf. She followed Kennedy's at a distance, trotting silently in the huge footprints he left in the frosted grass. If Kennedy noticed, she never mentioned it, and neither did I.

I've been to the river plenty of other times, too. I went a few days after the mating to hide whatever was left of my nest, but there was no sign of it. No whiff of scent left, neither his nor mine. The wind had blown it all away.

He was wrong about me. I'm not a coward. I'm afflicted with fear, and most of the time, it wins, but not always. They say courage is being afraid and doing it anyway. And I do. Sometimes.

So why not now?

I wipe my sweaty palms on my corduroy skirt and take off toward the north.

Don't be reckless. Don't be stupid. You know what happens. Fangs. Fists. Sightless eyes. Twisted mouth.

I lengthen my stride and pick up my pace. The voice is bringing out the big guns.

Most of the time, I hate her. But once in a blue moon, like now, I'm so sorry for her that my heart breaks. She can't ever be brave, even a little bit like I'm being right now.

I hurry along the edge of the nettle field, passing the trailhead where I usually turn and taking the next one a few yards further on instead. It's a patrol path, so it's as well-worn as the one I usually take. It goes straight up a steep incline at first, so I'm panting by the time I hear the river rushing in the distance. My heart pounds, harder than it should. The hill is steep but short.

Turn back. Now. Before it's too late.

Too late for what? A nice view?

I square my shoulders and trudge on, eyes on my muck boots. If I look at the rushing river or the darkening woods past the far bank, I might lose my courage, and it's not like this should require *bravery*.

I'm tromping through an overgrown field, stirring up crickets. Una attacked Haisley and claimed Killian in front of the entire pack. I'm taking the scenic route home.

And all I can look at is the green rubber toes of my boots peeking from the threadbare hem of my skirt.

Run. Home. Now.

The voice brays at the top of her lungs, but where's my wolf? She's quiet. Watchful.

Expectant.

She's on her feet, nose pressed to the border between us. Staring at the river.

Don't look up. Run.

My wolf whines. Softly.

I glance up. My feet sputter to a halt.

Run, the voice screams. A fresh surge of adrenaline crashes through my veins, sending my heart thumping into my breastbone. I moan.

He's there.

My hands clutch my skirt, my teeth sinking into my lower lip.

My mate is standing on the other side of the river.

Glaring at me.

My wolf is afraid to move. She plays a statue, her tail motionless in mid-air. Watching me.

I let go of my skirt, letting my shirt cuffs fall over my fisted hands. I should run.

Why am I not running?

Justus's long brown hair is snarled, but loose strands still fly when the wind picks up. His gnawed ears poke from his tangled mane, pointed and furry. Wolf ears.

His face is hard, every angle sharp, every plane spare. His beard hides his mouth. He's wearing a ratty pair of sweatpants and no shirt. My breath catches in my lungs. His chest is *fascinating*.

He's bigger than he was when we mated, but he's not beefy and bulging like our males. This must be what the word *sinewy* means. He's not pumped up; he's honed. Before, his right pec and bicep had been covered in tattoos, but now, every inch of skin on the entire right side of his body is covered in black ink. From this distance, I can't make out the individual pictures and patterns. It looks like lattice-work. Or lace.

His veiny arms hang loose at his side, but his chest rises and falls like he sprinted here.

And he's angry. His whole body declares it. The way he stands. The angle of his chin. The line of his jaw.

I can't get enough air. I need air.

The voice shouts *run* in the back of my head, like always. Like the boy who cried wolf.

She can't save me, though, can she? She can't make anything better; she can't protect me. All she can do is scream.

My mate waits, stock-still, but neither my wolf nor I are fooled—he's calculating. He didn't come this far to look at me. He's coiling, preparing to attack.

Our eyes meet. I can't tell the color or expression. He's too far away. But I can feel him in my chest.

I press my palm against the place where it hurts.

My wolf tilts her head.

He smiles.

No.

It's not a smile.

He bares his fangs, his muscles tightening. He's going to strike.

Run, run, run, run, run!

I whirl on my heel, trip, and pitch forward, my kneecaps grinding as they hit the ground. Behind me, I hear a splash.

I scrabble back to my feet and bolt for the woods, arms pumping, my skirt trapping my legs, hampering my stride. I hike it above my knees. Damn these boots. I curl my toes to keep from slip-sliding inside them. What was I thinking to wear these boots, this skirt?

The fresh spring grass squeaks against my rubber soles. I skid and lose a second. And then another. I pump my arms harder, as if that can make my legs longer or stop the splashes in the river from growing closer and closer.

What was I thinking? This is my fault. Again. I did this to myself.

If I can just get past the tree line, there are places to hide

—thickets, hollow logs, dead falls. It's so close. Three yards. Two.

One.

I plow into the underbrush. Vines whip around my ankles. My foot slips from the boot, and I turn, teetering on one leg as I flip the boot upright to shove my foot back in. More seconds lost.

There are no sounds to track him by now. No splashes, no steps. The wood muffles everything except its own chirrups and cracks.

I hold my breath and strain to hear him between the thuds of blood in my ears.

He hates me. Why would he come after me?

To kill you. To make you sorry.

A twig snaps.

I whirl.

He's there, ten feet behind me, water dripping from his beard. His pecs. The ridges of his hard stomach. His wet pants sag low on his hips and cling to his thighs.

He stares me straight in the eye and then very, very deliberately, he lifts his foot from the branch he snapped.

On purpose.

He ran a circle around me. In silence. In no time at all.

I'm no match for him.

Scream. Drop. Cover your belly. Cover your head.

I cannot be in this body, on the ground, small and powerless. I reach into myself and fling my wolf into existence.

I'm a quicker shifter than I used to be, but the pain is still searing, and if he wanted, there's more than enough time for him to rend me to pieces while my bones are knitting back together. The pain and the risk are worth it, though. Anything to not be small and cowering on the ground.

I brace myself for an attack. His hands have fisted, and his arms are drawn back, but he doesn't lunge for us. His face is darkening, though.

Rage.

"Shift back!" he booms, shaking the buds in the tree above his head.

There is no way on earth.

"Shift back now!"

My wolf plops onto her butt and peers up at him.

"You can't avoid this," he says, quieter, through gritted teeth.

My wolf's nose quivers. He smells like fresh-turned earth, mulling spices, and river water. She wants to wallow in the scent. Lick it. Rub her face in it. The lingering aches and tension from the shift dissolve, and she stretches, arching her back, yawning as big as her jaws will go.

Run. Run!

I add my voice. Run! You idiot, run!

"You *will* talk to me," Justus growls. "You've had it your way. Time is up. You're done turning up your nose at me and turning your back." His words drip with contempt. It's clear he's not saying what he really wants to say. The rumble in his chest gives him away. It's the same sound Quarry Pack males make in the ring when they're pummeling their opponent's face.

Why isn't my wolf scared?

She's just sitting there, blinking up at him, sniffing the air for traces of his scent.

"I've done what you wanted, Annie. Do you think I would choose to come here? You're a grown female. You can't speak to your mate?" His voice grows louder and louder. "You *owe* me this," he spits. "Shift! Back!"

My wolf licks her chops, trying to taste his scent.

"Are you even listening to me?" he bellows. The question rings through the woods, echoing in the crisp evening air. My wolf is still trying to catch his scent on her tongue until his wolf snarls in his throat.

That does it. My wolf panics, drops to her belly, and scrambles backward until her butt runs smack into a tree trunk. She got about three feet. She trembles and stares up as Justus closes the distance between us.

Run! Run!

The voice is still trying, but I know my wolf is frozen in place, even more stuck than I would have been. She's all animal, and she recognizes him as the alpha she needs to placate to get out of this alive.

My wolf and I watch, mesmerized by fear, as the anger seeps from his face, leaving his brown eyes unaccountably sad.

He sinks to his knees, sits on his heels, and sighs. His shoulders drop, and he hangs his head, his beard bunching against his chest. For a long time, he stares at the dirt. My wolf stops shaking, distracted by his silence.

Finally, he lifts his chin to look her in the eyes, and he says, "Annie, I would give anything for you not to be afraid of me. Your fear is the greatest shame of my life." He straightens, collecting a breath. "But we can't stay here if you won't shift. I'm sorry."

He rises to his feet and scoops her up, too quickly for her to do anything but stiffen into a plank. He tucks her to his chest, his forearm supporting her belly, her rump in the crook of his elbow. She presses her nose to his damp skin.

"I won't hurt you, sweetling," he says, his voice bitter and tired.

My wolf nuzzles him with her snout and inhales. All four of her limbs relax and dangle, swinging as he takes off toward the river.

He's going to drown us. Bite him! Fight!

The voice is fighting her corner alone. My wolf begins to whack Justus's bicep with her wagging tail as if she can't even hear it. Maybe she can't. The elders say the wolf and the man are one, but I can't imagine ever letting a male carry me like a football.

I should be panicking. He's heading toward the river, strolling smoothly through the thick brush like it isn't basically booby-trapped with vines, gnarled roots, and hidden ditches.

I've run out of adrenaline, though. I'm oversaturated. And also, for some reason, I can't stop picturing his sad brown eyes.

He's nothing like what I know, tattooed and long haired and walking on two legs through the woods as deftly as a wolf, but those eyes are familiar.

They're very much like the ones I see in the mirror.

6

JUSTUS

She's sleeping.

My mate is sleeping in my arms.

My anger is soot in my mouth. The bond is a knife stuck in my chest. Yet, somehow, my heart is soaring.

This time, her wolf knew me at once. I was furious and bellowing like an idiot, and she sat her ass down and tried to scent me. Why does she respond to me now when she fought me after we mated?

She was probably traumatized from the pain of that awful first shift, and her head was filled with Annie's revulsion. No wonder her instincts told her to fight.

I snuggle her closer, summoning a gentle rumble, the one I use with the little pups when they have their moments. I don't want Annie's wolf to think I bear her a grudge. She's too sweet. Her cream underbelly is soft as feathers, and her clean coat shines with health. Even her ears are silky and smooth.

It wasn't my plan to take her away, but I don't have an ounce of regret. I'm not prepared, though.

I'm going to need more blankets. And maybe some

pretty pillows like Max found for his mate's den. Annie's wolf probably won't like lying on the ground either, even if it is cool. Her fur is so well-kept, she must be fussy about it.

Will she want all those soaps like Max's mate? Elspeth has a different one for every part of her body, and they create so much suds that Max has to fill two troughs with water when she bathes—one for lathering, the other for rinsing.

I won't mind fetching water, but I will have to find another oak barrel. I only have the one.

Does Annie's wolf still have those small fangs, or have they grown?

I reach over, and rumbling louder to keep her lulled, I gently push her lip up with my index finger. Oh, they're so tiny. I've seen rats with longer and sharper teeth.

Can she even hunt with fangs that short? Maybe smaller prey. Rats and such.

I bet she doesn't know how to hunt. Lost pack males make their females stay back in their camps; we never see them when we track their hunting parties. They probably want to keep them weak and dependent so they don't run.

I'd run if I was kept in a box and forced to be thankful for what I'm given.

Of course, a female should never *have to* catch her own meat, but she should also never be in a position where she's hungry because she was never taught to hunt. It seems like common sense to me. It *is* common sense if you want your females to have the best chance at survival, but I get the sense it's more important to the lost packs that they *keep* their females—not that they keep them alive.

Didn't Lilliwen say as much? After we took her from the human males who'd stolen her, she wouldn't eat because she thought we'd expect to mount her in exchange for food like they do in Moon Lake. She said in that pack, low-ranked females have to trade themselves for food if they have no money. When we asked who had the money, she said the high-ranking males. When we asked why they didn't give the females money for food then, she cried. We stopped asking questions and had Elspeth feed her.

My mate is never going to have to trade anything to eat, but when I teach her to hunt, I'm going to have to catch the critters beforehand and hobble them. Slice an ankle tendon or something. She'll never catch them otherwise. She has the shortest legs I've ever seen on a full-grown female wolf.

I can't wait to run beside her. I'll have to trot. She won't be able to keep up. She's so low to the ground, I don't think she'll be able to see over the meadow grass we have to pass through at the base of the evergreen camp.

I won't mind going slow for her. Inside my chest, my wolf howls in agreement. He wants out, and he'll walk if he has to, even though he longs to chase her.

Catch her.

Take her.

I can't let him out. He's waited so long, and she smells so good. If I let him take our body, he'd be on her in a second. Annie would hate us even more, then, even though I don't think her wolf would mind—not with the way she's draped over my forearm, her tail swishing lazily across my abs as she snoozes. Her wolf recognizes me now, and she doesn't smell like fear.

She smells like rain on dry earth—like petrichor, my favorite scent, ever since I was a pup. I always loved thunderstorms.

I hike her a little higher in my arms so she's closer to my nose. Her scent is subtle, easily overpowered when we walk past a pine or a rotting log. I breathe her in until my lungs ache. Her scent teases my memory, reminding me of how the world smelled when I was a pup.

My wolf crowds the boundary between us. He wants a sniff, too. He wants to bury his snout in her fur as he mounts her.

He can't. Lost pack shifters don't fuck as their wolves. When Max's wolf first tried to mount Elspeth's, her wolf ripped a hunk out of his shoulder. When she was in her skin again, she yelled at him for hours about how it was wrong and dirty. When he asked her how she thought natural wolves had babies, she threw a piece of firewood at his head. I see their wolves sneaking off now during runs, but it took her a while.

Even if Annie's wolf wanted mine, I couldn't do it. Annie herself is still terrified of me. Her fear stench was so strong that I caught it while I was still on the far side of the river.

But she didn't run, though. Not at first.

Because she was frozen in fear?

Maybe. She wasn't quite like she was before, though. Her pupils weren't blown, and she fidgeted, tucking her hands into her shirt cuffs and biting her sweet bottom lip. I stifle a groan. Her blunt human teeth sank into her lip like they were biting into risen dough. I want to bite that lip, too.

My stomach growls, or maybe it's my wolf, bitching about how I'm keeping him locked up. The sun is sinking fast, and I didn't plan any of this. I have no food, nothing to make a shelter or a fire. We'll need to find a place to camp soon. Ferals hunt at night, and I can take at least two or three on my own, but I wouldn't risk it with my mate in my arms.

My mate.

I can't believe I have her. I don't *dare*.

Soon enough, she'll shift to her skin and hate me again.

Once we talk and figure things out, I'll have to let her go back to her pack. But until then, all I need to worry about is food, fire, shelter, and ferals.

And Killian Kelly and Quarry Pack coming after me.

I feel like I've dealt with that for now. I cut south once I crossed back over the river, left a few signs, and doubled-back. They'll likely think we're heading for the high valley camp. Good luck to them when they find the black bears that moved into the dens once we left.

For now, the most pressing need is a safe place to stow my mate while I catch her dinner. What I need is a good tree hollow.

I eye her narrow haunches. It won't need to be very big.

She seems to sense that she's being examined. Her breath quickens and her lazy tail perks up. She squirms in my arms, twisting her neck to blink up at me with sleepy eyes.

My body tenses. Will there be fear again?

She yawns so wide I can see the back of her pink tongue and every tiny little pointed tooth in her mouth.

I smile. "Good nap, mate?"

Her belly grumbles, and she whines.

"We'll stop soon, and I'll get you fresh meat."

This settles her, and for a few more minutes, she's content to be held as she surveys her surroundings, shivering and tucking herself to my chest whenever an owl hoots or a leaf rustles overhead. I scan for a good hidey-hole, but the trees are too sparse here to provide decent cover.

I hoist her high over my head as I scramble down a slope choked with waist-high brambles. At the bottom, there's a dry creek bed that I follow northward. When we've been hiking a while, she begins to wriggle.

"You want down?"

She yips. It's more an order than a request. I grin as I set her on her four short, delicate legs. She happily trips ahead, gets about ten feet, and skids to a halt, looking over her shoulder, accusation in her rich brown eyes. I guess I'm not walking fast enough for her.

Her eyes are the same exact color as when she's in her skin. So lovely.

The blade that's been stuck in my chest since our mating twists. They might be the same color, but until now, I've never seen them without fear. My anger rises, and I stamp it down. This wolf wasn't the one who made me think we were mating when she was just taking my cock so I'd leave.

"Waiting for me?" I ask, my voice catching. I clear my throat. I don't want my voice to sound bitter with her.

She yips some more, bossy and impatient. I catch up, and she darts ahead again. She'll only go so far, no further, constantly checking over her shoulder to make sure I'm following even though she must scent that I'm close. She has to hear me, too. I walk softly, but not silently. Her double-checking must be a nervous habit.

Her wolf is more confident than her human, but she's still twitchier than any other female I know.

No sooner than I have the thought, leaves rustle overhead to our left and wood cracks against wood. A dead branch must've fallen. She dashes back to me, burrowing between my legs. I quickly plant my feet so I don't squash her, and then stand in place as she crouches low to the ground, quivering against my ankle.

I squat and rumble to reassure her, running my palm down her trembling flank. "You're safe. It was just a falling branch. Pretty far away. No danger to us."

She barks unhappily, like I ought not have allowed it to

happen. I hide a grin. She glares balefully into the woods where the leaves keep rustling.

"It's just the night wind picking up, sweetling."

She whines. I press my lips together, hoping my beard hides the fact that I don't consider a thump in the woods to be as grave a danger as she clearly believes it to be. With the little toothpicks she has for teeth, it's good she has a healthy respect for possible threats. In reality, a decent-sized branch could hurt her.

"Let's keep going," I say. "I know a place a mile or so ahead that might do for tonight."

I wait for her to venture out of the bolt-hole she's made between my feet. It takes her a minute, but she eventually creeps forward, nose high in the air and working overtime.

She sticks close for the rest of the journey, weaving figure eights around my ankles, boldly venturing a few feet away on occasion when her energetic sniffing catches out a particularly interesting scent.

My mate's wolf is definitely braver than her human self, but she's still skittish as hell. Elis is a lot like that since Killian Kelly unzipped his belly. Both Elis and his wolf alert to everything now, and half the time, I swear, he's alerting to his own loud thoughts.

Before the debacle at the Quarry Pack dens, Elis was a typical young male—happy to tussle over nothing, up all night, venturing far afield by himself. When he deigned to show himself at the dens, he'd stroll around with his dick out as if that were enough to entice a female to let him mount. To be fair, I did the same when I had nothing else to recommend me except size and enthusiasm.

Then Elis took that claw to the belly. The wound healed, but he hasn't been the same since. Some days, his dam can hardly get him out of his blankets, let alone the den.

A picture flashes in my head—Annie almost slamming her cabin door shut, throwing the bolt home, and then peeking out between the curtains.

The hairs on my neck prickle.

When Elis is in his skin now, he covers himself head to toe with baggy sweats and long sleeves, even in summer. I figured he wants to hide the scar, so the females don't see it and think him weak, but now I wonder—why long sleeves? Clothes protect against claws worse than fur, but I suppose he thinks any layer of protection is better than nothing.

Annie doesn't dress any different than the other unmated females in her pack. They all wear long skirts and sleeves.

But weren't her thick flannel shirts always buttoned at the wrists? The sleeves were never rolled. The buttons were never undone at the neck.

And doesn't she hold herself like Elis? So carefully. Like she could tip over and pour out.

Like she'd been ripped open before.

I stop in my tracks.

Immediately, my mate dashes to hide between my legs, ears pricking, nostrils flaring. Hyperalert. Just like Elis.

My heart shatters.

Why didn't I see it?

I scoop her up, hold her in place with one arm, and comb my fingers through her fur. She yelps and wriggles, nipping my fingers, but she's as easy to handle as a squirmy pup. I don't see any scars. I gently squeeze up and down her legs. They're straight. If they were ever broken, they healed well.

"Where were you hurt?" I mutter, combing her fur one more time against the grain, feeling for puckered, jagged skin.

Now that the idea is in my head, I know I'm right. I feel it in my gut.

When Max first brought Elspeth from North Border, she startled whenever a male raised his voice or a wolf snarled. I was too young to remember, but folks still tell stories about how Max would thrash any male who shouted or growled around her, so to this day, whenever she's around, we all lower our voices out of habit like she's a sleeping babe.

Why didn't I make the connection before?

My pride.

That's why.

Annie mauled my pride, and I was a dumb pup, so I decided to be mad for the rest of my life rather than *think about* why she was acting that way for a single second. I assumed her fear was her fault because it couldn't be *mine*. I'm a good, decent male.

She must not want me because something is wrong with *her*. She's from a lost pack, after all, and there's something wrong with all of them. She was raised to hate my pack and isn't smart enough to see past the bigotry. Her fear was intolerance. An insult.

I haven't been a dumb, eighteen-year-old male in years, but I never revisited my reasoning, never tried to make sense of it as a grown male.

Because of my hurt pride. Fucking pride.

Shit. Did I shout or growl at her back then? Maybe, yes, maybe I did. Afterward. When she told me she didn't really want me, and I was disgusted at myself and angry at her. What did I say?

Horrible things. I can't remember my exact words, but I wanted to hurt her, and after I swore I wouldn't.

I feel sick and wrong, the happiness I felt in her presence snuffed like a candle, replaced with gnawing guilt.

What have I done?

I hold her wolf in the air, so we're eye to eye. Her little legs dangle and her tail swishes as she cocks her head, patiently waiting.

"Who hurt you?" I ask.

Her sweet face falls. She glances down and away.

"What happened? Were you attacked?" I try to keep my voice even. I wish it wasn't so gruff and rusty.

Her wolf growls low in the back of her throat, and wriggles in my hands. She wants down. She won't look me in the eye. My stomach sinks.

I set her gently on her paws, and she promptly turns her back on me and trots off down the creek bed trail.

That's a yes. Something happened.

I trail after her, allowing her a lead, but not too much. My brain races, my body tensing for an attack although my nose tells me there aren't any predators for miles.

How did I not piece it together before now? Annie was terrified from the moment she saw me, and her fear never ebbed, not even that last day by the river. Even during her heat, it flavored her sweat. Her slick.

Why didn't I consider that she might have a *reason* to fear? Elis knows none of us would ever slice him open, but he won't even play wrestle with the pups anymore. And I'm not so stupid to think that Elis is afraid of *me*—I know he's terrified because of what happened to him. So why did I never consider that Annie was afraid of more than me?

Oh, fuck. Did I abandon her to whoever hurt her?

My stomach cramps, bile creeping up my throat.

Did I leave her alone with whoever did this over and over again? All the hundreds of times I made the trip to Quarry Pack to stand at the edge of their territory just so I could scent her on the wind, I just *left*, never once considering that she might have call to be afraid?

I'm a fool. A careless bastard. How could I have gone so wrong?

I follow her slowly. The creatures who hunt in late evening are stirring, rustling in the undergrowth, but she doesn't seek shelter by my side. She's pretending I'm not here.

Because she thinks I'm a bad mate? Stupid and cruel?

My stomach churns.

Even out in the camps, we hear the stories from the lost packs. Sooner or later, the females we steal confide in each other, and the tales trickle down to the rest of us. Basements and abandoned trailers and storerooms. Cruel males who believe might makes right. Fireside in North Border. The Munroes and Blackburns in Salt Mountain. The ones they call "nobs" in Moon Lake, including our adopted pack brother Alban Hughes who fled there when we drove him out.

Declan Kelly in Quarry Pack.

My mate was a pup when the elder Kelly died, but we've seen how the lost packs care for their young. Some they treat like kings, and others they chew up and throw out like melon rinds. Alban Hughes was one of those they threw away. Our pack did its best, but the days he'd spent crying for his dam on the river bank where she'd abandoned him did something to his soul that couldn't be mended. When he left us for Moon Lake, it was a blessing.

Was Annie left to fend for herself too young? Like I was?

Every inch of my skin burns with shame. I can hardly bear it.

My wolf prowls inside me, seething and unsettled. I don't know how to ease him or myself, but I can scent his aggression on my skin, and I don't need to frighten my mate any more than I already have.

I need to get away for a minute. Run. Hunt.

Luckily, we've come to the hidey-hole I discovered years ago on a day I'd rather not recall now. Before it dried up, the creek carved a gully out under an old oak, exposing its roots and creating a shallow alcove. My mate sees it and immediately makes a beeline for it.

I hang back. I don't want to leave her—at least, I want to reassure her that she's safe here, and I'll be back soon—but I'm shy of her now.

She knows how stupid and shortsighted I am.

Has known.

All these years, all the times I made the trek to Quarry Pack to stand at the boundary of their territory to brood and feel hard done by, and I never considered that something must have made her so fearful, but she's known all along that I am the kind of male who would reject his frightened mate.

Can I bear to know what happened? How much more can I hate myself?

Until this moment, I was so cocksure, wasn't I? Such a big male. So tough. So *right*.

"Stay here," I tell her, the words heavy with command, and stalk off into the shrub brush. I ignore her soft, confused yip.

It doesn't take long to catch the faint scent of squirrel leading north. At least this is something I can do without embarrassing myself. It takes longer to run down prey on two legs, but I've always had a steady hand with a rock, and the woods are teeming with hungry, scavenging critters at this time of year who aren't quite as cautious as they'll be later in the season when they've got some fat stores.

I hunt until my mind steadies, and by the time I'm done, I've got four bushy-tailed squirrels in hand. Careful to keep a firm grip on my wolf, I shift to fur and gobble down three of them. Unlike the lost packs, I have no problem eating raw meat while in my skin, but it's quicker to chew with canines.

At first, my wolf fights me hard—he wants his mate— but I manage to distract him with squirrel and steal our skin back when he's logy from the meal. His stomach has always been his greatest weakness.

I take my time returning. The area is still clear of predators, and I haven't ventured far. If I tune in to the bond, I can tell my mate has stayed where I put her.

Because she's too afraid to leave?

Of course. I've stolen her, and she slept a long time, so we're miles away from territory she'd recognize. She's stuck with me.

I whistle when I'm a few yards away from the hidey-hole so she knows I'm coming. She doesn't come out to greet me. I don't suppose she would.

I can't see her until I get close to the alcove. When I do, my heart sinks.

She's dug herself a hole between the roots and covered herself with dirt and leaves. All I can make out is her black nose and solemn, accusing brown eyes.

I crouch and reach out my hand. "What have you done? Mud bath?"

She narrows her eyes and yips. Or was that a snarl?

I sniff the air. "We're alone except for prey. There's nothing to fear. You can smell that, right?"

She snarls. There's no doubt this time. She's displeased. Or offended?

I raise my palms. "I wouldn't want to make assumptions."

She wriggles out of her little nook and shakes herself off, sending dirt flying. Then she strides forward until she's almost stepping on my toes. She lifts her head and lets me have it, growling and howling and snapping until my ears ring.

She's pissed—either that I left her alone or that I was gone so long or both—and she's making sure I know it. I bite the insides of my cheeks and try to look contrite. She's adorable mad. Even with twigs stuck in her coat.

Mad is so much better than scared.

But that's why she's mad, isn't it? Because she was scared.

I'm an idiot. I crouch, but I guess I do it too abruptly because she jumps and skitters backward. "I'm sorry, sweetling. You were frightened, and I didn't hurry back."

She gives me a low, unplacated growl.

"I keep making mistakes, don't I?"

Her growl lightens, ever so slightly.

"I brought dinner." I hoist the last squirrel up by its tail.

Oh, that's caught her interest. Her throat quiets as her stomach takes up the rumbling. I grin.

"If he's like his brothers, he's got a good bit of meat on his bones," I say and rip off his head, pitching it aside.

Her eyes bulge.

I slide a claw under his pelt at the shoulder joint and do my best to peel him like an orange. It's not my best skinning work, but I don't have a knife, and I'm not going to make my mate pick fur from her teeth if I can help it.

She makes a strange noise. I glance up. She's not watching me. Her eyes are glued to the squirrel's head. It's kind of looking back at her.

She makes the noise again, a sharp horking sound.

Oh.

Shit.

I snatch her up and dash for the bushes. We make it clear of the shelter seconds before she loses the content of her belly. It's only water, but somehow, it keeps coming. I sort of aim her at a shrub and breathe through my mouth.

How does she have this much in her stomach? Did she sip from some puddle while I wasn't looking? She drank where I did, and I feel fine.

She hawks up air for a bit, and then she quiets, whining. I carry her carefully back, and I try to interest her in the squirrel, but she won't even open her eyes to look at it.

She's had enough for one day. I have, too. I suppose it won't hurt to sleep now and let her stomach settle. Tomorrow, we'll meet up with the river, and I'll catch her a fat fish. She can eat trout with the head on.

I clean things up and sweep out the alcove while she watches from a distance. She's so exhausted that she's listing on her thin legs. She makes no complaint when I pick her up and settle her behind me, my body between her and the outside. There is still nothing more dangerous than a raccoon out there, but I don't suppose that matters. The dark is terrifying when you're small.

I remember when I was young. Predators stalked at night, and I was already vulnerable enough without being blind, too—small, alone, and so many years away from shifting.

It's unbearable to think that my mate knew that feeling, but she did, didn't she? When I found her, she had no living blood family, like me, except she didn't have her wolf to come to her defense. And she is so delicate. Her weight is nothing against my back, the pressure of her chest rising and falling almost a flutter.

And I stomped away from her like a pup throwing a tantrum. I left her.

How do I make this right?

For one, I'll discover what hurt her, and I'll kill it. Then I'll teach her to shift correctly and fight so she doesn't have to be afraid ever again.

A stiff breeze picks up, and the temperature drops. I'm shivering, stuck in my skin, huddled in the dirt. When the wind blows just so, I catch the scent of my mate's vomit and squirrel blood.

I've just realized that I made the greatest miscalculation of my life.

But my mate's wolf is breathing softly on the back of my neck, and I can feel her heart beat against my shoulder blade.

I'd live in this moment forever if I could.

7

———

ANNIE

I'm trapped between my sleeping mate and a wall of dirt, but my wolf isn't panicking. I'm petrified, cowering in a corner of our psyche, but she's wriggling up against his back and snuffling at his neck.

I can't believe her. She nuzzles the skin behind his ear, rubbing her chin on his shoulder, *scent marking* him. I don't know how he hasn't woken yet.

There's drool.

Don't wake him. Don't touch him. Be still. Don't breathe.

The voice bellows commands while I moan and rock. My wolf ignores us both. She wants to bite her mate. Gnaw on him like a drumstick. Desperate to discourage her, I toss pictures of the headless squirrel into her brain. She freezes, mouth open, midway to a nibble.

Thank goodness she's squeamish. Quarry Pack males and their mates hunt and eat in their fur during full moon hunts, but I never have, since I've never gone on a run. The meat I eat comes wrapped in brown paper.

Her stomach rumbles at the thought, the memory of the

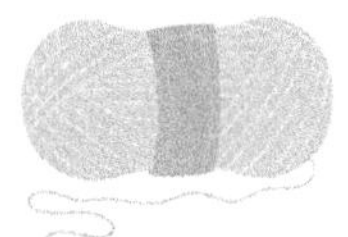

squirrel swiftly losing its ick factor as she stretches her jaw and gently locks it around Justus's muscular upper arm. His bicep flexes, almost imperceptibly, while his breath remains slow and even. He's pretending to be asleep.

It's a trap!

I focus with all my power on dragging my wolf away, but she's in full control, and she's lost all sense of self-preservation. There's meat in her mouth, and she's not letting go. She slowly sinks her teeth down, but not enough to puncture his flesh. She's just—*playing*. She knows he's awake.

My wolf doesn't play. She never has, not even when we were very little. She stays quiet and keeps her head down.

But now she's closing her jaw on Justus's arm, slowly shaking her head back and forth, gnawing his bicep like a marrow bone. Suddenly, with a growl, he flips to face us. She drops his arm and scurries backward, but there's no space, so she ends up plastered against the curved dirt wall with her paws braced on his rock-solid chest.

He grins, his fangs flashing bright white in his thick beard. He snaps them, playfully, pretending to bite my snout.

My wolf yelps.

I scream.

Fight! Run!

Immediately, a fog of fear swamps the small space, and I have a close up of his face as it contorts in horror and disgust. If he was wearing a shirt, he'd tug it up over his face like the males at Moon Lake Academy did when someone passed gas. My wolf screws her eyes shut and shoves her snout into the dirt as if that will get us out of this.

I smell *awful*.

Usually, for me, embarrassment is an aftereffect, and panic is the main reaction, but for some reason, even though the pecking voice is wailing in the background somewhere about how I need to claw my way out through the dirt, I'm not drowning in terror.

The reflexive fear is there, but for the first time, it's being drowned out by a desperate, terminal mortification. I stunk the place *up*. I can taste it in my mouth. That means *he* can taste it in *his* mouth, too.

"Sweetling," he says, low and cajoling. "Open your eyes, sweetling."

He doesn't sound totally disgusted. Actually, his voice is oddly nasal. I peek.

He's pinching his nose closed. My wolf moans like she's the most miserable creature alive. He grins again, flashing those long, wickedly sharp canines, but this time, I don't panic, and I don't look away. I can't. His teeth are so clean and pointy. His soft lips are so mysteriously curved as they disappear into his beard. I want to trace them with my fingers to see if they're as soft as they seem. Or if his beard is as scratchy.

"I'm not a danger to you. No need to smoke me out," he says, chuckling, and bobs forward to drop a quick kiss on my nose before he wriggles backward, out of our alcove. "Come on now before that stink settles into your fur. If I walk into camp with you reeking like this, the females will beat me with their brooms."

He's teasing. Females would never do something like that to a male his size. He's still grinning while he walks a few steps and pauses to stretch, arching his back and folding his arms behind his head.

His abs are taut. There is a smattering of hair peeking above the waistband of his low hanging sweatpants.

Run. Now. It's your chance.

The voice is so faint, like it's coming from under a bucket.

My wolf ignores her completely and pads over to stand next to him. She lifts her rump and lowers her forepaws to stretch her own back, cracking her spine, breathing through her mouth while her fur airs out.

It's very early. The gray light is only now turning mellow gold and every new green leaf is still wet with dew.

The voice is right. Now is our best chance to escape. I could trot off to the bushes. Pretend to need privacy to relieve myself. Get a head start.

Which he'd close in seconds.

He's fast and strong and somehow familiar with the terrain, even though it's not his territory. The area we've been passing through isn't marked by any pack. There are some signs of humans, the wrappers, cigarette butts, and bottles that follow their passage like the wake of a boat, but none of it is fresh. There's no one out here now except us.

If I ran, and for some reason he let me go, I'd be alone. It'd take a day to get home—*if* I could find my way. I can track as well as most, but he carried me for miles while I slept, and he doesn't leave signs. I noticed that early on.

Would my wolf even let me go?

No. I don't even need to ask her. She's fascinated by him. Even now, she's mimicking his side stretches, even though it doesn't work at all with her sausage-shaped body. If I want to run, I have to take back our skin, and then I'll be naked and slow. I won't get far if he comes after me.

Maybe he wouldn't. He seems fond of my wolf, but he hates me. His contempt burned in his eyes at the river. He didn't try to hide it. He wanted me to know how he felt. I don't need to dig the bond out of the deep hole I buried it in to confirm it and feel his hatred in my insides.

I don't care. It's good that he hates me. I don't want any of this. I want my morning tea, my toast and jam, and my bathroom. I'm so dirty. My fur is stiff, and I do not want to know what's in it.

I don't want to go to the Last Pack. Everyone says they live in dens like our ancestors, like animals, with no laws but strength and no justice except claws and fangs. At least that's what the instructors said at Moon Lake Academy. The Last Pack chapter in the textbook was short and mostly about how they steal pups and females.

Justus stole me. But why, if he loathes me?

To make you suffer. To kill you. Run now while you have the chance. Before it's too late.

The voice keeps up her ranting, but somehow, it feels almost...obligatory. Like even she wants to know what happens next.

If I were in my skin, there's no way I'd be going along with this without a fight. I'd be curled in a ball or tearing through the undergrowth.

But I'm not me. I'm my wolf, and whatever they say, the man and the beast definitely aren't one and the same. My wolf is a hundred times braver than me.

"Ready, sweetling?" Justus asks, cracking his neck to finish his morning warm-up. "I'll catch you something to eat along the way. How about a fresh fish?"

My wolf wrinkles her nose. She's not a fan of fish.

"I tell you what—in a few hours, we'll pass a supply cache. There should be flint. If you can hold out that long, I'll roast you a bird."

My wolf rumbles happily.

"Or a snake. Whatever comes to hand." He smiles.

My wolf's rumble turns displeased. His smile widens. "All right, then. I'll catch you a plump, juicy bird."

She rewards him with a yip, and excited by the prospect, she confidently takes off southward.

He whistles before he scoops her up, so she isn't startled. "Not that way, pip. We're headed north."

She yaps at him for awhile so that he knows she knew that, but he should have told her before she set off half-cocked anyway, and she's hungry, and she doesn't need him to carry her, but she'll let him for now.

Every so often, he murmurs soothingly. "All right then, pip. Just as you say. Not long now. We're making good time."

He's so different than he was when we mated, but what did I know about him, really? All I had to judge by are those horrible moments beside the river that I've tried so hard to scrub from my memory.

At Moon Lake Academy, we learned in science that a memory forms when your thoughts travel a particular neural pathway over and over again. I figured if I didn't let my brain do that, I could cut the thread, and all the bad things that happened in the past would float off into oblivion, but it didn't work. I'm so careful not to remember, but the bad memories loiter right at the edge of my awareness as if they're locked in orbit by the gravity of what happened.

I don't want to relive my mating. I refuse. But was he like this at all back then?

He was almost feral, wasn't he? Rough and cruel and single-minded. He hurt me. Took what he wanted.

My head aches, and my wolf squirms.

"Restless, eh?" he says and sets her gently on her feet.

She dashes ahead. The landscape is changing. We're following a deer path through meadows dotted with clusters of scraggly pines that rise from sprawling thickets.

She darts around a bush and hides, peeking behind to watch Justus. He hikes past, unconcerned, ignoring her and continuing northward. She lets him get a few yards and then races after him.

He strolls on, glancing down at her, bemused. "You've got a lot of energy for a wolf who slept rough," he says approvingly.

Does that mean he isn't accustomed to sleeping in a dirt dugout? Doesn't the Last Pack live in dens?

The question spurs a dozen others. The textbooks made it sound like Last Pack spends most of their time as wolves, but Justus hasn't shifted yet, except for his ears and fangs. Why is that?

And how does he keep his ears pointy? The low-ranking kids at Moon Lake would do that, too, wearing a tail or claws or chest fur while in human form. It was frowned upon, but I think the powers-that-be kind of liked it, too, since it gave them another reason to sneer at the ones they called "scavengers."

And why is it that Moon Lake pretty much forces its low-ranking pups to go to the Academy, as well as pups from Moon Lake, Salt Mountain, and North Border, but they leave the Last Pack alone?

Are they really as uneducated as everyone says? When we played "Last Pack" as pups, we'd always grunt and speak in monosyllables. Where did we get that idea? Justus is just as articulate as any Quarry Pack male. Maybe more so, honestly. We were probably imitating our own males with the grunts.

I'm still terrified—about ferals and his pack and what if something happens to him and I'm left alone—but for the first time in maybe forever, I'm also curious.

It's a good feeling. Different. But good.

At noon, like he promised, we reach a Last Pack supply cache. I was expecting at least a shed, but it's not much more than a lean-to made of stripped branches and woven vines, built against the side of a deep gulch.

Inside, there's a barrel packed tight with tools, clothes, and other supplies, including matches wrapped in oil cloth. Justus builds a fire, and my wolf naps beside it as he hunts down the plump, juicy bird he also promised. He plucks its feathers—and plucks off its head—before he returns, so my wolf is happy to snarf it down after a cursory browning over the flames. Apparently, she's not too fussy about whether her meat is cooked through.

She shows no concern that she's leaving none for Justus, but it makes me deeply uneasy. At the lodge, we serve the males first. They cause less trouble when their mouths and hands are full.

Justus doesn't seem to mind that my wolf is saving none for him. He watches her eat, arms folded, mouth lazily curved as he sits, resting against a tree trunk.

My wolf is pleased to let him watch her eat. I don't understand that at all. I can't eat if someone is watching me.

After the meal, my wolf lets Justus carry her again, and she snoozes in the mid-day sunshine. By the time she wakes up, yipping to be let down, the landscape has changed again. The meadows have disappeared, and the fields have turned into rolling hillocks, mossy and deep green. By late afternoon, we're hiking strictly upward, winding between rocky outcroppings and evergreens at least three stories tall.

The trees cast shadows, and my wolf's steps slow. She can smell his pack now. We're on his territory.

No one will find your body. Not out here.

The pecking voice, ever helpful, has found her second wind.

He'll throw you from one of those outcroppings. Break all

your bones. The moss will cover you. No one will ever know what became of you.

Justus must sense my growing wariness. His wolf rumbles at mine to stop, and he squats so we're closer to eye level.

"All right, pip?" he asks, wiping his brow. It's not hot, but we have been walking all day, and he did carry my wolf for quite a bit of it.

My wolf yips dramatically and plops on her rump, panting like she's also carried a grown female wolf for hours and hunted a partridge and went without lunch.

She's actually more or less fine, but I'm not all right. The stronger the scent of other wolves gets, the tighter my nerves stretch. I want to go home. This has been enough adventure. I want a cup of tea. My room with its locking door. The tire iron that I snuck from Liam's garage that I keep under my bed.

"I think—" He pauses like he's searching for words. His expression seems deliberately mild. "I think you should shift to two legs to meet the pack."

No.

There is no way.

Not ever.

No way.

No how.

I jam myself in a far corner of my psyche. My wolf physically backs away from him.

He blows out a long breath, raising his palms. "They'll want to talk to you, get to know you, find out how you came to be here. You'll want to talk to them, right?"

No.

I won't.

I only ever want to talk to Una, Mari, Kennedy, Old

Noreen, and Abertha when she's in a good mood. There are literally no other people on earth I *want* to talk to.

And they'll want to know how I came to be here? I was kidnapped.

Well, *I* was. I'm not sure about my wolf anymore. I feel like she went rogue somewhere along the line and decided she wanted to see the world, but I'm a hostage.

I could've fought her harder, though. I could have run, even if I didn't have much of a chance.

Why didn't I?

And what does "find out how you came to be here" mean? Do I need to say the right thing or else? Or *what*?

Is my wolf really going to strut into the midst of another pack? The *Last Pack*?

They'll tear you apart.

She's beginning to see the issue. A high-pitched whine rises from her throat, and she continues to creep backward, her belly dragging in the dirt, a fresh wave of fear perfuming the air. Justus squeezes his eyes shut, the tip of his nose flushing red as if the scent burns. It kind of does if you're not used to it.

They'll rend you limb from limb. Eat your flesh. Suck the marrow from your bones.

The pecking voice is back in her full glory, a tinge of vindication in her tone.

Your mate hates you. He'll hand you over to his pack and leave.

She flashes a picture in my head that I didn't even know existed in my mind—Justus walking away from my nest by the river, his back stiff, his muscles tensed, his hands balled in fists. Like he'd been hurt, and he was hiding it. I've seen plenty of males walk away like that when Killian has the males spar after dinner in the lodge. The ones who lose.

What do I do? I'm petrified, crouched low and shaking, terrified, with every reason to be, while this male waits for me, his palms raised, like I've lost my mind yet again.

How would he like to stroll into the Quarry Pack commons naked and uninvited?

My wolf whines. It's a question. Do I want our skin? Upon consideration, she doesn't want to walk into this, either.

There is no way in hell. I huddle in my corner, and she huffs a sigh.

At the same time, Justus seems to make a call. He huffs, too, scoops up my wolf, and tucks her under his arm like a football again.

"Never the easy way with you, eh?" he grumbles, more in resignation than complaint.

Little does he know how right he is—it is never, ever the easy way for me.

THE LAST LEG of the journey to the Last Pack is only about a half mile, so the voice doesn't have much time to predict our imminent demise, but she makes up for it with imagination.

They'll skin you, wear your fur, chew on your flesh until you're almost dead, then let you heal, and then do it again, night after night.

Her warnings come louder and faster as Justus climbs a steep, pebbled path that winds between craggy outcroppings and emerges on a kind of tableland.

My breath catches. This can't be real.

I've never seen any place like this before. We emerge from a narrow choke point between two sheer rocks, and all of a sudden, a sprawling glade and entire shifter camp is spread in front of us. Slabs of white rock rise like a natural amphitheater around it, dotted with deep green patches of tall hemlock, cedar, and cypress, and beyond and above the terraced rock, other ridges and spires tower to the north and west. Water burbles somewhere, but I can't see the source.

I don't see how it could possibly be man-made, but I also don't see how nature could make a place so clearly designed as shelter. It's a place out of time. Even the colors are enchanted. Every brown and green and white is bold—the brownest brown, the greenest green.

As my gaze darts around the clearing, searching for threats and escape routes, I pick out at least a dozen low, sloped entranceways among the rocks. Those must be the dens. Glowing almond-shaped eyes blink from the shadows, visible from hundreds of yards away.

Closer, and more terrifying, dozens of males have risen to their feet, looming beside rough-hewn stools, wooden crates, and overturned rusted buckets, glaring at me in spiky silence, poised to attack. I know that stance. I've seen it a hundred times in front of Killian's dais after dinner when he calls the males to fight.

Don't move. Don't breathe.

My wolf presses closer to Justus's side, searching for the feel of his low rumble. It soothes her. She trusts him to protect her.

I don't.

I cram myself in the furthest corner of the limbo where I exist, sliding down to scrunch myself into the smallest space possible, hugging my knees to my chest. I wish I'd run when I had the chance. I should have never taken a different way home. I should never have left my room in my cabin where I was *safe*.

Safe, but scared all the time, anyway.

My wolf peeks under Justus's arm at the males stalking toward us. Some are in full fur on four legs, but most have arrested themselves mid-shift, pointy-eared and fanged with various degrees of shag. None are in their skin alone.

When we arrived, two males were fighting, but they separated the instant we emerged in the glade. Now, they stalk toward us side by side, chests heaving. The skinnier one's ear is torn and bloody, half perked, the other half drooping like a leaf with a snapped stem.

Most of the males were clustered by the huge fire pit in the center of the clearing when we arrived. Now they approach us, carrying whatever they were working with. One elder carries a fiddle and bow at his side. Another holds a knife in one hand and a rabbit skin in the other.

They hold themselves the same way, and wear the same type of worn, low slung pants, but based on looks, they could have come from a half dozen different packs. Some are Black, some are brown-skinned, some are pale and ruddy. They're all tall, cut, and have the same natural confidence that Justus does.

They all have tattoos like Justus, too, the same intricate maze of lines and spirals that wind around the simple outlines of boats or trees or fish, draped over their right shoulder, arm, and torso like a shawl. The older the male, the further their tattoos stretch down their right sides to their thighs. Some have tattoos all the way down the tops of their right foot. Even the oldest males seem willing and able to shred an interloper to pieces.

There are so many cocks nestled in such thick pelts.

Where are the females? The pups?

The brawling males reach us first, pausing a few feet away the instant Justus's rumble takes on a note of warning. Like Justus, both of these males are in their twenties and wear their hair and beards long, but that's where their similarities end.

The taller one is brown skinned, and there's a glint in his dark eyes. He's smirking, his canines denting his lips. The only wolves I've seen with his exact coloring were some of the males from North Border who came to Quarry Pack to train with Killian.

North Border wolves don't have a single look, but they all carry themselves in a certain way so you can recognize them from a distance—like they'll attack first, without provocation. This male doesn't carry himself that way, though. He gives off assurance, maybe even cockiness, but not aggression.

The other brawler—the one with the injured ear—is pasty, red-headed, and freckled. He'd fit in fine at Quarry Pack. He has the confidence of a young, B-roster fighter, the kind of arrogance that reads as distemper and smells like bravado.

Both of the brawlers' expressions are suspicious, and their posture is almost hostile, but they toe the line Justus set with his rumbling. They clearly want to get into our space, but they stay back, pacing that invisible limit, nostrils flaring, tails whipping.

The other males gather closer, too, circling behind us, blocking the way out. My heart pounds faster.

They're cutting off your escape. Fight. Fight!

My wolf's fur bristles. She's with the pecking voice.

"This is my mate, Annie," Justus says calmly and sets me on the ground like he's presenting me to them as a gift.

He does it so quickly that there's nothing I can do. One moment, my wolf is cradled in his arms. The next she's standing on her own four, wobbly feet on the plush, mossy ground, mere feet from the prowling males, surrounded on all sides, frozen in terror.

See. You can't trust anyone.

My fear explodes.

The redhead's face instantly contorts like he's sucking lemons. "What did you do to her?" he asks as he tries to wave the smell away from his face.

Justus sighs. "She just smells like that sometimes. You get used to it."

"The females won't like it," the redhead says.

Justus doesn't reply, and I can't read his face. I'm paralyzed, staring at the pack as they circle us, gathering closer and closer. How many are behind me now? How close? I still don't see any females.

What have they done with the females?

Panic claws up my throat.

The redhead pinches his nose and asks, "Did you trade Kelly for her?"

"No trade. She's my mate."

The other brawler snorts. "You stole her."

"She's my mate, Khalil," Justus repeats more firmly. "I didn't steal her."

The redhead's pacing becomes more agitated. The gathered males mutter to each other, glowering in our direction. They look like the illustrations of ferals in the Moon Lake Academy textbooks—long, wild hair, lengthened fangs that dent their lower lips, furry chests, and wolfish ears and tails.

In the illustrations, ferals are always slavering or lunging or swiping at a cowering female with their claws. These males aren't acting like that at all, but they definitely aren't like Quarry Pack or Moon Lake males, either. I don't know quite how to describe it except that they don't stand like a pack at all.

Back home, when the males gather, they face the leader, usually Killian, and stand according to rank, higher in the front, lower in the back. This group is all over the place.

One lanky male is eating a drumstick. Toward the back, two younger males bump into each other, riling up the others nearby, trying to egg someone into a fight. A few elders have crouched to watch the proceedings from under the shade of an elm. Periodically, they bark when the others block their view.

There is a great deal of scratching among the furrier ones. A few who are fully shifted have padded to the front and plopped on their sides to watch. This pack isn't waiting for orders; they're waiting to be entertained.

"Well, did you take out Killian Kelly before you took her?" the redhead asks.

I turn to see Justus's reaction, and my heart jumps into my throat. The crowd behind me is five deep. I am well and truly surrounded.

Justus shrugs like the idea of taking Killian Kelly out isn't ridiculous—or out of the question—and says, "It wasn't exactly planned."

The one called Khalil snorts again.

"Well, what are you going to do, Alpha?" the redhead's voice rises, color creeping up his neck from his pale chest. "He'll come after her, mate or not."

"I'm not the alpha," Justus replies. He says it offhandedly, as if by rote. Isn't he, though? He seemed to be during the Byrnes fiasco. "And I laid a false trail."

"And how long will that delay the inevitable?" Khalil asks.

"Long enough," Justus answers. They share a speaking look and then Khalil shakes his head and backs off.

The redhead keeps pressing. "We don't need the trouble.

She's favored by Kelly's mate. You saw that. We all did." The redhead's face has flushed almost as bright as his hair. "Can't you just mount her somewhere else?"

The murmuring, muttering, scratching pack instantly falls silent. The redhead takes a huge step back, knocking the males behind him aside, and bares his neck.

"Apologies, Justus," he says. He's able to hold his tongue for about two seconds before he mumbles, "But what's wrong with high valley camp?"

"Black bears," the male with the drumstick calls out. "Can't fuck there until you clear out the bears."

Khalil snorts.

The redhead glares and continues muttering, "Why not take her to the red clay camp then? Killian Kelly isn't as stupid as he looks; he won't fall for a false trail for long. If we steal a female, we have to hold her at another camp until we're sure we got away clean. But I guess the rules don't apply to alphas."

He goes on and on, but he keeps his head bent, and the pack's attention is drifting away from him. There's movement coming from the caves in the terraces. Figures emerge and join together in a train that makes their way down a switchback path to the clearing. As they pass a tent near a tall sycamore tree, several more join them.

When they reach the gathering, the crowd shifts to make a path. My wolf's pulse picks up. Whoever is coming, they make the males nervous. There's a general shuffling of feet. The younger males posture, puffing their chests and throwing their shoulders back. The pitch of the entire crowd's muttering drops an octave.

The males gathered closest to us part, revealing a phalanx of females led by a black she-wolf, a gray-haired female in her skin, and another female, maybe in her late thirties or early forties, who is somehow both furry and all woman at the same time. She looks like the NSFW character art that Kennedy downloads on her phone—so much butt and boobs and hips.

My wolf draws herself up. She cowered like a pup in front of the males, but for some reason, she doesn't want to show these females her neck. She's trembling visibly, but she's holding her head high.

The voice is too freaked out to make any coherent warnings. All she can do is screech the kind of wordless, elongated, high-pitched "ahh" a person makes when they knock something over and it rocks back and forth, and back and forth, right on the verge of tipping. She's panicking, but I'm not.

Why aren't I?

By all rights, my wolf should be panicking, too. These females have the numbers, and most of them have a size advantage as well. Her best move is submission, and my wolf understands that, but she has no intention of giving an inch.

She's defending Justus.

But not because he's vulnerable.

Because he's hers.

"What's her name?" the gray-haired female interrupts my mental meltdown. I leap on the distraction, inspecting her as closely as she's inspecting me.

She has a North Border accent, and unlike the males, she's dressed. A skirt is wrapped around her waist and draped over her bare shoulder, somewhat like a sari or sarong. The blue fabric is clearly homespun and hand-dyed, but it looks as fine and soft as machine-made.

"Annie," Justus answers, lowering his voice respectfully

like he's been called to speak at an elders' meeting. "Annie, this is Elspeth."

My wolf inclines her head. It's an acknowledgment, not a show of submission.

The black she-wolf prowls forward, leaving a good distance as she anxiously sniffs in my direction. My wolf tenses, but she doesn't blink.

"This is Nessa," Justus says. "Annie's from Quarry Pack," he tells her.

She seems reassured by this and melts back into the gathering, tucking herself against the flank of a huge gray wolf. Three little wolf pups appear as if by magic between their legs. They gape at me, wide-eyed, their tiny tails thwapping the ground.

Instantly, my heart melts like cotton candy in water. Where did they come from?

They're shifter pups, but they're in their fur. How is that possible? Males don't shift until puberty, and females don't shift until they recognize their mates.

Except that's not always true, is it? Killian Kelly shifted when he was still a pup to save Una and Mari. Were these pups attacked? They can't be more than a year old.

My wolf growls and glares at Justus, displeased at the thought that he might've let them be hurt. His brow wrinkles.

Can the pups shift back and forth to human babies, or are they stuck as wolves until puberty? Somehow my curiosity allows me to relax enough to venture a little closer to the boundary between my wolf and me. The pups don't seem traumatized. One lies on her side, dozing off. Her belly is pure white. It looks so soft.

Another pup snuffles around the feet and legs of the males around him, yipping and nipping and head-butting at random until he gets a pat on his flank or a scratch behind his ears.

The third pup—the littlest one, a mix of her mother's black and her father's gray—seems as captivated by me as I am by her. She keeps padding toward me. The first few times, her dam yipped at her to come back, but when she just kept approaching, her dam gave a rumble, warning her to behave, and let her come.

She trots straight to me. Inside my wolf, I reach for her. It's a reflex. I've done it before I realize what I'm doing, and as soon as it registers, I drop my arms to my sides.

I don't get close to new people, not even the cutest little ball of fluff I've ever seen in my entire life. Her paws are no bigger than walnuts, and her nose is a black jelly bean. The others smile down fondly as she pads between their legs.

She keeps coming closer until she gets to the invisible line around Justus and me that no one is passing, and then she plunks herself onto her tiny rump and begins to groom her coat as she watches me.

An unsettling ache throbs in my chest. She is so small. So trusting. So defenseless. And there are so many males here, and so few females. They—we—are outnumbered ten to one. They could do whatever they want to us. They have the power.

You're trapped. You and the pups. There's no way out.

The furry, curvaceous female's snout wrinkles. "Justus, she shouldn't smell like that. Something's wrong."

I can't settle on where to look at her. The draped fabric serving as her dress is rigged so it only covers her nipples, and it doesn't cover her furry hips or thighs at all. It covers her privates, but every time she moves, the skirt swishes left or right, or bunches up in the middle, and somehow that makes her look more naked than if she wasn't wearing anything at all.

I don't want her to come any closer. Neither does my wolf, but she doesn't want to growl and disturb the pup. *I* don't want my wolf to growl and anger a Last Pack female who outweighs me by fifty pounds.

I force my gaze to settle above her neck because I was raised not to gawk, but her face is as arresting as her body. She has whiskey-gold human eyes with a wolf's muzzle, long whiskers, and lush human lips that are pillowy on top because of the snout.

In a way, she reminds me of the small band of human females who come to the farmers' market sometimes wearing fake tails, headband ears, and shirts that show off their breasts. Human males are all over them—and Quarry Pack males would be as well—but these Last Pack males keep their distance from her. She has an invisible fence around her, too, like Justus and I do.

The males closest to her are all standing at attention, their chests as puffed as possible and their stances so wide it looks like they're about to do the calisthenics that Quarry Pack males do before they go on patrol.

My wolf eyes Justus. He's not puffing anything, and his gaze is well above the female's neck, but my wolf isn't happy. She wants to bare her teeth, but the pup is watching.

"Annie, this is Diantha," he says. "Diantha, there's nothing wrong. Annie's just—she's quick to alarm."

"She's alarmed? *I'm* alarmed," the redhead mumbles. "Wait 'til Killian Kelly gets here. Everyone will wish they were more alarmed then." Despite the incessant smack talk, his head is still bent, and his neck is bared.

Justus growls a warning, not very loud and no longer than a second or two, but the redhead snaps his mouth shut right quick. My wolf and the pup startle. The pup whines. My wolf snaps her teeth at Justus.

He raises his palms and smiles at my wolf as he says to the redhead out of the corner of his mouth, "Weren't you the one who traded all our pelts and steaks for three Quarry Pack females just last year? That was you, wasn't it, Alroy?"

"He tried to," the male with the drumstick calls out, helpfully. "Wouldn't call it a trade, though, when y'all came back with nothing but your tails between your legs."

"I learned my lesson," the redhead—Alroy—mutters. "More than I can say for some. And it was Khalil's idea, too."

"Don't bring my name into it," Khalil says quickly.

"I don't think she should smell that way," Diantha says to Justus as if neither of the pack males have spoken. "You need to do something about it."

The other females murmur in agreement. It's strange—as the males manspread, they also made more room for the band of females in their center. The females are fanning out now, and I can make out more pups among them, in both skins and furs. They must shift then. My mind is boggled.

"What do you suggest I do, Diantha?" Justus asks, his voice dry, but not so dry that it's blatantly disrespectful.

Diantha props her hands on the lavish mounds of her hips. "I don't know. You're the alpha. Make her smell better."

"I'm not the alpha," Justus grumbles.

Diantha smirks. "Then we'll take her with us. Since you don't have any say. Since you're not the *alpha*."

She's *baiting* him—the male she calls alpha.

He's getting annoyed.

She better shut up. Someone will get hurt. The pup is right there.

"I'm her mate," he says. "She stays with me."

Diantha rolls her eyes. "That's not your call, is it?"

It *is* his call, though, right? Males decide where their females can go and what they can do. Even now that Una and Killian are mated, the males *allow us* to sell our wares in Chapel Bell.

"Do you want to come with us, Annie? We won't let any of them near you." Diantha turns her nose up at the males who have been subtly gathering closer to her. Immediately, they cast each other accusatory looks, projecting as much innocence as long-haired, tattooed, half-shifted males can.

"She's *his* mate." Alroy straightens, lifting his chest and hiking his chin so he can glower at Diantha. Standing tall, he almost seems like a different male. "You stay out of it."

Diantha's face gets shrewd and bloodthirsty, like a raccoon about to steal a dog's dinner.

"Where's my granddam's black bear pelt, eh, Alroy?" she asks in a singsong, projecting her voice so even the folks at the back can hear. "Oh yes, I remember. You traded it to Quarry Pack for three unmated females. Where are the females then, Alroy? Eh? Eh? Where are they?"

Alroy flushes beet red from his pasty chest up to the tip of his ears. The redder he gets, the more his muscles tense. Neither my wolf nor I clocked him as a big threat, but now, we both eye him warily.

"Don't try to be slick, Diantha," he sneers. "You want to take his mate so you can get him back."

Get him back? My wolf rumbles.

Justus is flushing now, too, under his beard. "Enough, Alroy," he says.

"That's right, Alroy," Diantha jumps right in to say. "Now show neck and shut up like a good boy." Her attention is trained on Alroy.

Justus's face darkens, his scent souring by the second,

and Diantha is so intent on riling Alroy, she doesn't notice at all.

Be quiet! Danger! Make her be quiet!

My wolf edges closer to the little pup who's watching wide-eyed like the rest of the pack.

Why aren't they bending their heads? At the first hint of Killian's displeasure, everyone in Quarry Pack bows their head like it's time to give thanks at a full moon feast.

None of the females seem concerned that there are two males growing angrier and angrier. It almost seems like entertainment to them. The male with the drumstick is sucking the bones while his gaze ping-pongs from packmate to packmate.

"You're not the alpha female, Diantha," Alroy sneers. "No matter how many times you've sniffed Justus's ass."

She snorts. "You *wish* a female would even sniff in the *direction* of yours, but for that to happen, you'd have to wash it, *Alroy,* more than once a season."

"I said *enough,*" Justus growls through gritted teeth.

He's angry. No one move.

The little pup rolls onto her side, stretching her legs and splaying her tiny toe beans. Exposing her belly. My wolf's muscles bunch, her heart in her throat. How does the pup not sense the danger?

When males fight, they don't care what breaks or who they trample. Where the hell is her dam?

"Next time, you should try trading for human females, Alroy." Diantha smirks as if Justus isn't even there, his wolf rattling his ribs. "They don't have much of a sense of smell."

A sharp snarl bursts from Alroy's chest.

The pup lets out a surprised yelp.

No!

My wolf leaps on top of her, rolling her away from the angry males and into the crowd. Packmates stumble back.

My wolf pops to her feet and crouches over the pup, hiding her, growling and snapping until the circle around her clears. She catches sight of Alroy's flaming tomato face, and she lets out a snarl so furious that it scrapes her throat.

He frightened the pup. He's the threat.

Kill him.

I can't. He's too big. My wolf looks to Justus expectantly. His eyes are dark with rage, his body tensed and menacing, but my wolf doesn't flinch. She yaps at him. He's bigger. He needs to handle this male. She can't do everything herself.

Justus growls. He's clearly threatening Alroy, not my wolf, but still, the sound has the force of an alpha's growl, no matter what he says, and it strikes terror in my human heart.

Shut up, wolf.

Oh, please, shut your mouth.

My wolf ignores us both and yaps at Justus even louder.

Pockets of smothered laughter bubble up from the crowd as if one by one, they can't hold it in anymore.

Justus steps to Alroy, his aggravation blaring like an air raid siren. Inside my wolf, I scurry back to my corner, huddle, and moan. My wolf bares her teeth at Alroy and rumbles in anticipation.

Alroy doesn't even notice. He's steaming mad, glaring daggers at Diantha, screwing up his mouth to say something else.

She smirks, waiting, her eyes sparkling with anticipation.

"We should trade *you.*" Alroy sneers. "Everyone's tired of your old ass anyway."

All laughter dies. Diantha's jaw drops. The sharp stink of

aggression rises from the females. The pup curls into a tighter ball beneath me.

My wolf lifts her muzzle and howls.

"That's it." Justus curses and lunges for Alroy.

In the blink of an eye, Alroy shifts and tries to leap away, but Justus is quicker. He snatches Alroy's full-grown wolf from midair with his bare hands and spins almost exactly like we were taught in human sport class at Moon Lake Academy when we learned the discus. Then he lets go.

Alroy's wolf goes flying. The crowd scatters, clearing a runway. He lands a good ten yards away and skids across the ground, tearing up the lush green grass. Eventually, he rolls to a stop with a sad mewl. He stays down.

Justus throws his head back, bares his fangs, and roars. His bellow echoes off the terraces rising around us. Loose pebbles skitter down the rock face. The entire pack crashes to their knees and bares their throats. Pups dart between their dams' legs to hide. The silence is sudden and absolute.

A breeze whips down from a high peak, ruffling fur like wind across a wheat field. My wolf draws in a steadying breath, bracing for the stench of fear.

The air is clear.

Almost *brisk*.

The entire pack is showing neck, and they're chastened —and wary—but they aren't afraid.

I don't understand.

Justus blows out his cheeks, clenches his teeth and glares beseechingly up at the sky for a moment, and then points at Alroy's wolf and says, "You watch how you talk to females. I'll skin *you* and trade *your pelt* to Quarry Pack. Try me. See if I won't!" He bellows the final words.

Alroy's wolf whines and tucks his snout into his shoulder.

Then Justus turns to Diantha. "You—" he snaps, then stops himself and starts again with a deliberately, teeth-grindingly even voice. "Mind your own business. Please." He surveys his pack and announces, "This is Annie. She's my mate. That's all. No need for all of this. Go on about your day now."

"Yes, Alpha," the pack mutters.

He growls. "I'm not the alpha." He strides forward, picks up my wolf and the little gray pup, and tucks one of us under each arm. "You don't need an alpha to tell you what to do. You need common sense, so some of you are out of luck, but that doesn't mean I need to step into the breach."

He keeps grumbling as he marches over to the black wolf and gently sets her pup at her feet. The black wolf butts his leg and rumbles her thanks. The pup whines and props her little paws on his other leg to try and reach me. My wolf bends over Justus's forearm and gives her a few reassuring yips that she'll see her soon. The pup isn't the least bit upset by the events of the past few minutes. If anything, she smells excited. Like a pup who's going to be hard to put to bed.

I watch from the boundary between my wolf and me where I've crept, stealthy and uncertain, so I can memorize the pup's twig of a tail and her downy belly fur and her tufty ears. She captivates me.

And it's not just that she's precious. Or that she's the first of her kind I've ever seen.

She's not afraid. She should be. She's small. Defenseless.

It's not that she's particularly fearless. Her siblings don't smell cowed, either.

Justus carries me away, and I crane my neck to see the pup join her brother and sister to tumble together and sniff and snuffle like it's been five years, not five minutes.

She's not afraid. Nothing's hurt her yet, not badly.

As Justus walks through the pack to the far side of the clearing, I watch as his packmates stand, dust off their knees, and start to chat and laugh and bicker again. They duck their heads when Justus passes, giving me a once-over from the corner of their averted eyes, but they're not afraid, either.

They're curious.

The atmosphere feels exactly like it did in class at Moon Lake Academy after a badly behaved student got it from the instructor—that giddy release of tension and effort to look innocent and obedient.

What is going on in this pack?

And where are we going?

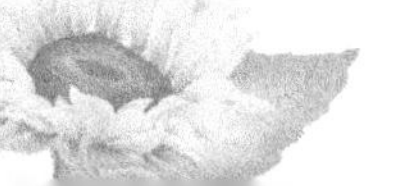
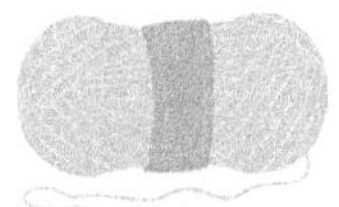

8

———

ANNIE

Carrying my wolf like a sack of potatoes, Justus hikes up a narrow switchback path that runs along the steep incline surrounding the clearing that acts as their commons. There are no buildings, but the higher we get, the better I'm able to make out how the camp is organized.

At the end furthest from the dens, there is an area for tanning with the lowest branches of a magnolia scraped smooth to act as a frame and drying racks. At the center of the clearing, around the huge bonfire, there are spits and barrels and long, sturdy wooden tables for cooking and eating.

Moving away from the center of camp, I see crescent-shaped herb gardens and vegetable patches, and various small groups of packmates. Elders in rocking chairs snooze or play a game with stones on a table carved with blocks like a chess board. Males wrestle or squat on stools, whittling and mending, or nap on their backs, gathered near clusters of canvas tents situated around small fire pits.

I only see one group of females, and they're mostly

hidden underneath a canopy of deer skins battened to posts sunk in the ground. They watch over pups who swarm a tall sycamore strung with ropes and ladders and swings.

When we reach the highest level, I can finally see the water source that I heard below, a rushing stream—not quite a river, but too wide for a wolf to leap across—that meanders the perimeter of the camp. I count three rough-hewn bridges at three different oxbows.

The stream's headwater seems to be the mountain to the north, and it enters camp via an unlikely opening through the rocks, visible now that we're above the canopy. It doesn't seem natural, but I can't imagine how a tunnel could be bored through the rock and then made to look like a haphazard arch of fallen rocks.

From this height, I can also trace the curving dirt paths that run between and among all the various areas of activity. Exactly like the males' maze of swirl tattoos.

The fur along my spine bristles. There is magic here. It tickles my nose like it does in Abertha's cottage.

If it were this time of day at Quarry Pack, no one would be outside. I'd be in the lodge's kitchen, prepping dinner with Mari, Kennedy, and Old Noreen—and the Z-roster males still under punishment from backing the traitors. The other males would be training in the gym, and the females would be working at the laundry or the commissary or in their cabins, tending their pups. No matter what exactly they were doing, they'd be busy.

Not so here. Some of the Last Pack folks are working on something, but most are lounging or chatting or napping or roughhousing. There's *lots* of roughhousing.

No patrol. No guards. Nowhere to hide but these dens. These traps.

The voice is back, and no surprise, she has concerns. My

nerves twist tighter—there isn't even a guard posted at the narrow entrance—but I can't tear my eyes away from the scene.

It's so peaceful. Like a lazy dance.

When I started watching, there was a single, older male at the long table by the fire, peeling carrots, naked except for his long, swishing tail. After a while, another, younger male joins him. He grabs a carrot and pops it in his mouth.

The older male cuffs him upside the head. The youngster, not chastened in the least, leaves with the carrot dangling from his lips like a cigarette. I figure he's been chased off, but he returns a minute later with a milk crate full of potatoes. He sits down and joins the older male to do the prep work.

A little later, a pup wanders over on two legs with paws for feet. The older male tosses him a raw potato chunk, and he snaps it out of mid-air, like a dog with a treat. The older male then asks him something, pointing to the far side of the clearing. The pup waits until the older male tosses another potato chunk before he heads off on his errand.

I track him as he meanders off. His route is not straight.

First, a gang of wolf pups race across his path, and he detours to chase them. When they shift to human and haul themselves into the sycamore like monkeys, the helper pup loses interest and continues on his way.

He passes the deer skin canopy, and a female calls him over and hands him a wide-brimmed straw hat. He carries it awhile, spinning it on a finger like a frisbee. When he passes a group of elders, he places it carefully on the bald head of a snoozing, gray-bearded male. The others raise their trembling, gnarled hands, and he brushes their fingers with his own, a brief show of casual affection, like bumping noses.

We don't really touch like that in Quarry Pack, not

unless the person is blood. I've worked with Old Noreen in the kitchens for years, but I don't think we've ever touched except by accident. The gesture is still familiar somehow, though. It reminds me of how the pack's wolves act after they return from a run when they're resting in the commons before shifting back.

We don't nuzzle packmates in our human skins. Our males spar. That's about it.

It's strange to watch as the helper pup passes his people. It's like a daisy chain of touch—his back is clapped, his hair riffled, his shoulder bumped in greeting, his leg clung to by a little guy with chubby arms and an octopus's grip. Except for the octopus hitching a ride, the helper pup hardly seems to notice. He reciprocates automatically.

Like it's perfectly natural to touch and be touched.

Like it never hurt.

Eventually, after dropping the octopus off with his sire, the helper pup arrives at his destination, the only solid structure I've seen so far, a tall and narrow wooden shack resting on a platform of stacked slabs of stone. Smoke puffs from a tin pipe on the roof.

Unlike the entrance to the pack land, the shed is well-guarded by a trio of grizzled males with full complements of claws and fangs, but not a patch of fur between them. There is a lot of conversation and gesticulation between the helper pup and the males before a haunch of meat is taken down from a hook and handed over on a platter that, from this distance, looks very much like an upside-down metal trash can lid.

The helper pup carries the meat back to the fire, knees bent and arms straining. He takes the direct route this time.

When he returns to the fire, others have gathered and formed something of an assembly line. It looks like they're making a stew. Besides the potatoes and carrots, they're chopping onions, mushrooms, parsnips, and some kind of green herb, maybe parsley. They fill one huge cast iron cauldron after another and hang them on tripods set about the fire.

The wind is too brisk this high, and it's blowing the wrong way, so I can't smell the cooking, but my wolf's stomach grumbles anyway.

"Once you're settled, I'll go fetch us a bowl," Justus says.

My wolf startles. We both forgot ourselves. How long have we been standing here, letting him hold us? A good while.

My wolf yips to be let down, but Justus lifts her a little closer and bends his head to talk into her ear. "The pup is Griff. He's Elspeth's oldest. He does take his good ol' time, but he can be relied upon not to nibble the beef on his way back with it."

Justus points my wolf at the older male who started chopping carrots. "That's Tarquin. If no one else makes a move to get dinner together, he'll do it once he gets hungry, but he only ever makes stew."

So the males cook in this pack? None of the females are helping. As far as I can tell, they're all still lounging under their canopy.

"The male with the black and white ears is Pierce. The skinny one thieving meat is Colm."

I watch Colm, who is tall and lanky as a beanpole, carve a haunch into bite-size pieces, pausing every so often when no one's watching to toss a hunk into the air, snap it up with his teeth, and scarf it down.

Why is Justus telling me their names?

It feels like the first day of school at Moon Lake Academy when the human instructors would make everyone introduce themselves and do something silly like tell two truths and one lie about themselves. The humans sailed through the assignment, but we shifters were various degrees of terrible.

I might have been the worst. One year, I said that my name was Mari, and I love knitting and gardening. The instructor said I needed to say one more thing, so I said I was looking forward to the class, which I figured she could take as the truth if she wanted, but it was a massive lie. She called me Mari all year long.

Anyway, we did introductions because we were going to be there together for a while. I am not going to be here long. This is a kidnapping.

I think.

Even Justus said I'm not going to be here long. When the wolf called Khalil asked how long a false trail would fool Killian, Justus said, "Long enough." That means he's going to take me back soon.

If it hurts my heart, it's only because of the reminder that I'm not going to get what other females have. A mate. A pup. A home of my own.

I could never belong here, even if Justus decided to keep me, which he wouldn't. There aren't any *doors*, any locks. There's nothing to hide behind.

Long enough.

The pecking voice won't let that rest. She wants to know —long enough for what?

I worry, and my wolf squirms. Justus sets her down. She wanders away from the ledge-side path, through a small, mossy patch with two skyrocket junipers growing like sentries beside a crack in the rock.

The place smells like Justus, as if this is where his scent comes from, this is the earth that exactly matches his earthiness. The ache in my heart turns to butterflies in my belly.

There's a rickety stool outside the den with a book sitting on it, a paperback that's gotten soaked and dried at least once, opened like a fan. A bookmark made of braided grass is tucked between the pages.

He reads?

What is he reading? My wolf can't read. All she can do to satisfy my curiosity is sniff the pages. They smell like they've been dew-dampened and baked in the sunshine many, many times. She bumps it off the chair with her enthusiasm, and Justus rescues it from the ground.

"Go on in," he urges her, nodding toward the low entrance. His voice has dropped an octave, but it's also shaky, in a rough, raspy way.

Is he nervous? He can't be, right? He's the male, and this is his territory. I'm female, smaller and weaker and surrounded by *his* people. And if I walk into his den ahead of him, I'll be trapped.

Still, I think he's uneasy, too. He thumbs the pages of his waterlogged book and stands in a very posed, very nonchalant way. Like he very much wants me to go into his den, and he's very worried I won't, and he doesn't want me to know that.

What's in there?

My wolf prowls a few inches closer to the entrance and pokes her nose in. It's dark inside and smells even more like him than the grove out front.

As my wolf's eyes adjust, the outlines of objects rise from the gloom. A pallet. A big, round woven basket with a lid. An apple crate full of books. A braided mat made of rags.

My wolf sniffs and takes a step forward. The pallet smells like sweet grass, and linen, and Justus—like the things he must do there, under the sheets. My cheeks heat. Whatever he does, he does it alone. His scent is the only one in the den. My wolf is pleased. She draws in another, deeper breath.

The basket is willow. The books smell like the one on the stool outside, but these also have a hint of tart sweetness, maybe from the apple crate. The rag rug looks clean, but it smells exactly like a long-faded version of the scent of the whole pack gathered around us—wolfy and earthy and warm. Homey.

Without a second thought, my wolf pads over so she can get a better sniff.

No! Stop! It's a trap!

My wolf whirls, but it's too late. Justus has followed us in, blocking the entrance. My fear explodes, the stink obliterating the straw, the apple, the mat, the sweet grass, the linen—everything.

Justus immediately drops to a crouch and raises his hands, but for once, his face doesn't show even the slightest reaction to the smell.

He's blocking the exit. You're trapped. Hide. Hide!

The voice shrieks, but my wolf doesn't take her eyes off Justus. She's well aware that there is nowhere to hide. She stands in place and waits.

We're afraid, but then again—we're not. He's not going to hurt us. She knows.

I know.

The voice is incapable of knowing that we're safe. It's a blaring alarm. That's all. It doesn't have some kind of insight that we don't have.

The night of the coup, when our cabin caught fire, Fallon rolled up on his ATV, saying Killian sent him to take us to safety, and the voice didn't warn me that he was part of the plot.

It can't see the future, and it can't read minds. It can only scream in the back of mine.

"Annie, please come out. Talk to me," Justus says, deliberate and calm, but rough underneath. Not with impatience. With yearning?

He lowers his arms to brace them on his thighs. My wolf is very quiet, like she's faded into a spectator.

"I'd like to hear your voice again." His lips curve in a rueful smile, there and then gone.

His eyes are so somber.

Behind him, the sun has sunk, its last rays backlighting him, falling across the center of the den, and illuminating the faded colors in the worn rug, so clean despite the packed earth floor. He must shake it out a lot.

The sun picks out gold streaks in his long brown hair. It's not groomed, per se. He clearly hasn't done more than run his fingers through it, but it isn't hopelessly matted like it was when his people tried to trade the Byrnes for us.

Come to think of it, none of the males in the camp are as unkempt as that crew. Last Pack males don't look nearly as recently showered as Quarry Pack males do, but they're not *dirty* dirty. I guess they look like folks who live in dens, bathe in a stream, and spend most of their time naked and outdoors.

"Where'd you go, sweetling?" Justus asks, a brief, soft twinkle in his eyes. "Won't you come out?"

How did he know I drifted off?

I'm so curious, and I'm not used to it. I don't usually have the bandwidth to have questions. I have to keep my eyes peeled. Be ready. Run down the list of all the horrible things that can happen, over and over again, ticking them off like the elders with their prayer beads.

"I won't hurt you," he says. A shadow crosses his face. Regret? Shame?

There I go, wondering again.

I could shift. Talk to him. Ask him when he'll take me home. If it goes to hell, I can shift back.

I prod my wolf for reassurance, but she remains quiet and passive. She's tired. She's had our skin for such a long time now. Quarry Pack wolves don't spend this much time in our fur. I'm going to have to shift back at some point.

Don't. You need claws. Fangs.

Even the pecking voice sounds tired.

If I shift, I'll be naked. In this small den. With a male. My mate.

The last rays of sun outline his wide shoulders. His upper arms. Sinewy. It's such a funny word, but that's what describes him. Sinewy and self-possessed and still.

"Listen," he says, rising to his feet. "I'll go get our dinner. You can think about it."

No.

My wolf stiffens. She doesn't want him to leave us alone, but he's already turning, and then he's already gone.

She whines and lowers herself to her belly. The silence is heavy. At the entrance, the wind blows faintly and the cedars' needles rustle, but the center of the den has that close, warm quiet that you make when you pull your winter comforter over your head.

Out of habit, I scan my surroundings, but there's no place for anyone to hide. I suppose a wolf could hide in the big basket, but I don't smell anyone except Justus.

Better check it anyway to be sure.

I don't see how I can unless my wolf knocks it over. The

lid is battened on with straps looped over the handles. If she knocked it over, he'd know we looked.

Still, better check. It's a big basket.

There's no nefarious, scentless wolf hiding in a basket. I'd hear him breathing.

Better check now.

This is the kind of baseless worry that I've gotten pretty good at ignoring. My common sense tells me it's bullshit, and the voice's heart isn't really in it. She's just doing her job.

But what *is* in the basket?

And what books does he have in that apple crate?

If I shift, I can snoop. Not in the basket—that would be an invasion of privacy—but the books are out for anyone to see.

But I'll be naked.

I could shift right back after I take a peek.

Justus has to walk all the way back down to camp and back up again. I have time. And my wolf needs a break. Is it fair to keep hiding inside her, especially now that she's dragging ass?

Curiosity wins.

I don't really take our skin. The instant I make the decision, my wolf dissolves into a puddle of fur with a huge sigh, and I have no choice but to mold us into legs and arms, rising up until I'm standing, shivering on two bare feet.

My body feels strange and rubbery, and my knees sway when I step toward the apple crate. The clock is ticking. My heart speeds up.

Run now. He's gone. It's your last chance. Run!

Through his entire pack, pups and elders and all? With these rubber legs? Butt naked?

I sink to my knees beside the crate and pick up the top book, a small white-covered paperback with a surreal picture of a sun with a human face on it. Jean-Jacques Rousseau's *Discourse on the Origin and Basis of Inequality Among Men*. The pages are sepia and brittle as fall leaves. I've never heard of it.

I'm not much of a *reader* of books. I'm too distractible. When the money started to come in from the farmers' market, I got into audiobooks, though. The sound doesn't exactly drown out the pecking voice, but I can kind of focus on the narrator, and it really helps the day go by better.

I like mysteries and psychological thrillers, but only if they're written and narrated by women. If a woman's reading it, I can listen to the most grotesque crime scene descriptions and think nothing of it, but if it's read by a man, I can't handle it. I can't explain it, but I don't have to, either, if I don't bring it up, and I'm not one to ever start conversations.

I sniff the paperback—old, musty paper, glue, and Justus—and set it on the pallet. The next book in the pile, Peter Kropotkin's *The Conquest of Bread*, has a picture of two men chopping down a tree on the cover. It smells the same. All the books are dog-eared paperbacks with yellowed pages—*Walden* by Henry David Thoreau, *Parable of the Sower* by Octavia Butler, *Critique of Practical Reason* by Immanuel Kant, several each by Ursula K. Le Guin and N. K. Jemison, and a massive hardback of Plato's collected works.

The Plato is the only one that looks like it hasn't been read a hundred times. There are dozens more. I haven't heard of any of them.

How did Justus learn to read? Can everyone in Last Pack? I was always told that they can't.

I flip through the book with the sun on the front. The font is small, and the paragraphs are long. I skim the first page, but none of it sticks. My eyes slide along the words like they're buttered.

I'm about to put it back when someone whistles outside the den. My fingers fumble, and the book falls, wide open and face down.

Another whistle rings out, closer this time. I pitch the book into the crate and scramble to sit on the pallet, wrapping my arms around my shins, tucking my knees to my chin.

Justus ducks into the den, and the second that he sees me, huddling in my skin, his eyes light on fire. A delicious spicy, muskiness fills the den. My heartbeat skips.

He has blue fabric folded over his right forearm and a steaming bowl in each hand, and he stands in the entranceway like he's forgotten what he came here to do.

Suddenly, I'm aware of my bare bottom on the edge of his pallet. How my breasts smoosh against my knees. The trickle from my pussy that is immediately soaked up by his cotton top sheet.

His chest is rising and falling like he ran back. His nostrils flare.

In the back of my mind, the voice is shouting, but he's not moving an inch, so I can ignore her.

He clears his throat. "Can I bring you this?" he asks, raising the arm with the fabric and a steaming bowl. My stomach grumbles.

I nod, keeping my eyes locked on him. In case he makes a sudden move. Not because he's so tall and muscular and tattooed and bearded, and he has fabric folded over his forearm and a bowl like a fancy waiter on TV.

He slowly sets his own bowl down at his feet and then approaches me, one step at a time, like he's stalking deer. My muscles tense and my belly explodes with butterflies.

I'm still shivering, but I'm not the least bit cold. The temperature in the den is actually pleasantly warm. Cozy, not stuffy. If I weren't so terribly, painfully, awkwardly naked, it'd be comfortable.

Justus stops a few feet from me, places the bowl on the rug, and then lays the fabric beside it. He tries to fold it, but he does it about as well as the Z-roster males working off their punishment in the laundry.

"I'll turn around so you can, uh—" He waves at the fabric and then goes back to the entrance and squats with his back to me, staring out into the dark.

His butt and quads stretch his pants tight. There's a crease that follows his spine all the way into his waistband, and those dimples. His tattoos swirl along his right arm and shoulder, wrapping around his right side, but the left side of his body is blank except for the lines his muscles make.

I don't realize I'm gawking until he fidgets, shifting his weight. I quickly bend forward and grab the fabric. It's lightweight, but there's a lot of it. I wrap it around me like a shower towel, and I'm covered from boob to ankle. I sit back on the pallet, but the fabric is too tight to pull my knees up, so I fold them sideways.

"I'm good," I say. My voice is soft like usual, but the cave is quiet, so he hears me fine. He turns and sits, knees bent and thighs wide open like males do without thinking twice. He drags a bowl to the space between his legs and digs in.

I wait—I'm not sure for what—but when he keeps eating and not paying me any attention, I grab my bowl and give it a stir with the spoon that came with it. I was wrong about the herb. It's not parsley; it's rosemary. It smells heavenly.

My stomach rumbles, and my wolf adds her two cents,

growling along. I take a bite. The carrot is mushy, and the beef is stringy, but it's easily the tastiest stew I've ever had.

Old Noreen says that hunger is the best spice. As I ladle spoonful after spoonful into my mouth, quicker and quicker, I acknowledge that's true, but I've been this ravenous before—we were always hungry during Declan Kelly's day—but nothing has ever filled my belly like this.

It tastes like a long time ago. Like when my mother was alive, and she'd take me to visit Abertha in her cottage, and there'd always be something delicious bubbling in the old black pot over the fire and a few other females gathered around the sturdy wood table, laughing and ranting and crying and whispering, while us pups filled our bellies, licked our bowls clean, and then got into every bit of trouble we could find.

I haven't remembered those days in years. The food stuck to your ribs, and Ma seemed younger there with the other females in that cottage, like a pup herself.

I actually whine when I take my last bite.

At the sound, a growl rattles Justus's chest, and he immediately springs forward. I startle, and my bowl clatters on the floor. Thank goodness it's empty.

Justus freezes mid-spring, lunging forward with his bowl in one hand and his other palm raised to assure me he means no harm. It's the world's most awkward yoga position.

"Here," he says. "More." He empties his bowl into mine and offers it to me, lifting it higher so I'll take it when I don't grab it right away.

His watchful eyes gobble me up. He really, really wants to feed me more. I've watched males fight each other for rank all my life. I know what it looks like when a male is trying to hide how desperately he wants something.

The warmth from the stew spreads from my belly, through my chest, and into my breasts. My nipples harden and poke through my toga. I hold Justus's gaze with all my might. Please, please don't let him look down and notice.

Partly to distract him, I take the bowl. I can't avoid brushing his fingers. I couldn't say how they feel, whether they're as rough as they look, because when I touch him, my whole body wakes up. A ball in my belly unfurls. My mouth waters. Tingles trip down my neck and spine, swirling around my tailbone until I feel like I have to pee even though I know I don't.

My body is glitching so badly, I wouldn't be surprised if smoke is coming from my ears, but Justus seems fine. Totally unaffected. He doesn't prolong the contact, not even a little. As soon as I have a good grip on the bowl, he backs off to sit exactly where he has been.

I start eating. He fixes his focus on my hand, watching me scoop up a chunk of potato like I'm defusing a bomb, not slurping soup. When I blow on a spoonful to cool it, his gaze darts to my lips, and his wolf rumbles.

The stew is hardly even lukewarm at this point, I don't know why I blew on the spoon in the first place—habit, I guess—but I do it again. The movement is mostly hidden under his beard, but his jaw definitely clenches. My pulse speeds even faster.

He feels this, too.

I usually hate being the center of attention. My whole life, I've done everything possible to avoid it. I'm an expert at position and timing, a choreographer at blending into the background. In any group situation, I make sure I end up standing behind someone else. I don't make work or ask questions. I'm never first in line or last to finish.

Attention is dangerous. But Justus's isn't. Not to me. Not

right now, at this moment. And I don't hate being here with him.

Maybe because he's keeping his distance, and he's not leering like a Quarry Pack male would. In a way, he reminds me of a scruffy pup who's come across something fascinating like tadpoles or an ant hill. His interest isn't creepy at all.

When there aren't any grownups around, sometimes Abertha will do tricks for the pups, pull buttons from behind their ears or make it seem like she's levitating a few inches off the ground, that kind of thing. The littlest, shyest pups don't crowd close and bug her to spill her secrets. They hang back, rapt.

Justus is looking at me like that. Like I'm magic, and he'd best give me room because I might be dangerous.

My spoon scrapes the bottom of my empty bowl.

"Do you want more?" he asks.

I shake my head and set the bowl down as far as I can get it from me.

Much more slowly than last time, he prowls forward, bracing himself on one hand. His forearm and bicep flex to take his weight, and then he shifts onto his opposite knee and that thigh tenses. With every move, every flex, my breath softly catches. I sound like the world's quietest chugging train engine.

If he kept coming, he could push me onto my back on his pallet and cover me. Pin me in place with his weight. I wouldn't dare try to push him off. He'd growl, but it wouldn't be threatening. It'd be more like a dare. If he pressed his chest against my swollen breasts, how would it feel?

What am I even *thinking*?

I squirm, shifting to a butt cheek so I'm not sitting

directly on my lady parts. I've never noticed the pressure a seat can exert on my bottom before, but I'm keyed into it now.

It's not like I *want* Justus to touch me. It would pop this bubble, ruin the moment, and bring the voice back with a vengeance. Justus doesn't take a second longer than he has to, plucking my empty bowl off the floor and immediately returning to his side of the den. He stacks my bowl on his and ducks out of the den to place them outside.

When he comes back, he lights an oil lamp, and instantly, the den feels different. Shifters can see pretty well in the dark, even in human form, so I don't see anything new, but the *feel* of the space totally changes.

The curl of smoke from the match twists mid-air like a thin, twirling ribbon, and the glowing flame is soft and warm, casting velvet shadows on the wall. I can pick out the colors of the rug now—coral and goldenrod and burnt sienna. The basket is made of willow, and Justus's sheets aren't plain white. They're super-faded robin's egg blue.

Justus returns to his seat barely past the den's entrance and goes back to watching me, so casual, like he could do it all night. I'm feeling the effects of a belly full of stew on top of a kidnapping. I need a bed.

Where am I going to sleep? Where is *he*?

"When are you taking me home?" I blurt because I don't dare ask him about beds.

His shoulder blades snap together. That amazement in his eyes flickers out. My stomach sinks. I've made things heavy again. I curl my toes into the rug and hug my knees tighter.

"Later," he says.

Never. They have you now. You'll never see Una or anyone from home again.

A fresh wave of fear bursts from my pores, overpowering the lingering scent of stew. Justus's jaw clenches, his lips curling back in a grimace.

"But you will take me back, right?" My voice rises with each word, my anxiety taking off like a shot, running wild, coloring everything until it's ugly and menacing—the den is a trap, Justus is my jailer, the bed is a threat.

I can't breathe. I gasp for air, my hands reaching for something to help myself, but there's nothing, nothing. I look to Justus, pleading with my eyes, my throat strangling my ability to speak.

"I will," he says, holding my gaze, his face both fierce and terrified at what's happening to me. His mouth turns down and his skin grows pale like I've asked him to do the unthinkable. Like he's my hostage. "I promise you that I will take you home when you ask. I swear it to you on my dam's grave."

My throat eases. Air fills my lungs.

I recover more quickly than he does, but then again, I'm used to panic attacks. There was a time when I'd have them almost daily. The trick is to tell yourself you're not really dying, and if you are, at least it'll end. This was a quick one, and I didn't go into a full-blown meltdown. Thank goodness for that.

I glance around the den to avoid Justus's eyes. I don't like that they're guarded now. It felt safer before, when I could read them.

It was actually starting to feel almost good.

I can't get in trouble for just thinking it. Not every positive thought can be a jinx. That's what I tell myself while I practice my deep breathing and search for something to say. My gaze falls on the apple crate.

"Where did you get the books?" I ask.

It takes him a second to realize I'm sweeping the past few minutes under the rug, but considering, he catches on pretty quickly. "The hedge witch. I trade her."

"You mean Abertha? You know her?"

He nods.

"What do you trade?"

He shrugs. "Meat, mostly. Odds and ends. Herbs. Stones. Eye of newt, toe of frog."

Oh, gross. "You cut off frog toes?" Our people will eat a fat toad if they come across him as their wolves, but they wouldn't pluck him apart for pieces. That's vicious. And besides, do frogs even have toes?

Justus's lips curl. It's a bashful smile, not mocking. "'Toe of frog' is from a book. A play, actually. It was a joke." He glances down. "A bad one."

Now I toss a shoulder, my cheeks warming. "I don't read plays. Or books like yours."

"You looked through them?"

Oh, no. What am I doing, admitting I went through his things?

He'll be angry. Shut your mouth before you make it worse. No. Beg forgiveness. Now. Before he loses it.

"I'm sorry," I rush to say. "I shouldn't have."

"Why not?" he asks. His brow knits. He's serious.

"They're your belongings." I might not have acted like it, but I was raised right. I know to respect other people's privacy.

"But you're my mate."

"But not really, though, right?" Why did I say that? I don't want to go there. Ever. Certainly not right now while I'm sitting on his bed, post-panic attack, wearing a sheet.

Heat sears my cheeks. I want to close my shutters and shut my door and turn the locks. Tuck myself into my shell.

My gaze dives to the ground. The flush seeping across my chest is so intense that it heats my chin. I don't want to talk about him and me.

Right?

So why did I say something? It's like my deepest fears are in charge of this conversation.

"This is real to me," Justus says, his voice low and even, not accusatory or angry. He leaves it at that, falling silent.

I could stop talking, too, drop the subject and shrink into myself until he gets bored and turns his attention to something else. That's what I do, right? Hide.

"But you don't want it to be," I say instead, and my face bursts into flame.

Justus holds himself very still while he answers. "I don't want my mate to fear me. Or hate me. Or hate my pack."

"I don't hate your pack." I blink up, accidentally meeting his eye. Instantly, I'm snagged, a fish on a hook, dry drowning.

"Just me, then?" His lip quirks, wry and bitter.

"Not you either," I whisper. "I don't know you."

"Can't you feel me?" He presses his palm to the center of his chest. My hand rises to cover my heart, mirroring the motion.

The bond is there, aching so very, very faintly, deep in the recesses of my mind with all the other ghosts and bogeymen I've shoved down there. And yet, somehow, when I focus on it, the gash the bond makes in my soul is still pink and fresh, the kind of walking wound that makes you fixate on the thinness of your skin and how impossible it is that something so fragile holds all your guts and bones together.

"A little," I say.

"But you can feel that I won't hurt you, right? I didn't

ever want to hurt you. Or frighten you. I'm sorry that I did. I —I was rough, and—I didn't understand that—"

He's talking about the nest beside the river. No, no, no. I don't want to talk about that. Not with him. Not ever.

"I've never heard of any of these before," I interrupt, scooting over to the apple crate and picking up the book with the sun on the cover. I thumb through the pages. "What are they about?"

He's thrown, but again, only for a second. "That one? Mostly about how once an individual claims to own his territory within pack lands, everything goes to hell."

"So you don't own this place?"

"I stay here," he says.

"But it's *your* den."

"No, it isn't."

I sniff to check, but no, I'm right—it smells like him and no one else. "Whose is it then?"

"Yours." He flashes another slight smile.

"You're playing." I pull my heels closer to my body. I don't like being teased.

"Dens belong to females. It's a male's honor and duty to provide shelter for his mate and their family, the elders and pups. He can stay, too, if he's welcome."

"But you're the alpha. Aren't you?"

"Wouldn't matter if I was, and I'm not."

I'm not sure if he's lying or not. The pack sure acts like he's in charge, albeit not at all the way we act around Killian at Quarry Pack. "Your people call you Alpha."

"To annoy me." He sighs, leans his head back, and stares at the low ceiling for a few seconds before he explains. "I've told them a hundred times—in nature, wolves don't have alphas or betas or whatever. That's a human thing. Humans put wolves in cages, and when the wolves didn't have enough room to breathe, and they couldn't hunt for their own food, they lost their minds. The strongest took everything he could for himself, and the others lived in fear. That's where alphas came from, and it's not the natural way of things. As shifters, it's sure as hell not *our* way."

Yes, it is. That's exactly our way. The strongest gets whatever he wants, and everyone else gets to be afraid. A snort that I meant to keep in my head somehow comes out my nose.

Justus raises his eyebrows. "You disagree?"

Never. Not with a male his size. I put the book down and pick up the next in the stack. "What about this one? What's this one about?"

His lips quirk. "Are you changing the subject again already, Annie?"

My heart rate kicks up another beat. He says that like he knows me. He doesn't. But the way he says my name like he's accustomed to it—I don't hate it.

I hold the book a little higher.

His lips curl higher. "It's about what packs should do instead of claiming to own land."

"Are all the books about the same thing?"

"Pretty much."

I return it to the stack.

"You're not interested?" He's still smiling. It's not a grin or anything, more like a soft curve, but he's clearly enjoying this—talking to me.

I shift position to rest on my other butt cheek. My fingers twitch. I wish I had my knitting.

"I like fiction," I say.

He kind of lights up. "Oh, I've got something you'll like," he says and makes to come over. Before I can tense up, though, he catches himself. "There's a book at the bottom I want to show you." He glances toward the crate. "All right?"

He waits until I nod and then prowls over slowly to sit beside me. His earthy scent follows him, filling my lungs, making me feel strangely greedy.

Quarry Pack females always complain when a male's wolf rolls in his kill and then trots into the lodge to let everyone know what he's found. I never understood why the males insisted on doing it since they could just shift and tell people what they caught. I get it now.

I want to roll in this scent. Wear it like a coat. Snuggle deep into it. I inhale quicker so I can get more into my lungs. It's not a particularly good smell—no one would make a cologne out of it—but it eases my chest and makes me feel languid and weightless, like I'm floating in space.

I'm hardly paying attention as Justus takes all the books out of the crate to get a hardback at the very bottom. I hadn't noticed it earlier. It's an old children's book. *Thumbelina.* The fabric cover is threadbare in places, and the gold embossed lettering is tarnished.

I remember the story vaguely from the early years at Moon Lake Academy. It's a human fairy tale.

Justus resettles himself on the pallet so that his thigh is pressed to mine. Now we're both perched on the edge, but I've folded myself up as tight as possible, and he's manspreading, knees bent and wide open, totally comfortable. And why wouldn't he be? It's his den—despite what he says—his bed, his pack, his territory. Whatever he wants to call himself, it's clear that he's the strongest here, the top of this particular food chain.

The pecking voice should be rattling off these facts, but she's grown eerily quiet.

"Look at this," he says, flipping to a full-page illustration.

A tiny woman, Thumbelina, is kneeling on an enormous lily pad. In the murky water underneath, huge wide-mouthed fish with bulging eyes swim among the reeds. She covers her face with her hands in despair. A monarch hovers in mid-air, gawking at her while she cries.

The colors are lovely in the lamplight—butter yellow, crimson, olive green—but I don't like the picture. Thumbelina is scared and alone, and the butterfly just gapes at her while the fish swarm underneath, horrified surprise on their fishy faces. Something terrible is coming, and she can't see it.

Justus smooths the page with a calloused thumb. "It reminds me of you. That's why I traded for it."

I feel like I've been socked in the stomach. "I have brown hair," I argue. The woman in the picture is a blonde, but I know why the sad, weeping lady stranded on a lily pad reminded him of me.

What was it that he said that day by the river?

"What a sad female you are. You stink like prey. You would make weak, spindly young." I don't realize I'm reciting the words out loud until he sucks in a breath and tenses, the warmth of his thigh disappearing from mine.

I brace for my own fear stink, but it doesn't come. His chest rumbles softly. I glance over. He's still holding the book open, but he's staring across the den, his jaw clenched.

"I was angry when I said that." He pauses. "I've wished a thousand times that I could take it back."

He means it. I can hear the regret in his voice, as well as read it clear as day on his face, but it doesn't make me feel any better at all. It actually stokes a strange, new anger in my chest.

"You don't have to say all that." I don't want a sincere apology that I have to graciously accept.

"I was young and stupid," he says. "It's not an excuse, but it's true, all the same."

I don't want excuses. We were both so young, after all, and I didn't react the way a female is supposed to with her mate, and he didn't *try* to hurt me, not 'til the end, and that was his bruised ego. I see that now that I've let myself remember the day, a little, in the broadest strokes.

"I am not proud of myself," he goes on. "You were scared, and I couldn't see past my own hurt pride. I am sorrier than you can know." He pins me with his soulful, earnest brown eyes. I drop mine, my fingers curling into fists.

I don't want him to be sorry, and I don't want to see things from his point of view. I want what I lost—a proper nest indoors with blankets and pillows and lavender sachets, excitement and anticipation and joy, a mate and a pup and a home of my own. I want what other people get, all the time, with no fuss at all.

I want a life where I haven't been afraid every minute of every day. I want to go back in time and leave Aunt Nola's bag on the table. I want my dam back, and Justus's "sorry" is a poke in the eye. It fixes nothing, changes nothing, and we both know it wasn't even his fault, not all of it, maybe not even most of it, but he can say sorry to me because he's so strong that he can afford to take the blame.

I hate him. I hate this. I hate myself.

"Annie?"

I clench my fists and glare a hole through an invisible spot on the rug. I wish I could say sorry, too. That I wish I'd done things differently, and I *do* wish that, but I also know I *couldn't* have. I'm a half-dozen coping mechanisms in a trench coat, and the only reason I function at all, day to day, is I do the same things with the same people and force everything that scares me deep under the surface like those ugly, terrified, teeming fish in the picture.

Justus exhales and flips ahead several pages. Then, slowly—so very slowly—he slides the book over so it's propped on my knees. He's flipped to a different picture. In this one, Thumbelina is riding a blackbird, gazing down with a serene smile at a miniature fairy prince lounging on a white morning glory throne. He's wearing baggy green harem pants, a vest with no shirt, and a gold crown with spikes like sun rays.

Justus taps the lady. "She reminds me of you because she's beautiful. Like you."

Warmth spreads through my belly. She doesn't look anything like me, but he's clearly not lying to flirt or flatter. Ivo and Jaime and their type will say things like that to try their luck with the unmated—and unhappily mated—protected females. Justus isn't like that. He's not slick in any way. He's what Old Noreen would call a 'rough instrument.'

He thinks I'm beautiful.

I let my gaze flicker to his face. He's watching me. My cheeks flame. He looks away for a split second, his face stern, but if I tune into the faint bond and listen closely, I can tell he's not mad—just bashful—and his eyes come right back. Like he can't help it, and he doesn't want to, either.

He lets his thigh touch mine again. His upper arm, too. I curl my fingers around the top edges of the book and grip it tight.

I'm not panicking. The voice is silent. My wolf is conked out. I'm tucked away in this cozy den, alone except for a male—my mate—and despite the earlier bump in the road, I'm okay. In fact, I'm so afraid of tipping the moment over that I don't dare move.

I watch Justus watch me.

"Our irises are the same color," I say.

"Yours have sunbursts."

They do. I have thin golden halos around my pupils, but no one's ever noticed them. I widen my eyes as big as I can and bat my lashes a few times, my cheeks reheating immediately.

What am I doing? I'm being goofy. I'm an idiot. My face catches fire. My bones are going to melt. I'm going to sink off this pallet and disappear under the rug forever, and I'll still be mortified.

Justus grins.

My gaze falls to his mouth. The bristles closest to his mouth are a slightly lighter brown than the rest of his beard. His canines dent his lower lip, but when his smile disappears, so do his fangs.

Is his beard as scratchy as it looks? Are his lips as soft?

Whistling softly, like he did when he was warning me that he was back with the stew, Justus reaches over and takes my hand, coaxing it from the book, and places it against his cheek. I let him.

The patrols at Quarry Pack whistle when they pass our cabin or Abertha's cottage, so I'm not startled. Is it a common thing, or did he pick it up from them when his wolf was stalking me?

He nuzzles my palm. His beard is coarse. I let the pad of my thumb rest on his bottom lip. It *is* soft.

He nips my thumb, gently, grinning for a brief second when I squeak. I snatch my hand away. But not too far. He chases my palm with his cheek until I cradle it again. Our faces are closer now. Inches away.

How did I end up sitting so close to him? I blame his scent; it's turned my brain muzzy.

It's a trap.

The voice is so far away, it's a whisper on the wind.

I raise my fingers to his long hair. It's thick and coarse, too, but it's not dirty and knotted like when I first saw him.

"This was all matted and tangled before," I say.

He hums in agreement. "I mudded it up."

"Mudded it?"

"To hide my scent."

"You did that on purpose?"

"You thought I kept it that way?" He smiles, but it doesn't reach his eyes. "Because I'm 'Last Pack' as your people say? And we're wild animals."

I drop my hand to my lap. That *is* what we're taught.

Justus's mouth curves down, his face shuttering. I clasp my hands in my lap.

"Worse than wild animals, I guess, since animals keep their coats clean." He braces his forearms on his thighs and stares across the den.

The air between us sours. I shift so our thighs aren't touching.

I stare at the picture of Thumbelina riding the bird. I can feel through the bond that his pride is bruised. That's when males are the most dangerous.

The voice is missing a trick. I had to remind myself this time.

Justus sighs. "I guess your pack only comes across us when we're, uh, hunting. I see where they might have gotten the impression."

Hunting or stealing females. I keep my eyes on the book.

Justus rumbles and tugs at my wrist—coaxing, not demanding—and I'm so thrown by the touch that I let him lift my hand.

"Don't stop because I'm proud and bad with words," he

says, pressing a bristly kiss to my inner wrist and then covering my hand with his and returning it to his cheek, cradling it there.

"People do say that about your pack," I admit.

"Is that why you didn't want me?" he asks tightly.

My hand trembles. Justus guides it lower to press against his bare chest. His heartbeat thumps against my palm.

"I was afraid." I splay my fingers, stretching them across his breastbone. His muscles tense. The line where his tattoos ends cuts straight down between my middle and ring fingers. He keeps his hand pressed on top of mine. Like we're staunching a wound.

"That I'd be rough with you? Or that I wouldn't be able to care for you?" His rumble grows jagged.

"That it would hurt," I whisper. "And other things."

"What things?"

I don't know how I'm doing this, speaking to a male I don't really know, far from home, surrounded by strangers, but my belly is full, I'm out of adrenaline, and the den is drowsily dim and warm like a dream or a fugue. Justus is so much stronger and fiercer than me, and I've let him so close, that he's not really a threat anymore. A brandished knife is a threat. Once it's been resting against your throat for a while, it's something else. A negotiation, maybe.

"Everything." I swallow a bitter laugh. "Mostly that you'd take me away." For the first time, I try to line all my anxieties up in a way that I can explain them to someone else, and I just can't. There are too many. So I try to explain a different way. "I've set my life up exactly the way it needs to be so that I can function. It has to be the way it is, or I'm a mess. It's just the way it is."

I wait for him to argue like Mari and Kennedy do whenever I say something like that. *Nothing is as bad as you make it in your head. You can't live scared. If you want to grow, you have to push yourself out of your comfort zone. Challenge yourself.*

Like every minute of every day isn't a challenge.

And yes, you can live scared.

Justus blows out a slow breath. "So what's the set up?" he finally asks.

I look at him, surprised. He's serious.

For a second, I feel too silly to tell him, but it's just us, and his earthy scent has somehow untied all my knots. "Well, I have my places and the things I do, and I know everyone, who's okay and who I need to stay away from. And I know where the exits are, and the hiding places, and what I can use for a weapon."

He's nodding. I decide to go on.

"And I have my tea and my knitting and my work with the bee hives and in the kitchen. I always know what's happening, you know?"

His brow creases. "I didn't think about any of that back then."

"Or now," I say softly.

He smiles ruefully. "Or now."

We sit a few moments in silence before he clears his throat and asks in a very careful, even voice, "What happened to you?"

Sightless eyes, staring at nothing. A twisted mouth frozen in a soundless scream.

"Something bad," I answer softly. "When I was a pup, I saw something, and eventually, most of the others who were there got better, and I just didn't." I shrug and hunch my shoulders. I'm squeezing the book so tightly, the edges bite into my palm.

"I didn't realize back then," he replies, his voice low, too, like we're telling secrets. "And I never really worried about how you felt. I figured you'd come around." He shakes his head. "My head was so far up my ass. I knew it all, right?"

I peek at him. His lips are curving again, like he's chagrined. I don't know any males like him. None of the males at Quarry Pack will freely admit that they're wrong. If they're backed into a corner, they sandwich their "my bad" in excuses and reminders of all the times they were right. Inevitably, they lose rank.

I've never heard a male say he's been mistaken like it wasn't costing him everything to say it, which is funny since females in the pack apologize all the time for things that aren't even their fault.

"We were young," I say, letting him off the hook because that's what you're supposed to do when a male humbles himself—preserve his dignity at all costs. A male with hurt pride is dangerous.

"I didn't think," he says. "I was so happy that I couldn't see what was right in front of me."

"Happy?"

He glances down at the rug, the hollows under his cheekbones darkening. "You were all I ever wanted."

I wish I could believe him—my loneliness *longs* to—but I was *never* naïve enough to take that kind of thing at face value. "You wanted a mate, you mean."

He's quiet for a moment, but then he draws a deep breath and gnaws his lower lip. "Stay here," he says.

Where would I go?

I'm expecting him to leave the den, but instead, he crosses to the big basket and begins to unpack it. It's a clown car. I have no idea how it holds so much. He takes out a stack of fluffy blankets and several quilts, two feather pillows squished flat in a plastic case, a leather knife roll, and an assortment of pants and shirts. No socks and no underwear.

My face heats, and I fuss with my blue sheet dress, arranging the hem so it covers my bare feet.

Finally, Justus reaches the bottom of the basket and takes out a round hatbox. I wouldn't recognize what it was except a vendor at the Chapel Bell farmers' market decorates them with decoupage and sells them for fifty dollars apiece.

Justus pushes the hatbox over to me with his knees and then sits on his heels so it's between us. His lips are curved in what I recognize as his usual, hesitant smile, but his shoulders are tense, and his eyes are carefully blank.

"Open it," he says.

I'm scared. A male has never given me a gift before, and I think that's what this is, even though the box is plain white cardboard. I look up at him.

His hands are firmly braced on his thighs like he's ready for something to go down. "Go on. It's for you," he says.

I take a deep breath and lift the lid.

It's yarn. Lots of yarn, hand-dyed, and by the look and smell, homespun, too. I raise a skein to my nose. Merino. I brush it against my cheek. It's so soft.

"Keep looking," Justus says, his voice low and gravelly, and nudges the box closer to me.

I pile the skeins on my lap. The colors are almost too bold for natural dyes, which must be what Last Pack uses. They aren't blue and red and green; they're indigo and crimson and emerald. "They're so beautiful. Who spun them?"

"The females," he says.

No shit. "Which females?"

He looks caught for a second, and then he says, "I'll find out. Keep looking."

I take out the rest of the yarn, and underneath, there's a rectangular leather case, about the size of a laptop. It looks handmade, too. The stitchwork is very neat and even, but not perfectly uniform like you'd get from a machine.

I unfold the case, already knowing what I'll find, and I'm right. There are slots filled with every size needle and crochet hook you could want, as well as a pouch with a thimble, scissors, and a random assortment of safety pins, straight pins, buttons, and a few threaders for good measure.

I take out a needle for a closer look. It's hand carved, either rosewood or maple, with little acorns carved into the tops. They're not perfect, either, but they'll work fine. "Who carved the needles?" I ask.

"I did." Justus's voice has gone downright gruff.

He's staring intently into the hatbox, and doesn't even look up when I ask, "What about the case?"

"Max made the leather. I did the cutting and sewing."

"Who's Max?" I don't remember meeting him earlier.

"He's Elspeth's mate. Gray wolf. Missing half his tail."

I vaguely remember a wolf like that watching the proceedings from under a tree, lying on his side and idly flicking his half of a tail.

"It's beautiful," I say. "Will you tell him thank you?" I feel like I've got a leak inside me—my heart is swelling, and my eyes are welling, but I'm too on guard to let myself cry in front of him.

My fingers flit from needle to needle. Their shapes aren't quite uniform, but they're all sanded perfectly smooth.

"There's more," he says.

I fold the case up carefully, and keeping it on my lap, I

reach back into the box. The next layer is all small tins and wooden boxes. *Tea.*

I take them out, one by one, stacking them like blocks. Each tin and box is absolutely charming. There's a red tin of Jasmine tea with a sailing ship on it. A tin of herbal tea with a koala wrapped in a blanket, pouring a cup in a eucalyptus tree. Several are decorated with flowers and birds— flamingos and hummingbirds and hibiscus and lilies.

I crack one of the boxes open. It's full of tea, wrapped in a wax paper pouch. I give it a sniff. Chamomile. My clenched stomach relaxes, and my cheeks flush.

A male has never given me a present before. There is no explicit rule against it, but Killian definitely wouldn't be okay with any of the males approaching an unprotected female that way. It's different for those with fathers or brothers. They have someone to tear a chunk out of a male's hide if he oversteps.

Even if it were allowed, males don't notice me like they do females like Haisley and Rowan, and I've never been anything but grateful for that.

I'm not sure what I feel right now.

"Where did you get all of these?"

He coughs, and with his eyes still averted, he says, "The others know I'll trade for them."

"How do *they* get them?" Don't Last Pack live totally isolated?

"Swap meets. Flea markets."

"*Human* swap meets and flea markets."

Justus shrugs. "Better humans than the lost packs."

"Lost packs?"

He shifts uncomfortably and glances up. "That's what we call you. Quarry Pack, Moon Lake, North Border, Salt Mountain. Like you call us 'last'. We call you lost."

"Why lost?"

"Why last?" he shoots back.

"Because your pack is the last one to still live in dens like the ancestors did."

His mouth quirks. "'Lost' because your people don't know how to be what we are anymore. You're losing the ability to shift. Your pups only shift if they're traumatized, and most of you've forgotten how to balance the forms. 'Lost' because you want to be human. You keep your wolves caged and only let them out on full moons like they're dogs that you walk. Because you don't know any more what pack means."

"What do you mean 'balance the forms'?" I ask.

He flashes a small smile, and before I can blink, his beard turns to fur, his face becomes a snout, his eyes rotate to slant at the diagonal, and his nose turns into a black nub. He grins, baring sharp white fangs and black gums.

I yip, startled. He cracks his jaws wide and lets his long pink tongue loll out of his mouth for a second before he morphs his face back into a man's.

"Did your wolf stick his tongue out at me?"

He grins. His teeth haven't turned back. "We did."

"We?"

His expression grows serious, and he switches to that teacher voice he used when he was talking about how shifter packs shouldn't have alphas. "Your people have such mistaken ideas about the wolf. You try to keep him in submission, same as you do your females and pups and elders. You act like he's a costume. Can you even hear him?"

I move the needle case to the pallet and draw my knees to my chest. I don't like how his criticism feels. It's not entirely unfair, I guess, but I just let him closer, and he thanked me by telling me that I'm bad at wolfing.

Part of me wants to shut my mouth, toss his yarn back in the hatbox, and pack myself up as small as I can, but the hard ball of spite forming in my gut won't let me.

"My wolf tells me to run and hide. That's it. That's what she says. Constantly. Why would I want to listen to that?"

Immediately, his expression changes as if he got lost in his own bullshit for a second and then suddenly remembered he's in a two-person conversation. Kennedy does the exact same thing when she goes off on Quarry Pack males. She'll be bitching about how they can never truly understand our perspective because they're so much stronger and then realize mid-sentence that her very legitimate complaints also apply to herself because of the killer he-wolf inside her.

He smiles ruefully. "My pack always say 'you have so many ideas.'" He lowers his head ever so slightly. "It's not a compliment."

The ball of spite dissolves, and my belly warms. I feel kind of low for making him feel bad about what he said—I was playing on his pity, and I despise pity—but I'm also surprised and delighted that it worked.

If a female pushes back on what a Quarry Pack male says, or tries to make him feel bad, he doubles down. Every time. Maybe later he'll bring a peace offering if she holds a grudge and he wants her sweet, but he'll never, ever show neck in the moment like Justus just did.

I don't know what to say, so I resettle myself so I'm sitting crisscross and draw the needle case back onto my lap so I can trace the stitches with my finger.

Justus's shoulders relax, and he nudges the hatbox toward me again. "There's one thing left," he says.

I guess we're dropping the subject for now. I look back in the box. There's a PlayStation controller at the very bottom.

Just one, sun-bleached and more than a little worse for wear. A knob is missing.

I take it out, glancing around the den in case I missed the TV and console—and electricity.

Justus tenses a little again. "I saw you with one of those at your cabin. I wasn't quite sure what it was for, but one of the pups found it out on a hunt, so I traded for it."

I turn it in my hands, that warmth in my belly heating up again. "What did you trade for it?"

Justus shrugs. "I can't remember. Maybe I let him come on patrol with me."

I replace it carefully in the box, and then I return the teas, examining each more closely. I'm getting tired, and I really have to focus to read the tins—oolong, black, chai, hibiscus, Darjeeling, Earl Grey. I'm a Tetley girl exclusively, but it's the thought that counts, and the pictures on the tins are so pretty.

"Thank you," I say as I arrange the yarns in the box by color. I'm too shy to look at him. My face is already permanently flushed.

When he answers me, his voice is almost a rumble. "I have an oak barrel. Someone's borrowed it, but I'll get it back, and I can trade for another. Whatever else you need, I can get."

Why do I need oak barrels?

All of a sudden, my nerves flare back to life. I don't need anything. I'm not going to be here very long. I'm going home. He said so. He swore on his dam's grave.

And that *is* what I want.

I can't stay here. I need my own bed and my locking doors and my friends. *My* things.

He's never going to let you leave. He lied.

"You said you'd take me back," I say in a rush, and it's like I douse the moment in ice water.

He jumps to his feet. I flinch and whimper. His face darkens, but he ignores the reaction and takes over with the box, shoving the lid on and returning it to the basket.

"I swore I would. I keep my promises," he mutters darkly as he stuffs the blankets, quilts, pants, and shirts on top of the box with complete disregard to whether the stacks are in the right direction. When he puts the lid on, it won't close.

I want to say sorry. I didn't want to make things weird—well, *weirder*—but I didn't have a choice either. When the panic hits, seeking reassurance is a compulsion. If I don't, I freak out, and then things get really, really weird. I wish I could explain, but he's an angry male, so I'm not about to open my mouth.

The air around me is tainted by a slight burst of my fear. Whatever gland or chemical in my body creates it—and I definitely wasn't paying attention that day in class—is still mostly exhausted. Justus's nose wrinkles, though, and he freezes, his arms braced on the basket lid as he tries to force it shut enough to loop the straps over the handles to keep it closed.

He sighs and straightens, opening the basket again and taking out two quilts. The straps go over the handles easily now.

He turns and comes to me, slowly but without hesitation, and kneels. I draw my knees back to my chest.

He sets one of the quilts next to me on the pallet. "If you want to go, I'll take you. Right now, if you want," he says and waits.

His face isn't angry anymore. He's wearing that supernaturally cool expression that he wore with his pack before he lost his temper. But he didn't really *lose* it, did he? He threw Alroy like a frisbee, and he yelled and threatened to skin them and trade their pelts to Quarry Pack, but that's not a real threat, is it?

I've heard real threats before. I've seen packmates beaten for real.

Sightless eyes, staring at nothing. A mouth twisted in a frozen scream.

Justus was *performing*.

He's performing right now, with me. Hiding his anger? Or something else?

I do something I don't ever remember doing on purpose before—I seek out the bond and listen very, very carefully. It's so weak. I have to close my eyes, focus with all my might, and weed through the bramble of fears, anxieties, regrets, and doubts that crowd my brain.

My eyes fly open.

He's scared.

He watches me with perfectly calm, unworried brown eyes, motionless, waiting for me to decide whether I want to leave, and he's terrified.

My heart cracks open.

Now, I'm scared, too. I grab the quilt and hug it to my chest. "I'm tired right now," I say quietly. "Maybe tomorrow."

He nods like his system isn't flooded with relief, but it is —I can feel it flow into my chest. Does he know that *I* know?

Oh, crap, is he feeling my feelings, too? Does he always?

I cover my absolute dismay with a yawn. Although it starts out fake, it soon becomes real. I am exhausted. I can't sort through all of this now.

His gaze softens. "I'll sleep out front. If you need something, call. I'll hear you."

Before I can argue about stealing his bed, he flashes a real, fond smile, and whistling softly through his front teeth, he leans forward and presses his forehead to mine. He stays there a moment, his nose bumping mine, our breath mingling. His beard tickles my chin.

His scent fills my lungs, and every muscle in my body relaxes as every inch of my skin comes alive.

My fingers itch, and suddenly, my ma's fudge comes to mind. She made it from scratch, and it was my pa's favorite. It took so long, she'd only make it for his birthday and winter solstice. You had to stir it continuously as you brought it to a boil, and then once it reached a certain temperature, you had to beat it with a heavy wooden spoon until it lost its gloss.

I was her helper, but I wasn't allowed to taste it until it cooled, and she cut it into squares. She'd always go sit on the porch to find a breeze, and I'd be left alone in the kitchen, watching the fudge like I was stalking my prey, its sweetness thick in the air. I remember the want, the *longing*, the fear of losing control, gobbling it up, and getting into deep, deep trouble. That's what I feel now.

I don't dare focus on the bond to see if he feels the same.

Would it be scary if he felt the same as me?

What if it felt good?

"Good night, Annie," he says, rising to his feet.

He leaves without looking back.

I lie down, pulling the quilt over me, and roll onto my side so I can see the den entrance. I see where he lays his quilt, and until I fall asleep, I keep my eyes on his shadowed form.

And I don't know if I'm watching to make sure he doesn't move from that place—or to make sure that he stays.

9

———

JUSTUS

I'm going to have to build a small fire pit outside the den. I'm walking as fast as I can back from the center of camp with a pot of boiling water, praying I get there before Annie wakes up and finds me gone, and I've managed to burn my hand twice.

She woke up a dozen times last night, and each time, she immediately looked for me, and I pretended I was asleep while she watched me until she drifted off again.

She's scared of me and also scared that I'll abandon her here alone. I don't need the bond to tell me. I can read it clear as day on her face.

She didn't insist I take her home last night, though, and she liked the gifts. Her fingers petted the yarn and the leather case like she was stroking a baby's cheek. She didn't care much for the plastic thing. Can't blame her. Still not sure exactly what it does, but it smells like human male in the worst possible way.

Things could be going a lot worse. Meeting the pack didn't go as smoothly as it could, what with Alroy being a dumbass, and Diantha not helping matters, but Annie's wolf was more or less steady, and she really took to Nessa's youngest.

Annie's wolf leaped into action when she thought the pup was in danger, crouched over her and bared those toothpick fangs and everything. And then she yapped at me to handle my dumbass packmates. My chest warms at the memory. My mate's wolf is a brave, bossy little cuss. She would be happy here.

And my shortsighted ass panicked when she got upset and promised I'd take her home when she asks. I *swore*.

The warmth inside me ebbs as dread trickles through my veins, and I force myself to focus on right now. I don't know what frame of mind Annie will be in, or how sharp she is in the morning, so I make sure to whistle and tread heavily as I approach the den.

She's just sitting up and scrubbing her eyes when I duck inside. The quilt is tucked firmly under her arms, covering her from her breasts to her toes. I keep my distance. Her fear scent reserves are probably full again after a good night's sleep—or whatever you'd call it with us waking and checking on each other every hour.

When I met her, I thought we had nothing in common, but now, I don't know—take away her anxiety, and we have a similar temperament. She's reserved like me, and more of a watcher than a talker. She's watching me now as I unpack my hamper yet again to get out the box with her tea. This time, I'll leave the box out and return things properly so I don't have to squash the top back on like an idiot.

I borrowed two strainers and cups from Elspeth. She said a lot of the folks in the lost packs put sugar and milk in their tea, but we're low on both at the moment, so Annie will have to do without until I get the chance to send Alroy out to get some. And it *will* be him who makes the run after what he said to Diantha yesterday. You can't talk to a female like that, even if you are more or less right.

My gaze slides over to where Annie huddles on the pallet, eyeing me with no less suspicion than she did yesterday.

Is she going to make me take her back today?

I bat the thought away. She won't. Not yet.

But what if she does?

My stomach aches. I ignore it, dig into the box, take out two tins, and hold them up. One has a swan on it, the other has a friendly, smiling teapot pouring itself into a smaller, smiling teacup.

"Which one do you want?" I ask, my voice still gruff from sleep. I didn't speak to anyone on my mission to boil water. Everyone awake this early is wrong in the head. I don't want to have a conversation at this hour with someone excited to start their day. They're going to ask me to help them with something.

Annie squints at the tins. I slowly step forward so she can see them better, but she still shrinks back as I get closer.

At least her scent is holding steady. It's delicious, even stronger than yesterday, rainy and muddy and musky in the best possible way. When I take a deep breath, I can make out traces of pussy in the air. I cough immediately to hide the groan that escapes before I can stifle it.

"The Earl Grey, please," she says. Her voice is husky with sleep, too. Shivers race across my skin. I want her to say my name like she says Earl Grey. I want her to say *please*.

Please, Justus.

It's never going to happen, not if she's in her right mind. The tightness in my gut spreads to my chest.

I busy myself fiddling with the little stainless-steel mesh balls, trying to shake tea into them without spilling leaves all over the rug. My hands feel like wool mitts. Her eyes on me makes all my blood rush to my cock, turning my fingers numb and clumsy.

"Can I help?" she asks softly, and my immediate impulse is to tell her I've got it, but thankfully, my brain cell sparks to life before I can open my mouth. If she helps, she'll come closer.

"Please," I say, sitting back, leaving the tea things for her.

Keeping me in her sights, she crawls forward. Her movements are awkward with the quilt wrapped around her, and when the fabric winds around her ankles, causing her to lose her balance, she gets frustrated enough to peel it off. She accidentally undoes the blue wrap underneath with the quilt, and for the split second before she gets it sorted out, I get an eyeful of bare breast, side, hip and thigh.

She curves like a fiddle. Like she has a handle at her waist. I want to cup her there, hold her until she warms to me, until she understands that I don't want to hurt her.

I drop my gaze to the pot of water. "Careful. It's really hot," I say to cover the fact that I saw, and she knows it, and now her face is blazing pink.

She resettles herself, making sure she's tucked tightly, and begins to gently shake tea into the strainers with her upper arms plastered to her sides to make doubly sure her wrap stays in place.

When our females approach the time that they become interested in males but don't want attention from them quite yet, they'll just wear their fur under their wraps for a few years. I guess Annie can't do that. It's all or nothing for her kind. I can't even imagine.

What do they do if they're in their skin but there's a sound in the distance, and they want to know what it is?

How do they crack bones to get to the marrow? What if they want to crack a walnut? Do they go ahead and lose a tooth?

Thankfully, by the time Annie passes me a cup, I've distracted myself from my hard-on so I can sit normally.

"I'll have milk and sugar for you tomorrow," I say and instantly regret it.

Her face blanches, and I clock the exact instant that the word *tomorrow* makes her remember that I stole her, and she doesn't want to be here.

She's going to ask me to take her home.

I can't.

Not now. Not yet.

I hop to my feet, leaving my cup of tea on the floor.

"We have to go," I bark. "I have something I need to do. Pack business. It won't take long, but I have to go now. I'm late." I'm making this up on the fly, keeping my mouth moving so she can't get a word in edgewise. I start fussing around the den, putting the tins away and folding the quilt, being really loud about it.

I catch a whiff of fear. Annie struggles to her feet, gulping down her tea. I feel bad—it hasn't had much of a chance to cool—but my chest is tightening, too, and my wolf is getting agitated. He doesn't want to leave her either, and he's pushing for our body. He thinks he's better equipped to keep her here. I push him back.

"I'll take you to the females' tent. You'll be comfortable there. They'll feed you, and I'll be back soon," I say as I rush her out of the den and down the trail to camp. I yap the whole time, basically repeating myself. Her fear scent is kicking up, and she's still holding her empty teacup. I didn't give her a chance to put it down.

"I won't be gone for long at all, and I'll send a pup to get your yarn and needles. I'll have them bring tea, too, and heat you up some water, whatever you want. It won't take long at all." I swear I've never babbled so much before in my life.

Thank goodness Elspeth is at the tent when we finally get there. It's still early, so I wasn't sure.

Elspeth was from North Border, so she'll understand how strange all this must be for Annie—and she'll make sure Diantha doesn't get too out of hand.

"Ho!" I call out as I approach the camp-within-a-camp that the females have set up so they can watch the pups as they play on the obstacle course we rigged up in the big sycamore. The females have their own small fire pit, a canopy for shade, and a thick canvas tent where the babes can nap undisturbed. Well, *less* disturbed. Pups at play are loud.

"Justus!" Elspeth calls back fondly. "And Annie." She smiles at my mate and gratitude fills my heart.

I didn't say anything about Annie when I came back mated without her, and I've said nothing since. In the absence of facts, packs make up their own. I've overheard the whispers—there was something terribly wrong with her, she was too weak, too foul-tempered, too messed up in the head like the rest of the lost packs—and I was so proud, and my pride was so bruised, that I never spoke up. It shames me now.

The itchy, restless feeling I had when I woke rides me harder. I need to get out of here. Just for a little while. I need to figure out what to do without Annie's scent in my nose, slowing down my brain and making my wolf rowdy.

"Do you want a cup, Alpha?" Elspeth asks.

I shake myself. "No, thank you." I don't correct her. My dam taught me better than to pick nits with elders.

While I was lost in my head, Elspeth urged Annie to a

rocker by the fire and filled her empty cup from the kettle kept hanging on the tripod. The brew smells like tea, but it's milky tan.

Annie sips and smiles. "Oh, this is lovely. You boil the leaves with the milk and sugar?"

Elspeth nods, dropping to sit in the chair next to my mate with her own cup. "We poured the water over the leaves in North Border, too, but here, they heat the leaves in the water and add the milk and sugar while it's still boiling. And they use evaporated milk."

Annie glances at the cup in her hand. "So that's what this is? An evaporated milk can?"

Elspeth laughs. "More than likely. We tend to make do around here."

"I was told we were out of milk and sugar," I can't help but grumble.

"*You* are out of it," Elspeth says. "*We* don't let ourselves get so low that we run out."

I could point out that the females only have milk and sugar—or any staples—because *we* hunt, gather, or trade for it, but I remember too well the day when I was a pup that I declared to my dam that *I* had provided the meat in her belly.

It had been my first kill, and I was so proud. The moment the words came out of my mouth, my sire snorted, shifted, and let his wolf snarf down the whole, juicy prime cut of steak on my plate. Once his wolf had licked his chops clean, he shifted back and said, "You might have given her a meal, but she gave you *life*, and if you think a piece of grizzled cow is worth anywhere near the same, you don't value yourself nearly enough." And then he ate my potatoes, too.

"Where's Max?" I ask to change the subject.

"Over yonder." She lifts her chin toward the bonfire.

Most of our elders gather there in the mornings to warm their bones.

"Well, I need a word with him." I shift awkwardly.

I don't want to leave camp, but if I stay, she'll ask to go home, and I gave my word. I've broken a solemn promise before, once, and I'd die before I did it again.

But how can I leave her, even for a moment?

Annie blinks at me, her brown eyes almost amber in the morning sun. They're beautiful. And unsure. She's looking to me for reassurance.

My chest tightens. I've never been so weak. She holds me in her hands. She could destroy me with a few words.

"You'll be fine here with Elspeth. I'll be back later," I blurt and stride off like my heels are on fire.

I'm a coward. I'm afraid of a hundred-and-thirty-pound female with a wolf so small she could probably fit in a groundhog hole. I hope she doesn't ever get that idea in her head. The animals flee when we arrive, but their tunnels are everywhere. If her wolf fled down there, I'd have to dig her out. It'd be a mess.

I should turn around. My wolf whines his agreement.

No. Annie isn't going to freak out and hide in the groundhog tunnels, and if she does, she'll be there when I get back.

I make a detour on my way to the bonfire and take great delight in sticking my head into Alroy's tent and barking, "Bonfire. Five minutes. Bring Khalil."

Alroy was dead to the world. He wakes up in a panic, fighting his blankets. I'm still smirking when I get to the elders sitting in their usual place on the downed log I planed and sanded into a bench for them a few years ago.

"Brothers," I say, taking a seat beside Max.

They mumble "Alpha" under their breath, and I ignore it. "What tracks have folks seen since I've been gone?"

They perk right up at the prospect of fresh meat.

"Possible bobcat down by the gulch where Colm snared that grouse," Max says.

Bobcat is not great eating, and in my opinion, their fur is a little too close to wolf to wear without feeling a little strange about it.

"My oldest said he saw pheasant in the mustard field," Tarquin offers. That's not far, only a half hour trek or so. I could be back before afternoon nap. If I fed Annie enough, she might doze off beside me, and I could watch her sleep in the daylight.

Or she could ask me to take her home.

"What about elk?" I ask. "Anyone seen elk?"

All the males shake their heads, and Rodric, our oldest packmate, rouses himself from a doze and shouts, "What did Alpha say?"

"He wants to know if anyone has seen elk," Max shouts back.

"No need to holler," Rodric grumbles, poking his finger in his ear to emphasize the point. It's a joke that he's been telling since I was a pup. He's fully aware that he's deaf as a doorknob. "I heard there's elk up by the lake."

"Oh, you heard, eh?" Max snorts.

"Which lake?" I ask.

"A big bull," Rodric confidently answers the question I didn't ask. "Fourteen points between both antlers."

"The lake by the boundary to Salt Mountain," Tarquin clarifies.

"The one with the bog worm?" I don't need to mess with a bog worm when I've got Annie here. Their blood is like sap. If it gets in your hair, you might as well shave it all off, and I don't know what I'd look like bald, but I doubt it's an improvement.

"No, the one west of that." Tarquin squints at me. "Why you asking? The smoker is stocked."

I stand and stretch, cracking my back. "I promised my mate fresh meat."

It's the truth, but every male on the log, including Rodric, looks at me like I'm full of shit. No male would leave their new mate when there's plenty of good food in camp. Thankfully, Alroy and Khalil arrive. Neither looks good. Alroy is clearly not fully awake yet, and Khalil looks like he didn't sleep. His dark eyes are red-rimmed, and he reeks of rotgut.

"I thought you were supposed to be the fresh meat, what with the new mate and all?" Khalil slurs as he takes the coffee Tarquin offers and swallows it in a single gulp. Alroy eyes Max's drink hopefully. Max tightens his gnarled hands around his cup.

"Ready?" I ask, ignoring the remark.

"No," Alroy groans. Khalil shrugs and stumbles, even though he was doing nothing but standing there.

"Ready." Max sets his cup down on the log and stands. He twists to crack his own back, winces, thinks better of it, and rolls out his shoulders instead.

"Griff," he calls to his son who's poking the fire with a stick a few feet away. "Go tell your dam that I'm going hunting."

Before the pup can dash off, I quickly add, "And run by my mate's den and take the box of yarn you find there to her at the females' tent."

Griff straightens and tries to hide the wide grin breaking across his face. I sigh inside. I try not to make requests because whenever I do, the younger males always take it as a sign of favor no matter how many times I tell them boot licking makes your breath stink.

"Yes, Alpha. I'll take it to her straight away," he says.

"And don't forget to tell your dam I've gone hunting!" Max hollers after his son.

Tarquin snorts. "That boy's already forgotten."

Rodric shakes his head. "That poor female will be looking for you all over camp by lunch."

"Well, then *you'll* tell her where I've gone," Max says, tying back his graying locs with a strip of leather.

"Don't count on me—I'll have forgotten by then, too." Rodric cackles, grabs Max's abandoned coffee, and sips.

"You'll keep an eye on things?" I ask Tarquin. He nods.

Tarquin has the best sense after Max, and he's better than all of us at soothing tempers. He'll listen to each side and ask so many questions, that by the time each person has had their chance to speak, everyone's either too tired, hungry, or bored to stay mad.

"Well, let's go get us an elk," I say, slapping Khalil on the back, snorting when his wolf whimpers. Must be one hell of a hangover if his wolf is feeling it.

I lead the way to the den that serves as our armory and help myself to the best bow and arrow, strapping a quiver across my back. I feel a twinge of guilt as Max grabs the second best, but I know he'd leave the best one behind rather than take it when I'm around. My sire taught me to respect my elders. He couldn't have imagined a world where they'd defer to me.

I didn't have my sire long, but I'm one to listen the first time I'm told, so his voice is still clear in my head. That's why I slow my pace as our hunting band leaves the camp, so we can walk side-by-side, and Max doesn't have to struggle to keep up.

I vividly remember traveling from our summer to winter camps one year, and how the alpha at that time took the lead of our long line. My sire hung back to bring up the rear, and I was impatient. I didn't want to be last.

Of course, I whined about it, and my sire said, "Would you rather be in the front with your nose up Alpha's ass or back here where we can actually *see* it if a feral snatches a straggling female?" It made sense to me then, and it makes sense to me now, although I think moving as a herd is safer than a line. Much quicker to form a defensive phalanx when you're already bunched together.

The way to the lake grows more difficult as the hours pass. At first, we travel through familiar woods, but soon enough the terrain gets steeper and rockier as we approach Salt Mountain territory, and I have to attend more closely to my surroundings.

I'm not worried about running into Salt Mountain wolves, but I am worried about the ferals and humans and other predators who've taken advantage of the land that Salt Mountain's left unprotected.

In reality, Salt Mountain doesn't have a territory beyond their town. The pack only ventures out to the woods to hunt. No patrols, fences, or anything. Our younger males have a game to see who can piss the closest to their front gate, and it's been doused a few times, and no one's been caught.

For a long time, all the shifter scents we come across are stale, and we don't see anything bigger than a possum. The sun is bright, but there's a breeze, and Alroy keeps his mouth shut. It should be a pleasant hike, but with every mile that passes, my nerves jangle more and more. I'm twitching at everything—twigs cracking, toads honking, birds casting shadows.

My wolf is torn. He loves hunting, but he hates that we're

getting farther and farther from Annie. I don't like it much either.

He's comforting himself with the absolutely unfounded belief that he could run back to her in five—ten—minutes flat.

I calm myself with facts.

She's fine. No one in the pack would let any harm come to her, and the land around the camp was clear of strange scents or disturbance. I hunt or scout all the time. This is no different. If she was my mate for real, I'd hunt. Probably more often than I do now if we had pups. Pups can *eat*.

But she's not my mate for real.

Don't I want her to be? Isn't that why I kept traveling to Quarry Pack and hanging out in the woods outside their border, sulking and stewing and pissing off the local wildlife?

What am I doing out here?

I should be home, tending to her. Making her more gifts. Listening to her talk, if she has something to say. Feeding her. Coming up with more excuses to sit next to her on my pallet.

It's not that I don't *want* to be doing that—I want it so badly that if I think about it, my chest will get so tight I'll start huffing and puffing worse than Max.

Shit. Max. I glance behind me. He's a good yard behind me. I force myself to slow down.

"Do we even want to get there before the sun goes down?" Alroy bitches when he realizes the pace has changed, and he has to wait for us to catch up.

"Sorry," I say. "Is there a specific time you have to be back to jack off alone in your tent?"

"Where'd you sleep last night?" Alroy asks. "Bet it wasn't in your den, was it?"

I leap for him, shifting my top half so he thinks I'm letting my whole wolf out, and just like I knew he would, he shifts all the way, and his wolf scurries away like his tail is on fire. I take my skin right back and grab the pants his wolf left behind.

"It's just too easy." Khalil snickers.

"Embarrassing." I shake my head. That's a prank we played as pups. He always fell for it then, too.

Alroy shifts and strides back, dick swinging, no shame. "If you wanted to watch my fine bare ass, you could've asked," he says, strutting ahead.

Khalil speeds up so he's ahead of us all. Max lets out a long-suffering sigh.

What am I doing?

Am I such a coward that I'll go this far to avoid a conversation?

Yes. I suppose I am. I never again want to see the trapped, terrified expression that she wore when she realized she was in heat.

I should have stolen her. It couldn't have been worse than what happened by the river. At least, she would have had her heat in a real nest in a den.

When do I get to stop feeling like shit about what should have been the best thing that ever happened to me?

I slow my steps so Alroy and Khalil pull farther ahead. When there's a decent distance between us and Alroy turns his attention to muttering to himself about the unfairness of life, I ask Max, "Do you remember when you mated Elspeth?"

He snorts. "My legs are slow, not my brain."

"She didn't want to come with you, right?"

He slides a glance over to me, his warm, brown eyes glittering. "What are you asking, Alpha? You know she didn't."

"I'm not the alpha," I reply without thinking as I try to figure out what it is exactly that I want to know. Has she really forgiven him? How long did it take?

Max blows out his cheeks and stops to catch his breath. Alroy and Khalil keep going.

"You know, I'm an old wolf, and in all my life, I have never met a male who thinks the way you do," he says. "You're the strongest male in the pack. It's not even close. Who would be next after you? Khalil?"

I nod. Khalil can fight. Alroy has the potential to be at least as good, but he's so fixated on his gripes and grudges that he doesn't have the confidence to dominate in a real fight.

"And Khalil isn't even a challenge, is he?"

"He might be, if he were disciplined."

"But he's not. Not like you. That's my point." Max skewers me with his sharp gaze. "You lead this pack, and you say you aren't the alpha. You have a mate, and you're acting like you don't. The sky is blue no matter what you call it, pup." He sighs loud and long. "What are we doing out here, Justus?"

I hold his gaze. I might be afraid of my mate, but I won't bend my neck to any male on earth, no matter how good a point they make. "Hunting elk," I say.

"Hiding from a female." He snorts. "And why? Do you even know?"

"I don't want to let her go," I say almost under my breath. Not because I'm ashamed, not in front of Max. He's the one who dragged my wolf out of the crevice I burrowed into at the back of my dam's den after my parents died. I was halfway feral by then, living in my own shit, eating bugs and slowly starving to death.

He'd held me by the scruff of the neck and scrubbed me

clean in the river while I fought and bit, and then he fed me and threw me in a pile with the other pups who'd lost everyone. He kept watch over us every night until Elspeth finally let him sleep in her den, and even then, he'd come to comfort us if a pup cried out from a nightmare. If *I* cried out.

I'm not ashamed to tell Max that I don't want to let Annie go, but I want it so bad that it feels dangerous to say out loud. The things you want the most—the things you can't live without—that's what Fate takes.

"So don't let her go," Max says. He drinks from his canteen and offers it to me. I take a sip and pass it back.

"It's not that easy."

"It could be. You should have heard Elspeth holler." He grins, remembering. "Knowing the female she is today, you'd never guess the pair of lungs she had on her. They must have heard her in Moon Lake."

In sync, we cap the canteen and continue hiking. Up ahead, Alroy has caught up to Khalil, and they're taking a water break, too.

"I don't want a mate who despises me," I say, aware that Max could take offense if he chose, and also that I'm lying. The years have worn my pride away. I could live with Annie's hate if it meant when I woke up in the night, she'd be there where I could see her.

Max says, "Pfft. She'll get over it eventually. Just tell her how things are going to be. Be firm and consistent. She'll come around. It's the natural order."

I snort. "You told Elspeth how things were going to be?" There is no way. That female rules him.

Once, she left her favorite comb at our summer camp one year, and she didn't realize it until we'd reached high valley. His wolf ran all the way back for it himself in a snowstorm, and then when she idly remarked that his fangs had scratched the wood when he carried it in his mouth, he carved her a new one, but not until he traveled all the way to red clay camp for more of the teak that he'd made the first comb from.

"Not in so many words," Max mutters. "But she knew."

I hide my smile as we reach Alroy and Khalil. We're getting close enough to the lake that if there's elk, we should start seeing signs of them. So far, I scent nothing on the wind but possum, raccoon, and the like.

"I'm not as brave as you," I say to Max.

"What are we talking about?" Alroy asks, falling into step beside us.

"How my balls are bigger than the alpha's here," Max answers.

I growl.

He raises his hands. "Sorry, my balls are bigger than *Justus's*."

Khalil and Alroy both hum in ready agreement. I roll my eyes.

"I was asking Justus here why he won't grab his balls—smaller than mine though they may be—and claim that mate of his. Tell her she's First Pack now, and that's that."

"That is not how females work." I'd love to hear him repeat that in front of Elspeth. He'd be out of the den, bunking with the pups again, as soon as the words came out of his mouth.

"Oh, so you know how females work now?" Max raises his bushy gray eyebrows, and Alroy snickers.

"He read about 'em in that book that said only wolves in zoos have alphas." Khalil smirks at me. He's spoiling for a fight. He must have sobered up.

"It's a matter of respect," I say, flagrantly ignoring our

long and storied tradition of stealing our mates from under their birth packs' noses.

"It's fear," Khalil shoots right back, holding my gaze with his laughing, red-rimmed eyes, daring me to deny it. "Brother Justus won't claim his twitchy little mate because he's figured out that if he has nothing, he has nothing to lose." He flashes me a wry smile that tells me he figured out the same thing himself.

I smack him upside the back of his head for calling Annie *twitchy*. He grins and ducks away. He knows he overstepped, and we all know he's right.

We're pack. We let each other spout our preferred brand of bullshit, but at the end of the day, we've run together our whole lives. We've shared hundreds of kills, breathed each other's farts, huddled together in the dead of winter to keep from freezing. We've stood together in six-foot holes, shoveling dirt so we could bury our dead.

We know each other to the bone.

It would kill me to really have her and lose her. I couldn't walk away from that. And then what happens to the pack? Who will remind them, over and over again, that freedom for safety is a bad trade?

I listen to the elders' stories. I know that history repeats, and we could so easily go the way of Quarry Pack.

When the lost wolves moved out of the dens to build their towns and cities—seduced by light at night, cold air in the summer, and fresh meat from a box at any time—some banished their wolves more thoroughly than others. Moon Lake built high rises so they didn't even have to smell the earth anymore. North Border built walls to cage their own people.

For a long time, Quarry Pack kept to many of the old ways. Some even lived in dens, and we still ran with them then during full moons. And then, when my parents were young, Declan Kelly came from nowhere, killed their alpha, and took over, in part by convincing them that we were the enemy.

Obviously, there were no more runs after that, but until the wasting sickness decimated our numbers, our males would still risk occasional incursions onto their territory. Twice they found runts left to die in the forest, and once, they rescued a female beaten and left for dead in a gulch. One of the runts died, but the other lived, and the female happened to mate the male who carried her back to camp and birthed Alroy before she was taken by the sickness.

I love my pack, but I know them. They're as susceptible as anyone to the lure of a strong male who promises to keep the bad wolves away. They want to believe that someone has the power to keep them safe, and if they were weak and scared again, like they were after the sickness, they'd follow any old asshole with a loud mouth and confidence.

No matter what they call me, I'm not the alpha, but I am the male sitting in the alpha's seat so no one else can take it. As long as I'm here, Alroy's dickishness is a nuisance. Khalil's fatalism hurts only himself. If I'm gone, what happens when Alroy realizes no one can tell him to shut up? What happens when Khalil's death wish tells him the pack can outrun a blizzard on the way to winter camp?

I almost didn't survive walking away from Annie the first time. I'm a flawed, flawed male, but I know myself. I wouldn't willingly live through that again.

But do I have a choice?

Already, thoughts of her run on a constant loop in the back of my brain—is she okay? Elspeth will keep an eye on her, and none of the males will dare go near her. The worst that can happen to her is boredom, but she doesn't know that. Is she scared?

Of course, she is. *What* is she afraid of? Or maybe she feels better without me around.

Is she relieved that I'm gone?

Is she thinking about me?

I march on, stiff as a soldier, and my mind spins. I don't know what to do. Fate is making all the calls, like she always does, and I need to make it right, and what do I *do*? Who do I fight? Who do I bark into submission?

Max must smell my angst because he snorts and says, "Oh, don't worry about it too much, pup. Soon enough, you'll be fetching her a snack at three o'clock in the morning because you were an asshole in her dream, and she can't stand smelling you for another second, and she's hungry."

Alroy and Khalil's faces twist in mocking disbelief.

Max laughs. "You *wish* you had what I have."

They can't say anything because we all know that yes, yes they do.

Finally, a strong wind gusts down from Salt Mountain, and I catch a faint whiff of bull. We instantly fall silent, our noses quivering.

Alroy jerks his head to the north, and I nod. We head off in that direction, careful to stay downwind. Alroy shifts and runs ahead to scout.

Khalil slides me a glance. "Winner gets the backstrap?"

I grin. "Loser gets the shank?"

He nods.

We bolt, Max's long-suffering sigh in our ears. We race between the towering pines, our steps silent, our breath ragged. The sun is so high that the sky above us is a blue wash, not a cloud in sight. The tension and dread seep from my body as the clean mountain air fills my lungs.

My wolf wants out, but he knows this moment is mine. I need it—to remind myself that I am sure of my step and my direction.

The elk's scent grows stronger. Khalil harnesses a second wind and pulls ahead, raising his bow. He's got the bull in his sights. I'm not going to outrun him.

A ridge rises to my left. I cut over, scramble up the steep incline on all fours, and then sprint along the crest, loose stones and dirt rolling under my feet, skittering down the sides. I see the elk in a stand of trees. He lifts his head, alerting at the ruckus I'm making.

His eyes darken, recognizing my wolf.

My wolf howls.

The elk's haunches flex.

Max's voice floats to me on the wind. "Idiot. He's gonna scare him off."

No, I'm not. I'm quicker than that. I raise my bow, notch my arrow, aim, and let it fly.

The elk's pupils blow wide. My arrow hits home, seconds before Khalil's splits mine in half and Alroy's wolf leaps from the brush, slitting the bull's throat with his claws. The animal falls to his knees and then collapses, eyes open, staring sightlessly at the perfect sky.

I jog down the ridge, joining Khalil. We go to crouch by our kill, resting our hands on his warm, motionless flank. Alroy's wolf comes to sit silently beside us.

Needles rustle in the limbs above us. We breathe in pine and sap, earth and air, our lungs fueling the muscles that his flesh will feed.

"Go in peace," I say.

"May I have so good a death," Khalil murmurs the words

we were taught to say when we were pups by males whose faces we can hardly remember.

We're silent on the walk back, except for Alroy's muted muttering whenever it's his turn to help haul the carcass.

I haven't figured anything out.

I am still walking back to a mate who doesn't want me. I'm still going to have to let her go again, and somehow, keep living.

Unless I can find the words to convince her to give me a chance.

To stay.

To leave my heart where it is—beating in my chest. For her.

10

ANNIE

Male! Approaching from your left!

I'm sure there is a male approaching. There are folks everywhere. I'm sitting among a dozen females, some gathered around the fire, others working under the canopy or resting in the tent. Pups swarm the ladders and ropes hanging from the branches of the sycamore tree in front of us.

Males meander the invisible paths around the camp, going about their business, none of which seems to be urgent. Wolves of all ages lounge and wrestle and groom themselves, and then set off at random on urgent missions that end with them lounging, wrestling, and grooming themselves in a different location.

Male! From your left!

The pecking voice is back, and she's been promoted to Captain Obvious.

LOOK! MALE!

I grind my teeth and glance up from my knitting to shut her up. Griff, the pup who brought the hatbox to me, strolls

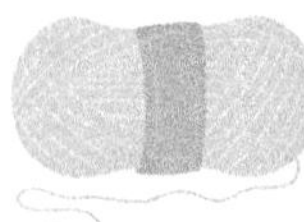

up to the fire. I wouldn't call him a male, but the voice has always gone by size, not age.

"All right, Ma?" he asks Elspeth, poking at the charcoal with a stick although it doesn't need stoking. "You need anything?"

"I don't. What about you, Annie?" Elspeth asks me.

"I'm good." I muster up a smile for Griff. This is the fourth or fifth time he's dropped by to see if we need anything. Justus must've asked him to, although it's possible that it's Griff's habit to check on his dam. The males do seem drawn to the females' camp like moths to a flame.

Already, a male has come by because he found a particularly smooth rock and wondered if any of the females had lost it, and if not, if any wanted it. Diantha took it. It was threaded with a neat green color, almost like jade. It was lovely. Another male came by to offer us fresh bread he'd made. It was delicious—nutty and warm.

Griff is still messing with the fire, waiting in case we change our mind, I guess, when a pair of males come by rolling a huge, wooden spool they'd found in the woods. I can't imagine how they got it up the narrow, rocky trail to the clearing.

I've seen something like it before. There's a bigger one at Quarry Pack in the field behind the nursery. We were told it was human-made, a device to hold the wire they use to run electric lines. Pups pretend it's a giant's dining room table or a stage.

As soon as they see it, the Last Pack pups shift to two legs and join forces to roll the spool as fast as they can with no regard for life or limb. They narrowly miss the canopy stakes. The broad side of the tent. The huge trunk of the sycamore. A babe in basket.

The babe is the end of the game. Before my brain even computes the danger, Diantha leaps from her loom, shifts to her wolf, and leaps onto the spool to shove it off course with her paws. Her wolf then chases the culprits into their tree playground, baying as ferociously as any male wolf I've ever heard. The pups scramble to the highest branches they can reach.

It isn't until she sashays back to the fire on two legs, her tail swishing, that I realize I'm standing, my knitting dumped on the ground, a needle clutched in my fist like a knife.

Elspeth gently takes my wrist and lowers my arm. "Listen to your wolf," she murmurs. "Diantha is not a threat to them."

I never *listen* to my wolf. I don't have to—she's not shy about letting her thoughts be known. Run and hide. Twenty-four seven, in any given situation. Run and hide.

Elspeth is still holding my wrist, though, and she's gazing into my eyes like she's waiting for me to do what she asked.

My face flushes. I can't tug my wrist free—that would be rude—so I do what she says and listen to my wolf.

She's on her feet, but she's not alarmed. She's excited. There was an enormous wooden spool rolling around, wreaking havoc. She wishes she could've rolled it around. She would've pushed it up the switchback trail to the dens and watched it roll back down.

My wolf has zero concerns about Diantha. In fact, she thinks Diantha's wolf went easy on the pups. She didn't even nip a behind, and the pups were being much too wild around babes and elders.

My wolf wouldn't have been so wild. She would've howled to clear a path before she sent the spool sailing.

I blink, meeting Elspeth's kind gaze. I don't understand. I was afraid for the pups. Why wasn't my wolf?

Elspeth pats my wrist as she lets it go and resettles herself in her chair. She picks up her own needles, smiles gently, and says, "I was the same at first. Always prepared for the worst. It helped to listen to my wolf. She was quicker than I was to realize that things are different here."

Different how?

I have so many questions, but I've never been good with strangers, and I'm too shy to ask in front of everyone. Now that the spool is settled in place under the sycamore, the females return to their conversation. It's been going pretty much nonstop all day. Back at Quarry Pack, we chat while we work in the kitchen or the garden, but nothing like this.

For one thing, not everyone is making themselves busy. Several females are lounging in chairs or blankets, doing nothing more than soaking up the sun. I don't think I've ever seen females idle in the middle of the day, especially if they have pups.

It's almost lunch, and the sun is high in the sky. Despite the shade, I'm sweating like a pig from nerves. Although the chatter and clack of the needles and the loom are calming, this is still a strange place, these are strangers, and my mate has left me here alone.

I'm not too mad about it. Or hurt. I just can't settle. The breeze is sweet, and the yipping and shouting of the pups as they swarm the sycamore are soothing in their own way, but as the hours wear on, it's getting to be too much. I'm home-sick. I want to lie on my bed with my fan blowing straight on me from my night table and take a few months to work through everything that's happened in the past two days.

The Last Pack females keep trying to be polite and

include me, but my calm is wearing thin, and every time they preface a comment with, "Annie," I jolt and drop a stitch. Being with them is nothing like being with Una, Kennedy, and Mari. They know how I am, and I don't ever have to worry about offending them with my startles or my silence.

My stomach aches with missing them, and it's not a new feeling. I've been missing them a while now. If I were home, they wouldn't be there. Una and Mari would be with their mates, and Kennedy would be out, training or scouting or hunting. She's grabbed freedom with both hands.

At home, I felt so left behind, so forgotten. And that's what feels like safety to me?

On a whim, I listen to my wolf again. She's drowsing with her head on her paws, perfectly content. What does she know that I don't? What's different now for her?

It's a wild thought—that things could possibly be different.

"Annie, you wouldn't believe what Max would have to do to keep Justus out of trouble when he was little," Elspeth says, and I startle, but I don't drop a stitch. I make myself focus on the conversation.

Diantha, Nessa, and the others chuckle like family who've heard a story a hundred times and knows what's coming. Most of the females' hands are occupied in our small circle. Nessa braids one of her pup's thick black hair in neat rows, the female named Lelia files her nails, and Diantha works her loom. It's an interesting cherry wood piece, foldable, with a built-in bobbin winder and shelf. If it's homemade, the craftsman was very skilled.

Elspeth waits for me to reply, but I can't figure out what I'm supposed to say quickly enough, so she takes pity on me and continues, "Max would take the pups out to teach them how to hunt, but of course, if you left Justus to his own devices, he'd tear off and kill everything in a five-mile radius before the others had a chance to sniff out a track."

Everyone chuckles fondly. Elspeth pauses for me to respond. I should chuckle, too, or make some approving sound. She's so obviously proud. Yet again, though, I don't manage to reply before Elspeth feels compelled to go on. My face burns. The embarrassment doesn't help the sweat situation. It's trickling down my neck.

"Well, it was so bad that Max would have to hunt down an animal the day before—say a badger—and then go out in the middle of the night and create a whole trail of badger sign—up, down, and all around, over hill and dale. Like a maze. Then, the next day, he'd take the pups out and tell Justus to have at it. Justus would tear off after the badger, and Max would tell the others, 'Today, pups, we're hunting fox.'"

She laughs. I can't imagine a male creating such an elaborate ruse when he could just bark the pup into submission. That's what a Quarry Pack male would do.

"Oh, remember the time Justus caught that skunk?" an older female named Mabli cackles. "Skinned it and everything and brought it to Alys proud as a peacock, the pelt reeking to high heaven."

"Who's Alys?" I ask. Several females glance up in surprise, but they recover quickly.

"Justus's dam," Elspeth answers.

I focus on my knitting so I don't see their expressions. They know Justus and I aren't really mates. It isn't so strange that I wouldn't know his mother's name. I'm not in the wrong, but you couldn't convince my stomach. It aches like it got kicked by a mule.

"Well, she soaked that pelt in tomato juice for days, scrubbed it with lemon rinds," Mabli recalls. "She tried everything to get the stink out, and she never quite could, so in the end, she made a pair of slippers out of it. She said her feet were the furthest she could get that foul fur from her nose." Everyone laughs, and again, it's the warm, easy laughter of people who've heard the story a hundred times.

I remember, one time when I was very young, when my father was still alive, Ma let me help her make a mincemeat pie. I was so careful with spooning the pre-measured spices and dumping the raisins and stirring, but rolling out the dough was beyond my coordination and strength. I kicked a fuss, though, so Ma let me do it.

In the end, she made the crust on top look pretty, but the dough on bottom was uneven, so some parts burned, and others didn't cook all the way through. I still remember how her face lit up when she ate her slice, how she hummed happily and sunk back in her chair, saying to Pa, "Our Annie's a natural cook, just like her mother, isn't she?" And he smiled and agreed.

My chest tightens. It's hard to imagine young Justus, skinning a skunk, while little Annie baked pies. He's been the bugbear of my life for so long, I've never considered that we were both young at the same time. We both had mothers who loved us.

Mabli talks about Alys like she's not here anymore. "Did she pass away?" I ask softly.

"Yes, during the great sickness." Mabli's voice roughens, and the females grow quiet.

"I lost my dam then, too," I say quietly.

We learned at Moon Lake Academy that the sickness tore through all the shifter packs, and that the wasting sickness was a virus, not a curse, but regardless, we should leave it in the past—don't dwell or ask too many questions—lest we somehow wake it up by talking about it. We've memory-holed the people we lost and the things we did when we were scared.

My heartbeat speeds. It feels dangerous to talk about it here, now. Like I should be crossing my fingers or knocking on wood.

The females shift in their seats. They're not tensing, although some straighten their spines. It's more like when Una, Mari, Kennedy, and I are sitting in our living room late at night, and we've all had a few tokes or nips of whiskey in our tea, and one of us says something real, and we all let our masks slip for a moment so we can speak and hear each other the most clearly.

"I did, too," Lelia says, scratching the back of a wolf lounging beside her with her freshly sharpened nails. "Her name was Ryanne. She was a great weaver."

"And so beautiful." Mabli's thin, feathered lips curve, her gaze growing distant. "Her hair was so long and red. Just like yours," she says to Lelia.

"It was down past her bottom," Diantha says. "She could sit on it."

"When she was little, the back would knot up like a beaver's tail, and she'd holler like you were killing her when you brushed it. Drove your granddam to distraction." Mabli reaches over and strokes Lelia's hair. "So soft. So lovely."

Lelia smiles sadly, her shining eyes rising to meet mine. "What was your dam's name?"

"Aileen Murphy," I say. I haven't said her name out loud in years. No one has.

A strange feeling untangles in my chest. Guilt that it's been so long. Gratitude that I had reason to speak her name on such a beautiful day with the sky so blue. Grief. Love. Regret.

"She was the best cook," I say.

The females hum and murmur, a kind of affirmation. Or maybe an amen. I blink, and maybe for the first time, I really see the people around me.

The tremor in Mabli's hand. Her swollen knuckles, her red chafed skin.

The steel in Elspeth's spine, how she won't let herself relax against the back of her chair, and how her eyes are always darting when she hears a shriek from the sycamore, a clang from across the clearing, or the caw of a crow flying overhead.

The dirt under Griff's fingernails as he crouches by the fire, pokes it with his stick, and pretends he isn't listening to our conversation.

This is all so strange, but is it that different, really, from home? Mabli's hands could easily belong to Old Noreen. Griff lingers just like Fallon used to do when he'd drop by for the video games we'd buy for him in Chapel Bell, like he craved the warmth of our company but some grown male voice in his head wouldn't let him show it.

And isn't my gaze darting, too, like Elspeth's, at each shriek, clang, and caw?

"Remember when Justus and Khalil went after that bog worm up by Salt Mountain?" Lelia changes the subject back to Justus's exploits. This time, everyone chuckles a little more gustily. I guess this one's even better than the skunk story.

"They really thought they could catch him with a net." Diantha snorts.

"They did catch his head," Elspeth says.

"More like they harnessed him." Diantha's furry, pointed ears twitch with humor.

"It was a lucky throw, though. I'm sure I couldn't tell a bog worm's head from its ass."

"That beast dragged the both of them around the whole lake at least a dozen times."

"You couldn't tell them apart afterward; they were both so covered in muck."

"And the smell!"

"Oh, Fate, the *smell*!"

"It was like they'd rolled in something dead."

"Like they'd rolled in shit and *then* in something that died."

"They had to scrape themselves clean with a putty knife."

"If I close my eyes, I can still smell it."

"I smell it in my nightmares."

"And that bog worm got away clean in the end, didn't he?"

"He's up there laughing still, mark my words, telling his little bog worm babies about the time he took two idiot shifters for a tour of the bottom of the lake."

They're all nearly falling out of their seats, cackling, their noses scrunched, tears gathering in their eyes. Griff has given up acting like he's not listening. He's cracking up, too.

Is this bog worm the same one that Darragh killed a little while back? I heard it was a monster. Should I mention it?

Join in?

Reach out?

I listen for the voice to tell me why I shouldn't, but she's silent.

I listen for my wolf.

She's grinning, her tongue hanging out the side of her mouth, giddy to be in the middle of chatty, happy females and fresh air and sunshine.

I open my mouth.

Before I can speak, Diantha's strong voice rings out. "I have a story."

The laughter immediately fades. Elspeth's eyes narrow, the lines at the corners disappearing. Mabli's mouth tightens. My wolf gets very quiet, her ears perking.

"Remember when Justus was—what—eighteen or nineteen? And he was out past the red clay camp for some reason, and he came across the scent of humans and some North Border males?"

Everyone's gaze shifts to Nessa where she's sitting by the tent flap, keeping an eye on her sleeping pups. A sourness taints the air.

"Diantha," Elspeth warns.

Diantha ignores her, looking past her to Nessa.

"Go on," Nessa says, her voice very deliberately even, her eyes cold as ice. I can recognize a mask when I see one. Hers is good. Much better than mine.

"He was alone and outnumbered, but he smelled a female in distress, and he didn't want to lose the trail, so he stalked them. It turned out to be a hunting party. The North Border males were guides. The humans were the paying customers. Nessa's brother was the prey. And Nessa was the bait."

Diantha holds Nessa's gaze as she speaks, and there's a challenge in the look, but no cruelty, at least not that I can recognize. Nessa doesn't flinch, although her face has gone gray. I think this hurts her, but at the same time, I think she wants Diantha to keep going. What is that like? For someone to know your story and tell it for you?

"There were a dozen of them. They tied Nessa to a tree by the top of a hill. They chained her brother, threw him in the back of a truck, and drove away. Justus was left alone with the two North Border males guarding Nessa. How long did it take him to kill them once the truck was gone?" Diantha asks.

"Seconds," Nessa says. "He cut their throats with his claws like *that*." She snaps. Her small, cold voice sends chills up my spine.

Diantha continues, "He freed Nessa, told her to hide, and went after her brother. He tried his best, but he was on four legs, and the hunters had a huge lead and guns and numbers."

Nessa takes over. "I found a place I could fit between the roots of an old oak by a dried-up stream. It felt like I was there for hours. Every so often, there would be a gunshot, and I would pray so hard for another one because as long as they were shooting, Bowen might still be alive."

The wolf on Lelia's lap jumps down and pads over to Nessa, winding between her calves. Nessa's fingers float down to trail through the fur on the top of the wolf's head.

"Eventually, there weren't any more shots. And then Justus came back, covered in blood. Weeping." Tears stream down Nessa's cheeks. "He said he was too late."

"He killed every single one of those bastards, though." There's a fierce light in Diantha's wolfish eyes.

"I wanted to see Bowen. I made Justus take me to him. There was a North Border wolf in the dirt near his body. The wolf was enormous. As big as a bear. His intestines were trailing from his belly. Justus was so young—not much older than a pup."

"Oh, he was fully grown," Diantha says, her gaze hardening as it turns to me. "He was newly mated. That's why he was out in those woods. He was trekking back to his mate's pack territory yet again to check on her."

My stomach knots. *Yet again?* How many times did he come back, and I didn't know?

"Diantha," Elspeth warns quietly.

Diantha ignores her, staring me down. "I have another story, since we're talking about mothers."

"Diantha," Elspeth hisses louder.

"Remember how Alys died during the worst of that winter, when we were losing one or two people a day? Everyone was either sick themselves or too busy nursing their own blood or burying the dead. Remember how no one made their way up to her den for days? How Justus had done his best to bury her by himself. Was he eight? Nine?"

Justus's words in the den echo in my head. *I swear it to you on my dam's grave.*

Diantha pauses, but no one answers her. They don't interrupt her, either. I'm going to be sick.

"His sire was already gone. How many days was Justus alone up there? No one remembers, do they?" She pins the others with her stare. No one will meet her eyes. "How long did he stay alone in that den before Max finally got well enough to go up and check on him?"

"Max had to drag Justus out," Elspeth says quietly. "He didn't want to leave her nest." Her cheeks are wet with tears.

Nessa is crying, too. And Lelia. Mabli. All the females are tense, weeping, staring at me, blaming me.

They love him, and I rejected him, but they don't want my blood. They want to tell me who he is. They want me to *hear* them, to *see* the pup who refused to come out of his dam's nest.

Come on, Annie. We've got to get out of here.

You've got to come now. What if they come back?

Please, Annie. Please.

My chest balloons with guilt and grief and regret and

rage. I didn't ask for this—any of it. They don't know me. Do they think this is what I wanted?

I want to shout that at them, but the muscles in my throat don't work—they've never worked—and besides, it's not them that I want to shout at, is it? These weeping mothers and daughters and sisters?

What do I do?

Where is the pecking voice now? Doesn't my wolf want to bark at me to run and hide?

I grasp for the fear—the familiar, reliable, insistent fear that doesn't leave room for anything else—and it's not there. All I have left is me.

And them.

And the blue sky overhead.

The pups yipping and yapping over in the sycamore tree.

The scent of woodsmoke and fur on the breeze.

For the first time in my life, it is crystal clear in my mind that—in this moment, at least—I have a choice. I can shrink down. Wrap my arms around myself. Or I can straighten up. Open my hand.

I did it once before, didn't I? I let go of the slat. Crawled out from my hiding place. Reached for the knife.

Inside me, close to the boundary between us, my wolf sits, quiet and watchful.

I meet Diantha's eyes. "We lost so many," I say. "So much." And even though it is very, very hard, I don't look away.

It's not a defense or excuse or platitude. It's the truth. No more, no less. It's all I've got.

"We did," Diantha says, her chin high. Her whiskers quiver. She's not crying, but her diamond eyes shine.

It isn't enough, but what else do we have?

Diantha sniffs and settles back down to her loom. She throws the little wooden boat through the threads and pulls the shaft firmly forward with a clunk. Slowly, as if she's waking up from some spell, Elspeth begins to rock her chair again. Griff, who'd been making himself invisible, stirs the coals with his stick.

Nessa ducks into the tent and reemerges with a yawning toddler with puffy black curls. The pup plasters herself to her dam's front and promptly falls asleep again, her head nestled in the crook of Nessa's neck.

A pup rushes over from the sycamore with a scraped knee.

A male drops by with a bucket of water to refill our kettle.

The moment passes.

I'm not sure if I said the right thing. My hands shake as I take up my yarn again. Actually, all of me is shaking.

The voice still doesn't have anything to say, though.

I didn't run. I didn't hide. I didn't close my eyes and keep my mouth shut. And the world didn't end.

The sun is still shining as I knit beside a fire, surrounded by this strange pack. They don't know me. I don't know them. But the same breeze dries our cheeks.

And when a pup shrieks in the sycamore, all our eyes flick over for a second, to reassure ourselves that everyone is safe. Everyone is well.

11

———

ANNIE

Justus still isn't back when the sun begins to sink behind the hills to the north. Most of the females ventured to the tables by the bonfire for dinner, but Griff brought a tray for Elspeth and me at the female camp. Nessa's youngest, the sleepy curly-headed toddler, kicked a fuss when the cowbell rang that summons the pack to eat, so she's here with us, too, picking off my plate.

Her name is Efa, and for some reason, she's as interested in me as her wolf. She's the cutest pup I've ever seen with her big round eyes and delicate tan whiskers contrasting with her warm brown skin.

She's been talking to me nonstop since she fully woke up from her afternoon nap, but she's still sporting baby fangs, so I can't understand a word. She doesn't seem to notice or mind. She babbles a few words in her raspy little growly voice, and I'll say, "Is that right?" Or "Oh. Is that so?" And she's happy. I wish all people were this easy.

She grabs a handful of mashed potatoes from the plate balanced on my knees. I glance around. Elspeth is messing around with the kettle. No one else is around to see my

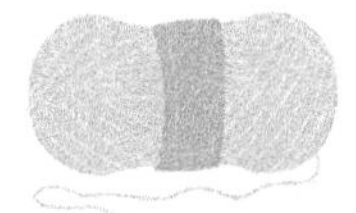

terrible babysitting. I wait until Efa licks her hands clean and then I gently wipe them on the skirt of my gown.

"How about we use the spoon?" I say, offering her another bite. She scoops the potato off the spoon with two fingers and sticks them in her mouth.

Elspeth chuckles over by the fire. "Usually, that one will only eat as her wolf. Count yourself lucky she's not licking the plate."

"Is that true?" I ask Efa. She's balancing herself with a chubby hand on each of my knees. She bares her tiny fangs in a shameless grin and yips.

I spear a hunk of beef with my fork and hold it up. She plucks the bite off, pops it into her mouth, and then before I can stop her, she licks the tines with her long wolfish tongue.

I'm not used to spending time with pups her age. At Quarry Pack, they stay close to their dams, and despite the changes Killian has made, the mated females still stick together and steer clear of lone females like me. The only little one I have experience with is Una's babe, Raff, but he isn't walking or talking yet.

Efa is the most nonsensical person I've ever met. She'll go running straight toward the fire on her thin wobbly legs to give Elspeth a piece of beef, but when an owl hoots overhead, she yelps and huddles close to me, hiding her face in my side. I don't get the fearlessness, but I understand about the owl. I startled, too.

Despite the good company, as the shadows grow longer, I'm getting anxious again.

Where is he? He left you here. He's dead. They'll blame you. He's dead.

And he's your mate, and you don't even know him.

I distract myself from my dread—and Efa from her infatuation with the fire—by playing peek-a-boo with the rectangular tablecloth-wrap-runner that I made today. When I started this morning, I was too nervous to make a conscious plan, so I started a second row both too late and too soon for a scarf, and then, hours later, when I was calm enough to take stock of what I was doing, I realized I'd already stitched too many rows for a placemat or doll's blanket. It's not my best work, obviously, just rows upon rows of garter stitches.

It makes for a good prop for peek-a-boo, though. Efa stands in front of my knees, and I raise it between us so she can't see my face. Her wolf growls. It's adorable, about as loud as a tummy grumble. I say, "Peek-a-boo!" and drop the knitting in my lap. She squeals, and her whiskers quiver.

No matter how many times I do it, she doesn't get bored. When I try a variation, covering my head with the knitting and then raising it to peek out at her, she dissolves in giggles and yips. I'm a comedic genius.

I'm about to do it again when there's a disturbance across camp. Males are howling. Voices are raised. There's a mass movement toward the entrance to the clearing.

Danger. Run. Run!

I stand, lifting Efa into my arms so I can bolt with her. She promptly grabs my face, accidentally sticking a finger in my ear.

Elspeth arrives at my side, laying a hand on my forearm. "They're back," she says. She squeezes my arm. "Nothing to worry about. If there's something wrong, the howls will let you know. You can't mistake it."

Is there often something wrong? *What* goes wrong?

Efa wriggles, wanting down, so I set her on her feet. She grabs my hand and immediately begins to toddle off toward the action. Everyone seems to be going to greet their returning packmates. The sycamore is free of pups for the first time today.

I let Efa lead me at her top speed, which is a very slow stroll for me. Elspeth keeps pace with us, and I'm grateful again for her company. I'd gotten comfortable at the females' camp-within-a-camp, but as I pass by the areas where the males gather, their mixed scents rattle my nerves.

You're outnumbered.

It doesn't help that it's that time before night falls when you realize that you can't quite see as far in front of you as you could a minute before, and your brain switches from relying on sight to relying on smell. Everything is swathed in shadows—the work tables, canopies, and stacked boxes marking the various males' territories.

A stiff breeze blows down from Salt Mountain. I'm still warm from lounging in the sun all day, so my skin is clammy where the wind cools the dampness on my chest and the back of my neck.

Wrong direction.

The pecking voice wants me to turn around. My wolf urges me to walk toward the commotion faster. She wants me to press through the crowd in front of us, find Justus, and let her out to tell him exactly what she thinks about him leaving us alone all day. She flashes her plans into my head. It's a picture of him on his knees, his palms raised in surrender, as she sinks her fangs into his neck.

Well. We're not going to do that. Mostly because in her imagination, she's about five times her actual size.

When we get to the back of the gathering, my feet slow and then stick in place. Efa strains against my hand, but I can't go farther. I'd have to weave through the males, and I can ignore the voice's incessant shrieks, but I can't do that.

Turn around now!

All of a sudden, Efa makes herself dead weight, trying to move me another step forward. She ends up dangling from my hand, parallel to the ground like an ice dancer. She whines. I get it. I want to see what's happening, too.

Danger. Better run now. Before it's too late.

The pack is excited, almost raucous.

"They must've got something good," Elspeth observes, rising on her tiptoes to try to see between the males' shoulders.

Efa wriggles her hand free from mine—my palms are weirdly slick, probably from leftover mashed potato slime—and bolts for a roughhewn picnic table a few feet away. She's folded over it, throwing a leg up, when I get to her. She's going to get splinters. I pluck her up. She wails. I freeze.

"Oh, no, little one. Don't fuss."

"Up!" she demands with a husky little bark. "Up, Annie!"

Oh. She knows my name. My eyes prickle. Oh, crap. I look over my shoulder at Elspeth. She shrugs. "If you don't help her up, you're going to be playing 'pull the howling baby wolf down off the table' until her dam comes for her."

"Where is Nessa?"

"I told her to leave Efa with us and take a break," Elspeth says. "Thank Fate I wasn't blessed with triplets." We share a silent moment of respect.

"Up, Annie, up!" Efa starts to climb me like a tree.

Even if I held her steady while she stood on the table, she wouldn't be able to see anything over the crowd of tall males.

I sigh. A draped sheet is not ideal for climbing. I tuck it tighter around my chest and step onto the bench, careful not to tread on the hem. Once I'm steady, I lift Efa next to me. I repeat the maneuver to stand on top of the table. It's sturdy with thick X-legs. Oddly enough, height isn't one of my fears.

Everyone can see you. Get down. Get down!

I'm surprised when Elspeth climbs up after us.

"Up!" Efa demands, and I set her on my shoulders. She digs her fingers into my hair to hold on, and I wrap my hands around her chubby thighs to anchor her in place. We both still as we catch sight of the hunting party.

The scene looks like something out of the first chapter of our shifter history textbook at Moon Lake. The sunset hasn't quite faded, but the burnt oranges and reds don't give off any light. The clearing is illuminated by dozens of small fires and the torches that some of the males carry.

They've cleared a path through the gathering for the returning males. The wolves have pushed forward, forming a kind of aisle.

Justus and Khalil come first, an elk hanging by its bound hooves from a thick branch that rests on their shoulders. The elk's antlers scrape the ground as they walk. It's a huge bull, big enough to feed a pack this size for weeks.

Justus's tan skin shines in the flickering torchlight. His hair is pulled back in a messy knot. His hands wrap around the branch, elongating his torso, throwing every single muscle into relief and exposing the whole tapestry of his tattoos.

I don't know where to stare. His obliques? The ridge of V-shaped muscle that disappears into his waistband? The black swirls and shapes that I can't make out from back here, but that my eyes can't help trying to decipher? My mouth waters. I swallow it down.

There isn't an ounce of arrogance or even pride in his walk. He walks no taller than usual; his back is no straighter. He carries his kill through his excited packmates like you'd haul a bucket or push a wheelbarrow. It's not fake nonchalance, either. This is a male who isn't trying to nurse a moment at all—he just really wants to put that elk carcass down.

I still can't believe he's my fated mate. I've never once been so unbothered in my entire life.

Maybe that's what Fate does when she pairs people— she matches you with your opposite. Una is nothing like Killian, and I still can't believe Mari and Darragh are mates. Whenever I see them together, I think of a video Kennedy showed me on her phone where a Doberman puts a kitten's head in his mouth and wouldn't let her go until his owner traded him for a hunk of cheese.

Max and the redhead, Alroy, follow the elk. They're both strutting, although Max is clearly low on gas. His swagger is a little creaky. I glance over at Elspeth. She's tracking her mate, the corners of her mouth curling in a fond smile.

The return of the hunters seems to be the cue for a celebration. A few scattered drums beat a rhythm for the males to stride along with, and a fiddle joins from somewhere over by the big bonfire. The volume of the chatter rises. Song breaks out.

The pack sways, swirling together in Justus and Khalil's wake, forming new patterns. Some folks dance. Some shift into their wolves to wrestle and race around the clearing. Others gather around the fires, laughing, drinking, and talking at the top of their lungs. A flute joins the fiddle. The moon comes out, big and round, balanced just above the horizon.

Efa bends over so her chin is resting on the top of my head and grabs my flushed cheeks. I gently turn from left to right so she can take it all in, gasping as a pattern appears before my eye. The tattoo is a map of the camp. I needed to watch the pack disperse from a higher vantage point to recognize it, but I can't unsee it now. The fires match the starburst shapes. The dens are the jagged triangles. The swoops and spirals are the worn paths the pack takes as they settled themselves in their accustomed places.

Above us, the stars are coming out. Everything seems to line up somehow. To connect. Maybe it's the music or the sweet weight of Efa, the pinch of her grabby fingers. I've never felt like this before, like a bird perched on top of a tree, not a mouse cowering in a hole.

"Oh!" Efa squeals, patting my cheek and pointing. Her attention has been caught by a group dancing by the bonfire.

The fiddler is bending his bow double speed, and the drums beat faster. The females hold their gowns high so their legs show, their bare feet moving almost too quick to track while they hold their bodies perfectly still from the waist up. The males dance around them, stomping, tossing their heads back, their wolves howling to the hills. This is a pattern, too. The females are the stationary shapes, and the males are the swirls weaving between them.

The singed, crackling scent of magic tickles my nose like at Abertha's cottage, but there aren't any pots bubbling with potions or herbs hanging well out of the reach of pups. I couldn't say where the scent is coming from. The ground? The people?

Efa giggles, her rump shifting back and forth on my shoulders. Elspeth shuffles beside us, her feet padding a dull rhythm on the table top. She's dancing. I glance down at my feet. Am I swaying to the music, too? There must be magic in the air.

Get down now. You're a target.

No one's looking at us. They're all absorbed in their own bodies, their own rhythm and partners.

Get down!

I sigh, reaching up to lift Efa off my shoulders and when I inhale, my lungs fill with the scent of freshly turned earth. My body reacts the way it always does in the spring when we till the garden—my chest rises and something deep in my bones takes note that we've made it around the sun and into warm days and blue skies again. Anticipation thrums low in my belly.

Justus emerges from the shadows to stand a few feet from my table.

Efa screeches, reaching for him, her weight forcing my head to fold forward, chin to chest.

"Affa!" she shrieks. "Affa!"

"Justus," he says, holding his arms up to receive her. I lift her up and pass her down. She snuggles right up to him, her face morphing into her wolf's so she can rub her forehead all over his face. She grabs a handful of beard, and to his credit, though she gives it a good yank, he doesn't even rumble.

"Are you keeping Annie company?" he asks her, looking up at me. Have I ever seen him from this angle before?

He's a few feet below me, so the whites of his eyes show under his dark pupils. They glow in the moonlight. The breeze whips his long hair, and with his height and honed muscle and inked skin, he looks like a wild male, like the ones in the fresco above the stage at Moon Lake's outdoor amphitheater that shows their Great Alpha, Broderick Moore, single-handedly fighting off the ferals who attacked his people on their way down from the dens.

Except Justus has a pup propped on his hip, she's half-shifted, and her wolf is licking the side of his face. And although the expression in his eyes is fierce, his lips curve, bemused.

"I'll take that little pupkin," Elspeth says, stepping down from the table so nimbly that neither Justus nor I have time to help her. "We need to go find her dam. I don't want her on my hands when she decides it's too far past her bedtime."

"I saw her over by the elm with Redmond," Justus says, tickling Efa's nose with his beard as she screeches with delight.

"Snuck off for some alone time, have they?" Elspeth smirks. "Well, let's go ruin your ma and da's fun, shall we, little one?" She takes Efa, and after a small fuss, she convinces the pup to wave goodbye to us and go find her dam.

I'm still on the table. Justus has me stuck up here, treed like a raccoon. To get down, I'd either have to jump—and risk losing my makeshift gown and my dignity—or I'd have to turn my back on him to step down to the bench. Something inside me won't let me do that.

"She's taken with you," Justus says, his voice low even though there's no one nearby.

My cheeks heat. I don't know how to answer him. There's too much weight to his words. I'm probably his only chance of having a pup of his own, and there could have been one between us, but not in this timeline, not the one that made me the way I am. That's a lot of baggage between two people who are virtually strangers.

But is he really a stranger now? He doesn't quite feel like one anymore. He just kind of feels *new*.

"She's taken with you, too," I finally reply.

He shrugs and grins. "She saw that elk we brought home, and she knows what side her bread is buttered on."

"You think she was being sweet to you for food?"

He nods very seriously. "Absolutely. She knows what I'm good for."

"I don't know. She seemed pretty taken with your beard."

His grin widens. "I do have a great beard."

My lips rise at the corners of their own accord. "Very yankable, it seems."

He takes a step closer. I clutch the sides of my gown with my sweaty palms. "Yes, I've been told that many times. Great for yanking and catching crumbs."

"Seems like a good thing to have, then." I don't know what I'm saying, or what we're doing, or what I'm still doing up on this table. Is this flirting?

"It serves me well." He closes the rest of the distance between us. "Want to give it a tug? See what everyone is talking about?"

My face catches fire. My lower belly squirms. I'm on my own. My wolf is hanging back, watching, and the pecking voice is missing in action.

I can't think of even a quasi-smart reply. I've run out, so I do what I have to do—I reach out, take a chunk of beard between my forefinger and thumb, and pull, very gently. The smile that breaks across his face steals all my air. Blood whooshes to my head. I'm a balloon about to pop. I'm a complete dork, and at the very same time, I'm utterly, totally, transcendentally entranced.

I drop my hand. Justus catches it and brings it back to his face, pressing my palm to his cheek. My skin is so clammy. My thighs clench, trying to tamp the squirmy sensation that's doing strange things to my pulse and breath and ability to think.

"I shouldn't have left you." I'm not sure whether he means today or back when we mated, and regardless, I don't know what I'm supposed to say to that. My wolf snorts. She agrees with him, and she's unimpressed that it took him so long to realize it.

"I was fine." I'm going to assume he's talking about today.

"I was afraid you'd ask me to take you home, so I made myself scarce."

My jaw drops, not much, but enough that I have to close my mouth. Males don't just *admit* things. They brood or stomp around or refuse to eat the dinner put in front of them, and then you have to go back to the kitchen and play 'guess why' with the other females.

Hold on. Back up. Focus. He bailed because he didn't want to take me home today?

"But you *will* take me back to Quarry Pack?" I ask, my anxiety spiking. I don't actually want to be anywhere else right now. I like his rough hand cradling mine while I stand on top of a table like I'm a bold female who's never obsessively worried about exposure, bolt holes, and escape routes. But in order to breathe, I need to know I *could* go.

"Yes, when you say it's time," he says, his eyes shuttering. He lets go of my hand, and I let it fall to my side. There's a fraught moment while he braces himself, waiting for me to ask, and I try to think of something, anything else to say instead.

I do want to go home. But not right now. I'm afraid to tell him that I want to stay. That he'll read too much into it.

He's afraid, too, though he's doing a good job not showing it. The bond is giving him away.

I stare down at him. He stares up at me.

He blinks first. "Will you come for a walk?" he asks, his voice gruff and tentative.

I nod, my throat too tight to say yes out loud.

He reaches for me, but he doesn't grab my waist. His

hands stop and hover a hairsbreadth over my hips. I have to step forward into them.

He cocks his head and lets me see into his eyes again. He's nervous. Relieved. Excited.

I am, too. I step into his hands. His fingers curve around my sides, and he lifts me like I'm made of cotton fluff. I instinctively grab his shoulders for balance. His wolf rumbles. I draw down a deep breath, my nose quivering. Oh, lord. His *scent*.

When I was a girl, we'd till the garden behind Abertha's cottage as soon as the ground was soft and dry enough, usually in March when the weather still felt like winter on most days. The sky would be stark gray, there would be a bite in the wind and only the barest hint of buds on the trees, but with every spade-full of turned dirt, a delicious springtime scent would rise in the air. That's Justus.

When I breathe him in, I can hear the crunch of my boots on the cold dirt, the scrape of the hoe hitting rocks, the thunk of steel hacking through clumps of earth. I can feel my palms burn from the rough wooden handle.

His scent confuses the past and the present in my head. He wasn't there. It's a trick of the senses that he smells exactly like my memories.

Or is it something else? Out of all the males in the world, Fate picked him for me. Why?

He takes my hand and leads me in the direction of the bonfire, his pace so slow it's almost bride-like. His grip is strong and certain. I hope he doesn't notice the clamminess.

We take one of the worn paths that winds between the various areas of activity. We pass by a workbench with the tools left out and some sort of wooden contraption left in the vise. A little further on, someone has left a bowl on a pottery wheel, the rudimentary kind made from wood discs that you kick with your foot. Farther still, there is a circle of empty chairs, whittling left in one, a pipe left in another.

We pass through scents—sawdust, clay, tobacco—but Justus's rich earthiness travels with me. My steps feel light, and my head swims. I've never felt like this before. So *not alone*.

When we walk by the dancers, they holler and howl and call to Justus. He smiles and waves them off, but two females —Ashleen and Brigid, two young mothers who spent most of the afternoon chasing after their pups—make their way over and block our path, their feet flying, sweat streaming down their smiling, ecstatic, moonlit faces. Several males follow in their wake, stomping out their part of the dance, winding between and around them.

"Come on, Alpha, Annie!" Ashleen calls.

"Alpha! Annie!" the others echo.

I freeze. There is no way my feet can do what theirs are doing. They'd twist off at the ankles.

"Not tonight," Justus says kindly.

"Come on, Alpha!" a male shouts, and then his wolf bays, calling Justus to join the pack.

Justus shoots me a rueful grin, and then as smooth as butter, he breaks into the steps. His shoulders dip, his feet stomp, his rhythm perfect. Effortless. The dancers erupt in shouts and howls of approval. Justus throws his head back, tossing his hair. It's the first time I've seen him cocky.

My lower belly winches and something flutters in my chest.

I've never seen a male dance up close before. I've spied from the kitchen at Quarry Pack when our mated females put music on the radio after dinner. If they'd had enough to drink, some of their mates would dance after they got the sparring out of their system. There weren't really *steps* to their dancing. They'd kind of grind on the females and grab whatever part of them was closer at hand—boob or butt.

This is different. These males had to *learn* this. The females, too. And it doesn't look like foreplay at all. It's more like a model you make in science class—the females are the sun, the males are orbiting planets. The females are the nucleus. The males are electrons.

Justus winds in a figure eight, looping the other females, and then looping me. The males fall in line behind him, their wolves' sharp yips punctuating the drumbeat.

My heart thumps. The males are big and loud and close.

Don't move. Don't breathe.

Or run? Maybe run?

I'm an island in a stream, and I'm scared, but also, I'm outside of it all. This is so far beyond my experience that I can't do anything but watch and listen and try to orient myself in this strange, strange moment.

Life is work, right?

Bed, bath, kitchen, garden, greenhouse, beehive, kitchen, bath, bed.

Work, punctuated with episodes of sheer, unfounded terror.

Life is swimming, and if you stop, you drown, and if you think about what might be underneath you, you'll sink.

You don't leave your work out on the table or your pipe on the seat of your chair. In order to *dance*.

I don't know how it's dangerous, but it has to be. My *soul* says so.

Justus passes behind me and then in front of me again. He stops, the males fanning out behind him, furling into a new configuration. He steps forward and back, one foot, then the other, his lips curled up in invitation.

I suddenly feel disproportioned. My feet are cafeteria trays. My arms are fence posts.

He does the sequence of steps again, a shuffle closer, a quick hop back. Isn't this what male birds do to attract their mates? What do the female birds do back? Stand there awkwardly and wish they'd stop?

Close by, a female yips.

Behind you!

Ashleen appears at my side and bumps me with her hip. "Like this, Annie. Look at my feet."

She slows her steps, so gracefully, until it seems she's dancing in slow motion. "There are eight bars." She begins to clap. "One-two-three and two-two-three and three-two-three and four-two-three."

She bounces in time to her counting, and since she's watching my feet, and I've always been the most well-behaved student in any class, I bounce, too.

"Okay, now, start with your left. Heel. Toe. Heel. Toe. Tap, tap, tap, tap."

I heel. I toe. I tap. My feet are clunky wooden marionettes at the end of strings.

"You've got it," Ashleen says. "Now dip with your knees between the heel and toe."

That's when it falls apart. My feet stutter to a halt. I'm already flushed and breathless, and now my cheeks are on fire.

"Oh, no, don't give up. Here, let's do it how we do with the pups," Ashleen says and slides in front of me, so she's facing Justus. She swipes behind her back to find my hands and plants them on her hips. "Okay, now do what I do with my feet, and when you feel me dip, you dip."

My wolf rumbles. She doesn't like Ashleen between Justus and me.

Ashleen lets out a gusty peal of laughter. "Settle down, lady. Tell that wolf of yours I don't want your male. I've got my own, and he's trouble enough. Now, on three. Ready? One, two, three."

It is easier to follow the steps with her in front of me, and after a few minutes, I can let her hips go, and a little after that, she calls, "Double time!" and I don't completely fall apart.

Then she dances off, and the males who'd been weaving around us trail after her like the tail of a comet, and I'm left alone with my mate. His eyes fall to my lips, then slip helplessly to my breasts, and finally plummet to the calves and ankles I'm showing by holding up my gown.

I watch him take me in like I'm extraordinary. A statue come to life or a Pegasus. Something that defies the laws of nature. Scary like that. Jaw-dropping like that.

His feet come to a rest. He's breathing hard, his bare chest rising and falling, his tanned skin flushed ruddy in the white space between his tattoos.

He's tall and strong and hewn like rock, but staring up into his gentle, smiling face, with the sparkle in his eye, I can see the pup who brought his dam a skunk. My lips curve. I can't help it. He's happy.

He's happy to be here *with me*.

He grabs my hand and lifts it, pressing my knuckles to his lips, only for a second, but I feel it deep, deep down, like I'm a whole other Annie who'd been raised in a place where it was safe to want to be beautiful, to want a sweet, wild male to kiss her in the moonlight.

I want him to kiss me again. On the mouth this time. I want a restart. What's it called in golf? In human sport? A mulligan. I want us to start *here*, instead of where we did.

Justus squeezes my hand. "Let's keep going," he says and leads me on.

We pass a group of rambunctious pups who've been left to their fathers' care, and it's pretty much a scrum of enormous male wolves being climbed and ridden like horses by punch drunk little ones up way past their bedtime.

When the pups see Justus, they race to him, and he drops my hand to toss them in the air or carry them like a package under his arm for a few steps while they squeal and howl. Then he puts them safely back on their feet, shoos them to their fathers, and takes my hand again. Each time his fingers twine with mine, it feels less strange, and more— safe.

Nothing is ever safe. It's a trap.

Lest I forget, the voice flashes pictures in my mind—the basement's low ceiling, the old leather sofa, the green and white checkered tile floor, the pool table, Aunt Nola, Iona Ryan, Orla Sullivan and the other females, everyone, everything, familiar and safe. And then boots sound on the stairs. Then the door slams shut.

Pool of blood. Sightless eyes. Twisted mouth.

My clammy skin goes cold, my fear scent erupting from my pores.

Justus holds my hand tighter and swings our joined arms. "Whatever you're afraid of, I am strong enough to kill," he says, soft and sure. "And if I can't, I have a pack behind me."

For a minute, I don't think I'll say anything, but then, surprising myself, I do. "It's just in my head," I whisper.

"Good," he whispers back. "If I had to ask Alroy to back me up, I'd never hear the end of it."

He smiles again. I can't smile back, but the small

muscles in the corner of my mouth twitch, and I get the sense he can tell, even if he can't see.

We keep walking. The moon rises, and the temperature drops. I'm not tired at all.

Toward the edge of the clearing, by the stream, we come across a group of males sitting on overturned crates, playing a game with cards and what looks like piles of buttons and human coins.

"Alpha," they all say as we pass. Justus's wolf grumbles in his chest.

"Nice kill."

"That's one big bull."

"Can I get the tenderloin, Alpha?"

Justus chuckles. "Get your own, Calvus."

"Aw, come on," Calvus whines good-naturedly. "Play me for it."

"You think I'd trade my mate's company for yours? For what? What's he wagering?" Justus asks the others.

"He's laid down a chit," another male answers.

"For what?" Justus asks.

"The next squirrel he catches."

"You want to bet me a squirrel you *don't have* for a tenderloin that I *do*?" Justus snorts.

"It'll be the best squirrel you've ever had. I guarantee it," Calvus says, laughing.

"You've got a lot of confidence for a male with the smallest pile at the table."

"Hey, Alpha," Calvus protests. "Don't talk about the size of my pile in front of our new female."

Justus's wolf straight-up growls, vibrating his voice as he says, "*My* female."

Trouble. Show your neck. Show neck!

I stop myself from bowing, but all four males at the table dip their heads. They're still smirking, though.

"Yes, Alpha," Calvus says, his grin the biggest of them all. "As you say."

Justus clears his throat. "All right then. We'll let you get on with your game. Calvus, I'll make sure to tell Tarquin to give you the shank."

"Oh, come on, Alpha," Calvus whines. The males are still laughing as we walk away.

Despite the growl, Justus doesn't smell angry at all. I take a deep breath through my mouth. I can pick out scents better that way. Maybe his earthy smell is covering the anger.

If you can't smell his anger, you won't have any warning.

"What's wrong, Annie? Do you scent something?" Justus asks.

I glance over. He stops in place, frowning, scanning the area for a threat.

"No, I—I just—" I shake my head, flustered. I'm not used to people noticing my little freakouts. My roommates are used to it, and everyone else at Quarry Pack are too busy impressing each other to pay attention to me.

I wish he'd just let it go, but he's waiting, not moving, so I blurt out, "You were angry, but you don't *smell* angry."

His brow wrinkles. "I'm not angry."

"Your wolf growled. You made them show neck."

He glances up at the sky, blows out a breath, and then looks me in the eye, grabbing my other hand so he's holding both. "I'm not angry, and neither is my wolf. We were just —" He pauses like he's searching for words. "That was just my wolf pissing on a tree."

Oh. I'm the tree.

Gross.

My cheeks heat. Justus's gaze shifts awkwardly to the side, and he clears his throat.

"It would take more than Calvus' big mouth to piss me off," he kind of mumbles.

I overreacted. My brain leapt to the worst-case scenario. Like always. My cheeks burn hotter. "I'm sorry," I say.

He opens his mouth, and I know he's going to tell me not to apologize—which is what Kennedy and Ivo and Tye and everyone always says when I act like they're monsters because they had the audacity to come upon me around a corner without warning or ask me for something from across the lodge in a loud voice.

For some reason, I don't want Justus to sweep it under the rug like everyone else.

I tighten my grip on his hands. "I get jumpy," I tell him. Yeah. And the surface of the sun is a little hot. I exhale. "I worry a lot. I get anxious."

To his credit, he doesn't say *no shit*. Instead, he bends forward and presses his forehead to mine. "Maybe one day you'll tell me why."

I would shake my head, but I'm held in place with the pressure of his noggin.

"I would die before I let anything hurt you," he says, so softly that the warmth of his breath hardly reaches my lips.

"I don't want you to die."

He squeezes my fingers, drawing my arms to his side, and runs his temple down my cheek and along my chin. Scent marking me. I'm so hot and trembly. I feel like my knees are going to give out.

"Then how about I worry with you?" His nose brushes my jawline, right in front of my ear, and every nerve in my body jolts awake.

"I worry enough for ten people," I say. "I have it handled."

"I worry," he says.

I've heard this a hundred times before, too. People love to tell you about their anxieties and how they conquered them, and the only time it hasn't both irritated and depressed me was when Kennedy told me how weed gummies helped her get over her fear of accidentally shifting into her he-wolf in public, and she followed the confession up by sharing one with me, and we spent the night watching videos of cats being weird on her phone.

"Yeah?" On the one hand, it's past time I changed the subject, but on the other, his beard is brushing along my cheek, and it's scratchy and comforting and strange and lovely, and I don't want him to stop.

"I worry that something will happen to me, and I won't be here to protect my people. Or we'll be attacked, and I won't be strong enough, or the sickness will come back, and like last time, there won't be anything I can do."

Oh. Wow. His voice is even, but it's deadly serious. I worry about bad things happening to the people I love and not being strong enough all the time, but no one *expects* me to protect them. I'm not an alpha.

"Is that why you don't want your pack to call you alpha?" I ask before I can stop myself. I don't mean to suggest he's scared. I brace myself. Males don't like you to insinuate they're less than, even if you don't mean it.

"I guess," he answers, completely unfazed. "I don't believe that one of us is somehow superior than the others or destined to lead, but I'd let them call me alpha all day, if it made them happy, if it didn't make us weaker as a pack."

"What do you mean, weaker?"

"My decisions aren't any better than anyone else's. Well,

they're better than Alroy's, but other than that—I'm just as shortsighted, just as prone to careless mistakes as the others. I lose my temper. I miscalculate. My pride makes me stupid." He pauses there and flashes me a look I can't quite understand.

He goes on. "And the second I *let* them call me alpha, half of them are going to stop disagreeing with me, and there won't be anyone to point out when my ideas are bad. Or dangerous. A lot of them will rely on my judgment, and theirs will get rusty. If you know our history, you know what can happen."

"Whose history?" I know more about Moon Lake's than Quarry Pack, and that's very little. I know nothing at all about Last Pack.

Justus takes my hand, and we continue our walk. "Ours. Shifters in this part of the world."

"We didn't really learn about that at the Academy. Except for Broderick Moore and how he led Moon Lake Pack out of the dens."

Justus snorts. "Nothing about First Pack?"

"Who is First Pack?"

He smiles ruefully. "You call us the Last Pack. We call us First Pack."

"Oh. No. Not much. Just how you wouldn't leave the dens."

He laughs, and there's a bitter edge to it. "That's more or less the story."

We've gotten to the pups' sycamore playground. It's abandoned. There are still quite a few dancers by the big bonfire, but I don't see any little ones running around. They must've been herded to bed.

Justus pulls himself up on a swing made from a wood plank and rope and bends over with his hand out to give me a boost. I ignore it. I can do it more gracefully under my own steam.

I brace a palm on the plank, grab the rope, and jump with both feet, throwing my upper body forward. My chest slams the wooden edge so hard, I knock the wind out of myself. This was so much easier when I was six.

Justus chuckles and tries to roll me over and help get my butt on the seat, but he ends up just getting in my way. My wolf snaps at him. He laughs and backs off, scrunching himself into the rope on his side to give me as much space as possible.

By the time I finally get myself in position, I'm a mess. My gown is twisted and winching my waist. I'm breathless and sweating. My hair is all over the place.

Justus is grinning at me like the Cheshire Cat. He reaches over, tucks a loose tendril behind my ear, and quickly pulls his hand away. My heart thumps harder.

"Hold the rope and kick when I say," he orders.

"Yes, Alpha." My eyes bug wide at my own audacity.

He laughs from his belly. "One, two, three, *kick*."

We manage to lift our heels and lean back in sync, and in no time, we're swinging with hardly any effort. I haven't done this since I was little, and never two abreast. Back on the playground at the Quarry Pack commons, I'd sit on a black rubber swing, and Mari would sit in my lap since she was smaller, and then she'd make me do all the work.

My chest aches with homesickness. I miss that place, that time, and I can never go back. Homesickness doesn't feel like enough of a word. What do you call it when your heart longs to rewind time?

To distract myself, I ask, "Why didn't your pack leave the dens when the other packs did?"

He frowns, confused. "Well, we weren't a pack before the others left the dens."

Now I'm confused.

"They don't tell you who we are?" he asks.

I shake my head.

Justus doesn't seem that surprised. "We're you. Well, some of us are you. Lelia would've been one of yours. Ashleen. Alroy." Justus smirks. "He definitely comes from Quarry Pack blood."

"I don't understand."

He blows out air like he's thinking about how to put it. "You know how some of us came over on boats, right? Because the humans were blaming us for the famine where we came from, and they were eating everything down to the squirrels and rats, so we were starving, too?"

I vaguely remember a brief mention, an instructor describing how our shifter ancestors had to pass as human on ships, which is how we first began to learn civilized ways. I think it might have been during the field trip we took to Moon Lake's old den.

"That's how my people got here, and yours, but of course, there were shifters already here, and some in the area who had escaped from the south during slavery. Max's people came all the way from Louisiana. Twelve in their group—males, females, and pups—all the way from Bayou Lafourche. Max's great-grandsire didn't lose a single soul on the trip."

I've never been taught any of this, and I would know if I had—I paid attention in class like my life depended on it.

"All the shifters who settled here established a territory and lived in dens. We ran together on the full moon, and sometimes we fought, but mostly we lived in peace. We were too busy trying to survive and steer clear of the humans to mess with each other much. And then the Great Alpha, Broderick Moore, came along."

Of course, I've heard all about him. He was a footnote to every lesson at Moon Lake. I swear, even in math class, there would be questions like "The Great Alpha, Broderick Moore, had three apples. He ate one. How many apples did he have left?"

"Broderick Moore looked around and saw the humans with their horseless carriages and electric lights and indoor plumbing, and he wanted it. And if he was good at nothing else, he could paint people a pretty picture, so his people followed him out of the dens to Moon Lake, built themselves a human town, and convinced their wolves they only needed out once a month because wolves are shit at carpentry and laying brick."

I like electricity and plumbing, too, but we were taught that leaving the dens was more noble than that—like shifters had been living in squalor, uneducated and lawless, and when we moved into houses we became better somehow. And there was this unspoken insinuation that Moon Lake was the best, the *rightest*, and the other packs were good only inasmuch as we were like Moon Lake.

"So the other packs wanted to be like Moon Lake?"

"Well, an alpha can't let another alpha outdo him, can he? The first Alpha Fireside set his pack to building North Border. Malcolm Shaw had his build the compounds on Salt Mountain. Lorcan Bell settled by your quarry."

"But the alpha of Last Pack didn't want things to change?"

"There was no alpha. There was no Last Pack. Just a bunch of folks who didn't want to jail their wolves and break their backs to live like humans."

So that's why Last Pack looks so different from each other, like they could be from all the packs. They *are*.

"So these dens—they used to belong to one of the packs?"

Justus nods. "This was Salt Mountain's. Our winter camp belonged to North Border. Moon Lake and Quarry Pack kept their dens."

Little pieces are clicking together. "And this is the way we used to live?"

"Mostly. When we joined together, our ways kind of mixed."

"Is that why you steal females? Because they're descended from the same pack?"

"Sometimes." He grins. "Sometimes a male sees a female with a piece of shit for a mate and figures he can do better."

"And the females don't waste away, separated from their mates?"

He shakes his head. "Why would they? We feed and care for them well. They aren't left alone."

Everyone knows that the loss of a mate is devastating. I've seen elders who've lost their mates refuse to eat, bathe, leave the house. On occasion, Old Noreen has sent Mari or me to their cabins to coax them out, and sometimes, they come, and they sit in the lodge, staring blankly into the fire or nodding off. Alone.

Because we were busy in the kitchen, and everyone else was occupied with keeping or improving their rank. No one was keeping them company. There were no rocking chair circles gathered around small fires, no pups running wild among them, no dance parties breaking out and weaving among them.

"Why don't we know all this?" It takes a second for me to realize that I spoke the thought out loud.

Justus shrugs. "If I had to guess, a male who thinks he knows best isn't keen on people learning there are other ways. A male with a plan doesn't want to hear about how it was done before. If he thinks his way is better, he doesn't appreciate evidence that it's not."

I think about this and swing, letting the breeze cool my face. The sycamore leaves are a dark umbrella above us, rustling while the camp quiets. High overhead, pinprick stars dot the sky.

Is that why this place feels strange, but also like a long-lost memory? Females didn't sit together and chat while they worked when I was little—they wouldn't have dared look idle or like they were telling tales about the males. But sitting with Elspeth and the others did feel familiar, didn't it?

When I was young, weren't there stolen minutes—in the laundry or on the porch behind the lodge—when my mother and her friends would gather to fold linens or shuck corn or shell peas, and they'd murmur to each other and giggle behind their hands?

What would it have been like if I'd grown up here? What would *I* be like?

My thoughts float back to stealing females. "Were your people Quarry Pack, then?"

"My dam was. My sire was a wanderer from parts unknown."

"He didn't steal her?"

He chuckles. "The way Max tells it, he hung around like a stray, bringing her geese and rabbit and frogs and piling them up in front of her den until my dam took pity on him and let him sleep inside."

A smile tugs at my mouth. "Like your wolf. He brought me a goose."

I glance over. In the shadows, it's hard to read his eyes, but his voice is low and raspy when he says, "He did. And he only took a bite or two before he left it for you, and that was revenge."

"Revenge for what?"

"For the bites the goose took from him."

I giggle, and a grin breaks across Justus's face, bright in the dark. "I like that sound, pretty Annie. Sounds like bells."

My face heats. Out of some kind of synchrony, we both swing our legs slower and ease to a gentle back and forth.

The clearing is calm now, and silent, except for a few males sitting way over by the bonfire, keeping it stoked.

A question bursts to the front of my mind, like a wolf pup busting free from a thicket, all forward momentum, no caution, slipping my good sense and leaping out of my mouth without looking.

"Why did you steal me?" I whisper.

The swing stops. I force myself to look over. Justus meets my gaze, calm but confused.

"You don't feel it?" he asks. "You're going into heat again."

12

ANNIE

R *un!*

Yes. Don't need to tell me twice. I'm already gone.

I leap from the swing, landing hard, jarring my ankles, and I bolt, sprinting past the banked ashes of the females' fire, deaf from the blood rushing in my ears.

Heat.

No.

Hell no.

Faster!

I cut across the packs' curving, worn paths, making a beeline for the exit, pushing harder and harder until every muscle in my legs screams. As I pass the bonfire, I hear a male say, "Alpha?" But by the time the sound reaches me, I'm yards away.

Don't look back!

I won't. I feel Justus on my heel, his breath hot on the back of my neck.

My gown comes untucked, so I gather the fabric and clutch it to my chest, freeing my legs to pump faster. The pecking voice shrieks in my brain, dragging memories from the back of my brain to flog me with so I'll go faster.

My brown flannel shirt, sweat soaked and reeking of cum.

A sad nest of dry leaves.

The cold, rushing river.

What a sad female you are.

I don't want such a pathetic coward for a mate.

What would my pack say if I brought you back?

You smell more like food than female.

You stink like prey.

A female like you would make weak, spindly young.

I want to puke, but I don't dare slow down, not even a little so I can bend over and retch. Justus's steps thud behind me.

I reach the narrow camp entrance and burst through, instantly losing my footing on the steep, rocky trail that leads down to the woods below. My arms windmill as I desperately try to find my balance. Justus growls.

"Easy, easy," he says, so close, too close.

I don't have time for balance, so I lurch forward, surfing the loose pebbles down the slope, keeping upright by staggering from tree trunk to boulder. Almost at the bottom, I trip on an exposed root and crash to a knee. I cry out, scrambling forward on all fours until I can scrabble back to my feet.

I'm out of my mind, and I can't stop.

Sightless eyes.

Green and white checkered tiles.

Red blood.

The voice hurls bombs at me, dredging deep in my memories, like horror is fuel, like that's what I run on.

Camphor.

Rattling lungs.

A white sheet almost flat except for the knobs of Ma's knees and the ridges of her hips.

The voice scrapes the very bottom.

Declan Kelly at our door, smirking, with a palmful of fangs. "Sorry, Aileen. This is all that's left of him. Had to pick these out of my leg. The rest of him is in my belly."

Ma falling to her knees as Declan Kelly belched.

Why am I back here again? I've already lived through all this. I grew up. I've come all this way, miles and miles from where I started, and here I am, fleeing, but *back*, not *away from*, and I can't stop. My momentum has the force of a super magnet.

The trail levels, and I find my stride again, even though I'm favoring my right leg since my left knee is scraped and bleeding. I'm not running as fast as I was, but Justus isn't gaining on me. The trees become sparse, fields of wild-flowers opening on either side. Their stalks and new buds are dark outlines in the moonlight.

Where am I even going? I can't outrun my own body.

But I can't stop, either. The voice has hijacked my control center—I don't even know where my wolf has gotten to—and I've never learned the trick of calming myself down. Box breathing, balloon breathing, visualization, counting items, listing colors, naming a thing I can see, smell, hear, taste, and feel, plunging my face in cold water to stimulate my vagus nerve—I can panic through it all.

I'm doing it right now, slow jogging through this field of bluebells and Jack-in-the-pulpits and Dutchman's breeches. I can see the past clear as a picture—me, out of my mind, naked in the dirt, ass up in the air. I can smell my shame, hear the river, taste the blood from where my teeth bit through my cheek.

I can't do it again.

My fear spikes, the scent charring my nostrils. I trip over my own feet, cry out, and pitch forward.

A howl rings out. Something darts around me.

I land hard, face down, on a huge heap of fur, the air knocked from my lungs.

Freeze!

I do not need to be told.

I'm lying across a wolf. Justus's wolf. He's on his side. I'm sprawled on top of him. He slid underneath me while I fell like a baseball player stealing home. He's very quiet and very still except for his flank that lifts and lowers me as he breathes.

I tilt my head so I can see his face. He's already craning his neck to look at me, his soulful wolf eyes watchful and guarded.

I haven't seen this wolf in years. A fist squeezes my heart.

He caught me a goose. He made himself a pair of alien antennae out of sunflowers. He sat beside me on the porch. Before he figured out what was wrong with me, he tried to hunt down my bad mental health.

I've missed him, and I didn't even know it.

With his eyes locked on mine, he slowly rolls under me so he's on his back, so I'm lying on soft belly. He slowly sprawls his legs in an X, rests his head back on the ground, and lolls his long tongue out of the side of his mouth. He's pretending he's dead. Like I killed him when I fell.

I giggle.

He snuffles and picks his head back up so he can see me. Wolves can't smile, not really, but it sure seems like it, with his golden eyes dancing.

"Hi," I say, softly, and try to push myself up without squishing his belly by accident.

He rumbles, lifts his head, and licks my face, chin to forehead. Right up, in, and over my nose.

"Oh, gross!" I roll off him, landing on my butt. He scrambles to his paws, backs off maybe three feet, and sits on his haunches. Was he always this huge?

I draw my knees to my chest, doing my best to cover myself with my mess of a gown. A strip hangs off where I stepped on it, and there's mud on the hem and grass stains everywhere.

Justus's wolf flops onto his belly, laying his chin on the ground and gazing up at me with his golden eyes. Did they always glow like that?

His tail thwaps the tall grass behind him. I startle. He drops his tail with a whump.

I watch him. He watches me.

He slowly folds his ears back until they are flush against his head. He looks almost like a pup. A gargantuan, razor-clawed, sharp-fanged, oversized pup.

Very, very slowly, he raises his right ear. Just his right ear.

What does he hear? There's a mouse rustling in the underbrush and a bullfrog croaking over in the woods, but otherwise, there's nothing but the wind and our breath.

I frown.

He slowly lowers his right ear and lifts his left.

What is he doing now?

Even more slowly, he lowers his right ear and simultaneously lifts his tail straight up in the air like a handle.

He's kidding around. I've lost my mind, run a mile in a bedsheet, and now I'm sitting in the dirt, and this wolf is joking with me. Oh, and lest I forget, I'm in heat. Explains why the other females today were enjoying their hot cups of tea by the fire while I was desperate for a breeze.

I can't do this again.

My panic rises, and Justus's wolf whines. He drops both tail and ears and wriggles forward on his belly, his furry rump working side to side.

I stretch my legs straight, my shoulders slumping. He's not going to hurt me. He's a sweet wolf. *Justus* is sweet.

I'm the problem.

Justus's wolf sidles up and plops his head on my thigh. He stares up at my face, the angle making it look like he's giving me a rueful smile.

"I wish I wasn't like this," I tell him, my eyes prickling with tears.

An owl screeches in the distance, and I glance away. In that split second, the wolf disappears, and Justus is there instead, sitting cross-legged beside me, knees up for modesty.

I hang my head, my cheeks heating. I was talking to the wolf. I didn't mean to say that to *him*.

"I don't wish you were any different," he says, gruff and gentle.

I sniff. "You can't possibly feel that way. *I* don't."

He shrugs. "We see things differently."

That's his story now. "'Pathetic coward,' remember?" I spit at him. "'A female like you would make weak, spindly young.'"

I don't want to be bitter like this, not anymore. I know I'm throwing his words from years ago in his face, and he's apologized, and I believe he meant it. I don't want to make him feel sorry again. I just want him to be honest.

His head bows forward, his long hair falling in his face. My stomach knots. I don't want to hurt him. I don't want to hurt *me*, either, but I've got a multi-tool in my brain, and it's all knives, and every edge is serrated.

His bare chest rises, and he lifts his head back up, skewering me with his gaze, shining gold in the dark. "Something happened to you," he says.

My lower lip trembles. I don't have to answer. He's not asking.

"You survived." He takes a deep breath, and his nostrils flare. "I hadn't found you yet, and I wasn't there to protect you, and you survived. Then I found you, and like an idiot, I walked away, and you kept surviving. Our young will be tough as hell. They'll be so, so strong." His deep voice is too ragged to be bullshit.

I mash my lips together to stop the trembling, but all that does is make my chin wobble.

"And they'll be fast as hell on two feet," he says, his lips quirking, coaxing me, inviting me to believe his fairy tale where the tiny thumb-sized female ends up riding a sparrow to her prince rather than being eaten by any one of the monstrous goldfish or butterflies that stalk her like dinner.

We can *run.*

The pecking voice sidetracks me for a second. For once, it's not an order or a warning. Is it *bragging* on us? Is it *agreeing* with someone? A male?

I give my head a shake to clear it and then look around to distract myself from the need to answer him. When I fell, we left the trail and landed in the wildflowers. The air around us is sweet from the stalks we crushed, the night air punctuated with honey from the goldenrod, vanilla from the milkweed, and carrot from the Queen Anne's Lace.

Justus sits alongside me, facing south while I face the opposite direction. We're surrounded by tall grass and new spring blooms, blue and purple in the dark. Even this close, butt naked and sitting cross-legged, he's clearly a dangerous dominant male who smells like alpha no matter what he says, with wild hair and tattoos, fearless and assured—in the middle of a bunch of buttercups and bluebells.

He gazes patiently at my profile, waiting for me to say something.

"You were following me," I say. "You could have caught me at any time."

"I wasn't trying to catch you. I was following you wherever you were going. I'd follow you anywhere."

Is he sweet-talking me? Males don't talk to me like that, but I've overheard Tye with Kennedy, and Ivo with about every unmated female in the pack.

I scrunch my toes in the dewy grass and clutch my gown tighter to my chest, balling the fabric right above my heart. "You *say* that."

After we mated by the river, he bolted like his tail was on fire and stayed gone for years. Although that's not what Diantha said. She said he came back to Quarry Pack to check on me. The thought calms my heart.

Justus reaches to his side and picks a panicle of aster from its peduncle. The only reason I know the scientific terms is because when we were pups, Abertha would call us things like *panicle* and *peduncle* and *bugbane* and *warty goblet*. I thought they were weird witchy nicknames. I didn't realize until I was older that they were real words for plant parts.

Why am I thinking about that now? When Justus is reaching over and offering me the aster?

While moonlight is falling on his face, illuminating his expression like a spotlight on a dark stage, and the bond shimmers and flows between us?

He *wants*, he *hopes*, but he can't let on, and he doesn't— not by the cast of his jaw or set of his mouth or even by the look in his eyes. He has to be above desire like a monk. The stakes are too high to put any skin in this game at all.

I know how that feels.

His longing and mine both thump in my chest, off rhythm, a staccato beat that feels familiar and new and scary and right. I splay my palm flat on the hot skin above the gown.

"Can you feel me there?" he asks.

I nod.

"I feel you, too." He fists his empty hand and presses it to his chest.

"What's it like?" I ask.

He takes a breath. Swallows. Lowers his hands to rest on his knees. "Like I'm not alone," he finally says, eyes lowered, shoulders braced, muscles tensed.

Defenseless.

I don't want to leave him alone, but I *can't* change. Fate knows I've tried, but I can't—not the past or the voice or who I am. But I don't have to, do I? He's not asking me to fix myself. He's just offering me a flower.

The aster is dangling from his hand like an afterthought. Like I've left him with it.

How can I leave him like that? When he's mine? When all I need to do is reach out my hand?

I get a good grip on the gown with one hand, and careful not to move too quickly—he's a big male, after all—I reach over and pluck the aster from his fingers.

He glances over, surprised.

I tuck my knees closer to my chest, trying to hide from a sudden feeling of exposure.

A smile like a sunrise breaks across his face.

I delicately sniff the flower because that's what you're supposed to do. "Thank you," I say and smile politely.

"You like that one?" he asks, his whole manner changing, his shoulders relaxing, the furry tips of his pointed wolfish ears perking up.

"I do. I like asters."

He reaches into tall grasses around us, plucks another flower, and offers it to me, grinning. "How about this one?"

"Queen Anne's Lace."

"That's what it's called?" he asks as I take it.

I nod. "Sometimes you'll hear folks call it wild carrot." That's the name I learned from Abertha. Queen Anne's Lace is what the humans in Chapel Bell call it, but I think the name is prettier.

"You can eat it?"

"There's a little root, and you can, technically, I guess, but I wouldn't."

"Why not?"

"Looks too much like poison hemlock, and it doesn't taste good enough to risk the mistake."

He growls low and says, "All right. Give that back here." He takes the Queen Anne's Lace, tosses it into the field, and picks me a new flower. "What's this one?"

I take the delicate stem that he nearly crushed to a pulp when plucking it. "That's Blue-Eyed Mary."

"Can it kill you?"

I giggle. "No, it's just pretty to look at." I pair it with the aster. The blue and purple complement each other well.

"That makes two of you," he says and holds another flower, a snow trillium, under my nose.

I roll my eyes and take the white bloom with the yellow in the middle. "You're as silly as your wolf, aren't you?"

"He's much worse. He has absolutely no dignity when it comes to you."

He picks and passes me a bluebell and another aster. I

arrange my little bouquet and blush. My skin is hot, the night air is cool, and the heat from Justus's body warms my left side.

"I like him," I say softly without looking up from my flowers.

"He likes you, too." Justus's voice is tinged with wolf.

I glance over. He's already looking at me. Our eyes catch.

I feel so small beside him, but not in an intimidated way. More like how it feels to curl up with a book and my lunch at the base of the huge red oak that grows by the greenhouse at Abertha's cottage.

A wave of mellow warmth washes from my head to my toes. My lower belly twists. This is really happening. I'm going into heat again.

Like he senses my panic gathering, Justus leans over and presses our temples together. I close my eyes and breathe him in.

"I'm scared," I whisper.

"Me, too," he says.

I draw back so I can see his eyes again. "What are you scared of?" It's not a challenge; it's a serious question.

His face darkens, but he doesn't look away. "I can't do it—I can't make you hate me again."

"I didn't hate you," I say. "Neither of us had a choice. I knew that."

"I would never have chosen *that*," he says. The pain and shame, the *damage*, in his voice are jagged claws, and they snag my heart and slice me open. I wouldn't have, either. I wish I could have saved us both.

"What do we do?" I ask.

He's quiet for a moment, wrapping his arms around his knees and staring into the distance. His bicep brushes my upper arm. Some kind of gravity urges me to lean into him, but I don't dare.

Eventually, he clears his throat and meets my eyes again. "When we scout, we go in pairs," he says. "We could do that. We could be scouts together."

I understand what he's saying. If we're going to do this—and we *have* to do this—it can't be like before. There can't be a bad guy. So we'll be in it together. "Okay. How do scouts work?"

Some tension leaves his body. "Well, usually, one of us keeps an eye out for threats while the other looks for signs of prey."

"Dibs on being the one who keeps an eye out for danger," I say.

He smiles. The tightness in my chest lightens. I made a joke, and he got it. This is good.

"Good. I'm really good at tracking."

"Elspeth told me."

"She did?"

"She said when you were little, and Max was teaching the pups to hunt, he had to put out a decoy trail for you so you'd leave some animals for the others."

He smiles, bashful but clearly pleased. "I wasn't that good. I was just a bad listener. Max probably figured I'd learn better on my own and out of his hair."

His arms loop loosely around his knees now as the atmosphere has eased. He is so unlike Quarry Pack males. They take compliments as their due—or at least they act that way. Modesty is weakness.

And no Quarry Pack would sit beside a female in a field of wildflowers, not unless he was about to mount her.

My face catches fire, and I catch a whiff of my slick in the air. I immediately clamp my thighs together, my gaze darting over to Justus to see if he noticed.

He is very obviously pretending that he didn't. His pupils are blown, the gold only a thin ring, and his muscles strain again, his cheekbones coloring. He makes a great show of sifting through the tall grasses at his side, humming under his breath.

"Here's a good one," he says, plucks a geranium, and passes it to me. "See, I'm a good tracker. You don't have that one yet."

"It's a wild geranium."

"Yes, he was. Very wild. He was a very wily foe. Don't expect me to bag you one of those every day, now."

"I'll keep my expectations low." I struggle against a smile.

He leans over, plucks another, and gives it to me. "Not too low," he says.

I stop fighting and grin at him. His mouth curves, mirroring mine. "Okay, mighty hunter," I say.

"Now we're in accord," he says, rising to his feet, brushing bits of grass off his hairy, bare thighs. I quickly avert my eyes.

"Ready to go back to camp, Scout?" he asks, low and gentle. "We don't have to decide anything tonight. It'll keep for tomorrow."

I guess it will. I clutch my bouquet in one hand, hold my gown closed with the other, and let Justus help me up by the elbow.

"Okay," I say.

I let my mate lead me back to his den, and I am bad at my job because the entire way, despite the pecking voice's best efforts, I don't dwell on any dangers.

I hold my flowers, and I walk beside my mate in the moonlight.

I hardly sleep at all, and I'm up before the sun to get hot water for Annie's tea. I don't know how long we have, and time is nipping at my heels.

I wake her up by being as loud as I can when I come back from the bonfire, and despite her blurry eyes and grumpy face, I can't feel bad. I don't want to miss a second with her.

She grabs whatever is at hand to cover herself and ends up under a haphazard pile of yesterday's gown, a quilt, a thermal blanket, a pillow, and the sheet that she kicked off the pallet in her restless sleep. My den overflows with the scent of her approaching heat, so thick and delicious on my tongue, so heady.

I can't afford a fuzzy head. If this is all the time I get with her, I want to remember it all. And I need all my wits to convince her to stay, or at the very least, if nothing else, not to fuck up the mating like I did last time.

I wracked my brain all night for a strategy. Flowers seemed to work, so maybe Max and the other happily mated males are onto something. I don't want to leave her to rustle up chocolates and treats, though, and it just doesn't seem like enough.

How do you make a female fall in love with you? In one day, maybe two if you're lucky?

"Tea," I say, ducking and cautiously entering the den.

She rubs her eyes, frowning, and makes grabby hands. I smile and pass the tea. She still has the spark from last night. Good.

She sips and tries to raise herself to sit cross-legged, but the blankets are hopelessly tangled, and there's no way to sort it without spilling the tea. She glares down at the messy pile of blankets around her, her willowy arms raised, the mounds of her lovely breasts showing over the hem of an old patchwork quilt.

She looks like a princess from a picture book with one of those big, poofy dresses, but even better than that because her hair is a complete wild mess, and instead of sparkles and satin, she's surrounded by my things, saturated in my scent. She looks made for me.

She *was* made for me, so I must know somewhere deep down how to make this work. If I were a female, what would I want?

I am not going to think about Annie slipping her graceful fingers into her wet slit while she bites her bottom lip and whines my name. That's not helpful. I am going to stop picturing it now.

Right now.

Fuck.

I get up, turn my back, and rummage in the basket like I've got a sudden basket emergency.

What would I want? Well, I would want pants for a start. I couldn't stand walking around in a bedsheet.

I paw through the contents of the basket with renewed

purpose. I have a pair of pants with a drawstring that'll do for her, and a thin sweater I wear when it's too cold to go shirtless but not cold enough to go full fur. It'll hang off her, but it smells like me. Maybe she won't mind.

I noticed how she has the blankets piled close to her nose so she can tuck her head and take a good whiff of my scent. I'm doing the same, but since her scent is so thick in the air, I'm pretty much breathing twice as fast, once for oxygen, once to soothe the need gnawing in my belly. It's not doing much for my clarity of thought. I root right past the pants I'm looking for twice before I grab them.

"You can wear these," I say, setting the sweater and pants on the edge of the pallet. "And then we can—"

We can what?

What do females like to do? Long baths in the stream with no one asking them for anything, talking with the other females, hell, I don't know—Lelia likes throwing knives with the males. Ashleen likes dancing and cards. Mabli likes propping her feet up and tippling from the flask of moonshine she keeps in her knitting bag.

None of this works for courting. What do I like to do? My mind is blank.

I like her. Annie. My pretty, perfect mate.

She gazes up at me with big brown eyes and delicately sips her tea, a knotted hunk of hair sticking up from the side of her head. I would love to do anything that this female would let me do.

"We'll do the rounds," I say. That's all I can think of. We'll do what I usually do.

Why is this so hard? It's Fate, right? And nature. I'm supposed to be born knowing how to woo this female.

Annie stares at me. She's set her tea down on the floor,

and she has the shirt in her hands. Oh. She wants me to leave so she can change.

"Right," I say, wiping my palms on my canvas pants. Well, I'm proving Plato wrong, moment by moment here. My soul has knowledge of jack shit, at least when it comes to females. "I'll go."

Her scent sours.

"Not far. Just outside. I'll be right there." I drag a hand through my hair, and then, after a few more excruciating seconds, my feet take pity on me and walk our ass out of the den.

I stride over to the ledge and survey the camp below, hands on my hips, pretending that I have some dignity left. Folks are slow to rise today. They usually are after a successful hunt.

I see little Leon has beat his dam awake. He's snuck from her den and toddled all the way down to the clearing and across camp to the bonfire where he's begging bread from Rodric. When Annie comes out, we'd best stop there first and take him back before Delphie wakes up, misses him, and panics.

Just as I make the plan, Annie clears her throat behind me. I spin, overeager, my heart catching in my throat. In the daylight, she's twice as lovely. My faded gray sweater swims on her, and the pants bag around her legs like potato sacks. She tamed her hair and tied it back with what looks like a strip from yesterday's gown.

With her brown hair and eyes sparkling in the sunshine, she looks like a forest sprite. She clasps her hands and rocks on her small feet, bashful but enthralled, just like me. She takes me in, too. I can't help but straighten my shoulders while her gaze darts to my chest and then slides down.

My cock swells, and her eyes snap back to mine. I smile

—very, very careful not to let it turn into a smirk—and say, "Ready?"

"Okay," she answers softly.

I gesture for her to go ahead of me down the switchback path. As we pass the dens, I call out a greeting if I hear rustling within and tread lightly if it's quiet. When we pass Delphie's, I hear her stirring, so I call in to her that Leon is down at the fire with Rodric, and then I urge Annie to hurry on before Delphie can pop her head out, and I catch the scolding meant for Leon.

On a normal day after a hunt, I'd check on the butchering first, so when we get to the clearing, I grab Annie's hand and lead her toward the smoke shack. She lets me keep hold of it as we walk. My heart soars. I am very careful not to strut or grin like an idiot. If I act like this is an everyday thing, maybe Annie will see how it could be.

When we get to the smoke shack, Tarquin greets me, ducking his head at Annie. She blushes and shrinks closer to me, but she does say good morning and gives him a shy smile.

The elk has been skinned and sectioned, and the shank, shoulder, ribs, and brisket are already smoking. Tarquin has Elis slicing the top and bottom rounds for jerky.

"How is it going?" I ask Elis, not expecting a response. Like usual, he startles when I speak, even though he's been watching me this whole time. I act like I didn't notice. That's how we handle his twitchiness.

Annie picks up on it, though. She frowns, her hand tightening on mine.

Shit. Does she think he's afraid of me? That I've given him a reason? Or does she see me ignore his distress and remember how I didn't credit hers?

Mates are a fucking landmine.

Maybe it doesn't need to be that dire. I'm the dominant male here, Elis is scared, and despite her own fears, Annie has a strong protective instinct. She showed that when she leapt on little Efa's wolf to save the pup from Alroy when he snarled like a bitch because Diantha got the best of him again. Annie's wolf was defending the pup while she waited for me to handle shit.

I can do that. Handle shit is more or less what I do all day, every day.

I let Annie's hand go, and padding forward very slowly, I approach Elis where he sits on a bench at the table we use for processing. His fear scent bursts into the air, strong enough to cut through the smell of smoking elk.

"What are we doing this time—garlic or honey glazed?" I ask, crouching beside him so I'm lower than his eyeline when he answers me.

He clears his throat. "Just a pepper rub on these."

My stomach growls, totally unintended. Elis grins, his shoulders dropping a notch away from his ears.

"I get dibs, right?" I ask.

"Sure thing, Alpha," he says, flashing me a faint smile. That's better, but it's not quite right.

My wolf pushes forward, and I follow my instinct and let him out, fully expecting him to scarf down a few of the elk strips piled on the cutting board.

Instead, he kicks his hindlegs free of our pants and proceeds to headbutt Elis in the armpit.

"Wha—?" Elis tenses, preparing to lose it, but before he can, my wolf props his paws on Elis's shoulders and marks his face with such enthusiasm that Elis gets both a mouth and nose full of fur.

My wolf rumbles, and I can almost scent Elis's remaining tension seep away. My wolf laps his face, and Elis chuckles, a deep, rusty creaking sound. Until I hear it, I don't realize just how long it's been missing from camp.

It makes sense in a horrible way. If the world is out to get you, best to be invisible, quiet and small. That's how my Annie was living, wasn't it?

I can't let her go back to that.

And I can't stop her. I swore.

A rock lodges in my chest, and at that same moment, my wolf realizes Elis's hands are covered in elk juice.

Apparently, that's the line, because Elis leaps to his feet and throws his hands in the air to escape my wolf's tongue, groaning through a belly laugh. Tarquin and the others crack up. My wolf takes advantage of the confusion to snarf up a few elk strips, gets a snoot full of pepper, and sneezes for a half minute straight.

My job is done here.

I shift back, find my pants, and pull them back on. Thankfully, my wolf didn't rend the seams like he usually does in his struggle to free himself.

"Shall we get breakfast?" I ask Annie, holding out my hand.

She takes it like she's been doing it for years. That has to be a good sign.

"Didn't you just eat yours?" she asks.

"My man stomach is still empty."

"Your wolf and your man have different stomachs?" She raises an eyebrow, meeting my eye without hesitation. It's gentle and teasing, but she's still challenging me. That's very good.

"Absolutely. Wolf stomach, man stomach, and dessert stomach. Don't you have three?"

She giggles softly, and my heart beats double time.

"We were always taught the wolf and the man are one," she says.

I snort. That's some lost packs bullshit. It's how they brainwash their people. If you can convince someone to believe things that are obviously untrue to anyone with eyes or a brain, you own them. Reality is what you say it is.

"Oh yeah?" I say. I'm not about to get into an argument with my mate over it, though, not while she's smiling and smelling sweet.

Annie is quiet for a while as we make our way toward the long tables by the bonfire.

When we pass the sycamore, she says out of nowhere, "My wolf isn't afraid of you."

I blink, surprised she's still on the topic. "No, she isn't," I agree.

Even when we mated, her wolf wasn't scared. She wanted to tear my throat out. She wasn't actually frightened until she got herself trapped between me and the river.

"But *I* was scared."

I keep my eyes ahead so she doesn't see the hurt, but then one of her words snags my brain. *Was.* As in not anymore? I school my face so she doesn't see the flash of hope. Now isn't the time. She's working something out in her head.

"My wolf always howled at me to run and hide," she says. Her forehead wrinkles, and her pace slows. I slow mine to match. "But I don't think *she* was scared. I think she was scared for *me*."

I nod. It makes sense. Even a small wolf can defend itself better than a young female. Considering how long it takes Annie to shift, she'd need a decent head start to give her wolf any chance of shifting in time to launch a defense against a predator.

She falls silent, deep in thought, and stays that way until we get to the bonfire. I seat her at a family table next to Nessa and her pups and then go to fetch our plates and a cup of tea. Redmond has made a hash of potato, apple chunks, and onion. I heap two plates high and score two rounds of bannock hot from the skillet.

When I return, Efa is standing on Annie's lap, playing with her hair. Annie's face is pink, and despite the cool morning, her upper lip is beaded with sweat. Her brown eyes have a feverish shine. I don't think we have days before her heat takes over. More like hours.

Dread clutches my chest as adrenaline sends a rush of blood through my veins. My wolf howls at me to take her away from these other males. I breathe through it, willing my muscles to relax. She's still in her right mind. We're going to keep calm as long as we can.

I set our plates down and slide onto the bench beside her. Efa gives me a big smile that's mostly gums except for her new baby canines. She looks like a little vampire.

"Affa!" she shrieks.

"I'm not Efa," I tease her. "You're Efa." I tickle her snout with my beard, and she lets out a peal of delight.

"Affa!"

"Apple? Is that what you said?" I pierce the softest piece of apple with my fork and offer it to her.

"No!" she giggles. "Affa!"

"Okay." I shrug. "No apple." I pop the bite into my mouth. She laughs like I'm the most hilarious, outrageous male on the planet and tries to pry my lips open to get the apple back. I glance over her mussed head of fur to see if my mate thinks I'm funny, too.

Annie's mouth quirks, and if I'm not mistaken, her eyes shine even brighter. She is the prettiest female I've ever seen. Now that I've watched her up close without the rut hormones of a young male messing up my mind, I see she isn't like the little fairy in the children's book at all. She's more like a wood nymph with her beautiful brown hair and willowy neck and delicate fingers, like Daphne from the book of Greek myths I inherited from my dam. She turned herself into a tree to escape her mate.

In the story, he got to stay near her and wear her leaves as a crown. I'm going to have to return my mate to her people. Never see her or our possible pup again, except from a distance. How can I? What power could force my legs to walk away from her now?

But how could I keep her here with me, make her miserable, destroy the trust she has in me now? Break my solemn word, again, when I don't have the excuse of being young to temper my shame?

My gut aches. Annie's smile falls as she senses my pain.

Will it hurt her when I leave her with her pack and tear my own heart from my chest?

I can't let her hurt. Her people would never accept me, not after we tried to kidnap their alpha's mate. And I couldn't abandon my people. How would I live with that shame, either?

Worry fills Annie's eyes as she scans my face, trying to figure out what's bothering me, and probably whether she's safe. I need to stop. Focus. I flash her a reassuring smile.

These are tomorrow's problems, after all. Tomorrow's grief. She is here beside me now. In this moment, I have all I need.

I spear another apple bite.

"Bite of Affa?" I say, offering the chunk to Annie, intentionally passing the fork near Efa's mouth. Her snout goes full wolf, and she snaps the apple off the tines, scarfing it down with a very self-satisfied smacking of her lips.

Annie laughs, low and sweet, and my muscles swell, whether from pride or the excitement she stirs in my belly, I can't tell.

"That was one for you. This one is for Annie," I warn Efa. I do a little defensive maneuvering as I offer my mate the next bite. It makes it to Annie's mouth, but it's a close thing.

"Me now!" Efa demands, but when I offer her the next chunk, she pinches it off the fork, and with no warning, tries to feed it to Annie by ramming it through her closed lips. Annie's head jerks back, her fingers flying to her face. I tense.

Annie recovers almost immediately. "Oh, delicious," she mumbles as she collects mashed apple from her chin and shovels it into her mouth. "Thank you for sharing with me, Efa."

Efa, pleased with herself, reaches down, grabs another handful of hash from my plate, and is halfway to smashing it into Annie's mouth when I catch her by the forearm. "Whoa, sweetling. Too much of a good thing."

Efa, quick on the pivot, twists her little arm like a snake and crams the fistful of food into her own maw.

"Oh, Efa, no," Nessa sighs, noticing what her littlest is doing. She's got her other two sitting nicely beside her with handkerchiefs tied around their necks as bibs. They're scooping up their breakfast with their own spoons, delivering most bites with an admirable deal of accuracy, and here we've got her youngest, standing half on Annie's lap and half on mine like she's driving a chariot with chunks of hash in her hair and potato smeared on her face and under her nails.

I am not bad with pups, but I usually work with the older ones, teaching them to track and hunt. I'm not useless with a baby, though. I don't want Annie to think I'm inept.

"No worries, Nessa. We'll get her cleaned up," I offer. The moment the words escape my lips and the eyes of every dam at the table light up, I know I've made a mistake.

"Oh, thanks, Alpha." Nessa widens her eyes at me and blinks. "Little Bowen and Maeve could use a washing, too, if you're going down to the stream."

Her other two pups immediately clamber down from the bench, breakfast forgotten, their wolves yapping.

"If you're heading down to the stream, could you take Noctiluna, too?" a female calls from the end of the table.

What have I done?

"Leon, finish your food. Alpha is taking you all to the stream," Delphie says to her little one.

"Auggie, clear your place," Lilliwen tells her youngest. "Don't make Alpha wait for you."

By the time we leave, I've managed to get us saddled with seven little ones. Annie doesn't seem to mind the company. Efa insists on holding one of her hands, and Auggie wins the tussle to hold the other.

The other pups shift to their fur, leaving their drawers and dresses behind for their dams to pick up. They trot along with us, weaving around Annie's legs, brushing her calves and generally doing their best to trip her. I keep a hand on her elbow.

"Is this too much?" I ask her quietly as we make our way down the grassy slope to the stream bank.

She shakes her head. "It'll be nice to wade. Is the water cool?"

I nod. "It comes down from the peaks past Salt Mountain. This time of year, it's mostly snow melt."

She lets out a soft, longing sigh. The sound twists my belly tight. Her demeanor is definitely changing, even since last night. She's less guarded, more distracted. She was like this last time, too, toward the end. Back then, I thought she'd accepted that we were mates, but she'd resigned herself.

A surge of acid burns my throat. I can't do it again—not knowing that she doesn't really want it.

But I'll have to. I could never leave her to suffer alone.

My wolf rattles my chest. He wants out to fight off the threat to his mate. He doesn't understand. Maybe that's a blessing.

The pups squint at me and scrunch their snouts, wondering what my wolf is rumbling about. The more skittish ones trot away from me warily. They scent my distress. Annie must as well. I have to hold it together. The world isn't ending yet. We're going for a swim.

When we get to the stream, I dart behind a thick blackberry bush to shuck my pants. I toss them onto the brambles and shift. My wolf takes a second to sniff the air, reassuring himself that whatever upset me wasn't a real threat like a feral or a rabid, natural wolf. Then he takes another second to munch a few of the unripe berries before concluding that they are, indeed, unripe before bounding back around the bush.

He rumbles low in his throat to herd the pups toward the stream. The males race full tilt into the freezing water and then yowl and shiver dramatically, affronted by the cold. The females hesitate at the edge, gingerly dipping their paws into the water and yipping among each other.

The pups can all swim, but they're still small, reckless, and rambunctious. Auggie, who's made of more daring than muscle, makes an instant break for it, sailing the current almost past the sharp bend downstream before my wolf can bound through the water to fetch him back. Meanwhile, back by shore, Bowen slips on a slick stone and stages a dramatic slow-motion drowning in the five-inch shallows like a turtle stuck on his back.

Annie bends over and rightens Bowen, her top getting soaked in the process. The thin fabric molds itself to her body—the flat of her belly and flare of her hips. I force my wolf's gaze away, and good thing I do, because Leon is stealthily floating past like a log, trying to get past me. My wolf plucks him out of the water by the scruff of his neck and carries him back to the wide, deep spot by the willow where most of the pups are still gathered.

My wolf chases the males back onto the bank, herding them until they're huddled in a pile of unchastened, wet, wiggly fur. My wolf plants his paws in the stream, lifts his head, and howls. Every single pup freezes, ducks his head, and peers up at me with big, round, innocent eyes.

Annie freezes, too. Shit. I've frightened her. My wolf snaps his jaw shut. She scans the shore quickly left and right. Is she going to run?

My wolf and I hold our breath.

She steps forward on frozen legs, like how the female pups walk the little rubber dolls with big tits that Alroy brought back from a trading trip to the human village. Her fear is etched on her face, but she keeps coming, placing herself in front of the pup puddle.

She stares down my wolf, her neck stiff, her hands shaking. She's protecting them from me, defending them with her body.

PRIDE SWELLS MY HEART. There she is. There's my mate.

My wolf plops his butt right down in the cold current, landing right on the pokey edge of an underwater rock. He swallows his yelp and tucks his ears down.

Annie curls her trembling fingers into fists, her chest rising as she draws in a long breath. The fear recedes from her eyes as she realizes there is no real threat.

She clears her throat, turns to face the pups, and says in an impressively even voice, "No floating past that bunch of blue flowers there, okay?"

The pups blink up at her in unison. My wolf lumbers back to his feet, flicking water from his ears as they pop back up.

"You bigger pups pick a little partner. If your partner falls over, you have to help him up, okay?"

I can say with confidence that none of the pups—except for maybe Leon, who is wickedly advanced for his age—understands her. Little ones, when they're in their fur, are all animal instinct. They recognize her authority, though. After all, my wolf submitted to her.

"Do you understand?" she asks them.

Efa's wolf yips, scampers over, and leaps up on Annie's legs. Annie takes that as agreement. "All right, then," she says to the others. "You can go back in, but don't go past the lobelia."

The pups burst back into action, the females racing rings around Annie's ankles, yapping for her attention, while the rest bound into the stream, splashing and paddling their way toward my wolf.

I sigh. I knew this was coming. At least it's my wolf's dignity at stake here, not mine.

For the next hour, the pups swarm my wolf like he's the sycamore tree. They climb his flanks, playing king of the mountain and wrestling each other for a seat on his back.

When they've got a quorum, they howl until my wolf obliges and paddles in circles like their very own boat.

Of course, when the pups least expect it, my wolf rolls or dives under, and they all tumble off his back and into the water, yowling with delight and then whining at him to let them do it all again.

The females stick close to Annie, longingly watching us from the bank as we play. Our females aren't wary of males or averse to roughhousing, but they're loyal like their dams, and Annie isn't joining in the fun, so they're going to stay with her.

Annie's gaze darts from pup to pup to pup like she's keeping a constant count of them. She's standing guard. I understand. Don't I do the same all day as I wander the camp and our territory, making sure that all the elders have made their way to their usual spots, that yesterday's scouts have returned and today's have left, that no tripwires have been tripped, no signal stones have been knocked over?

You can't keep watch every minute. Your eyes get blurry and your brain dulls. I won't nag Annie into joining us, though. No one could stop me from my rounds.

Efa's wolf is the bold one who tires first of the status quo. She bites Annie's pants and tugs with all her strength toward the stream, and Annie finally realizes there's a posse of female pups waiting for her to get wet.

"Oh, you want to swim with me?" she says, and the female pups bay in a chorus of sweet, high-pitched, slightly aggrieved howls. Annie chuckles. "All right then."

She bends over and rolls her cuffs to her knees. The females zig and zag around her legs as she makes her way to the edge. My wolf immediately shakes himself free of pups and bounds over to meet her, splashing through the water, soaking her in a wave of spray when he skids to a halt.

She laughs like chimes. He slaps the water with his happy tail.

"Hi," she says softly.

He watches her take one tentative step and then another into the stream. When the water is mid-calf, she exhales and says, "Oh, it's so cool. That's so nice."

The female pups step daintily into the water beside her. Their decorum lasts a solid ten seconds before one of the males—Auggie, I think—bowls into Noctiluna as he chases a tadpole, and the other females set after him for revenge like born huntresses. Efa's wolf is the only one who stays with Annie, imitating my mate's watchful supervision of the scene.

Annie will be a wonderful dam.

My wolf is captivated. He stalks over to her, careful to move slowly, and kneels with his forelegs to offer his back.

She laughs. "Oh, no. I'm too big for a ride."

She's wrong. My wolf is huge. I crouch as low as I can.

"I couldn't," she says, but the pups have taken notice, and they think it's a brilliant idea. They swarm her, yapping, nudging her forward.

My wolf growls a sharp warning, and they give her a little space, but they still splash and yip and yowl and whine, a frenzy of wet fur, slapping tails, and cold, black noses.

My softhearted mate gives in, flushing even pinker as she mutters, "I can't believe I'm doing this."

She clutches the fur at my shoulders, throws her top half across my back, and swings her leg over my flank until she's riding my wolf like a horse. Her toes dangle below the stream's surface, but I was right—there's plenty of room between her feet and the stream bed.

My wolf strides away from the bank, the pups cavorting alongside us, more excited than I've ever seen them.

Annie's nails dig into my thick hide, her knees gripping my sides like a vise, but she doesn't smell like fear. Her fresh rain smell mixes with wet fur, cold stream, and sunshine. It's the kind of scent that somehow makes you remember a time before you were born.

My wolf cranes his head to look back at her and accidentally breaks her grip on his scruff, so she loops her arms around his neck and scoots so she can lie flat on her stomach.

Triumph, pride, and anticipation ignite my wolf's blood. Our mate trusts us. He stalks further into the stream until he can float and paddle lazily in circles. One by one, the pups lose interest, and we lose our escort as they venture off to chase dragonflies and harass crawfish.

Annie's breasts and belly press against my wolf's back with every breath she draws. We're a pack of two. Gradually, she relaxes. She lowers her cheek to rest on his shoulder and trails her fingers in the water, sighing. Her heat radiates through my wolf's fur. He splashes her legs gently with his tail to cool her off.

We float around and around while the sun rises higher. In the distance, a hammer rings out. Voices carry from a gathering of males nearby planning a scouting run. Over by the curing hut, a ribbon of musky smoke curls into the blue sky. Annie rests her chin on the folded arms she's propped on my shoulders. If I twist my ears in the right direction, her breath bathes their ragged edges and rustles the white fur inside.

This is happiness. And peace. It's a soap bubble, lighter than air and rainbow bright.

She idly kicks her feet in the water by my haunches. Her

toes brush my hind paws. I wish we could float here in circles forever.

But already, time is moving on. It's well past midmorning. The females would leave me to watch their young all day, but their males won't dare leave me saddled with their pups for too long. My wolf's nose twitches, and he lifts his head, narrowing his eyes at the males scrambling toward us down the slope. Murtagh, Redmond, and Griff come to stand at the edge.

"The pups clean yet, Alpha, or do you need another hour or so?" Redmond calls, grinning.

My wolf snorts.

Murtagh whistles at his pups to come. They immediately dive into the current, so they can pretend they didn't hear him. My wolf grumbles. It's easier to catch a bird with human hands than a pup when it's time to get out of the water.

Annie is rousing herself to sit up, but her movements are languid and awkward. My wolf paddles to the shore and lowers himself to his belly so she can climb down safely. She still stumbles before she finds her footing. Her heat is coming on quickly now. I need to get her to the den.

I leave her for a second to shift and snag my pants before one of the males sees them and tosses them into the stream.

"Sit and rest," I tell her when I come back. She's trying to coax the pups out of the water, standing at the edge on wobbly legs. Her face is rosy red.

She isn't behaving like other females entering their heat. She isn't shooting me sidelong glances, and her wolf is silent in her chest. She sure as hell isn't grabbing my hand and dragging me away like Elspeth has been known to do with Max.

She's not running from me, though, and she doesn't

smell like fear. In fact, she ignored my order to sit and waded back into the water to scoop out a wriggling, splashing Auggie. She tucks him in the crook of her arm and whispers in his ear. His tail starts wagging, and he licks her cheek. She smiles and hands him over to Murtagh.

"What did you say to him?" I ask her.

"To be good, and we'll play later."

I want that. With every fiber of my being. I want to take my mate to our den. I want us to lose ourselves in each other, and in a day or two or three, when her heat breaks, I want to walk my rounds with her, feed her breakfast, play with the pups, and then watch her while I work, counting the hours until I can take her to our den again.

I want to do it every day while her belly grows round with our young, until the pup we play with is our own, until we're too old to work and walk, and we spend our days instead together by the fire, talking for hours about nothing, happy because we're not alone and never will be again, not in this life, not in the next.

And I promised her that I'd take her home.

I swore.

The males lead the pups back toward the sycamore, and when the last straggler is gone, I offer Annie my hand. She takes it.

"Should we go to the den?" I ask.

She glances down, her cheeks flaming.

"Okay," she says. Her voice trembles, but her steps are sure as we climb the grassy slope.

It feels like everything I've ever wanted.

It feels like the end of the world.

14

ANNIE

It doesn't feel exactly like last time. I'm hot. My clothes, my skin, the breeze, the lack of breeze, the brightness of the light—all of it irritates the hell out of me, but this time, the pecking voice doesn't have much to say, and I'm not shivering.

Last time, I remember shaking so hard that my teeth chattered, but I feel more tipsy than feverish this time. How much of the shaking was heat, and how much was fear?

I'm not afraid now. Nervous, yes. Trying desperately not to think about what happens next, absolutely—but I'm not scared.

This is Justus. He leads me through camp toward the dens, as confident and unhurried as always, with a measured word for anyone who speaks to him. His palm is as sweaty as mine, though.

It's strange. Justus is nothing like Killian, but he's every bit an alpha, albeit in his own way. At both Quarry Pack and here, males straighten when their alpha walks past, but at Quarry Pack, males stiffen their spines, and here, the males puff their chests.

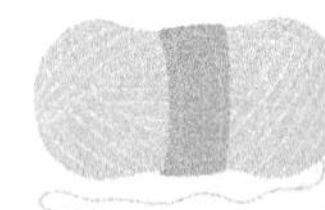

At Quarry Pack, until Una, unmated females would do anything for Killian's attention—tight tops, short skirts, dropping things and picking them up by folding over at the waist. Here, females are just as demanding, but they want Justus to taste their cooking or side with them in an argument or lift something heavy, and the males are just as likely to jockey for his attention.

I trust Killian not to hurt me, but I've never been comfortable around him, not even for a second. With Justus, I can forget for whole minutes at a time that he's a powerful male who could kill me in a single blow.

I am going to let this male mount me. It's going to happen. And it might be awkward and uncomfortable, but it'll be okay.

I clutch his hand tighter, and he glances at me, the corners of his mouth sneaking up. He's pleased that I'm clinging, but he doesn't want to let on. Another way he's different than the males back home. I've never known so strong a male to be so reserved. I like that about him.

I like everything about him. He's the most handsome male I've ever seen. I feel like his hair and beard are so wild to cut the sweetness of his deep brown eyes. The same with his build—his body is so hard to counteract the softness of his lips.

I want to kiss them.

Because I'm in heat, but also because I want to know what it would be like. How would he look at me afterward? I bet he'd be dazed.

I want him to be dazed.

Justus stops our progress at the bonfire to fetch a bucket of water, and Tarquin gives him a wrapped bundle that smells like smoked meat and dried fruit. Provisions for my heat.

If my face got any hotter, it would burst into flames. Tarquin knows. I scan the folks nearby. Everyone is deliberately going about their business, very careful not to look at us, except for when they dart curious, surreptitious glances our way. I catch Mabli's eye by accident, and she gives me a thumbs up.

She knows, too. They all do. I yank Justus's hand, tugging him toward the trail to the dens. He tries to smother a grin and fails. Does he think I'm impatient to mate? Oh, no. I whine, embarrassed and anxious, and my wolf chimes in with her own yip of complaint about his unimpressive lack of urgency.

That's it. I'm going to self-combust.

"Want to race to the den?" he asks me in a low, laughing voice.

"No!" I hiss.

"I'll give you a head start." He winks.

A wave of slick gushes from me. I'm not wearing underwear. Am I soaking my pants? Justus's light tan pants?

I drop Justus's hand, clamp my thighs together, and duck walk to the trailhead like my tail is on fire. Somehow reading my mind, he falls in behind me, blocking the packs' view of my wet butt as I scurry up to his den. Are they thinking I can't wait to get on all fours for him?

Why does all of this have to be so undignified?

I'm so flustered by the time we reach the top that I don't know what to do with myself. I lean against the cedar next to Justus's reading chair, gasping for breath and raising my hot face, desperate to catch a breeze. The sweet scent of resin and pine mixes with Justus's earthiness as he comes to stand beside me.

"You okay, Scout?" he asks.

I close my eyes and drop my head back. It thumps

against the trunk. My stomach swirls, and my heart pounds. My body is running away with me, and I've lost my hold on the reins.

Justus's wolf rumbles. The wolf has never let anything bad happen to me.

And the man? I was left hurt, but did he hurt me?

The past is there. It never goes away.

If I were brave enough, I would crack my memory open and call to mind a much younger Justus. A much, much younger me.

I'd recall how he tried to impress me—or reassure me— by bragging about the quilts he had at home, and his den, and the barrel he had for bathing. I open my eyes, searching for his. They're already on my face.

"The first time we mated, you said you'd bring me an elk."

He nods, clearly thrown that I'm bringing it up now, but willing to go along with me. I've never met a more patient male.

"I did," he says. "And I delivered, didn't I?" He flashes a grin, and it's wry, but there's pride in it still.

"You said you'd bring me a cow." The memories are tumbling out of their box now. Justus's hands stroking my ass. His fingers inside me. How careful he tried to be, and how futile that was.

"Did I? I still owe you then." He steps closer to me, reaching for my hands, placing them on his chest. It's rising and falling as fast as mine.

"You called me pretty."

His brown eyes crinkle, and he smiles, like I've told him something nice. "You have always been the most beautiful thing I've ever seen," he says.

I wasn't searching for compliments—I don't do that—

but he's given me one anyway, and I don't know what to do with it. It feels like I've got an egg cupped in my hands with no shelf or surface where I can put it down.

For lack of a better idea, I pass it back. "I think you're pretty, too," I say, flushing immediately.

Pretty? I couldn't have said—

He kisses me. Bends over, braces his hand on the trunk above my shoulder, and steals my breath.

His lips are firm and certain. The bond sparks to life.

He wants this, and he's not shy. He's not asking, he's *telling* me that we're doing this, and it'll be fine, better than fine. I'm beautiful in his eyes, and he's been waiting. He'd wait longer, but is that really what I want?

I should trust him.

I should trust *myself*—the evidence of my eyes, my experience. He is a good male. Safe. Such a thing does exist, and it's here, in my arms.

He tugs my lower lip with the very tips of his teeth. I gasp. His tongue slips inside my mouth, searching, coaxing. He wants me to seek him out, too, because even though he's bigger and stronger, he wants to belong to me. He wants me to slide my tongue past his lips. Past the points of his incisors.

He wants me to want him back so bad that I dare, so I do. He groans. His wolf rumbles. I melt. He cups my nape, stroking the pulse throbbing in my neck with his rough thumb. My knees wobble. My thighs tremble.

What are we doing out here?

I wrest my head away from his grasp and scan the sky. It's too wide open.

My wolf grumbles in agreement. There are too many smells out here, and despite our high vantage point, too much territory to defend.

"Come on," I tell Justus, striding for the den. I don't bother grabbing his hand. He'll follow.

I duck into the den and take a deep breath. This is exactly right. There is the apple crate of books, the rag rug that smells like pack, the pallet that will make a fine nest.

Nothing in here smells like a place where I've been afraid, and besides, I have a good, strong mate. He won't let anything get to me.

I go to the willow basket and unpack the sheets and blankets and clean but threadbare clothes that my mate has worn all these years when we were apart. Why was that again? I can't remember now. My brain isn't working right.

All of a sudden, my certainty flees. My eyes blur with tears.

"What's wrong, Annie?" Justus asks from the entranceway. He's lingering there, waiting to be invited, as he should.

"You left me. Where were you?" I face him, clutching a patchwork quilt to my chest.

His face falls, and he steps forward. My wolf snarls in my throat. He has not been invited. The nest is not ready.

He curls his hands into fists, and for a moment, he seems to fight himself, and I'm not sure who won, but his moment of inner turmoil ends when he falls to his knees. "Never too far away, Annie. At least not for long. I couldn't leave you. I always came back. You're here." He beats his chest once, twice.

My heart twists. I don't want him to hurt, and even though I don't remember how, exactly, I know it was my doing, too. Or it was the work of an evil neither of us were old nor wise enough to fight.

Yes, that's what happened. "We're safe now," I tell him.

"Yes," he softly agrees, sitting back on his heels. The

tension ebbs from his broad shoulders, his fierce jaw. "I won't hurt you. Nothing will hurt you."

Lies.

"Oh, stuff it," I snap at the voice, turning to my work. She's not needed right now.

I prop my hands on my hips and survey the pallet. It's all wrong. There's no help for it. I'll have to start fresh.

I sink to my knees, strip the bed, and pile the linens to the side. I saw a blanket that would make a good foundation, a fuzzy, soft one with a silky hem. I grab it from the stack and bury my nose in it. Yes, this is perfect.

I shake it out over the pallet, lay it flat, and tuck the corners under, humming to myself. Then comes the hard part. The arranging. I fold and fluff and fuss and change, and it's daunting, like a puzzle with no picture on the box for reference, but it's also deeply, deeply satisfying.

Everything is falling into place.

My mate watches me make our nest, fascinated and proud. His muscles twitch with anticipation, but he'll wait until I'm ready. This is how it's supposed to be. He guards me as I work. His strength and the wolf inside him are mine.

I'm not small and weak and alone. I'm a female, where I'm supposed to be, doing what I was made to do.

I punch a pillow and prop it in place. There. Done. I turn to Justus, smile, and reach out for him.

For a second, he stares at my hand, his brown eyes dark and wide. Poor male. I bend at the waist so I can snag his wrist and pull him to the nest. I know he's not rejecting me. He's just overcome. I understand.

I can hear his heartbeat in my ear. Our blood rushes along in our veins at the exact same speed.

My yank gets him moving, and he climbs into my nest

with the enthusiasm and grace of a moon-drunk wolf. He manages to undo everything.

My wolf growls, and a little too late, he notices there's a system of organization. He settles himself in the middle of the nest and gives me a rueful smile. "Sorry about that."

I shake my head. "Now I have to do it all over again. Stay there. Don't move."

He hangs his head, but he's still smiling as I replace pillows and rearrange sheets. It's much more difficult with a huge male plopped right in the middle.

Finally, after a few more tugs to make sure my tucks will hold, I sit back and sigh. Perfect again.

And then I see the pillow. Justus is holding it in his lap. It's supposed to be at the head of the pallet by the apple crate. I frown.

He grins.

He did it on purpose.

I growl.

His wolf growls back deeper, stirring a strange excitement deep inside me.

Unacceptable. I dart forward on my hands and knees to snatch the pillow back, but he holds on tight, and I tip forward and smack into him.

I jerk the pillow, but his grip is too tight. "It's not funny," I say.

He laughs low. "Say please."

My breasts are crushed against his hard chest, and our arms tangle in the narrow space between our bellies. Our legs are a jumble. I struggle for the pillow, but for some reason, my muscles are the kind of weak you get from laughing.

"Give it back," I pant.

He wrangles the hand holding the pillow free and raises

it high over his head. "What will you trade me for it?" he asks. His brown eyes sparkle.

I climb full on top of him, bracing one knee on each thigh, and rise up until we're face to face. My bare forearm presses against his as I strain to reach. My skin is soft against his hard muscle. Our wrists touch, pulse to pulse.

His pupils blow, and I can make out my reflection in the shine of the black.

"Ask me for it," he teases, smirking, testing me. He's not in charge here. This is *my* nest. I allow him here.

I let my hand fall and turn my head away.

He snarls. He doesn't like that.

I drop back so I'm sitting on the pallet, lift my chin, and fold my arms. His wolf rumbles unhappily. He shouldn't have let his man mess with my nest.

He dips his head and looks up at me from his lowered eyes, a wolf playing at a lamb. "I'm sorry, Annie. Here it is."

He holds the pillow out.

It's a trap.

Of course it's a trap. I reach for it anyway. As soon as I grab the pillow, he yanks and falls to his back, dragging me with him. I tumble on top of him. He quickly nips the pillow from my grasp, tucks it behind his head, and grins up at me.

I push up on his chest, struggling upright until I'm straddling his waist. He crosses his arms behind his head.

I lean forward and try to pull the pillow free, but his head is too heavy.

"Just ask nicely, Annie." There's a new note in his voice, a gravelly depth that has nothing to do with his wolf.

I prop myself on his folded biceps. They're hard and velvet and flexing under my palms. He's doing that on purpose.

I stare down into his face. He winks.

I curl my fingers around the bunched muscle. They're at least twice, maybe three times, too big for me to wrap my hands around. All of him is huge. My thighs are stretched to aching from sitting on top of him.

He could crush you.

But I'm on top, and he's lying so patiently underneath me, even as his cock throbs against the seam of my pants. He's huge there, too. And insistent.

I sit tall and gaze down at the smirk half-hidden by his beard and the need swirling in his dark eyes.

I squeeze my thighs together, just a bit. The need swirls brighter. My lips are curving now.

"Annie," he groans.

"Ask nicely," I whisper. I don't know where my boldness is coming from, but it somehow feels familiar, like this is who I am, too, underneath it all.

"Please, Annie." He cranes his neck to stare at where I'm straddling him.

"I don't know what to do," I whisper.

This time, when he groans, there is plenty of wolf in it. "Come here. Lie back down."

He takes my forearms and draws me forward. I lean over until we're nose to nose. My hair falls in his face. His palms smooth down my sides to rest at my waist.

"Does this feel good?" he asks as he flexes his hips.

I gasp. My eyelids drift closed as all my attention refocuses on the pressure and heat between my legs.

He does it again.

I whimper.

"It feels so good to me," he says quietly, his lips brushing mine as he speaks.

He pulses his hips, and every time, it feels better and better, until I feel my own hips rocking to meet his thrusts.

His grip on my waist tightens, his fingertips pressing into the swell of my bottom. My toes curl.

"Open your eyes," he whispers.

I don't hesitate to do what he asks. He knows what he's doing, and he's on my side. He wants this, too. I blink, meeting his smoldering gaze. He wants it as badly as I do.

I grind harder, but what I need is just out of reach. "What do I do?" I pant. If I were alone in my bedroom, I'd touch myself to get there, but he's here, and my brain is fuzzy as hell, but I'm not so far gone that I'd shove my hands down my pants with him watching.

"Trust me?" He's panting too.

"Yes," I gasp.

He slides a hand between us so he's cupping my butt with his thumb pressing right over my clit. The fabric dulls the sensation, but it's still exactly right. My gaze darts from his fingers to his face and back again while my lungs constrict and a knot coils tighter and tighter in my belly.

"Come now," he growls, and I shatter, throwing my head back, a wolfish howl ripped from my throat.

I'm bathed in the absolute best feeling on earth—better than a warm bath, an electric fan on sweaty skin on a summer night, a mixing bowl with lots of batter left to lick.

I gaze down at Justus in wonder. I've made myself come before, but that was nothing like this. This is magic.

"All right, Scout?" His eyes twinkle.

I smile. "Yes. All right."

He tugs me to his chest again and holds me close, stroking my spine as his wolf rumbles and my heat comes over me again as gently as a blanket.

I am so hot. Why am I still wearing clothes?

I wrestle free from Justus's hold, peel off my shift, and kick off my pants, toeing them out of the nest.

Yes. I can breathe better now. I stretch my arms over my head and roll out my shoulders.

Justus growls. He's on his knees, and his pants are gone. Good. I'm ready. It's time.

He strokes his thick cock as he stares at my breasts.

I cup them and squeeze as my nipples tighten. It aches so, so good.

"Are you showing me your beautiful tits, Annie?" he asks, his voice gruff and scratchy.

I hum, hefting them in my palms so he can see them better. Of course he wants to admire me. I'm his mate.

"I want your mouth," I whine. What is he waiting for?

He shuffles forward and lowers his head to suckle me, his tongue winding around the aching tip, his beard and sharp teeth scratching and nipping my exquisitely sensitive skin. I whine louder, arching my back. I want more.

He switches his attention to my other breast, and I glance down, admiring the red rash he's left and the glistening, swollen nub. I thread my fingers through his wild hair, holding him close to the place where our bond flows between us like an electrical current.

This male was made for me. The pressure of his hands, the temperature of his breath, the tension and tremble of his muscles against my skin—it's all exactly right.

I want him inside me.

I want him to ease this gnawing ache, but also, I want him to come back to me. We belong together. Like thread through a needle. I'm delicate, and he's sharp, and that's how we're made. Exactly how we're supposed to be. Built for purpose.

"Justus," I sigh, longing, demanding.

"Yes, Annie. Yes," he murmurs, low and rough, as he hoists me onto his lap, urging my legs around his waist.

This isn't the way it's done. Shouldn't I present?

"Justus?"

"Trust me," he shushes, the hot head of his cock already notching at my entrance. He flexes his hips and sinks into me, a groan of pure relief torn from his throat. He fills me so completely that I ache where I take him, but I love it.

I pant through the strain, and he gathers me close as he thrusts, cradling me to his chest, kissing my lips, my brow, my cheeks, the tip of my nose. I start to rock my hips in time.

"You're so beautiful, Annie," he rumbles in my ear. "So perfect for me. My Annie. Mine."

I sigh and ride his bucking hips, his cock stretching me until I feel like a glove made for him.

"Come for me, now," he growls. "*Now*, Annie."

Hot cum floods my womb, and his knot catches and swells, tearing a raw shout from my throat. His fingers find my clit while his fangs sink into my shoulder.

I scream, bucking against him, but I'm caught, so he moves with me, hushing me.

I hover another second on the edge, somehow above myself, watching his strong arms tremble as they wrap around me and listening to his strong heart race as he fights for air. And then, like the world is tipped on its side, I'm knocked over, shattered, coming apart in a million, billion beautiful jagged pieces, and when I land, deliciously boneless, I'm whole again and safe in his arms.

He nuzzles my shoulder, mouthing his bite mark clean, mumbling words I can't quite make out that sound like promises. Like vows.

I burrow into his chest, tuck my head into the crook of his neck, and murmur back at him. I don't know what I'm saying, but I know what I mean.

Yes, the wait was too long.

Yes, this is where we belong.

Yes, Fate was right all along.

I WAKE up sometime in the wee hours, tucked between Justus and the blankets and pillows bunched against the den wall. It's the same position we slept in on the trip here in the gully under the oak.

It's toasty warm, but my heat has broken. I'm flat on my back, and I couldn't roll over or move a muscle if I tried. I'm a limp noodle. I can't even open my eyes. I orient myself by the smell of earth, the pressure of Justus's arm around my waist, and the ghosting of his breath on my cheek.

Justus is on his side, facing me.

When he speaks—so very, very quietly that he must think I'm still asleep—his beard tickles my jaw.

"Stay with me," he whispers. "Please, Annie. Please. Stay with me."

I'm searching for my words when I slip-slide back into a deep, dark, dreamless sleep.

I return to the den with water for Annie's morning tea like I'm heading to my own execution. She was curled like a shrimp and snoring when I left her. I covered her with a quilt. She wouldn't like her bare ass hanging out even if there was no one to see it.

She was so beautifully bold and demanding in her heat. Would she be like that all the time if she felt safe?

She doesn't feel safe at Quarry Pack.

She belongs here. I am the male made to protect and care for her.

But I swore I'd take her home. I won't break that promise.

I won't.

My heart cracks and my stomach roils as I hike up the switchback trail, balancing a pot of boiling water that I've overfilled yet again.

She is likely carrying my pup. Am I really going to let her leave to raise the babe on her own? Who will make sure she has enough sleep? Who will make sure she drinks enough so that her milk comes in? Who will watch over her and tend her if she comes down with the affliction that makes some of the new dams take to their beds?

We've welcomed enough females with young babes to know the lost packs have forgotten everything they used to know about caring for new pups. They tell the dams to "sleep when the baby sleeps" as if little ones don't sleep as randomly as bullfrogs honk in the night—and as if there aren't perfectly capable packmates living to their left and right who could rock a fussy babe or give them a bottle of expressed milk.

I vividly remember how Lilliwen woke up every time Auggie cried, and the consternation and offense it caused when she sent away the females who came to help. There were many bitter feelings I had to smooth over before we figured out that in Salt Mountain, she was expected to do all the night feedings herself, and if she'd asked for help, it would've been considered shirking her duties. As if making sure a baby is fed and a dam recovers from birth isn't the duty of the whole pack?

I can't let Annie go back to the pack who let her live in fear. I can't leave her to fend for herself, caring for our young alone. It's unconscionable. Unbearable.

But I swore I would.

I can't do it.

She'll settle in. In time, all the stolen females do. She'll be happy. I'll make her happy.

I'll learn to live with myself when she looks at me with betrayal in her eyes. And if she cries? Calls me a liar? Hates me?

If I break my word now, then am I as weak as I thought I was all those days I hid in my dam's nest, too ashamed to face the pack? I'd sworn to my sire that I'd keep her safe when he was gone, and I'd failed.

And I am going to fail again. No matter what I do.

I reach the grassy ledge outside my den and stand there, water cooling in the pot, frozen in place. I can't take another step. I can't let the next part happen, and there's nothing I can do to stop it.

Annie rustles as she moves around inside.

Alphas are supposed to be invincible. They are the strongest in the pack. The wisest. They fix problems and right wrongs and protect the vulnerable, and here I stand, as I've always been, the strongest and smartest of my people— and still outmatched and outmaneuvered.

I couldn't save Nessa's brother from the hunters or Elis from the consequences of Alroy's stupidity or my dam from the wasting sickness.

There are no alphas. There is no one strong or wise or brave enough.

There is only me, as flawed as I am.

And another impossible choice.

I can't hurt her.

And I can't let her go.

My grip on the pot handle tightens. Water sloshes over the sides. My jaw clenches, my guts knot, and my dry eyes burn.

I can't do this.

I have to.

"Justus?" Annie appears in the den entrance. She's wrapped herself in a light pink sheet, and she's holding a cup. "You brought water." She smiles, padding toward me on bare feet.

And then she stops. Her smile falls aways.

She blinks in the sunshine, the bleariness of sleep disappearing as she takes in my grim face and desperate hold on the pot. If I had dignity, I'd find a way to smile back. Say good morning. Act like everything is fine.

Her chest falls as she lets out a long, silent breath. She looks me straight in the eye. Her fear and doubt are clear as day.

She's going to ask me to take her home now.

She takes a step closer to me, and then another, until we're toe to toe. She gazes up at me, and for a second, all I can see is her beauty—her graceful neck, her delicate pointy chin, her soft, curving lips—and then I notice the expression in her eyes has changed.

It isn't quite fear. It's courage. And it's not doubt, not exactly. It's caution.

She draws in a deep breath and wraps her hand around mine, tilting the pot to pour water carefully into her cup. She already has a strainer filled with tea in it, the chain hung on the side with a fish hook.

She lets go of my hand and blows the tea water, although it's hardly steaming now.

"I think I'll stay here," she says, her cheeks pinkening, her eyes glued to the hands wrapped around her tin cup. "If it's all right by you."

My heart shoots up like a rocket. My wolf howls in triumph so loud the water ripples in the pot I'm still holding.

Annie's mouth quirks, but she keeps her eyes down and flushes a deeper red, plunging ahead like she's afraid to hear what I'm going to say back. "I can help with the meals while you attend to your business. And I can do laundry and mending, as well as gardening and canning and beekeeping. But you don't have hives." She finally stops and glances up, flustered.

I'm grinning like an idiot. "Will you stay with me, Scout?"

She jerks a bashful nod, but her lips curve higher. "Yes."

"It's settled then," I say as if she hasn't just given me everything I've ever wanted. As if this isn't the best moment of my entire life.

I water the cedar with the cool tea water and set the pot on my reading stool. Annie turns to watch the sun finish rising over Salt Mountain. I join her, and we stand side by side in silence.

It rained during the night, but now the sun is the warm yellow of a baby chick, fuzzy as the morning mist burns off. The sky overhead is a bracing blue.

It's going to be a beautiful day.

I TAKE Annie on my morning rounds, careful to keep my pace leisurely. She's walking a little slower than usual. I can't think about the reason why, or I'll get hard, and the knowing looks are bad enough without me adding any fuel to the fire.

My feet are so light, I'm surprised I'm not floating, but I'm scowling and snarling like I've just come back from one of my stalking trips to Quarry Pack. Good-natured joking is tradition after a mating, but the smirks immediately soured Annie's scent, so I'm having to warn our bigger idiots off left and right before they can open their mouths.

I'm mostly successful. I'm not sure whether Rodric can't hear or see my posturing—or whether he doesn't care—but when we pass the bonfire, he bellows, "Why is your pretty mate up and out of the den so early, Alpha? Speed isn't a virtue in everything, pup. Sometimes you've got to take your time."

Thankfully, Nessa has the grace to intervene and calls us over to join her at the breakfast table. Annie winces when she sits on the hard bench, and I make a note to send Griff for a pillow before lunch.

Efa is excited as always to see her favorite female. The pup has decided to be on her best behavior this morning. She sits primly next to Annie and makes a game of offering Annie every other bite from her biscuit. Annie thanks her for each piece, rubs her stomach and exclaims, "Yum. Thank you. So delicious." For some reason, Efa finds this to be the best entertainment ever.

When Efa runs out of her own biscuit, she steals mine by ordering, "Look away, Affa."

She's such a confident little thief that she doesn't even wait for me to turn my head before she nabs the biscuit from my plate.

After breakfast, Annie and I continue on our rounds. We accept the elders' congratulations, Annie smiling prettily as the females make the effort to stand and embrace her. The females are more ribald in their comments, and I don't dare growl at them, and they wouldn't mind me if I did. When we leave them, Annie is flushed bright red.

I chase a few squealing, giddy pups up the sycamore as we pass, and then we swing by a secluded bend in the stream for a quick dip. Annie makes me turn my back when she slips under the water, and I don't even sneak a peek. She has me leashed. I would follow her to the ends of the earth.

As the hours pass, she becomes more talkative, and I am more and more enraptured. After lunch, when she asks to go back to the wildflower field to pick some lavender, I'm happy to go.

The afternoon is as beautiful as the morning. The air is fresh, the wind carrying an earthy note from last night's rain. Annie picks flowers, and I pretend to do the same, but really, I watch her and wonder at my luck.

"This is purple. Is this lavender?" I hold up a bluebell. I know damn well it isn't. I just want to see her hide the smile that says *foolish male*.

"Lavender is light green this time of year. It doesn't bloom until June or July."

"What are you going to do with it now then?"

"Make a sachet. The scent mostly comes from the oils in its leaves."

"Make a sachet for who?"

I wade through the tall grass to stand close to her and inhale her sweet rainy scent.

"For the den," she says, glancing bashfully up at me from under her thick brown lashes. She's wearing my old sweater and another pair of my drawstring pants. Her pulse flutters at the base of her throat. She's excited, too.

Maybe we should cut this trip short and head back to the den.

Or take a detour into the woods.

She probably wouldn't do that, but I think she'd agree to return to camp. I draw in another deep breath. Her arousal teases my nose.

My wolf snarls.

Annie startles.

It takes my brain three seconds too long to catch up.

Underlying the rain and slick, there is another scent. Earthy, yes, but not the *right* earth. It doesn't belong. I've smelled it before. A long time ago.

I sniff deeper with my shifted snout. It's not mud. It's muck. Like from the bottom of a lake. And every second, the stench is getting stronger.

Lakes don't move.

I grab Annie's arm, spin her toward camp, and bark through my wolf's descended fangs, "Run. Raise the alarm. Intruders. Go to Khalil. Go!"

She's frozen in place, staring over my shoulder, her eyes growing larger and larger.

I spin.

At least two dozen wolves, caked in muck from head to tail with moss and leaves stuck to their matted fur, stalk out of the tree line, no more than three or four yards away.

"Run!" I roar at Annie as I shift.

The steadily blowing wind eases for a moment, and their scent smacks me in my face. Quarry Pack. And Salt Mountain. They circled our camp to approach from the east, staying upwind.

I crouch, readying myself to spring and buy Annie time.

The wolves stop at the far side of the field, a huge, golden-eyed male in the lead. Killian Kelly. He's come for my mate. He can't have her.

My wolf bares his fangs.

And then his balls shrivel in their sack.

Annie runs *past us*, toward the Quarry Pack alpha. The breath is torn from my lungs.

"No, Killian," she shouts as she runs, waving her hands, the rancid scent of her fear trailing behind her like a train.

My wolf bolts after her.

"He's my mate!" she yells at her alpha. "He's my mate!"

Killian's wolf doesn't understand her. She's running to him, and he smells fear. He does what I would do.

He tears toward me through the wildflowers. My wolf, no coward, rushes him. They crash mid-air, a collision of hard muscle and bone, and fall to earth, grappling and snarling in a frenzy of fangs and claws.

Killian's claw slashes through my flank, slicing through

the scar left by the feral that killed my sire, as I sink my fangs into his haunch, ripping through muddy fur and flesh.

We plow through the field, tearing chunks from each other, rolling and fighting for dominance, but neither of us can hold position. He's bigger, but not stronger. I'm quicker, but nothing slows him down.

The broken stalks drip with blood, and the other wolves hang back, watching, while my wolf sinks his teeth into Killian's shoulder, and his wolf shakes himself free. His wolf slams into my flank. Mine twists onto his back, dragging his claws along Killian's wolf's underbelly as his momentum carries him past.

The world around us fades, and the daylight dims, the other wolves' howls muting as if lost in a thick fog. Time slows. There is nothing but this alpha and me, nothing but the taste of copper in my mouth and the cast iron certainty that even if I'm skinned to the bone and gutted, I will win this fight.

I can't lose.

Annie is mine.

As the minutes pass, and even the muted howling fades, it becomes clear—my wolf can't lose, but he can't win, either.

And neither can Killian's.

My wolf clamps his jaws around a foreleg. Killian's wolf sinks his fangs into mine. In perfect synchronization, we shift to human form. Killian throws a punch at the side of my head. I duck and kick out at the leg I had in my mouth a split second ago.

We trade blows, landing some, blocking others, discovering each other's weaknesses and exploiting them, recovering and compensating, faltering and rebounding in turn. We flash between forms, throwing punches while we snap our fangs, leaping with four legs to bowl each other over with our full human bulk.

Killian's talent and experience can't overcome my intuition. My instinct can't prevail over his skill.

We will kill each other in this field, watering the wildflowers with our blood, before either of us wins. Or concedes.

Killian slams his fist into my side at the same instant I drive an uppercut into his chin. And then, in the distance, screams cut through the red mist in my mind.

Females. Pups.

Killian and I both whirl to face the direction of the screams, our ears lengthening. They're coming from camp.

Annie is gone, but so are a dozen of the mud-matted wolves. The ones who smell like Salt Mountain.

Killian and I leap and land on four legs, and we race toward the sound of screams.

16

ANNIE

un! Run! Run!

I squat as low as I can in the wildflowers and tear off my clothes.

A few yards away, Killian and Justus are murdering each other. Tye, Ivo, and the rest are just watching, and no matter how much I scream, no matter what I say, their wolves don't listen.

And the Salt Mountain wolves are up to something. They're edging away from the fight toward the trail to camp. Quarry Pack is so intent on the fight, they either don't notice or don't care.

I have to get to Khalil, and my wolf is faster.

Run into the woods! The woods!

I huddle in the tall grass and summon my wolf. For the first time in my life, she's ahead of me, bursting through our skin before I'm ready, assuming form like she's surfacing from water rather than tearing herself free from bone and muscle.

She runs away from the woods, toward the trail. The Salt

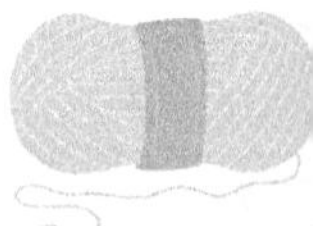

Mountain wolves have gotten ahead of her, so she hangs back, keeping low and downwind.

Turn around! Now!

What are they doing? They can't think to attack Last Pack. They'll be vastly outnumbered. By old Rodric and timid Elis and Tarquin the cook and sweet Max and—

They aren't fighters. Not like Quarry Pack and Salt Mountain. These skulking males who reek of aggression are going to spill into camp, and if our males are at the bonfire, maybe Alroy and Khalil and the others can head them off, but if the Salt Mountain wolves head straight for the sycamore, they can get to the females and pups before anyone has the chance to stop them.

My heart sticks in my throat. I need Justus. I need to get him to help. I'm not big or strong enough on my own, never, never strong enough. I scream and scream, and it's like my voice is the crickets chirping.

Hide! Hide!

Get Khalil.

The Salt Mountain wolves pace so stealthily, and every second I'm watching them, Killian might have killed Justus. My mate might have killed my alpha.

Turn around!

If I turn around, what can I do? I can't stop them. I'm too small, too weak.

Hide!

The voice throws up a memory, the underside of an old leather couch, the warped slats, the dust cover ripped at the seam. My stomach revolts. My wolf swallows the puke down. No time for this. No time.

The Salt Mountain wolves have reached the crest of the hill and are gathering at the narrow entrance to camp. They exchange greedy, sly glances. Their rancid eagerness wafts behind them, singeing my wolf's nose, searing her eyes.

What do I do?

What *can* I do?

I've got no witch, no knife. I'm small and weak and alone. Again, again, again.

Go back. Hide. The voice is whispering now. Cajoling.

On some silent signal, the Salt Mountain wolves burst into motion, streaming through the gap in the rocks, howling a rally cry that echoes off the hills and freezes the blood in my veins.

Turn around and run!

In the distance, a pup screams.

I run.

My wolf pumps her legs so fast that she skitters and stumbles and then staggers forward until she regains her balance, and then she sprints into camp, straight for the sycamore.

At the bonfire and smokehouse and work sites and tents, Last Pack males shift, their wolves racing for the pups and females, too, but they're coming from every direction toward a single place, in essence, funneling themselves, and the Salt Mountain wolves anticipate it.

Every Salt Mountain wolf but one forms a line to lasso the Last Pack males, their two strongest quickly engaging Khalil and Alroy's wolves while the others outflank our males to the left and right.

Salt Mountain's line can't possibly hold against our numbers, but it's holding for now, and their lone wolf, a supernaturally large beast, is loping unchallenged for the sycamore tree. For the pups. Efa.

Run!

I race for the females' fire.

Faster!

My wolf's lungs and legs burn. The air rings with guttural growls and screams and howls.

On your left!

I dodge right, narrowly missing a Salt Mountain male. Two of ours were on his tail, and they tackle him, rolling together in a ball of fur and fangs.

My wolf's paws eat up the yards to the sycamore, but the lone wolf is already there, herding the females and pups together under the canopy. He bays and snarls, pacing and darting until our people are huddled together.

Diantha, Nessa, and Elspeth have shifted into their wolves and stand shoulder to shoulder, blocking a dozen pups behind them. Lilliwen cradles two babes, crouching to shield Auggie, Efa, and Leon with her body. A grizzled wolf that must be Mabli's stands with her front on an overturned rocker, howling, baring her toothless black gums.

The lone wolf lifts his massive head and lets out a blood-thirsty, mad roar. The female wolves snarl back while the females in human form do their best to block the pups with their bodies, but there are too many little ones to hide them all. The babes wail, the pups in fur whimper, and the pups who can speak, cry for their mothers and fathers.

Kill him. For the first time in my life, the pecking voice is perfectly calm.

My wolf skids to a halt several feet away and then slinks forward, keeping the fire between her and the Salt Mountain wolf, letting the smoke block her scent. When she's too close to dare creep closer, she huddles close to the ground, staring up and up at his tremendous mud-caked haunches. She's a miniature in comparison. All the females are, and we all stare, powerless, as the wolf's bones crack and a strapping man rises from the hulk of his beast.

His blond hair shines through the dirt. I've seen him. Leith Munroe. The new Salt Mountain alpha.

He rests his hands on his hips as if there isn't chaos all around him as his wolves play a game of distraction, breaking after our slower, smaller, or older males and mauling them until our strong males are forced to turn back, away from us, to rescue them.

Leith takes no notice of our wolves, even when they get close, or me, skulking behind the fire. Why would he? I'm no threat—skinny and small and stinking of fear.

Instead, he's intent on someone behind the line of female wolves.

"Lilliwen Boyle, is that you?" he says. "Imagine finding you here. Are those pups all yours?" Lilliwen shifts to hide Auggie, and Leith cranes his neck to see around her. Auggie doesn't help by poking his snout out and growling. "Oh, that one's yours for sure. And his sire's a Munroe, too, if I'm not mistaken?"

Leith squats and reaches out a sculpted arm, wiggling his long fingers. "Come say hello to your uncle, pup."

Lilliwen snarls. The female wolves press tighter together, lowering their haunches, readying themselves to attack.

"L-leave us alone," Lilliwen stammers, shoving Auggie behind her. Efa peeks out her other side. My heart lodges in my throat.

"Ah, but your new pack won't leave *us* alone, will they? Always thieving our females. Pissing on our territory and running away." Leith rises back to his full height and spits in the grass. "I think turnabout is fair play, don't you? Don't worry. If you want to stay here, Lilliwen, you can. We don't have much use for a—used—female." He makes a show of peering past her. "But this pack of dogs can't keep stealing our good females with impunity. I think you'll understand if we help ourselves to a few of these pups to balance things out. Seems a fair trade. Don't worry, we'll raise them right." He winks.

Our females break into a ferocious snarling and howling that raises my fur.

Leith is unconcerned. There's no tension in his stance, no shred of anxiety in his scent. He knows, as we all do, that we're no match for him.

His back is turned toward you.

He flashes the female wolves his eerie fake smile and coos to Efa's wolf where she pokes out her head. "Come out, come out, little lady. Don't make me come through your dams to get you."

Nessa's wolf snarls and glances over her shoulder, gauging the distance between her and her pup, weighing the danger of breaking the line to protect her.

Leith snarls back, louder, longer, with all the force of an alpha at the height of his powers.

Efa's wolf whimpers and hides her muzzle in Lilliwen's skirt.

That won't save her.

Efa's terrified, shivering, her fur bristling.

She did nothing to deserve this.

She's going to remember this forever.

She's going to wear this fear, from this moment, like a second skin. It's going to burrow into her brain and torment her, dogging her steps, stealing her peace, tainting every good thing that will ever happen to her until she runs away from hope. From love. From life.

And this male doesn't care. He's smirking. He wants her to be afraid.

For all of us to be afraid.

He snaps his fingers. "Send the pup to me now, or I'll come get her myself."

He's a male, and we are nothing to him. Nothing.

No.

Not again.

Never again.

The needles. By the chair.

I see them, the two medium needles I absentmindedly left stuck in a ball of orange yarn the day before my heat. They're sticking out of a burlap bag beside the place the rocking chair had been before it became a barricade.

I can't. I'm too scared.

Yes, you can. You can run.

"Now!" Leith barks.

Now!

I shift. No bones break. No muscles tear. I lift my paw and my bare foot hits the ground. I blink and the grays and browns of the sycamore turn bright, spring green. It's not a shift; it's a flip. Like a flip of a switch.

I stumble, but I don't lose momentum. The voice is right. I *can* run.

The females notice me, see where I'm heading, and they break into a single-throated cry of deafening howls that shakes the ground. They lunge forward and scramble back, distracting him. Nessa dashes for Efa, throwing her body of top of her pup.

I'm close. So close.

My fingers wrap around the needles, one in each hand, and I whirl, setting my sights on the enemy. He still has his back to me.

I'm small. Weak. Not a threat.

Aim for his throat.

I break into a sprint, and when I'm just close enough, I leap, my wolf powering my legs, and I drive a needle into the place where his shoulder meets his neck, sinking it all the way to the acorn carved on the top.

He spins, blinking in surprise.

I raise the other needle.

Stick it right in his eye.

A male roars behind me. Bloody arms wrap around me like a vise, the scent of earth and copper surrounding me.

Justus.

Other howls ring out, other scents descending from all directions, mixing with the smoke from the dwindling fire.

Killian. And Tye, Ivo, Gael. Khalil, Alroy, Max.

Justus shoves me behind his body, the other Last Pack males rushing to stand at his left and right, blocking me from the Salt Mountain alpha swaying on his feet.

He didn't even go down.

He bares his fangs, yanks the needle from his neck, and blinks at it, bemused.

"Did you stab me with a fucking *knitting needle*?" He holds it up. Blood oozes from the wound, dripping down his bare chest. I didn't even hit an artery.

Justus snarls, squaring his shoulders and bending his knees, readying himself to attack. Every inch of his body is covered in mud and blood, gashes and purpling bruises. White bone shows through a jagged slash on his forearm.

A male coughs, clearing his throat. "Can we just take a beat?" Killian raises his hands, raw flesh where his nails should be.

I wouldn't have thought it possible, but he's as battered as Justus, and he seems to be favoring his left leg, like his right can't hold weight. Our males spar constantly. I've seen all of them beat up at some point, but I've never seen any of them mangled this bad. I can't believe either he or Justus are still upright.

"That bitch stabbed me." Leith points at me with the knitting needle.

Justus howls and steps toward him. Khalil and Alroy grab his arms. He shakes them off like flies.

I dart forward and snatch his hand. He glances over his shoulder at me, his wolf blazing gold in his eyes. A snarl rattles his chest, but he stays put.

"That's Annie Murphy," Killian says to Leith. There's a note of exhaustion in his voice that I've never heard before.

"The female we're stealing back?" Leith's lip quirks. He's amused.

My wolf growls. The Quarry Pack males gape at me in surprise. The Last Pack wolves add their growls to mine.

"Can I ask what you were doing?" Killian asks Leith.

"Taking the opportunity to get a little of our own back."

"Efa isn't yours!" I shout. I have to be loud in order to be heard over the female wolves howling their own objection.

Justus tightens his hold on my hand, and I realize I've stepped forward, lifting the needle still clasped in my fist. He lifts his chin and growls at Leith in a register I've never heard before from any male, any alpha. It's wolf and man, a resonance that's both and neither and something else besides, a rumble that's more thunder than voice. I catch a whiff of singed air.

And I realize that while we were speaking, the Last Pack wolves have been stalking closer and closer. All of them. Griff and Elis and Rodric and dozens of others, old and young, big and small. Somehow, Leon snuck from behind Lilliwen and circled around everyone so that he's now approaching our rear with the others. The Quarry Pack and Salt Mountain males are outnumbered easily twenty to one.

And when my eyes dart to Killian's face, I see that he realizes it, too. His gaze meets mine, and for the first time in my life, I hold it without flinching.

"You're not stolen, are you, Annie?" he asks.

I shake my head.

He blows out a long breath before turning his attention to the female wolves still bristling in a line, defending the pups huddled under the sycamore.

"None of you were stolen, were you?" he says to them.

They bare their fangs and snarl at him low in their throats.

Killian looks to Justus. "She's your mate?"

Justus growls in the affirmative.

"I can't believe *I'm* the one talking shit out," Killian groans. Tye snorts, but he shuts up real quick when Killian glares at him.

"Look," Killian says to Justus. "What are we going to do here? Because if I kill Annie's mate, *my* mate is going to cut off my balls. And unless I'm seriously mistaken, if *you* kill *me*, Annie isn't going to be happy either."

Justus narrows his eyes, like he's weighing the idea anyway. "My mate won't mind if I kill *him*," Justus says, jerking his chin at Leith. "Will yours?"

"You can try," Leith says, squaring up as he drops his hand from where he was pressing it to his neck like a tourniquet.

Justus's wolf replies to Leith with a desultory snarl, but Justus's attention stays on Killian. Leith is a huge, strong male, an alpha from a long line of alphas, but the balance of power is clear. Every single wolf gathered in this clearing is looking at Killian—and Justus.

I'm used to everyone deferring to Killian—he'd accept nothing else—but I'd never understood until this moment that Justus is as dangerous, as strong, as pure born alpha as Killian. Justus may not carry himself that way, or avail himself of the privileges, or even call himself Alpha, but wolves *know* the best among them, they look to that wolf when push comes to shove, and right now, every Last Pack eye is on my mate.

And my thoughtful, judicious, even-tempered mate is looking at Leith Munroe like he's going to rip out his beating heart and eat it.

If he does it, the Salt Mountain wolves will fight back. It'll be a bloodbath. I can't let this happen.

This is my pack. This is happening because of me. It's up to me to defuse the situation.

Me, Annie Murphy.

Shit.

I take a step forward, clear my throat, straighten my spine, and open my mouth.

Run!

"You have to leave," I say to Killian.

Hide!

"And take them with you." I jerk my head toward the Salt Mountain wolves.

In my head, everyone holds their breath. Annie spoke to the alpha. *She* told *him* what to do. The world must surely end.

In reality, the Last Pack wolves rumble, backing me up.

"Are you sure, Annie?" Killian says.

Justus snarls. It's my turn to squeeze his hand.

"Yes. I belong here." The crackling scent thickens in the air, and I know the words are more than true. They're a stake, a claim, a kind of magic. I wasn't stolen. I was stolen *from*, but I can take things back. My peace, my place, my power.

My voice.

"This is my home," I say. "This is my mate."

I twine my fingers with Justus's, and his mouth widens in a gap-toothed, bloody smile.

In all my life, I've never seen a male so happy.

My perfect, beautiful mate does not like surprises, so she knows exactly where we're going as we trot through the woods that run along the human highway. At first, I was sad that I couldn't spring this visit on her, but I love watching her wolf get more and more excited the closer we get to Chapel Bell. Her short little legs are moving so fast, I almost don't have to slow my pace.

Alroy, Griff, and Diantha don't have my patience, so they're several yards ahead of us. Poor Griff has to be the buffer between them, and he keeps getting caught in the crossfire when their wolves decide to break the monotony by sniping at each other.

I was worried that Annie would be too nervous to venture this far from camp, but she gets more confident every day. I'm pretty sure that's because when we were out for a walk two months ago, she saw me take out two ferals that were encroaching on our territory to the north, so even though Killian and I pretty much fought to a draw, she knows I can handle any other comers.

She says she's more confident because she's been talking to her "pecking voice." I don't quite understand the whole thing. She explained it one night when we were snuggling in the den after sampling Mabli's new batch of moonshine.

Apparently, there's a voice inside her that warns her of possible threats, and she is adamant that the voice is not her wolf. Two voices in your head seems like overkill, but I'm not complaining. She's everything to me. The more alert my mate is to danger, the better I sleep.

Anyway, she used to ignore the voice or argue with it, but she's on friendlier terms with it now. She says it's quieter now that *it* knows that *she* knows it's trying to keep her safe. I told her to let *it* know that keeping her safe is *my* job, so it can take a break, but Annie just laughed and said, "You go ahead and tell it that."

I'm not talking to the voice in someone else's head. That's moon mad.

I smell the town before I see its church spire rising in the distance. Gasoline, trash, frying fat, and myriad attempts to cover up the stench of it all. That's what human towns smell like.

I remind myself to breathe through my mouth until we're out of here.

I've ventured among humans before, but not often in recent years. There's always a younger male excited to go when the need arises.

Now that Annie and I are properly mated, I'm going to all kinds of new places. I had to parlay with Killian out at an abandoned shack with a moss roof and a chimney made of mushrooms. We talked about females we'd stolen over the years, and his sire, and the old days that he doesn't remember when our packs ran together.

Annie made me bring various gifts she'd knitted—

scarves for her friends Kennedy, Mari, and Old Noreen, a blanket for Una's pup, and a shawl for Una. It was such a big package, I had to sling it over my back and travel on two legs, which meant I had to be away from camp longer than I wanted.

It was good, though. Killian and I talked about the hunters who killed Nessa's brother. Killian didn't know that males from North Border were their guides. He said he didn't know what Salt Mountain planned to do the day he came for Annie, either, and I believe him. He seems like the type too sure of himself to bother lying.

For this trip to Chapel Bell, the package Annie has set me to carry is small enough that my wolf can hold it in a bindle from his teeth. When I begin to hear the humans' cars, I growl at everyone to stop and nose Annie's wolf behind a tree for privacy.

Annie is still very shy of shifting in front of others. Her wolf is as unconcerned about nudity as the rest of us. This has caused a few moments of consternation, especially since her shifting ability is spotty. Sometimes, she can shift the normal way, like she did when she stabbed the Salt Mountain alpha and took twenty years off of my life, but other times, she shifts like a lost packer, which I swear hurts me more than it hurts her.

Today, her excitement seems to have the upper hand because as soon as her wolf ducks behind a tree, she's reaching out a graceful bare arm and snapping for her clothes.

I toss her one of the short, baggy dresses she made herself during our first week together. That sewing session was spurred by an unfortunate incident when Alroy trod on the back of her wrapped gown as we walked up the trail to the dens, yanking it clean off of her, and I was not able to keep my usual sense of perspective. She had to shift, bite my wolf's tail, and try to drag him off of Alroy before he accidentally ripped Alroy's head off.

I quickly draw on my own pants and shirt, so I'm fully dressed when Annie emerges from behind the tree like a nymph, smoothing her pale pink shift. I hold up the slippers I made from the hide of the first elk I bagged for her. She slips her feet into them and grins at me.

"Ready?" I ask.

She nods and grabs my hand.

I carry the half-emptied bindle and swing her arm, playing off my nerves. I don't like being so close to humans, and if I'm being honest, I'm not entirely comfortable with our visit today. Annie says she's happy with me and our pack, and she smells happy, but I know she misses her friends.

What if she decides she wants to stay with them?

Then, I guess I'm moving to Quarry Pack. It wouldn't be the worst life, spending my days kicking the snot out of arrogant wolves who think they're fighters. Beats hunting down Leon for the hundredth time while his dam loses her mind. He's much too good a climber for a pup his age. Last time he disappeared, I found him curled up asleep in an eagle nest at the top of a white pine.

Alroy, Diantha, and Griff fall in behind us as we enter town. I have to rumble at Diantha to get her to tuck her ears behind her hair. She'll wear full skin when she has to, but she refuses to do human ears. I'm not sure if she can anymore.

The humans know about shifters, of course, but there's no need to draw more attention to us than we already do, as strangers in such a small town. Folks already gawk as Annie leads us to the village commons even though the streets are busy. It's market day.

As soon as we reach the grassy expanse filled with tables and tents, Alroy and Diantha peel off, heading in opposite directions. Griff seems torn, but when he sees that Diantha is making a beeline for a booth with racks of female clothing, he hurries to follow Alroy.

Annie leads us down the makeshift walkways, smiling when she's greeted by name. My mate is still shy, but there's no trace of fear in her scent. I breathe her happiness and excitement in, letting it flush my lungs clean of the oily town air.

She sees her friends before I do and lets go of my hand to run toward them.

My mate. My Annie. Running with a smile lighting her face.

This is a good, good day.

Two females rush around their table, the third making her way more slowly. I know them immediately from Annie's description.

The female with the limp is Una, Killian Kelly's mate. She's a plain female with a quiet confidence, and her mate watches her like she's charging into battle unarmed, not greeting a friend.

The blonde with curls who looks like a doll is Mari. She's mated to the Haunt of the Hills. It's hard to imagine a female so sweet and small would be with such a brute. According to Annie, he's not as fearsome as the tales would have you believe. I won't be sharing that with the pack, though. A healthy fear of the Haunt is the only thing currently keeping Leon from venturing even further afield on his adventures.

The short-haired female is Kennedy, the blessed one.

She races to meet Annie and wraps her in a hug, swinging her in a circle.

My wolf's instinctive snarl trails off midway as he tries to wrap his brain around the situation. His eyes and nose tell him a female is spinning his giggling mate, but his sixth sense knows a male when he comes across one. He won't tolerate a male touching his mate, but the person smacking kisses on Annie's cheek has breasts, and although they're slender, a female's hips.

I prepare to rein him back, but in the end, I don't have to. He figures whether the shifter hugging Annie is male or female or both, Annie counts them as family, so they're family to us, as well, and he can go back to sniffing the smells coming from the food vendors and wondering which meat they've ruined with their human sauces.

"What are you doing here?" Kennedy squeals, giving Annie no time to answer before she squeezes her again.

Mari and Una reach them, and the circle expands to four babbling, laughing females. I raise my eyes to meet the gaze of the three males standing with their arms crossed behind a table covered with jars of honey, candles, salves, and a dozen other crafts, all stamped or stickered with a wolf logo that reads "Cottage Industries."

Killian Kelly, his beta Tye, and the Haunt himself stare at me stonily and then turn their heads to watch the happy females, their gazes softening. I sent word we were coming. I see they decided to keep our visit a surprise from their mates.

"I can't believe you're here," Mari says, bursting into tears. The Haunt's jaw clenches.

"Oh, don't cry, Mari," Annie says, wiping her friend's face with her thumbs. "Look. I brought a present." Annie rushes back to me, takes the bindle and grabs my hand, dragging me forward with her.

She sticks out the parcel, smiling proudly. Una takes it and unknots the fabric to reveal the morel mushrooms Annie and I discovered on one of our walks.

"Morels?" Una's eyes round.

Annie grins. "There are tons more where they came from."

I guess this trip to market isn't a once off. Seeing how big Annie's smiling, I can't mind. I'll have to figure out a way to bring her once her belly begins to show, and she can't shift anymore. It's too far a trip to make on two legs, especially pregnant. I'm not buying a car, though. Could I rig up some kind of cart? My wolf would look like an idiot pulling a wagon, but I get the sense he'd love it.

Annie squeezes my hand and pulls me closer to her side —and closer to her friends. My wolf and I ignore the chorus of rumbles that erupt from behind the table.

Mari and Una roll their eyes. Kennedy blushes.

"This is Justus," Annie says.

I show the females my neck, and their males rumble louder. Lost packers are so lost. They read respect as insolence and guard their mates by glowering from a distance. Utterly backward.

"Nice to meet you," Una says, baring her neck briefly to me in return. Killian Kelly's snarl scatters the humans rummaging the nearby tables.

I shake my head. I still can't believe that Quarry Pack has the audacity to scare their pups with cautionary tales of the big, bad Last Pack when their own males act like that. When Annie told me, I thought it was funny, but the more encounters I have with their males, the more I'm convinced that it's a scheme to keep their females grateful for the bare minimum.

The females almost immediately forget about me, bursting into an animated, overlapping conversation about everything at once. Eventually, they decide to go for tea at a human café, and I'm relegated to standing with the silent, brooding Quarry Pack males next to an enormous statue of a cow.

It's miserable until I realize that the cow is an advertisement for a shop that sells a sweet dessert swirled on a cone. I wave Alroy over when he passes and get him to give me human money. I'm not sure where he gets it, but he's never without.

When Killian sees what I'm up to, he finally deigns to speak. "That shit's dairy," he says like he's warning me.

"What's wrong with dairy?" I ask.

"Wolves don't like it," he says with the impatience of a man who thinks he's telling an idiot something obvious.

"My mate would literally eat her weight in cheese," I say. "Yours doesn't like it?" I thought all females had a thing for cheese—like either they're in their chocolate mood or their cheese mood, depending on the phase of the moon or whatever.

"Mari loves cheese," the Haunt of the Hills says. "Sometimes, all she'll eat for a meal is cheese on apple slices. She calls it girl dinner."

Killian's forehead furrows, and he doesn't answer. Looks like he's grappling with some cognitive dissonance. It is unpleasant being wrong.

I buy a chocolate ice cream. It's delicious, with the added bonus that when Annie notices me eating it, she blushes bright red. The other night, she let me settle between her legs and lick her until her thighs shook. I think she might let me do it again when we get back to camp if the brightness in her brown eyes is anything to go by.

The afternoon passes quickly enough. I try two more ice cream flavors—vanilla and peach—but neither is as good as the chocolate, so I have another one of them before we leave so the memory is the freshest.

Annie cries a little when it's time to leave, but I promise to bring her back on the next market day, and the kiss she gives me in front of everyone—totally trusting and unashamed—makes it seem like a small price to pay.

We begin our hike home on two legs. The sun sets, the woods turn a deep blue, and lightning bugs come out, flickering like fairies among the trees.

Alroy and Diantha run ahead. Griff trails behind. It's been a big day for him. He's going to sleep like a log when we get back.

The summer leaves rustle overhead, and the critters who hunt at night venture forth in search of prey.

Annie twines her fingers in mine and sighs.

"Did you ever think it would end this way?" she asks me dreamily, her voice husky with exhaustion. I'm going to end up carrying her at least part of the way if I'm not mistaken. I won't mind at all.

"I didn't even dare hope," I say.

"Sometimes magic needs time." She smiles at me, her heart in her eyes.

I smile back, my heart in mine.

THE FIVE PACK saga began with *The Tyrant Alpha's Rejected Mate.*

It continues with *Ravaged Wolf.*

WANT MORE?

Sign up for the Cate C. Wells newsletter at www.catecwells.com for a bonus epilogue to *The Wild Wolf's Rejected Mate* and other exclusive content, updates, and special offers.

If you already subscribe, a link to the bonus epilogue is at the bottom of every newsletter.

ABOUT THE AUTHOR

Cate C. Wells writes everything from motorcycle club to small town to mafia to paranormal romance. Whatever the subgenera, readers can expect character-driven stories that are raw, real, and emotionally satisfying. She's into messy love, flaws, long roads to redemption, grace, and happily ever after, in books and in life.

Along with stories, she's collected a husband, two daughters, and a cat along the way. She lives in Baltimore when she's not exploring the world with the family.

facebook.com/catecwells
instagram.com/authorcatecwells
tiktok.com/@authorcatecwells